# AWAKEN THE FIFTH ORDER

BOOK THREE
OF THE IMMORTAL
ORDERS TRILOGY

ACW

AWAKEN THE FIFTH ORDER
Copyright © 2022 by Allison Carr Waechter

ISBN 979-8-9860604-6-0 (hardcover)
ISBN 979-8-9860604-7-7 (paperback)
ISBN 979-8-9860604-8-4 (paperback)
ISBN 979-8-9860604-5-3 (ebook)

Cover Image by Christin Engelberth
Design by Allison Carr Waechter
Editing by Kenna Kettrick & Shelby Godwin

*for the babes who cry over the kitchen sink & keep going:*
*i love us.*

# Content Guidelines

*Please note that you may find what could be considered "spoilers" in the following content guidelines. Additionally, while I make every effort to be complete in my guidelines, I do not always correctly anticipate what may be sensitive topics for some people. If you feel I've missed an important guideline, please feel free to contact me via my website with suggestions at www.allisoncarrwaechter.com*

**DEMOGRAPHIC:** Adult

**HEAT LEVEL:** Spicy scenes, including explicit descriptions are present in this book.

**SENSITIVE CONTENT:** One implication of a threat of gender-based violence against women. Non-specific, but a threat of sexual assault may be inferred here. Some gore/fantasy violence. Vivid descriptions of anxiety, depression, trauma, and sensory issues. Descriptions of child abuse and neglect, as well as descriptions of complex relationships with parental abusers. Implications of torture, both in the recent and distant past.

# THE PEOPLE OF OKAIROS

## THE ILLUMINATED
*a race of immortal humanoids, also known as the Ventyr who conquered
Okairos by dubious means 2000 years ago*

## THE ORDER OF MYSTERIES
*sorcière, also known as witches*

## THE ORDER OF MASKS
*shifters, some more "mundane" as well as the Heraldic, shifters who were
present on Okairos before the Illuminated arrived*

## THE ORDER OF NIGHT
*vampires and incubi*

## THE FIFTH ORDER
*a group of immortals and humans fighting for a better world, formerly known as
"the Rogue Order"*

## THE VESPAE
*humanoid aliens with a hive-like social structure that were set loose on Okairos
at the end of*

## HUMANS

# Prologue

Frigid wind whistled through the open slats in the walls of the barn. Once, someone kept animals here, but no longer—now, monsters overran the little farm. They'd been here for six days, the longest they'd stopped moving since Finn and Larkin had been separated. Finn knew the Vespae were hungry, but for whatever reason, they would not touch him.

Nor would they release him. The creatures had a stinger containing a poison that suppressed his connection to both aethereal and celestial magics, and they'd kept him alive but sedated as they moved from place to place. Finn was weak, but not as groggy or unconscious as he'd been at the beginning; he'd cataloged their movements as well as he could. From the pattern of incoming and outgoing parties, he'd concluded that they were searching for something. The Vespae were violent—brutal, really —but they were not unthinking creatures.

In fact, he believed they had language. Outside, in the barnyard, several huddled in a circle. Soft clicks and hisses passed between them, and from what Finn could discern, there was a pattern to it. They didn't seem to be cold, but they crowded together like that when daylight became too harsh.

Finn peered out from between the rough wooden slats at the Vespae gathered in the barnyard: they were the group he thought of as "drones"—the ones who gathered food, which consisted solely of plant matter, and were the advance guard for any of the swarm's maneuvers.

The Vespae were pale creatures, with silvery-gray skin, who walked upright like the humanoids of Okairos. Their features were strikingly different though, with huge, dark eyes that resembled those of a moth, and tiny noses and mouths. The drones' long arms allowed them to drop to the ground and run at alarming speeds, while the swarm's elite were proportioned more like the humanoids of Okairos. All had long, graceful limbs that reminded him of the Illuminated's true forms.

In fact, there was something eerily similar between the Vespae and the Ventyr. Something that bothered Finn to think about, when he could think clearly enough to do so. That was rarely enough, as the noise the drones made was incredibly disorienting. He might not be groggy from the poison any longer, but that sound—both the constancy of it, and the pitch —was enough to make him want to clap his hands over his ears.

Though the drones were terrifying, they were the least of his problems. The queen and her guard were the ones whose poison kept him disconnected from his sources of strength. He hadn't seen the queen since they arrived at this farm, but one of the guards visited him every day before sunset to dose him again.

Typically, daylight hours were the most peaceful for him, since the drones were usually dormant, but today they couldn't rest. They'd been "talking" in the barnyard for hours, so much so that he couldn't think. The intermittent hissing wormed into his mind and grated on his nerves, bringing back the memory of being separated from Larkin—something he used any mental acuity he had to suppress.

Now, memory flooded him, detaching him from the frigid wind howling through the barn. They'd traveled in the limen for nearly a day after being ripped from Harlow and Cian in the catacombs, Morgaine and Ashbourne both helping them to navigate. It had been strange to spend time with an uncle he'd never known existed, especially because he hadn't acted like they were related in the slightest. Even now, that stung, though Finn understood that the Warden had been locked in Nihil with the Ravagers for longer than he could even conceive.

Guarding a prison for ancient elemental horrors like the Ravagers seemed to have dulled Ashbourne's emotions, or perhaps he just disliked Finn on sight. He'd certainly been unhappy to see Connor. If it were just that, Finn could understand, but it was a deeper indifference that had stung. Unlike most of the Illuminated, who were typically extremely reactive in comparison to humans or the lower Orders, Ashbourne was practically stoic.

The Ventyr General had treated him like a problem to solve, and even now, with all his other problems, Finn wished it had been different. It would be nice to think that somewhere, he had a blood relative who cared for him. That not everyone he came from was a monster. Though on that front at least, he had no complaint with Ashbourne, who despite his obvious disinterest in Finn cared deeply for Larkin, and the worlds he kept safe from the Ravagers.

Morgaine and her cat, Bayun, had been different. It was obvious the human girl had been worried about her mission, but they'd been kind to him and Larkin, trying to comfort them both. As bizarre as it had been for the cat to speak, it had distracted both him and Larkin from the terror of being locked in the limen, violently isolated from everyone they loved, while the world fell to pieces on the other side of the breach.

That seemed like a faraway time now, those days of hope that he'd see Harlow again soon. Finn wasn't sure how long it had been since then, and—whether it was the effects of Vespae poison or the limen itself—his memories of what had happened inside the limen were more impressions than anything else.

The days blurred together and he thought he'd been with the hive for more than a month. They'd moved from location to location for what felt like weeks until settling here. Finn estimated they'd been here for ten days, and he thought he remembered most of them. Unlike the rest of his recent memories, the day they stumbled out of the limen was vivid in his mind.

Morgaine had disappeared back into the portal with Ashbourne. From what Finn gathered in the short time they'd traveled together, Morgaine needed Ashbourne's help to find the next world she was to visit, a place called Sirin. Finn had learned more about her mission to ensure that the Ravagers could not access aethereal worlds by closing the unnaturally opened portals, but thinking about that was confusing now.

Sometimes thinking about anything but his failure to protect Larkin was physically painful. They'd been woefully unprepared for travel through the mountains of Falcyra when they exited the limen, given that they'd been dressed for a mild autumn evening in Nea Sterlis. His first order of business had been to get them to the shelter Morgaine had located for them— a hobby farm a few miles away from the opening to the limen. It had seemed like such a good thing at the time, a place to rest and procure cold weather clothing the original inhabitants had left behind.

If only they'd gone as soon as they'd geared up for the cold. The day had been sunny, a rarity in Falcyra that lulled Finn into a sense of safety. With no Vespae about, Finn decided to explore the property to see if there was a vehicle somewhere they could use for its radio. He'd known he needed to try to get in touch with the Rogue Order, and Morgaine had given him their radio codes. She'd assured him the Rogues would easily find the farm once he got in touch with them, but he hadn't found a way to do that in the house. He'd searched for hours, failing to notice when the sun began to set.

All they had to do was stay warm, radio the Rogues, and everything would be fine. If only he'd stayed out of the barn. Or if he'd gone in at noon, rather than twilight. *If, if, if.* There were so many ways he could have avoided fucking things up, if he'd been more careful. If he hadn't been so curious about the buzzing coming from deep inside the barn. If he hadn't woken them.

His only hope now was that the Vespae hadn't been able to get into the basement where he'd shoved Larkin. He'd done everything he could to draw them off, to get them to pay attention to him instead, and he thought it had worked, but of course he couldn't be sure. They'd kept him mostly unconscious since capturing him, and things blurred together.

Outside, the drones' hisses and clicks blurred into a buzz. Finn struggled to his feet. He wasn't bound or confined. The Vespae's poison kept him weak enough that he couldn't leave. They'd easily catch him if he tried to escape again—several early attempts had confirmed this. He'd been dragged back to whatever gods forsaken camp they'd been sheltering in. Now he bided his time, hoping that soon he'd learn *something* that would be the key to his escape.

A rumble in the distance suggested a vehicle—multiple vehicles—approached. *Was he being rescued? Had the Rogue Order found him?* Hope lit in his heart. *Thank all gods for Kate.* As the Rogue Queen, he knew she'd find him, and maybe Harlow was with her. He gathered his strength. If there was going to be a fight, he'd be as useful as he could.

Finn stepped out of the barn, expecting to find the Vespae preparing for conflict. In daylight hours, they did this by hiding. Instead, the full swarm gathered in the yard, buzzing excitedly as three SUVs barreled through the snow about a mile off. Finn squinted, trying to make out who was within, but the vehicles' heavily tinted windows obscured his view.

Glancing around, dread seeped into his gut. The Vespae weren't preparing for a fight—they were *excited*. All stood upright instead of crouching near the ground. And the queen's guard stood on the steps of the house, though the queen was nowhere to be seen. Finn saw his chance in this moment of distraction—every drone and guard were focused on the approaching vehicles.

He might not get far, but he had to try one more time. He owed that to Larkin—and he missed Harlow more than he usually allowed himself to admit. Thinking of her, when he could do nothing to find her, nearly drove him to distraction, something he couldn't afford right now. Moving slowly, he backed away from the swarm. All the usual guards were in the barnyard, and all he needed to do was slip into the woods to get away. It had been a little over a full day since the last sting, and the poison's effects were wearing off. They'd never let it get so low in his system before, and his body's ability to heal rapidly kicked in—he felt stronger by the moment.

Typically, the queen or one of her guards dosed him sooner, so his access to magic never returned, but now he could feel the threads that made up reality again, and all the power of the universe behind them. If he could put enough distance between himself and the swarm, he might be able to shift and teleport out. His limbs dragged as he focused on moving silently, creeping out the back of the barn towards the woods. To his surprise, none of the Vespae followed him. They were all more interested in whoever, or whatever, was coming in those SUVs.

Finn narrowed his attention—staying quiet and moving quickly had to be his priority now, not looking back. He had no recourse if they caught him; he knew he was still too weak to fight, so getting away had to be his only goal.

The little farm nestled deep in a tall, wooded grove. Finn

knew exactly where the darkest parts of the forest were, and he stayed away from them now. He'd tried that before, mistakenly thinking he was providing himself with cover, but now he understood daylight was his best advantage. So he stayed with the light, his strides lengthening with every step he took away from the encampment, some of his strength returning.

Though Finn had no idea where to go, or what he'd do when he was away from this place, his heart sprang back to life for the first time since he'd been taken. As a child, he'd learned to shut down during the long stretches of time that his parents' machinations involved him too directly, or too intensely. He'd found out early that hope could be a weakness, as it gave opponents something to destroy. Now, he couldn't escape it, couldn't pen it back in, or wrangle it into submission.

Away from the near-constant buzzing of the Vespae, Finn's head cleared. His movements grew stronger, more confident. He wasn't back to full strength, or anywhere near it, but he could think—try to make a plan. When he was younger, his father had taken him on trips to the dense forests of Castel des Rêves and Falcyra alike, dropping him in the middle of nowhere, with only his wits and a directive to find his way out of the forest. There had never been a clear destination, just "find your way to safety," and though Finn knew he'd been watched, Connor didn't rescue him from being injured or going hungry. Finn assumed his father would have stepped in if his life had been truly threatened, but there had been plenty of times he'd been afraid, and Connor never intervened.

As terrible as all that had been, it prepared him for this moment as he crested the ridge of the valley the little farm sat in. He looked behind him to find that he could survey his prison perfectly. The SUVs had parked in the barnyard now, and a dozen vampires and several witches spilled out of them. A murky feeling of doom soured the hope he'd felt moments before. *Why were sorcière helping anyone associated with the*

*Vespae?* The group moved quickly into a guard formation as they yanked a hooded figure forward.

When the queen finally appeared, emerging out of the farmhouse, one of the sorcière pulled the hood from the vampire's face, exposing him to the queen. Her ragged wings flexed with excitement as she smelled him carefully. Her huge eyes gave nothing away, but the wrinkle of her tiny nose showed what she thought of the vampire's scent. The Vespae themselves smelled of flowers, which always struck Finn as odd, given their ferocity.

The vampire shrunk away from the queen, his eyes fearful. From the state he was in, it was clear he'd fought his captors. Finn recognized Jareth Sanvier, one of the leaders of the Humanists. The queen stepped forward, and Finn didn't have to watch what would happen next; she would incapacitate him with her poison.

Finn turned in the other direction. There was nothing he could do for the vampire, not alone and weak as he was. He didn't like the Humanists' methods, but he would have helped Jareth if he were capable. Larkin and Harlow had to be his only concern now. Finn wouldn't risk his chance to find the people he loved, his family, for someone who condoned outright terrorism.

Ahead of him was a vast mountain range, which he was in no way prepared to traverse. Already, the sun was low in the sky and cold crept into his bones. He was slightly more resistant to cold than other immortals, but he would still freeze in his mortal form. The only option he had was to shift and fly. He attempted to drop his glamour, but it wouldn't budge. Deep in his veins, there were still traces of the Vespae's venom, keeping him from shifting to his true form. His burgeoning hope deflated.

"Frustrating, isn't it?" a familiar voice rang out from the trees. "There's really nowhere for you to go."

Finn whirled around to find Mark Easton leaning against a tree. Every instinct he had edged on a knife's blade, and he dropped into a solid crouch. It wasn't possible for Mark to be here. Finn had watched Harlow disembowel and decapitate him during the Solstice Gala, last spring. There was no way he'd survived. No immortal could survive without their head.

"Keep trying to figure it out, McKay," Mark hissed.

Finn's vision blurred and now Mark stood before him in his incubus form, his glamour dropped, revealing ghastly gray skin and hungry, bloodshot eyes. When he smiled, his teeth were pointed razors. Finn's head felt as though it might split open, it ached so deeply. His ears rang until he was sure he bled from his eyes and ears both, driven to his knees in the snow.

The incubus' face swam before Finn's eyes. He attempted to muster his strength, but Mark just laughed. Finn saw the punch coming, but could do nothing to stop it as Mark's fist met his face with full impact, and all went dark.

# CHAPTER ONE

Blood filled Harlow's mouth, the metallic tang coating her throat as she resisted the urge to duck away from her attacker. A pale creature hissed in her face and threw its right hand back, a long thorn-like spine pushed out from its palm, glistening in the silvery light that shone through the arched windows of the enormous hallway. The creature was preparing to sting, but Harlow drew her shadows around her, honing them into daggers—extensions of her arms. She punched up fast, driving the shadow dagger through the bottom of the Vespae's chin, sending it straight into its brain.

Dark, viscous blood spilled from its mouth as it screamed, but as soon as she drew her shadows back it fell to the ground, dead. Another was on her as it fell, launching at her from the fray that surrounded her. They swung at one another, evenly matched, for the moment. Harlow slipped, the blood from her former foe slick on the smooth marble floors. The creature lurched towards her, its movements erratic and wild as she fought it off, struggling to right herself, her senses blurring with the stress of the fight. There were so many of them, and she was getting tired.

Luckily, the Vespae she fought was already injured, a gash oozing fluid down its pale, bony chest, seeping through the thin rags it wore as clothes. It was breathing hard, dazed and unable to get its bearings as it gripped her arms. Perhaps it was as tired as she was. Harlow caught herself, using the struggling Vespae to steady her body.

The second she regained balance, she thrust a shadow-dagger into the creature's already injured chest, pinning it in place long enough to separate its head from its body with shadows she wrought into a longer blade. The creature fell to the floor, and there was an exhausted part of Harlow that envied it. Its fight was over, while hers continued.

Yet another of the drones jumped at her, but before she could convince her body to move against it, Tomyris and Samira worked in tandem, ripping it apart. Tomyris leapt back into the melee, her three pairs of draconic wings spread out behind her as she sliced through two Vespae drones with a pair of short swords as easily as if they were butter. Sam shifted out of her Feriant form, catching Harlow as she stumbled, her avian features melting into her familiar humanoid face. "You okay?"

Harlow nodded, woozy. *Maybe she wasn't just tired.* She glanced down at her thigh, where blood and milky white Vespae poison oozed from a tear in her armor. That last one she'd killed must have gotten a sting in without her noticing. Sometimes in the heat of battle, she lost her ability to track every moment. "Got my ass handed to me."

The poison seeped into her, dulling her senses as she looked around to see how the rest of the team was faring. Harlow often lost track of everything but the next move in a fight. She was still a novice, and sometimes that meant tunnel vision when it came to her awareness in combat. Soon she'd lose any ability to use her magic, or shift into her Feriant form. The Vespae's poison acted as a magical immobilizer, temporarily freezing its victim's ability to connect to Okairos' source of aethereal power.

Samira helped Harlow to a velvet-cushioned bench at one end of the hallway. The fight was beginning to die down. Max, Mirai and the four others they'd come with had disappeared to chase down the last of the Vespae, lest they get back to their swarm and bring reinforcements. Harlow had been the only one of them stung, which frustrated her to no end. The Feriant Legion was having a hard time accepting her into their ranks, and she worried that every mistake would be held against her. She took a few deep breaths, trying to focus on the beautiful snow-covered courtyard outside the giant windows the bench faced.

The Austvanger Institute for Geological Research was a lovely facility in an old palace at the center of the city. Harlow's team had come here on a mission to help a group of refugees make their way to the Rogue Order's sanctuary, but their team had arrived too late. The Institute was meant to be a good place to hide, with its maze of hallways and gardens. The refugees had believed they were safe here—and they should have been.

But the Vespae got here first. They were looking for something, and the refugees had been nothing more than collateral damage. "Are they all dead?" Harlow asked, hoping Sam knew she was talking about the refugees, not the Vespae.

Samira's dark eyes widened with sadness. "All but one human. Tomy's talking to her now." Sam nodded towards a huddled figure on the floor near the doorway to the courtyard, and the muscular Ventyr woman who spoke to her. Harlow blinked several times. The Vespae poison was making her groggy and she hadn't noticed them at all. Tomyris, Sam's partner, spoke softly with the injured human. They recited a familiar prayer to Raia the Mother in unison. Tomy was honoring her last rites. "She won't last long."

"Poor thing," Harlow murmured. She watched, her vision still blurry, as Max, Mirai and the other returned. They dragged corpses, Vespae and refugee alike, into the courtyard.

Samira, who had become one of her best friends in the Feriant Legion, fished a syringe out from a pack at Harlow's waist. "Why didn't you take this sooner?" the Strider asked, as she stabbed Harlow's arm with it.

Tomyris' venom, the antidote to the Vespae's, flowed into her. It burned through her, cleansing her vital systems of the creatures' debilitating poison, but it hurt. Tears stung her eyes, and not from the pain.

Sam sunk down next to her on the bench, her sturdy body a warm comfort as the venom did its work. Though the rest of the Legion remained chilly with Harlow, Tomyris and Sam, and the Legion's strategist, Audata, had become friends. Friends who knew that every mission that wasn't looking for Larkin and Finn tortured Harlow.

"We'll be back on the search soon enough," Sam reassured her.

Harlow closed her eyes against the pain of Tomyris' venom, but it did nothing to help the ache in her heart. "It's been so long since we had a lead," she whispered. She didn't want any of the team to hear her complaining; she felt enough like an outsider as it was, and didn't want them thinking she resented being sent on missions like these.

Sam's hand closed around hers for a moment, and Harlow felt blessed for the thousandth time since that last day in Nea Sterlis for her easy friendship. She and Tomyris were a binary system: Samira, with the gravitational pull of a dark star, and Tomyris the brightest point in any room. They'd taken her under their wings and taught her the ways of the Warbirds, letting her grieve the loss of Finn and Larkin and her family in whatever ways she needed.

Her sisters had been none too happy about it. Thea especially, who wanted nothing more than for Harlow to forgive Aurelia quickly and move on. If Selene couldn't forgive the fact that Aurelia had secrets that might have kept Finn and Larkin from disappearing into the limen, then neither could Harlow. Things had been tense between the Kranes since their arrival in Sanctum, the Rogue Order's compound. So tense that the twins had left with the Wraiths, Nox and Ari Flynn, on covert missions to Nytra and Avignonne, respectively.

Tomyris' venom did its work, and the pain eased. Harlow tried not to think about what Finn's would have done for her, as her Claimed—how fast it would have healed her, or the euphoria she would have felt at his bite. This was the best she could get, and she should be grateful for it. She stood without much of a struggle. "Let's go help them with the bodies," she said, pulling Sam up from the bench.

Sam groaned. "Noooo, I was enjoying a break."

They headed for the courtyard anyway. As they neared the door to the courtyard, Harlow could hear the conversation Tomyris had with the dying refugee. The Ventyr grabbed Sam's hand as she was about to push through the courtyard door, squeezing her partner's hand hard. "There's children in the catacombs."

Sam nodded, rushing outside to tell the six other members of their team. They followed her back inside, a big Ventyr named Max leading them. He crouched over the human, taking her hand with gentle grace, his voice lowering. "Can you tell me where the children are?"

Harlow was impressed with the way the Ventyr in the Feriant Legion were able to present their true forms to humans without frightening them. Their faces were impossibly beautiful, of course, but they were still winged, fanged creatures with a variety of skin colors not seen before on Okairos.

Max, like Finn, had pale opalescent skin with a blue cast to it in some lights, and long onyx hair that hung down his back in a plait. His partner, Mirai, was a short, pear-shaped sorcière with a square jaw and bronze skin that glowed from within. She peeked out from behind Max's wings to glance at the refugee. When she turned, she murmured the directions the dying human gave to the others, glancing at Harlow, trepidation in her eyes.

Harlow was used to that look by now, the vague message that while they didn't believe she'd outright betray them, they didn't fully trust her either. It was the exact same look the sorcière of the Order of Mysteries continued to give her after she'd been with Mark Easton, a human, for two years. Harlow was both utterly exhausted by the politics of Okairos' many factions, and understood completely. When everyone was liable to turn on others for even a miniscule amount of power, this was how things were. People only trusted those they considered their own—and outsiders had to prove themselves.

"I'll stay here and finish with the bodies," Harlow said. She'd found that every time she offered to do an unpleasant task that Mirai softened towards her. She got it—she needed to earn her place.

A small smile played on Mirai's generous lips, so maybe her efforts were working. "Thank you, Harlow. We'll see you back at Sanctum."

Max looked to Samira, who shook her head. "Me and Tomy'll help with the dead." Her voice dropped. "It's going to be a few with that one anyway. We won't leave her 'til it's over."

Max clapped a hand to Sam's shoulder, squeezing it once, before motioning to the team to follow him. Harlow didn't watch them disappear. She just got to work, following Sam out to the courtyard. Tomyris stayed inside with the human, holding her hand and talking softly to her as the woman relaxed more and more. The Ventyr woman had a way with people—all people—that Harlow admired. She was brash and confident, but warm and genuinely kind. She was, Harlow thought, the best of what the Illuminated could be.

*If only the rest of them could be like Tomyris...*

*...and Alaric, and Petra... and Finn.*

Harlow pushed the thought from her mind as she piled the

rest of the refugees' bodies. There were about a dozen of them, though Harlow didn't like to count the dead. Each was a tremendous failure in her eyes, an incredible loss that she couldn't bear to think of specifically in times like this.

There was so much they still needed to do, and Harlow didn't have time to grieve the way she wanted to for these lost lives. Before the season last spring, she'd never thought about death, especially not on this scale. She certainly never expected she'd have to learn to fight, to protect others with both her magic and her skills. It was overwhelming at times, but most of the Warbirds had been thinking this way their whole lives, and it didn't do her any favors with them to show how much this disturbed her.

Snow drifted down in the courtyard in huge flakes. It was pretty enough here, protected from Falcyra's incessant, frigid winter wind. The courtyard was quiet. Austvanger was quiet—too quiet for such a large city, but most people had either fled, or were deep in hiding. The Vespae and the Illuminated alike were a constant scourge here, though in different ways.

They didn't have time to bury the dead, so Harlow and Samira held hands, pulling aether from the threads of magic around them. Together, they transformed the marble statues that looked over the four corners of the courtyard into a tomb for the fallen refugees. Their last companion wouldn't rest with them, but Tomyris would give her all the help she could, and she deserved every moment of the Ventyr medic's help.

Sam's smile was sad when she turned away from the tomb. She squeezed Harlow's arm once. "It's the best we can do for them."

Harlow didn't say that the best they could have done for them would have been getting here sooner, when the call came in over the radio, instead of waiting for the Rogue Council to approve the mission. But like everything on Okairos, the Rogue Order had its processes and traditions. And while those ways were leaps and bounds more progressive in comparison to the immortal Orders, they weren't foolproof. This tomb was evidence of that, but there was no point in saying so. Samira knew as well as she did that making decisions this way saved lives as often as it lost them.

They dragged the Vespae bodies into a pile, searching each one as they went. The Warbirds' top strategist, Audata, had discovered that sometimes the Vespae carried things with them. Her talent was pattern-recognition, and she'd found there was something connecting these items, though she hadn't worked out what that was yet. As such, the Warbirds were tasked with searching all Vespae bodies before burning them.

Sam pulled a small handful of silvery rocks from one of the Vespae's ragged vestments. She dropped them almost immediately. "Shit," Sam swore.

Harlow rushed over to check Sam's hand, which showed no injury. She picked up one of the rocks, and felt what Sam must have: It was as though the rocks were repelling her. Something about them felt *wrong*.

"They were in that little bag," Sam said, pointing to the body she'd retrieved the stones from. A small black bag lay on the ground next to it. Harlow picked it up. The fabric was rough, but had a toughness to it. She examined the threads that made it up, and found they were odd. Stifling. On a hunch, she bent down, using the bag to pick up the rocks Sam had dropped. She felt none of the repelling feeling she had before.

"The fabric blocks whatever gives off that *feeling*," Harlow explained as she filled the bag.

Sam's eyes widened. "You don't think they were here *because* of those rocks, do you? Are they smart enough for something like that?"

Harlow shrugged. "You know what Audata would say."

"Don't question the impossible..." Sam began quoting their strategist.

"Figure it out," Tomyris finished as she came over. "I think the human might recover... But if we take her back together..."

"We won't be able to figure out what's going on with these rocks," Sam finished.

*They finished each other's sentences. It would be cute if it didn't hurt so fucking much to watch,* Harlow thought.

"You take her back then," Sam reasoned. "Harlow and I will look around. We can make the jump together once we set the Vespae ablaze."

Tomy nodded, though there was worry in her eyes. The Dominavus, the Illuminated's elite squad of enforcers, had been spotted in Austvanger recently, and the Rogues' intelligence reported they'd been hunting for both Harlow and Finn.

"Maybe Harlow should take her," Tomy said.

Sam sighed. "If Harlow hadn't been stung, I'd agree with you, but she won't be strong enough to teleport with a human for another couple of hours. You take her, and Harlow and I will finish up here."

Tomyris drew a long breath, then nodded. "Okay. See you both at base."

Sam kissed Tomyris, long and hard. "We're right behind you. Promise."

# CHAPTER TWO

T omyris blinked out with the human, and Harlow and Sam got to work searching the rest of the Vespae. They found nothing, until Harlow searched the last body, and found a scrap of paper, worn and faded. On one side was the number 317, on the other an image of a building with a domed roof that looked vaguely like the planetarium in Nuva Troi.

"What's this, do you think?" she asked Sam, handing her the scrap of paper.

Sam examined it closely. "It looks like an observatory."

"I was thinking planetarium, but that tracks too."

Sam glanced at the number, then strode inside, waving at the bodies. "We can come back to burn them, before we go."

Harlow followed the Strider, who set a quick pace inside the building, her footsteps silent on the marble floors. She stopped short in front of an arched doorway. The stone around it, and all the other doorways, was ornately carved in a delicate pattern, but that's not what Samira focused on now. She tapped her fingers against a gold plate on the door.

A number. This one was 72. Harlow nodded to show she understood and followed Samira to the next door in the long hallway, which had an identical gold plate that read 71. They didn't speak. This was a rule with the Warbirds on missions—always assume the enemy can hear you, and always assume they're where you won't expect them to be. Harlow and Samira turned in the other direction and found door 73. Samira broke into a light jog, which Harlow kept up with.

The building was nearly as cold as outside, so jogging not only made their search for room 317 quicker, but also warmer. Harlow stopped by a stairwell door. A sign showed that offices 300-399 were on the third floor. They were on the "ground level" currently.

"Third floor," Harlow mouthed to Sam, silently tapping the sign.

Sam nodded once, and they crept into the stairwell, careful not to slam the door. They made their way up the stairs, feet quiet on the marble floors, both conscious of the fact that any noise would echo horribly in the enclosed area. Just as they reached the third floor, Sam reached back, gripping Harlow's arm. They froze, listening.

For a long moment, Harlow heard nothing, but she trusted her friend's instincts implicitly. Samira's primary talent was sensing any and all disturbance in the threads that made up reality. It was a little like she "saw" her surroundings in her mind, though many factors affected how much and how far she perceived.

Harlow heard it now. Many floors below, in one of the sub-basement levels, someone—no, *several* someones were creeping up the stairs. Sam's eyes widened pointedly. Harlow nodded affirmation that she'd detected what Sam had. Samira gripped her hand and they worked with their combined power to muffle the noise of their steps as they raced up the last flight of stairs.

Neither were exceptionally good with the kinds of spells that most sorcière found simple, like muffling spells or wards. Aethereal power was trickier, purer—more suited to generative work, like creating the tomb in the courtyard, or magical perception, rather than manipulation of the threads themselves. But they were good enough to dampen the already quiet sound of their steps. They strengthened the muffling when they came to the door, slipping through in silence.

When they were on the other side, Sam waited as Harlow focused. Just as she had done so many months ago in Mark Easton's apartment building, she manifested her desire for a locked door, to which only she held the key. Both appeared, and she felt the threads shift as Sam muffled the sound of the lock turning.

Harlow pressed her hand to the door, melting the lock. "We'll have to find another way out," she whispered.

Sam nodded, tracing a finger over the map next to the door. "This is the only way up to this floor. We'll fly out—do you think you'll be able to make the shift?"

Harlow shrugged as she followed Sam down the hallway. She felt better, and was able to use her magic now, but shifting took more power and her body was still recovering from the Vespae poison. They had theories about recovery timing, but only theories; the variations in how long complete recovery took were unpredictable. Furthermore, it was different for the other pairs in the Feriant Legion than it was for Harlow, who didn't have access to her Claimed's blood or venom. Finn could have healed her, almost completely, in an instant.

That was a forbidden thought, though—Harlow pushed it deep into the recesses of her mind and focused on her surroundings. The third floor was not as grand as the ground floor had been. Here, the hallways were narrower, and certainly darker, as there were rooms on each side, rather than an enormous courtyard at the center.

If the electricity in the building was in working order, the mahogany of the paneled walls would likely give off a warm glow. But the ruling Illuminated had cut the whole world off. As far as anyone knew, power grids were only on in Nuva Troi, parts of Nea Sterlis, and in select cities in nations like Avignonne and Castel des Rêves, where there were large concentrations of elite Illuminated families. As well, those cities had advanced wards that kept the Vespae out. Falcyra had been utterly abandoned, and the Illuminated were determined to punish the entire world for even *thinking* of rebelling against them. The cold, flat light coming in from the window gave the Institute an unnerving, claustrophobic feeling.

Sam stopped in front of 317 and tried the heavy wooden door. It didn't open. She closed her eyes as she pulled a kit out of one of the interior pockets of her jacket. Deftly, using her perception of the threads inside the lock, she picked it in seconds. Harlow envied the skill. She could create all kinds of things with her Strider abilities, but that wouldn't allow her to unlock a locked door. Whatever her perceptive capabilities were, they hadn't emerged yet.

Grinning, Sam stood, pushing the door open for Harlow. Inside, they found what Harlow felt was a fairly typical academic's office: messy, filled with books and papers piled on a heavy desk in the center of the small room. The walls were lined with bookshelves, with one enormous arched window that showed an excellent view of Austvanger, even if it looked over the alleyway that housed the building's many full dumpsters.

Harlow shut the door behind them, knowing it would muffle the sound of their location, if whoever was in the stairwell was attempting to suss them out. She wasn't sure how they'd get up here, but in a building as old as this one, she didn't doubt there were other ways up to this level. The Institute was a former vampire palace, and there were sure to be hidden passages for servants and other clandestine purposes everywhere. They'd bought themselves time, but if their pursuers were even somewhat knowledgeable about this building, they'd find another way to this level. In silence, the two of them riffled through papers and books as quickly as they could, not knowing what exactly they were looking for,

other than something that would give them information about the observatory.

"I'm not finding anything about the observatory," Sam said.

Harlow sighed as she finished searching the desk. "Me either."

Whoever's office this was had been doing surveys of gold mines in Castel des Rêves for decades. Lucrative, but completely uninteresting. Harlow shoved the drawer she'd finished searching shut. It closed differently, hitching halfway through, instead of gliding smoothly as the others had done. Harlow opened it and closed it again, watching it hitch in the exact same spot. She stopped the drawer, then felt along the edge.

Sam turned from the bookshelf she was searching, her movement sharp. "There's something there. Something different about that drawer."

Harlow's fingertips grazed the edge. There it was, a nearly undetectable irregularity. She placed her other hand underneath the open drawer on a hunch, and pressed in on the miniscule bump. The bottom dropped out of the drawer, accompanied by a slim manila paper envelope.

Sam froze, her eyes getting that faraway look they got when she was using her perceptive abilities. "They're here. We've gotta go."

"Where?" Harlow asked, clutching the envelope to her chest.

Sam closed her eyes to focus her extrasensory ability further. "Shit. They're on the other side of the floor, moving fast." She rushed to the door, locking it once more as Harlow threw open the window, feeling inside herself for the telltale spark that told her the Feriant was ready to emerge.

There was a flicker there, but not enough to shift. There must still be traces of Vespae poison in her system. She pushed the window open wide and shoved the envelope into Sam's arms. She looked down at the dumpsters. It was a long drop, but she thought she could cushion her fall with some quick magic. And she'd been taught to fall without taking too much damage, as shifting from her Feriant form quickly in battle scenarios was fairly common.

"Go," Harlow urged. "Get this back to Sanctum."

Sam shook her head. "I'm not leaving you."

The sound of boots on the floor, moving fast was louder by the second. They didn't have time to argue. Harlow lied. "I should be able to shift in a few minutes. All I have to do is fall and run. *Go*."

Sam's dark brown eyes were full of suspicion, but she tucked the envelope into her jacket and stepped onto the windowsill. She was graceful as a dancer, leaping into the air, the lines of her body blurring as her Feriant form took shape. Feriant were sleek, raptorial, and as big as a small SUV. The feathers on the double crest on Sam's head rippled in the wind as she looked back, hesitating as Harlow jumped into the windowsill. Someone was at the door now, and they had lock picks. They might not have Sam's talent with perception, but Harlow had to assume they knew how to use the picks. She regretted not melting the lock now, but there was no help for it; she needed the little reserve of aethereal power she'd built up to cushion her fall.

Closing her eyes, she stepped off the ledge, willing the dumpsters below to soften into several piles of giant beanbags. When her body hit soft velvety material, rather than hard metal, she knew she'd succeeded. Her nose wrinkled. They still smelled like trash though. Above her, Sam hovered, flapping her wings hard.

A figure appeared at the window, and Harlow recognized the face immediately—one of the vampires with the Dominavus squad Rakul Kimaris usually led, recognizable from the hours of footage Nox and Ari had procured over the summer in Nea

Sterlis. Harlow didn't know her name, but the vampire was yelling Harlow's.

"Go," Harlow screamed to Sam as she righted herself, struggling to escape the pile of beanbags she'd created. "Go!"

Harlow was on her feet and running, unable to keep track of Sam above her in the dark, narrow alleys. Somewhere, on one of the streets surrounding her, boots hit the snow-covered cobblestone, running just as fast—faster even—than she was. The Dominavus were a combination of vampires and the Illuminated, after all. They'd use their superior speed to catch her and take her back to Nuva Troi. To Connor McKay, who she knew wouldn't hesitate to harm her if he thought it would get his son back, or if he simply blamed her for his disappearance.

Harlow rounded corner after corner, completely lost, struggling not to panic. From the sound of things, they were closing in on her, though the incoming storm muffled noises, distorting them in ways that made Harlow unable to track her pursuers accurately. Snow was funny that way, she'd learned, and Falcyran winters were terrifying both for their brutality, and the uncanny way storms altered both sight and sound.

And then something wonderful happened.

The astronomical clock sounded its bell. It was one of Austvanger's most storied tourist attractions, having been built almost a thousand years prior to track the movement of the stars and planets in their system, as well as the days. Its bell was one of the loudest in creation, and it would mask the sound of her feet. She ran towards it. If she could make it across the square the clock was located in, she might be able to lose the Dominavus and buy herself enough time until she could make the shift.

The sound of the bell grew louder; she was getting closer. She couldn't hear the Dominavus, so perhaps they couldn't hear her either. The narrow street she was running down widened as she rounded a corner. The way was clear, and she was nearly to the square. A clear view of the clock was directly in front of her, with dozens of street openings to choose from to make her escape. It was two o'clock, which meant the clock was nearly done ringing, as it had already rung eleven times.

The hope that lit Harlow's heart ablaze snuffed out as soon as she tracked her potential path across the square. None of the usual public services were functional, and the snow in the square was an untouched canvas, waiting to be marred. While the blizzard was growing worse by the second, it wasn't yet coming down hard enough to mask her prints. No matter what path she chose, the Dominavus would see the direction she'd gone if they followed her to the square. She didn't have enough power in reserve to mask her footprints either.

Her heart beat wildly, trying to think of another way out as she drifted into the square. Helplessness threatened to take over. There had to be some clever way out of this. There just had to be. She couldn't let them take her back. She hadn't once made it through Audata's tests for resisting torture: she was a risk to everyone she loved.

Tall, imposing figures emerged from half a dozen streets. Harlow's mouth went dry—she was surrounded. Of course, they'd still been able to track her, even despite the bell, which sounded one last time. Laughter skittered across the square, echoing in the new silence.

"Hello, Ms. Krane," a voice said, softly enough, though her words carried. It was the vampire who'd looked out the window at the Institute. "We've been looking everywhere for you."

Harlow thought fast, shoving her clammy hands into her jacket pockets to keep them from visibly shaking. "Is Rakul with you?"

The vampire, whose platinum blonde ponytail swung to and fro as she stalked forward, laughed again. "Rakul won't help you, witch. Give up and come with us without a fight."

"No one here wants to hurt you," one of the Illuminated

said. He was a redheaded giant, nearly seven feet tall, and his voice boomed across the square.

The blonde vampire raised an eyebrow. "Speak only for yourself. *I* want to hurt you." Harlow refused to let her fear show, squaring her shoulders as the vampire took step after excruciating step towards her. "Just give me a reason. I dare you."

The six warriors strode towards her with an insulting lack of urgency. They were relaxed, confident in the fact that she was theirs. Harlow was trapped. Even with her training, she couldn't fight six of the warriors on her own. She'd gotten good enough to fight the Vespae, but this was different. The Vespae fought by instinct, not training. The Dominavus were the most elite warriors known to Okairos. Her shoulders slumped in defeat.

A gust of wind hit her face, as something dark shot out of the low cloud cover of the storm. Talons dug into her shoulders before she could fully register what was happening. *Samira.* Her feet lifted off the ground as her stubborn friend lifted her into the air. The Dominavus moved quickly, but Sam was already rising above the tops of the buildings in the square. As she hit the cloud cover, the spark Harlow had been looking for returned.

She didn't have much power left, but she'd only slow Sam down, and the Dominavus were sure to shift and follow them. "Drop me," she yelled. "I can shift."

Sam hesitated. "I mean it, Sam," Harlow screamed.

One of Sam's talons tapped three quick times on her shoulder then paused. Harlow understood the message; she'd release her in three. The talon tapped her again now, at a slower pace. Harlow closed her eyes and focused on the dark spark of aethereal magic inside her as Sam rose higher into the storm.

*One.*

*Two.*

*Three.*

Harlow fell, dropping quickly as she touched the spark within. As she shifted, her Feriant senses picked up their assailants, not far behind. She beat her wings hard, catching up to Sam.

*Glad that worked*, Sam said in her head. In their Feriant forms, they were able to speak mind-to-mind.

*Me too*, Harlow replied. *Thank you... The Ventyr among them are following.*

*I feel them*, Sam assured her, banking hard heading north.

With Sam's talent for sensing her surroundings, and the cover of the storm, Harlow was sure they'd escape. *Let's go home.*

# CHAPTER THREE

The blizzard cleared about twenty miles south of Sanctum, revealing the forgotten valley that had once been one of Falcyra's most luxurious ski resorts. Fifty years ago, a group of industrious vampires had bought a little fishing village, right at the edge of a fjord, and converted the entire thing into a posh resort, where Okairons could enjoy quaint scenery while indulging in ridiculously expensive spa treatments and the best skiing this side of the Apennine Mountain range. Twenty years after opening, the resort was overrun with ghasts, several nasty poltergeists, and a shade. The shade's murderous howling had been the last straw for the original owners.

The owners sold the resort at an unbelievable loss to Lou Spencer, the Rogue Queen of the time, and she'd made a very big show of having it destroyed to rid the area of the plague of spirits that inhabited it. There had been a television program and everything, though Lou's involvement had been obscured. It had all been a hoax. The television documentary had been the first of the Rogue Order's forays into media manipulation—all to hide this place from the Illuminated, and the Falcyran vampires, in preparation for using it as a large sanctuary.

And it had worked. The area was so remote, and so rumored to be haunted even after the resort's "destruction," that the world had gladly forgotten it existed. Lou had invested in advanced warding. Rogue sorcière from a securities firm in Avignonne, Lou's home nation, had created a series of wards that made Sanctum extremely difficult to perceive, unless you knew exactly the right counter spells to use.

Now it was a bustling village, filled to the brim with a bizarre intermixing of immortals and humans alike. Lou had the rougher elements of the poltergeists and shades banished immediately, which was easy for her to do, despite the former owners having hired the most expensive mediums in the world to fix the problem, to no avail. It was so easy for Lou because she was the one who'd summoned them in the first place.

The side effect was that the ghasts were permanent features of the resort, which was rather unfortunate for Harlow, who was unsettled by them. But aside from that, she was endlessly impressed by Kate's sire, and adoptive mother, who'd used the fortune she'd made from her vineyards to buy this land and make it a sanctuary for the Rogue Order.

As they drew nearer, Harlow's heart ached to see the charming stone houses dotting the valley floor, the snowy, cobbled streets, and the twilight lighting of the gas lamps throughout town. Electricity and most of the basic services that Okairons were accustomed to were still unavailable to them, though Sanctum had a generator that was used sparingly. Near the fjord beyond the village lay an enormous silver firedrake, napping in the snow. *Cian.*

The great dragon raised their head as Sam and Harlow began their descent and stretched, much like a cat would, before launching into the air in one long bound. It took Cian barely any effort to reach them, and they circled just below them, spinning a few times in the air to delight the crowds of children that had come into the streets to watch their flight.

Cian didn't get out much these days, except to complete their assigned patrols, which enchanted the children of the village as much as the abundance of ghasts did. Cian was wracked with guilt and sorrow over what had happened with Finn, but Harlow thought these flights brightened their spirits.

*When you didn't return with the others, I worried*. Cian said. Like the Feriant, in their alternae, they could communicate telepathically.

*I'm sorry to have worried you*, Harlow replied.

Samira's wings tucked close to her body as she dove. Harlow watched her trajectory, spotting Tomyris, who was waving at the center of the village square.

*You worried your parents as well*, Cian said.

Harlow hissed. It was a raptorial noise that she loved making —its violence was satisfying. She could all but hear Cian's inner sigh. She was still not speaking to Aurelia, and though Selene had not reconciled with her wife yet, Harlow knew the day was coming. They'd headed out on long snowshoe hikes several times in the past few weeks. They were talking, and while Harlow had no desire to see Mama miserable forever, she wasn't ready to talk to Aurelia yet.

They'd actually talked too much, in her opinion, when they'd first arrived in Sanctum. Things had been said that Harlow couldn't take back now, nor could she manage an apology, or accept another from her mother. Space was what everyone needed right now, which was difficult in the tiny village. Harlow missed Nuva Troi endlessly, for hundreds of reasons, but the ability to *not* see someone was topping her list right now.

*Go on without me*, Harlow said. *I want to stretch my wings*.

Cian did not reply, but made lazy circles in the air before landing just outside of town in the empty training fields. The children who'd been watching screamed, running towards the field in excitement. Harlow made circles of her own, watching as they piled atop her friend. Cian's only duties were their patrols and babysitting, as there was no safer place within the compound than with a dragon.

Harlow's wings rarely got tired anymore, now that she had daily training sessions with the Warbirds. She took another giant circle around the village, enjoying the feeling of the frigid wind in her face. In her Feriant alternae, there was a kind of peace she'd never known. It wasn't that her humanoid self was gone, but rather that all its concerns were lessened, their immediacy gone to the ultra-present worldview of the Feriant. The Warbirds were teaching her that mentality could be brought into her true form as well, that the two needn't be separate, but like working around the effects of Vespae poison, Harlow struggled to achieve mind-body alignment tasks. Her mind wandered too easily, got too lost in worry, or she was distracted by the sounds around her.

Finn would have ideas about how to make that easier for her when he got back—he always had a hack for her busy mind. *When he got back.* The thought hurt, but in a way that surprised Harlow. The ache had grown familiar, comforting almost. It wasn't that she enjoyed him being missing; there was nothing pleasant about her fear, but there was a painful kind of comfort in musing over what he'd think about the ways the world had changed when he returned.

Harlow would be expected at the Dairy in an hour or so. The standard for mission debriefing was to meet up at the Warbirds' headquarters, and then Audata would report out to the Council. She should head in and shower, but it was so quiet up here. Down there, there were hundreds of people, many of whom were suspicious of her, given her relationships to Aurelia and Finn both.

Everyone knew the ways her mother had kept the Illuminated's secrets, as head of the Order of Mysteries, and though Aurelia had been allowed to stay in Sanctum, she was not automatically trusted, and neither were her children. Harlow had watched her sisters and friends overcome the Rogues' wariness in different ways, but Harlow was having trouble doing so. Aside from Larkin, she'd always been the most introverted of her family, often feeling awkward in social situations. She was never certain how she'd offended people, but she often found out later that she'd made some misstep that couldn't be forgiven.

Okairons had what felt like thousands of subtle rules about how to interact that confused Harlow endlessly. She didn't understand why just being honest about things and respectful of one another wasn't enough, but the intricacies of tone, phrasing and even body language were often beyond her. In situations like these, where everything was further fraught by issues she *did* understand, like the Rogues' completely valid fear of the McKays, who were notorious for their cruelty, or the wariness of the immortal Orders' leaders like Aurelia, everything became even harder for Harlow. There were just so many social cues to parse out, and she often didn't understand what was happening in a given moment, but realized her mistakes later—long after the time had passed to do things the way Thea or the twins would have.

The village buildings grew larger as Harlow descended, though she still felt blessedly removed from the reality of the compound. With her enhanced sight, she spotted Riley Quinn and Enzo walking towards the cottage the three of them shared and she swooped down to greet them. Like Thea, Enzo had integrated nicely into the community here at Sanctum, given his relationship with Riley and all his natural charm. People had always liked her best friend. He had an easy way with people that Harlow lacked, because of his empathic abilities.

Riley was the same, and they reassured Harlow that no one

hated or feared her. As they put it, "They just need time to get used to you being around."

Harlow shifted as she landed, appearing silently behind Riley and Enzo. Axel, who sat in the window, watching for all of them, gave her away. He stood, scratching rapidly at the glass, meowing. Riley turned, their locs fanning out behind them as they spun. "Harlow! You're all right. We were worried when you and Sam didn't come back with Tomy."

Harlow tried for a smile, though she felt the way it only pulled at her lips and cheeks, as she took the chameleon shifter's gloved hand, giving it a quick kiss. Enzo pressed another to her forehead. "Glad you're back. We heard about the trouble from Sam, just now."

Harlow nodded, following them through the garden gate. The three of them had elected to share a small house in the village with Cian, rather than breaking up into one of the tiny ski cottages further out.

"I need to get to the Dairy, but I can pick up our grocery allotment on the way home, if you want," she offered.

The two of them held up the canvas bags that held the week's allotment of food for their house. Luckily, Sanctum had been operating off the grid for a long time. While their generators weren't powerful enough to light each of the village's buildings, the greenhouse had priority of power and the human hedgewitches had made quick work of using their newfound access to aether to encourage winter growth.

The human practitioners astonished Harlow. She'd been taught in school that humans were capable of doing magic, but that they would struggle with it terribly, given their inaptitude for it. Since the breach under the catacombs had been released, and aether flowed freely into the threads of the world now, she'd found something quite different from what the Illuminated had taught them.

"Oh, you got them already," Harlow said, taking a bag from Riley and another from Enzo.

Riley wrinkled their nose. "You smell of Vespae guts."

Enzo's face matched Riley's. "I'll get your gear cleaned up while you wash your hair. You've definitely got Vespae goo in your braids."

Harlow glanced at the dark mess in her honey-blonde hair and shrugged. It was a part of fighting the Vespae she'd learned to ignore. Thinking about it for too long turned her stomach. As they entered the little stone house, Axel wound around their legs, chirruping and purring, as everyone took the groceries to the tiny kitchen at the back of the cottage. Each of the village cottages was furnished in a similar beige and cream palette that had been all the rage when the resort was built, and was equipped with a minuscule, but functional kitchen. Though the refrigerator was all but useless except for storage, the rest of the amenities worked well enough most of the time.

Enzo picked Axel up, kissing his head as he filled his bowl with fresh kibble. "I'll start the water heater for your shower, if you want to send your gear down."

Harlow nodded, then simply undressed in the kitchen. Enzo shook his head, smirking. "Cheeky," he murmured as she shot through the house and up the stairs in only her bra and underwear.

She hadn't wanted to stink up the house, though. Some combination of citrus, rosemary and vanilla infused the air here, making it smell homey and comforting, while Vespae blood carried the distinct smell of death. Enzo, who was adept with any magic regarding garments, would have her gear fresh in no time.

It took a few minutes to assess the damage she'd taken in the fight in Austvanger, but there was nothing that needed attention. *Surely the water heater had filled by now,* she thought. But she didn't really know how long it had been. It was hard to keep track of that kind of thing these days. Harlow had never been good with time to begin with, and without the constant aid of her phone, she was often adrift. She tried the shower water, pleased to find it was the perfect temperature, but it wouldn't be for long, so she hurried to rinse herself off before the hot water ran out.

The tiny bathroom had enough room for a sink, a toilet, and a tub, which had a clever showerhead on the ceiling that Harlow stood under, closing her eyes against the sight of the blood washing away. Quickly, she scrubbed with some of the faintly herbal smelling soap that Selene had brought over last week. She had been working with the human hedgewitches, sharing knowledge—learning together about the different ways to use magic.

Harlow couldn't deny she was proud of Mama—how quickly Selene had adapted to the idea of humans using magic. Though she was loath to admit it, she was proud of Aurelia too. Mother had volunteered to share all she knew with the Rogue Order's governing Council in the spirit of cooperation between immortals and humans.

They'd always been told the Rogues were mostly unhappy immortal outcasts, but in truth, humans were primary in leadership. Samira hadn't been exaggerating when she'd said Kate's title as "Queen" was largely nominal. While Kate was the immortal liaison for the Rogues, her title was little more than a nickname here. She was a member of the Council, which was run in an egalitarian fashion, with each member having an important role.

Each of the immortal Orders had representation on the Council, along with representatives of all ancestries that organized committees for necessities like food, combat training and education of Sanctum's children. While the Rogue Order took in anyone who didn't want to be a part of the Illuminated's strict social structures, there was a fair amount of wariness regarding anyone who'd had heavy involvement in the governing bodies of the Immortal Orders, so people like the Kranes, or any of the

Knights of Serpens, weren't privy to the inner workings of the Rogue Order.

Until coming to Sanctum, Harlow hadn't realized how much Aurelia's position in the Order of Mysteries had affected her life. Now, she and her family were just like everyone else, citizens who were expected to pull their weight. All of her concerns about finding Larkin and Finn were forced to be secondary to whatever the entire Rogue Order needed. She understood it, but it infuriated her all the same, and in moments like these, when she was alone in the shower, she let it make her as angry as she actually was.

Furious sobs wracked through her as she raged against the futility of showing she was trustworthy on missions like the one she'd been on today, when her sister and Finn were out there somewhere, alone, fending for themselves. She didn't know how she was expected to carry on, and pretending like she was handling things was almost more than she could manage.

Cian had made it clear to her that the Council's choices were appropriate a thousand times, that she needed to grit her teeth and prove herself—as the rest of her family had done. She'd tried to understand, but after being ostracized by the sorcière for being with Mark, she was tired of not having community. Tired and lonely—especially without Larkin and Finn, who'd always understood her best.

Harlow rinsed her hair one more time for good measure, breathing in the lingering steam to calm her fury. The water was starting to cool. Finn would love the way the Rogues approached hierarchy, as it was the same as how he ran the Knights. Leaders ate last and fought first, running the most dangerous missions and taking care of their people first and foremost. A stray tear slipped down her cheek as she tipped her head back and shut off the water before it got cold.

Another sob threatened to break free from her chest, but she didn't have time for her tears—for the aching void inside her where Finn and Larkin should be. She dried off quickly, padding down the hallway to the room she and Cian shared. The air was cold, but the room itself was cozy, decorated in calm, creamy whites. It was out of vogue to decorate with such bland colors, but they soothed Harlow's mind, which was a riot of thoughts and fears these days.

Harlow dressed in thick leggings and an ancient sweater that was somehow completely soft, rather than itchy wool. Enzo and Riley had been careful with the fibers they'd chosen for her when they were allowed to procure clothing for their house. Harlow was struggling with irritating textures, or fits that felt as though they were too close to her neck. Since there weren't many choices for everyone, she had few things, and Enzo often altered them for her so that her senses wouldn't be overwhelmed.

No one was sure why Harlow had grown so sensitive to things like light, sound, and fabrics. It had always been like this for her to a certain extent, but now it was worse. When she'd expressed horror at strong scents, Selene forced her to take a pregnancy test, despite the fact that Finn was protected.

She wasn't pregnant, which had been both a relief and a strange sadness. Finn didn't want children, and neither did she, but in that moment, knowing she might never see him again, there had been a sharp pain in her chest. It faded, but a child would have been part of him, a continuation of *them*.

Axel jumped onto the bed next to her as she pulled on a pair of heavy snow boots and laced them up. He purred loudly as he bumped his head hard on her arm. She scooped him onto her shoulders as she went downstairs and he curled around her neck like a scarf, rubbing his face against hers happily.

Downstairs, Enzo and Riley made a richly herbed wild rice soup together in the kitchen. The way they moved comfortably around one another elicited an ache in Harlow's chest as she settled into a kitchen chair. Axel stepped off her shoulders and sprawled out on the tiny kitchen table, blinking slowly at everyone and purring. After glancing at the kitchen clock, she determined she had a few minutes before she had to go debrief and she wanted to soak in as much of this domestic bliss as possible.

Despite their glamorous lives in the real world, Riley and Enzo were domestic deities here at Sanctum. Riley baked bread and arranged branches of various winter foliage into vases that cheered the entire compound. Enzo took in mending and restyled clothes for folks who had differing needs like Harlow's, and he could often be found by the fire, knitting hats and gloves made from the yarn the Rogues crafted from the wool harvested from their herd of hardy mountain sheep.

He said he liked to do it by hand, but he'd devised a way of making three of the same at once, knitting needles clacking softly next to him, floating in the air in concert with his hands. "Hush please. This is my meditation," he'd say if anyone interrupted him.

The comfort she got from sitting in the kitchen as they cooked made her ache for home. For Aurelia and Selene on Friday nights in the kitchen, making big bowls of pasta and drinking wine. The tears she tried to keep in leaked silently from her eyes. But even as she stifled her sobs, she couldn't hide from Enzo and Riley's empathy.

Both turned as a ghast seemingly emerged from the useless refrigerator, attracted to the intensity of her sadness. Harlow was familiar with it by now, as it seemed comfortable here: a former fox-shifter, who spent most of its time as a decomposing vulpine atrocity that often screamed wildly when she cried. It didn't matter that it couldn't actually make noise on this plane—it was disturbing.

Riley handed her a cloth napkin, smiling sadly. "You have to let some of the grief out, love."

They ignored the ghast entirely, which was what nearly

everyone did. It wasn't so easy for Harlow. Axel faced the rotting fox, arching his back, his fur poofing out in an attempt to intimidate the ghast. It simply opened its mouth and maggots fell out. Harlow winced. They weren't real, of course. They weren't even solid, but it was disgusting all the same. Axel hissed at the creature. Perhaps it was intimidated, or just bored, but it dissipated into a little poof of smoke.

Enzo nodded, stirring the soup, completely oblivious to the drama that had taken place behind him. "If you don't, it's going to come out in a storm eventually."

Harlow glanced at the clock, and then let out the sobs choking her in a soft torrent, desperately praying to Akatei to not let the ghast return. Neither Riley or Enzo comforted her with touches or words, but went back to making soup and focaccia, waves of love and acceptance washing over her as she cried.

*She was safe to cry. She had plenty of time for her grief. She was held.* Harlow repeated these ideas to herself several times, but they didn't take, not really. No matter how hard she tried, she did not feel safe, nor did she have enough time. The only thing she knew for sure was that here, in this house, she was most definitely held. That did ease her pain somewhat.

As her sobs slowed and her breath came more naturally, Riley handed her a cool cloth, which she pressed to her face. It smelled of rosemary and well water. She smiled up at them, her mouth still shaky and stretched-feeling from her sobs.

"Thank you," she whispered.

Riley glanced at the clock, then pressed a kiss to her forehead. "You'd better go, or you'll be late for your debriefing."

# CHAPTER FOUR

Harlow's meltdown made her late, despite her best efforts. She made it across the village, to the Dairy, with haste, but Audata was still waiting at the split door with a vaguely impatient look on her face. The Strider was the only one of the Feriant Legion without a Ventyr partner, and though some people found her to be prickly, Harlow liked her immensely.

Audata always said exactly what she meant. She was herself in a way that made Harlow envious. The tiny sorcière was just tall enough to rest her elbows on the half-door. As Harlow approached, relief flickered across her serious face.

"We got started fifteen minutes ago."

"I know," Harlow replied. "I'm sorry."

Audata stood up, stretching her spine to her full height, which was still nearly eight inches shorter than Harlow. Like Harlow's, her hair was braided into two jet black fishtails that hung down her back. This was standard for the Warbirds with long hair.

Audata searched her face. Though her expression didn't change much, her eyes softened. "You've been crying."

Harlow rubbed her runny nose with the back of her hand, sniffling a little. "Yes."

It was always best to be honest with Audata. Sometimes the tiny witch didn't understand subterfuge, even if it was self-protecting. She was like a walking lie detector, and when she couldn't determine *why* someone was lying, Harlow sensed that it caused her deep distress. Harlow had no desire to confuse or upset Audata. She was one of the few people who'd taken her at face value—who believed what Harlow said about herself without question, so long as she was honest. Harlow thought they might even be friends.

"Are you all right now?" Audata asked.

Harlow nodded. "May I come in?"

Audata looked vaguely surprised for a moment, as though she'd forgotten she was blocking Harlow from entering the Dairy, and then stepped out of the way. She held the door for Harlow, who followed her inside. The Dairy was enormous, having housed dozens of cows when the resort was operational, as well as an artisanal cheese store. Now it was the Warbirds training facility and home base.

There really wasn't any difference between the common room and the training area—the inside of the Dairy was one open room, its gorgeous wide-planked floors its only real luxury. But the common area had a semi-circle of couches and uphol-stered chairs they'd taken from the cafe that abutted the former cheese shop. The seating area surrounded a giant board that everyone called Audata's "string wall"—the place where she'd pinned up everything they'd collected from the Vespae, since Audata began to notice a pattern.

Small cards with Audata's precise handwriting on them affixed to each of the items and actual string connected them in a pattern that only Audata understood. The tiny Strider carried the little scrap of paper that Samira found, along with the bag of rocks, and another one of her cards. Everyone else was seated already, chatting amiably and drinking various beverages.

Audata pinned the things Harlow and Sam had brought back from Austvanger to the board. The manila envelope they'd retrieved lay unopened on the enormous stone coffee table in front of her. Samira beckoned, having saved her a seat on one of the couches. Tomyris was sitting on the floor in front of her, reclining against Sam's knee, piling three plates high with the various goodies everyone had brought from home.

Harlow had forgotten to pick up one of the loaves of focaccia Enzo made. The sting of having made yet another social misstep pierced her chest. Debriefings were usually pleasant, with beverages and food to accompany any of the information they'd gained on their enemy, and Harlow should have remembered the bread. She tried to distract herself from her emerging guilt by watching Audata pin her new treasures to the center of the board. Harlow saw their importance immediately as Audata connected a piece of string to each of the other items on the board.

"This is what we've been looking for," Audata explained as everyone quieted. Tomyris handed Harlow a plate of food. She plucked out a globe of cheddar from the selection and nibbled at it, savoring the sharp taste on her tongue as she listened carefully to everything Audata said. "Each of these items was a piece of information about the same thing— I just didn't know what. But I'm sure now—the Vespae are looking for *this* place." She pointed to the observatory in the figure.

"Do we have any ideas about where—or what—it is?" Max asked. He'd changed back into his human alternae. Now he was a tall, dark-haired man, with soulful brown eyes and burnt umber skin that glowed in the lamplight.

Audata shook her head. "Not yet, but I think each of these is a clue." She gestured to the other pins. "They're like pieces of a puzzle, but they all connect, and that envelope may hold the rest of what we need to know."

Mirai's hands fluttered impatiently. "Okay. So let's open it already."

Several glances shifted towards Harlow. They'd been waiting for her. Guilt over inconveniencing them, when they still didn't like or trust her much, seeped through her so virulently that her hands ached with the power of her emotion. Lest she attract another ghast, Harlow breathed deeply, attempting to calm herself.

Audata watched Harlow closely. Harlow knew from talking with her about such moments that she was processing every detail of the room. The furtive glances, the flush of annoyance at her lateness, and Harlow's reaction to it all. What she gleaned from connecting the dots, Harlow didn't know, but Audata stepped forward and carefully tore the sealed envelope open, pulling out a thin stack of papers.

Audata's eyes darted over the information quickly, discarding page after page in a neat pile on the table. A blonde Strider with a heavy, muscular figure stretched across the table, picking a few of the pages up and glancing through them.

"What do they say?" Mirai asked.

The blonde, Vero, shook her head. "Beats me. It's some kind of technical report."

"It is a detailed survey of a mine," Audata corrected, placing the last sheet face down on the table. "An iridium mine, to be precise."

"Iridium?" Max asked.

Audata went to the board and removed the little bag of rocks. She dumped them onto the table. "Pick them up," she suggested when Max leaned forward to examine them.

He did so, and just as Samira had done, he dropped them immediately. "What the fuck is wrong with those things?"

Then everyone had to try it. The eighteen remaining Striders and Ventyr all picked up the iridium, each having a similar reaction, though they passed the handful of rocks between them, rather than dropping them. When Tomyris had her turn, she calmly put them back in their bag, with barely even a wince. She'd held them longer than anyone else.

Harlow hid a smile behind her hands. Tomy was like that, braver than everyone, with a better poker face too. Audata's face didn't change, but again, there was a softening around her eyes that let Harlow know she too was pleased.

"What does this have to do with the observatory?" Vero asked.

Audata took a long moment to look at the board, then back at the papers she'd discarded. "I believe the observatory is near the minefields. Where that is—I don't know, as much of the report has been redacted. But it's a distinctive landmark, wouldn't you say?"

She pulled the illustration down and passed it around. Each of the Warbirds committed it to memory. The building was built from stone, with a top floor that looked to be an elegant glass solarium, and a solid, rounded dome that likely hid a powerful telescope. It sat atop a range of peaks that jutted out into a valley, surrounded by higher, more imposing mountains. In the distance, beyond the valley, lay a fjord. The perspective was a little off, as though an amateur might have drawn it, but none of the landmarks looked familiar to Harlow.

As she watched the Warbirds react, she understood that like her, none of them immediately recognized the location. Audata sat in front of her board, facing the group. In the light of the oil lamp that was placed near her board, her rosy copper skin glowed. She shook her head finally, as though ruling something out.

"It has to be here. There's no fjords in Avignonne."

Everyone looked as though she'd spoken in some language they didn't understand. Audata's eyes flew to the ceiling. She was often mildly frustrated that no one kept up with her ability to both remember vast amounts of disparate information and put it together in a meaningful way. "Avignonne has the only other mountain range where iridium has been found on Okairos, but it doesn't have fjords. Wherever this is, it's *here* somewhere." When no one spoke, she clarified. "In Falcyra."

Tomyris fought back a smile. "Yes, love. I think we're all wondering why we haven't found it yet, with all the patrols and searches we've done over the past months. We must've flown everywhere by now."

"Especially looking for that portal," Peyton complained.

The sturdy Ventyr was one of the Warbirds who liked Harlow the least, and didn't mind showing it. She was never cruel, but she'd made it clear that she and her partner Vance didn't trust Harlow. They'd asked to be taken off searches for Finn and Larkin, long before the portal had disappeared completely.

Harlow took an even breath, reminding herself of the maggot-vomiting fox ghast in her kitchen. Now was not the time to get upset. She'd been teased enough by the Warbirds for the way the ghasts followed her around.

Audata shrugged. "Unless you've been flying in a precise grid pattern, which you have not been, there is no way you've seen the whole of this country yet. Or even the mountain range we're located in. There's only twenty one of you. Twenty-two if you count Cian. It would take about—"

"We get it," Peyton interrupted. Then a bit more gently. "I just meant..."

"I know what you meant, Peyton," Audata replied.

There was no softness around her eyes now. Audata despised being chastised for her tendency to elaborate on the finer details of the things. Thea had a similar reaction at times, and it only endeared Audata to Harlow further.

"I think we're done for tonight," Audata said. "It suffices to say that the Vespae are looking for this observatory, though we cannot yet say why."

The group of twenty-one Warbirds all nodded, one by one. To her credit, Peyton looked guilty. Harlow couldn't hate her, or even dislike her. She wasn't mean, only protective of this special group of people. Harlow hoped that someday she would be accepted fully among them.

"So we keep looking," Samira said. "We keep an eye out for the observatory on patrols, and we stay careful about searching bodies after a skirmish." Samira was a great diplomat. Often her words ended conversations like this, smoothing over the rough edges of the group's many strong personalities.

Audata nodded. "Yes, I think at this point we must be close to something. And the Vespae certainly think they're close to finding the observatory—because these types of items aren't being found elsewhere."

"No?" Max asked.

"No," Kate Spencer said from the doorway. "I've had my people searching since Audata started the string wall, and nothing like this has been found in Nytra or Castel des Rêves."

Kate strode over to the group. "Sorry I'm late, Aud. Petra said to bring you these."

Kate set a stack of three crates of wine down on the table. Petra had just returned from a supply run to her parents' obscenely well-stocked mountain house a few hundred miles away, with all sorts of goodies, as well as essentials. Peyton stood up, heading for the kitchen for glasses and a wine opener as the Warbirds combed through the wine.

Harlow got up, taking a bottle for herself. Kate watched, mouth open, looking as though she'd like to say something. Harlow stuck a shadow dagger into the cork, pulling it out in one fell swoop as Kate watched, aghast. A few other immortals trickled in, all bringing booze and more food—it wasn't unusual for the Warbirds' friends to join them after a debriefing for parties. The Dairy was big, and far enough outside the residential area of the village to not be a nuisance.

A small team of the Warbirds left to join the ground forces for guard duty, but everyone else clearly meant to let off some steam, and for once, Harlow planned to join them. She pushed through the little crowd forming, tossing words over her shoulder as she went. "Tell Petra thanks for the wine."

# CHAPTER FIVE

H arlow made her way to the little conservatory off the back of the Dairy as more people filled the open space. The tiny glass room used to be a greenhouse for fresh herbs used in the artisanal cheese, back in the days before the vampires had turned the village into a resort, but was now used as a meditation room. The big fireplace connecting the conservatory to the main Dairy was used to heat the entire building.

Harlow dragged one of the beanbags that dotted the room towards the fire and plopped into it, listening to the sounds of a party starting up in the common room. Someone had brought a battery-operated boombox, and music was playing. It was old music from thirty years ago, clearly a dance mix that had been played at parties up at the main Lodge, which the Council used for offices now. Not long ago, this would have been Harlow's cue to leave. She and Finn would have gone home and cozied up the cottage, where she'd be sharing a room with him, rather than Cian.

She wasn't sure if she was going to actually *drink* the wine she'd placed in her lap until she was gulping it down, straight from the bottle. Not one person had asked her if she was all right. If being pursued by the Dominavus had scared her. If she was worried that they'd come so close to taking her.

It was certainly more than Harlow could handle. She'd avoided thinking about it the entire trip back, and until the meeting had wound down. But now, it all rushed back—how close she'd come to being taken. She looked through the glass fireplace at the Warbirds dancing in the Dairy. None of these people would have come after her if the Dominavus had taken her. Not even Tomy or Sam, much as they cared for her.

It wasn't that she thought they *should*. If she'd been taken, it would have been foolish for *anyone* to try to get her back. The Dominavus were that formidable. But Finn would have. Finn, who followed her little sister through a breach between worlds, who would have destroyed *this* world and any other to get to her. Who was still out there somewhere, maybe hurt, maybe even dying. Finn would have come for her, and she couldn't do the same for him.

A little voice inside her whispered that Cian would have come for her, but her body was eager for relief from the rage that coursed through her. She took another long gulp of wine, letting the warmth it elicited washed over her. The edges of everything happening in the present got fuzzy as she drank again and again.

The leads had all dried up when the portal closed. It had been nearly a month since the Council had approved a search. Cian still looked, she knew, but she'd been strictly forbidden from going out on her own. When she'd railed against the idea, screaming at the Council that she'd never back down, they'd had the nerve to threaten her with a Binding to stop her from leaving.

It was too dangerous for her to go out on her own, with all she knew about Sanctum—and the Warbirds were needed for missions like the one to Austvanger. The worst part was, she understood. She didn't even disagree, not really. She'd learned so much about leadership from Finn's example that she got why they'd slowed the physical searches, hoping that magical searches might yield better, safer results.

At least they'd kept their word about that. Harlow brought the bottle to her lips again, almost draining the last of the expensive white wine. It had a slightly floral scent, with a buttery finish that was intoxicating. She laughed bitterly to herself. Of course it was intoxicating. It was wine.

Someone tapped Harlow's shoulder and she twisted in the beanbag chair to find Kate, looking concerned. "Are you drinking?"

"Obviously," Harlow replied, shaking the bottle at Kate. It was an excellent vintage, and she hoped it made Kate sick to see her gulping it down like it was water.

"Slow down," Kate pleaded. "You'll be wasted."

Harlow laughed. "That's sort of the point, Kate."

Kate dragged a beanbag next to Harlow's, clearly meaning to sit down and talk to her. That wouldn't do. They weren't in as bad a place as they'd been when they'd first arrived here, but they hadn't made up either, which put a strain on her relationship with Petra, given that they were living together now.

Harlow took another long pull from the bottle—it was almost gone. Had she really drunk nearly the whole thing already? She stood, and the room spun a little, though she righted herself quickly. There was no way she was staying here to spill all her feelings to Kate, of all people. Harlow pushed past her ex, who followed her back into the seating area in the main Dairy. Max and Mirai were setting up rows of shot glasses, pouring a clear, sparkling liquid into each vessel on the coffee table.

Harlow squeezed back in between Tomyris and Sam. Kate followed, frowning. "She doesn't drink."

Tomyris raised an eyebrow at Kate. "Are you the boss of Harlow, Majesty?"

Kate sighed, exasperated. She pushed a hand through her short reddish-brown hair in obvious frustration. "No, but..."

Sam tilted her head as she turned to Harlow. "And do you have a problem with drinking too much that we don't know about?"

Harlow shook her head, choosing lies over the truth to get her way. Audata wasn't here right now, she reasoned. It was just a little lie, anyway. "I don't like the way it makes me feel anymore."

"And you're still choosing to drink tonight?" Sam asked.

Harlow nodded.

Sam shrugged as Kate opened her mouth to say something else. She knew Harlow was lying, and she didn't care. "Stay out of it, Kate. We've got her."

Harlow swiped three shot glasses from Max and Mirai's rows, downing each in rapid succession. Kate's mouth fell open, this time in shock. "They've got me, Kate," she said with a smile.

Tomyris and Sam each took their own trio of shots and then stood, dragging Harlow onto the dance floor. "Be careful, okay?" Sam shouted into her ear over the music. "I know today was bad, and you're hurting, but don't hurt yourself, okay?"

Harlow nodded. "I just need to forget for a little while."

Tomyris spun her around. "We all need that sometimes, babe."

The booze hit her bloodstream hard and she found herself coasting on waves of music, high off her friends, liquor and the strength of her pain that simply would not relent. She didn't forget—she remembered more, the drunker she got.

Fragments of time and memory wove together in a symphony of torment that beat in time with the rhythm of the music, pulsing through her in agonizing clarity. The room had faded to a blur of color and sound, but her memories were all too clear, and all of Finn. Every touch that passed between him. The flex of the lilacs on the tattoo that covered his arm. The lilacs that were for her. The reminder of what he'd lost. And now what she'd lost. What they'd both lost.

Her heart cried out for him. *Where was he? Why hadn't he found her? Why couldn't she find him?* Harlow knew she was drunk, and that things were about to get ugly, but she couldn't seem to stop herself from going down this path.

Vaguely, she knew Kate had parked herself in a chair, and was monitoring her, but when she looked back to glare at her, she'd finally gone. Harlow danced for so many songs, she lost track, trying to drown her pain in the thumping bass. The music pumped hard, and someone passed a bottle of Lethe around, a rare and legendary brew that was rumored to erase sorrow for an evening.

She had no idea where it came from, but she found it pressed into her hands and she took a long swig before passing it on to someone else. Sam and Tomyris glanced at one another. Tomyris slipped into the crowd, while Harlow danced with Sam. Her body felt lighter than air, and she was sure she could fly. She *could* fly. She could become a giant bird.

That thought made Harlow smile. A slow song came on and Tomyris returned, taking Sam into her arms. Harlow's heart hurt more than she could bear, though she wasn't sure she remembered why now, though she knew who'd caused the pain. She turned to find a tall Ventyr standing before her, backlit by the candles in the chandelier.

"Finn?" she whispered as arms went around her.

"Sorry, love. Just me."

Harlow looked up into Petra's onyx eyes. Her wings spread out behind her. Petra was using her true form. In the dim light of the Dairy, Harlow made out a dusky rose tone to her skin, and hair the color of deepest fuchsia. Of course, Petra was pink in her true form—this was the first time she'd ever seen it.

Harlow began to laugh, until tears streamed down her face.

Petra held her closer. "I miss him so much," Harlow sobbed into her friend's shoulder.

"I know," Petra replied. "I do too."

"Why aren't you hanging out with Kate tonight?" Harlow asked, swaying gently to the music with Petra. It was playing softer now, so it was easier to talk. It must be getting late, if someone was turning the music down.

"I wanted to hang out with you."

"Liar," Harlow said, choking on a sob. She was too drunk.

"Am not," Petra insisted. "You never want to hang out with me anymore, so I had to wait for you to make an epically bad choice."

"You're always with *her*."

Petra sighed, taking a swig of Lethe herself, as the bottle was being passed again. "Yeah, that's true. You're gonna make up with Kate eventually, right?"

Harlow nodded, reaching for the bottle.

"Nope," Petra said, passing it on. "Absolutely not."

"You had some!" Harlow whined.

"So did you," Petra argued back.

"Are you drunk too?"

Petra grinned. "Yep. Kate sent me to get you."

"Were you about to have a big romantic night?"

"Absolutely not," Petra lied, grinning. "We were definitely *not* going to stay up all night drinking my parents' nicest sparkling wine and fucking."

Harlow laughed, twirling her friend around. "Take me home so you can get back to your night."

Petra shook her head, twirling Harlow in what was likely an ill-advised spin. When Harlow was safe again in her arms, and hadn't vomited, she said, "No, you need me."

Harlow threw her arms around Petra, hugging her tightly. "I needed you. You came." She pushed her friend away, shaking her shoulders a little. Petra was *so* tall in her true form. Harlow giggled, though she didn't know why. It was time to go. "Will you take me home?"

The Ventyr woman who'd once been her bully, and was now one of her closest friends, nodded solemnly. Harlow let Petra lead her out of the Dairy and into the quiet streets. Most of Sanctum had gone to bed, or was up at the Lodge, socializing at the bar there, or in one of the libraries that was used for games in the evenings. Petra took her hand and they walked home arm in arm, in complete silence. Harlow still felt the music vibrating in her ears and her chest. At the garden gate, she hugged Petra again.

"Thank you," she said, her words slurring slightly.

Petra shook her head, opening the gate and striding across the garden quickly.

"Your true form is soooo pretty," Harlow cooed as Petra went.

Petra glanced back, then did a little spin, her wings spreading out behind her. "I know, right? I'm gorgeous." She knocked on the front door. No one answered, and so she knocked harder.

"Riley and Enzo are out," Harlow remembered. Loudly. She was shouting.

Cian opened the door. "But I am here." They wrinkled their nose. "And the two of you are drunk."

"Her more so than me," Petra said with a grin, shooting into the air. "Night, babe!"

Cian sighed, as though they had never been so tired. "Come inside."

Harlow followed them into the living room, where Cian pushed her into a chair near the fire. "Stay put."

Axel snored softly on the little couch across from her. The arrangement of pillows and blankets told her Cian had been sleeping there, or maybe reading a book. There was one on the floor. She leaned forward, trying to read the title, and fell out of the chair. Axel opened one eye, seeming disappointed at her state. He closed both eyes tighter.

Harlow pointed an unsteady finger at the cat. "Don't be so judgy."

Cian appeared out of nowhere, with a tall glass that smelled of bitter herbs. They sat cross legged on the floor in front of her. "Drink this, please."

In their other hand, they held two thick slices of toast, oozing with butter. "You can have this when you've finished that," Cian promised.

Harlow drank the whole glass in a few long gulps. The liquid was cool and fragrant, but also sharp. "What is that?" she asked, her head feeling a little less spinny right away.

"Something Finn needed frequently when he drank too much as a teenager. He always liked the toast too."

Harlow stared at Cian. Their face was drawn and they looked older than they ever had, as though stress had turned them ancient. The sadness of losing Finn and Larkin was eating at them as much as it was her, and through her drunken haze, she regretted forcing them to care for her.

"Eat your toast. I'll get you some water," the firedrake said, kissing the top of her head.

Harlow munched on her toast, feeling sleepier by the second, but enjoying the idea that Finn liked toast too. Something about the thought was cozy, like he was just in the other room, though of course that made no sense. She didn't make it to the second piece, setting the plate on the floor under the couch. Her heavy head fell on the couch next to Axel, who purred gently as he slept. Harlow was asleep as well when Cian scooped her into their arms and carried her to bed.

# CHAPTER SIX

Harlow woke before dawn, some disturbance in the
threads bothering her. Axel was asleep curled against
her, snoring loudly, but otherwise all was well. She
stumbled out of bed, peeking out the window. The last flares of
a beautiful aurorae display were dying in the sky, the feeling that
had woken her fading as the lights did. She let the curtains fall
shut. Remarkably, she didn't feel as terrible as she expected to.
Her head wasn't even fuzzy, just slightly sore.

She glanced over at Cian's bed, which for the first time in a
long time actually had the firedrake in it. Their silver eyes
opened, glowing faintly with celestial light.

"You slept," she said.

"Yes," Cian murmured. "I need to rest for a few days, I
believe."

Cian had been as restless as she had, and since they were not
restricted by the Rogue Order, they'd run themselves ragged
searching for Finn and Larkin. As much as she wanted to find
them both, she didn't want Cian destroying their health to do it
—and they had been. There were dark bruises under the

Argent's bloodshot eyes again, which had become an altogether too common state for them.

"That would be good for you," Harlow replied. "Can I get you anything?"

Cian shook their head, but sadness infused every motion with a dull heaviness she felt in her bones. She was shivering by the window. The cottage got chilly overnight, despite the heating spells that kept the fireplace smoldering. When she'd tucked herself into bed next to Cian, a heavy thump signaled that Axel had joined them, settling in behind the shifter's back. Harlow laced her fingers through Cian's, kissing them.

"You were *very* drunk last night." There wasn't a trace of judgment on their face, only the tiny wrinkle between their eyes that appeared when they were worried.

"Yes," Harlow agreed. "Not something I plan to do again anytime soon, but it's been a lot lately."

Cian's eyes glazed over, as though they saw something far away that she did not. "It has. I am so grateful the Dominavus were not successful yesterday, sweet girl."

The pain in Cian's voice nearly broke her. "I love you," she whispered, unable to speak at full volume without sobbing. "You know that, right?"

Cian nodded. "I made so many mistakes."

"We all have."

The Argent growled, a low rumble in their chest. "You haven't forgiven your mother as easily."

"That's different," Harlow reasoned.

"It isn't," Cian said, squeezing her hand. "But I appreciate you all the same."

"We'll find them," Harlow said, sounding more confident than she felt. "I'm on another patrol today, and I'll keep a close eye out."

"You always do." Cian's voice was flat.

Harlow wasn't sure how to respond. They were both

exhausted from the highs of hope that only crashed when they didn't find them. "You'll rest?"

"I'll rest," Cian promised, kissing her fingers the same way she'd done.

"Okay, when you're ready, we found something interesting for Audata's string wall. I'd like you to take a look."

But Cian had already fallen back asleep. She could tell them about it later. Harlow fumbled in the dark, donning her clean fighting gear, grateful for Enzo's magic that left it smelling fresh and kept the lining soft against her skin. The old Harlow, before she lost Finn, would have hated herself for getting drunk last night. She would have gone over every moment in her head, worrying that she'd embarrassed herself. And that impulse was there, but she firmly set it aside.

Many nights since coming to Sanctum someone got a little too drunk, a little too sad, or even sometimes a little too angry. It was against the rules to cause repeated issues, but there was a lot of leeway and acceptance here for people grieving the loss of so many Okairons deeply. Nearly everyone at Sanctum had lost someone they cared for in the Vespae's initial surge, and people needed a variety of ways to work through that grief. What she was feeling wasn't special, or unusual. Harlow did her best to let it go. She'd needed to let off a little steam, and that was that.

When she'd finished braiding her hair, Harlow kissed Axel's head. He let out a sleepy little squeak, following her as she crept out of the bedroom. Everyone would be asleep for hours still as the compound was deeply settled into their winter routine. The Rogue Council knew everyone was drained from what they'd endured, and it was common knowledge that spring's arrival would mean the start of an unrelenting conflict.

Axel nearly tripped her, winding through her feet as she made her way to the kitchen to feed him. Absently, she scooped food into his bowl, going through the motions of her morning routine as she obsessed. She turned on the battery operated radio on a low volume in the kitchen. Everyone had one, and the batteries got recharged weekly by humans learning to channel aethereal power.

Sanctum had a very localized radio channel, blocked from the outside by their magical wards, and there were as many updates to what was going on in the outside world as the Council would allow, playing on the hour each day. As the human who read the updates gave the weather report, Harlow zoned out, watching Axel eat. She wanted to hear the overnight report—to find out if the Dominavus had been spotted anywhere outside Austvanger. The host would go through the weather, and then the schedule of volunteer activities for the day, before they got to any of that.

The Rogue Order had every intention of offering an ultimatum to the Illuminated, come spring: join forces to fight the Vespae, and agree to a complete reformation of the way Okairos was governed, or there would be open war. No one expected them to agree to collaboration. It would be war.

*War*. With the Illuminated—the Ventyr and the Vespae both, on two fronts, at the same time. They didn't have the numbers or the firepower, but there was little other choice at this point. The Vespae were ravaging Okairos, and the Illuminated were holding all the resources hostage. War was inevitable, if only for survival. It was a terrifying notion, but it was still a way off. Deep winter had descended on them here in the high reaches of Falcyra, and it was hard to imagine the season ever ending. The Council encouraged residents to recuperate, to sleep whenever they could, to read books, and to congregate for recreation.

Life here in the Falcyran wilderness was hard, and rest was integral to making certain Sanctum ran smoothly. But Harlow couldn't rest. She couldn't sleep for longer than four hours at a time, most nights. Lately, she was sure to be up long before the sun. But there was someone else in her family who'd be up at this early hour—she knew that much, as she slipped out of the house.

*Thea.* Her sister would be awake, performing locator spell after locator spell in the little workshop attached to the cottage she shared with Alaric and the maters. Harlow jogged through the frigid morning air, making her way across the steep hills of the village quickly, and let herself into the cozy workshop.

Thea sat at a rustic table, sipping tea. She barely acknowledged Harlow's entrance as she stared at the topographical map in front of her. Blood-red sand was scattered across the table. Thea's slender right palm was covered in the sand used for the locator spell, as though she had slammed her hand down on the table in frustration.

"Nothing still?" Harlow asked as she poured herself a mug of tea, stirring honey into it as she sat across the table. The witchlights in the workshop put off the perfect balance of light. Not so bright that Harlow's eyes strained, but a warm glow that filled the little room entirely.

"Not a godsdamn thing," Thea answered. She tucked her dark brown hair behind her ears. It had grown since her summertime bob, but still didn't quite graze her shoulders. "I don't know why it's not working. I can track you all over creation. I know where Connor is. Where Pasiphae spends her days... But *them*. I can't find them."

Thea's talent with locator spells had been a surprise. But Selene's mother had been adept in this kind of magic, too. Selene hadn't inherited her skill, but talents often skipped generations. Before the twins left, they'd tried, but were only decent at them. Thea had proven to be the gifted one.

Harlow missed the twins. She'd been grateful when Arebos and Meline had joined them at Sanctum, but they'd left again with Indigo and Nox almost as soon as they'd arrived. The Wraiths were needed elsewhere, and the twins were now a part of their unit, running intense intelligence missions for the Rogue Order in both Falcyra and Nytra.

"What about Rakul and Vivia?" Harlow asked.

They'd tried to find the leader of the Dominavus and his wife, as well. The two of them likely knew more about the Vespae and the Illuminated combined, given their age and the fact that Vivia Woolf was the Empress Lofrata's daughter. She was a living legend—a firedrake who'd known the world before the Illuminated came. She'd fought the Vespae alongside her mother, and the other Heraldic shifters, before Okairos was forever changed by the Ventyr's arrival. Vivia and Rakul knew things that could change the Rogue Order's standing in the world order, if only they could find them. But so far, they'd had no luck.

Thea shook her head. "It's the same. I can't find them either. People with access to some of the most sophisticated magical cloaking on Okairos, I can find, but the people we need to find most..." Thea's voice broke over her words.

"Hey," Harlow said, rising to hug her elder sister. "Hey, it's not your fault. We don't know what's going on."

Thea nodded, her chin quivering. She pulled a few threads rapidly, and the sand piled itself up, the map curling around it to contain it as she scowled. "It makes me so *angry*."

Thea truly hated not knowing something. It was one of her best qualities, but also the one that tortured her most. It wasn't unusual for her to fall down tunnels of information for weeks, only emerging sporadically for rest and sustenance—until her curiosity was satisfied. But these last few months, between the Merkhov book, the Scroll of Akatei, and now Finn and Larkin's absence, was about more than serving her own desire to know. It was the cornerstones of her world at stake. Harlow had watched as her eldest sister descended, slowly at first, and quicker since they'd arrived in Falcyra, into obsessively ferreting out the root of things.

Thea got up from the table, pulling a few more threads to clean up her mess. It was a trick that made Harlow endlessly jealous, as cleaning wasn't something she could manage with her own magic, and it made things so convenient for her sister. A metal rack that was probably meant for sorting mail held several of Thea's projects in organized rows on the buffet behind them. Thea plucked a little book from one of the slots. She handed it to Harlow.

It was *The Warden*—the story of how Finn's ancient ancestor Ashbourne had come to guard the most dangerous elemental creatures the universe had ever known—the Ravagers. The story read more like a love story than anything else, a tragedy really, but there were several pages missing that might hold the key to something more substantial about the Ventyr. Harlow couldn't help but wonder if Larkin and Finn might know those secrets after traveling through the limen with Ashbourne, but the dull ache that spread from her chest to the tips of her fingers when she thought about it too hard was enough motivation to shove the thought into a deep hole in her mind.

Thea's eyes narrowed, watching Harlow struggle. "I failed here as well. I can't find anything else out about the missing pages, or the person who wrote this."

"That's okay. It was a long shot since we don't really have access to archives of any kind here."

Thea hummed in affirmation, but her beautiful face clouded with worry. Harlow noticed the hollow in her sister's cheeks, the dark circles under her eyes, and the sallow tone of her skin. Thea didn't look well. In fact, she looked downright queasy. And then she lurched for a trash can, heaving several times before vomiting. Harlow moved quickly, kneeling behind her sister, pulling her hair back from her face. She said nothing, but focused instead on the threads between them, sending cool aethereal light through them to soothe Thea.

"Thank you." Thea slumped next to the trash can, her back resting against the buffet. "That's a neat trick."

"You're sick. We should get you to bed."

Thea's smile was wan, but happy. "I'm not sick, pal."

Harlow bit her lip, a frown crowding her face for a brief moment. Then, as she put the pieces together, the first genuine smile she'd had in weeks stretched her cheeks. "Are you..."

Thea nodded. "Twins."

Harlow threw her arms around her sister, tears pricking at her eyes. "I am so happy for you."

Thea squeezed her back. "Thank you. We're thrilled."

Harlow pulled back a little. "I am too. Congratulations."

Thea stroked Harlow's cheek. "I wish you'd try to hear Aurelia out."

"Please. This is a happy moment. Let's not ruin it."

Thea frowned. "She was trying to protect us."

Harlow groaned. They'd been over this dozens of times since the catacombs. Her shoulders slumped and her head fell into her hands. "But if she'd told us what was going on, Larkin never would have been there—I never would have brought her—and Finn wouldn't have followed her through the breach."

Thea was silent for a moment. When she spoke, her voice shook a little. "Are you angry with Aurelia, or *yourself*, for bringing her with you on such a dangerous mission?"

"So now you're blaming me?"

"No!" Thea insisted. "I'm not blaming anyone. What happened in the catacombs was terrible—but I'm not sure it's anyone's *fault*."

Thea. Always the peacemaker. Harlow sighed, searching her sister's face. For what, she didn't know, but what she found worried her. Thea was too upset, too overwrought about all this. It couldn't be good for the twins.

"You shouldn't be out here doing these spells," she scolded. Magic was safe enough during pregnancy, but like anything, it took energy. Energy Thea clearly didn't have right now. "Let's get you to bed."

Thea began to protest, but the door to the workshop flung open, interrupting her. It was Alaric, and though his usual calm demeanor was firmly in place, his eyes were wide. He rushed to help Thea up off the floor. "We talked about this," he murmured. "And you snuck out here anyway."

Guilt flickered in Thea's eyes. "I had to try out a theory..." she whispered back. "But I was wrong."

Alaric didn't seem to be listening to what she was saying, only waiting for her to stop speaking—too polite to interrupt his wife, even if he had something important to say. As soon as she was quiet, he looked pointedly at Harlow. "A swarm is mounting an attack against Sanctum. You've got to go. They'll be ringing the alarm any minute."

Harlow sprang up, tucking *The Warden* into her jacket. "Get her and the maters to the Lodge."

Alaric nodded. They'd worried this was coming for a few months, especially when Audata obsessed over the objects they'd found. She'd been concerned at first that the Vespae were searching for humans, specifically, like vampires might. But they learned quickly that the Vespae didn't feed off humans, or any animal matter at all. They ate a strictly plant-based diet, despite having evolved into what appeared to be apex predators.

Now, Harlow worried that the advanced wards on Sanctum might actually be working against them. If the Vespae were looking for that observatory, and it was somewhere in this mountain range, they might believe it was hiding behind the wards that obscured the village from view. If they overran Sanctum, everyone here would be dead in a matter of hours.

She kissed her sister and made a split second decision to teleport home. Inside her own cottage, everyone was still asleep. Quickly, she opened the door to Enzo and Riley's room. They were curled up together in their big bed, covered by a fluffy linen duvet.

"It's happening," she hissed, her voice suddenly choked with fear. Enzo, likely feeling her terror, woke immediately, sitting up as Riley woke more slowly.

"The Vespae?" Enzo asked, eyes worried. She nodded, noticing only now that Axel was asleep between them. Harlow scooped him into her arms, kissing his fuzzy cheeks as he purred, a low thrum of comfort.

"I've got to go. Don't worry about taking anything—there's plenty of supplies. Get Cian up, and get to the Lodge. Now. They're going to ring the alarm any moment."

"I love you," Enzo said, her terror reflected in his eyes. He knew exactly how much danger they were in, just as she did.

"I love you too," she said. "Get them out of here. Now."

Riley grabbed her hand. "See you in a few."

It was exactly what she needed to hear. She nodded, and teleported straight to the Dairy, which was abuzz with activity. Audata outfitted everyone. As the only Strider amongst them who hadn't paired with one of the Ventyr yet, she couldn't transform into her Feriant form, but in addition to being their resident genius, she was also the armorer—and she took the job of kitting everyone out for a fight seriously.

"How many?" Harlow asked as soon as Audata spotted her and went to work fitting a pack of something around Harlow's left thigh.

"This is Tomyris' venom. Drop out of the fight to inject yourself if you're stung, okay?"

"How many?" Harlow asked again. Audata was avoiding her eyes.

"A whole swarm."

Harlow's heart sank. That was too many for the Warbirds to fight on their own. They would inevitably come here—and then they'd find out if Sanctum's wards would hold. They weren't meant to keep the Vespae out. Their force was largely in averting perception. If they didn't hold... well, Harlow wasn't going to entertain that thought.

She wished desperately that there were more aerial fighters available—that they'd been able to find more of the Heraldic shifters. As it was, the ones they had found were children. None were older than twelve, and they had no place in a fight like this. As she thought this, she felt a distinct disturbance in the threads around her.

Slowly, she turned. Cian stood in the middle of the barn, looking tired, but alert. Their eyes met and her head began to shake. "No," she insisted, stepping towards them. "No. You haven't been well."

Peyton scoffed. "They've been on patrols, and guarding the children. We *need* them, Krane."

Harlow stepped forward, ready to give Peyton a piece of her mind. More than a piece, actually, a whole damn diatribe. How fucking dare she try to insert herself into this conversation?

"Harlow." It was just one word, but it was a subtle command. Cian outranked her, and loyal as she was to the Warbirds, the Knights were her first affiliation.

Cian took her hands in theirs. "I am well enough for this fight. The Vespae will feel my fire."

She couldn't lose Cian though. If Finn returned and she'd allowed Cian to be harmed, he'd never recover. *When* Finn returned, she corrected herself. When he returned, he would be devastated *if* he found his closest confidant and mentor had been harmed. These little corrections were important for staving off despair.

"I will be fine, Harlow. More than fine. You'll see." Silver flame flickered in the limenal space between them. Harlow felt it, more than saw it.

"What *is* that?" Harlow breathed.

"That's a beast the Vespae won't soon forget," Max said,

clapping a hand to Cian's shoulder. "My gran'da fought with the Heraldic in the Great War. I heard stories of your kind my whole life."

All of the Ventyr here were descendants of Ventyr who'd fought in the War of the Orders—they had never been "Illuminated," only ever devoted to the cause of freeing Okairos from oppression. It was the reason the Rogue Order trusted them. Their ancestors hadn't been Knights of Serpens, of course, since all of the Ventyr Knights had been executed, but rather the Ventyr that had been less important to Connor and Pasiphae, the ones who'd gotten away and never returned to Illuminated society.

Cian smiled. "And today I'll give you a story to tell your children."

Mirai wrapped her arms around Max's waist. "Thank you, Cian. I'll feel better if you're with us."

"It will be like the old days," Cian murmured.

Harlow still didn't like it, but she knew better than to argue further. In truth, she didn't want to fight. She wanted to go home. Home to Nuva Troi, not back to the cottage. To a year ago, before any of this had happened. She'd thought that was the worst time in her life, right after she and Mark had split up, but so much of everything that had happened since had been terrible. Not reconnecting with Finn, of course, but the world had changed in ways it would never recover from, and a part of her wanted nothing more than to return to the days when her worst problems were what Section Seven had to say about her.

Audata clapped once, returning everyone's attention to her. "We need a quick briefing on strategy, and then we need to get out there."

The Warbirds quieted, surrounding Cian and Harlow, who still held hands. Cian dropped one hand, so they could turn to face the group. The other, they held to their heart. "Thank you for having me with you today. I am honored to fight with you."

Despite the fact that she didn't want Cian to fight in their exhausted state, she was proud of them. There was no doubt that they were brave. Braver than she could ever be, and an obvious example for everyone in this room, who idolized the Heraldic shifters—firedrakes especially. Once, Okairos had been ruled by what Cian described as a servant-monarchy of Argent, dynasties of silver firedrakes whose only function was to protect humans. Cian was a mythological protector to them, not one of their closest friends. Harlow bit her bottom lip and tried to focus.

Audata spoke about needing an adaptive strategy to beat the Vespae back. Though many of the refugees at Sanctum had survived swarm attacks, most had been too busy fleeing for their lives to stop and analyze how the Vespae were so coordinated and effective in the face of magical wards. The Rogues were going in without vital information about how to win, and would have to bank on the element of surprise with Cian's presence.

They would pull the village's wards back from the edge of the compound to surround the Lodge, while the Legion and the ground divisions would hide inside various strategic points in the village to block the Vespae's approach. Since their numbers were so much greater, a more covert approach was necessary. Everyone was fitted with battery operated walkie-talkies, with old-school headphones. They only worked in close range to one another, but they would allow for the Legion and the ground fighters to adapt as needed during the fight.

It was a risky, terrible plan, as plans went. Harlow hated it. She was so frightened she thought she might have circled back around to bravery, numbness over the unreality of what they were about to do settling over her, as it did before every mission she went on. First came the fear, then the period of feeling absolutely nothing at all.

"Find the queen," Mirai reminded everyone, as the Legion

split up. They had minutes until the wards would withdraw from the edges of the village. "The Council thinks that if you take her out, their telepathy will be damaged, and their efforts less coordinated. It should make them easier to deal with."

Everyone nodded. There was nothing left to discuss.

"See you on the other side," Audata said, her voice solemn.

"On the other side," the Warbirds echoed back.

# CHAPTER SEVEN

Harlow peeked out the dormer window of the stables at the edge of town. The animals were sheltering at the Lodge, with everyone else, and it was odd not to hear the chickens chatting to one another, or the soft sounds of the goats and cows as they moved through their days. Harlow had always been a city girl, and it surprised her how quickly she'd grown accustomed to the sounds of livestock in the village.

The stillness was ominous, the feeling made worse by the waiting. She slumped back against Samira's shoulder, shaking her head. Nothing had changed since the last time she looked. There was no sign of Max or Mirai, who were scouting the Vespae's approach. The rest of the Legion was scattered throughout the first ring of rooftops behind them, Cian another few streets closer to the Lodge. The Argent was their secret weapon, their big surprise for when they were overwhelmed by the Vespae's numbers.

Not if. *When.* A whole swarm was more than anyone had ever fought and lived through outside of the big cities, as far as any of them knew. Harlow had to believe that today would be different though. A crackle came over her walkie talkie, and then Max was speaking in her ear. "Harlow?"

She hit the button that allowed her to speak. "Yeah, I'm here." She was surprised Max had contacted her, and not Tomyris.

"No one else's walkies are working. Something's interfering with the signal," Max explained.

Harlow swore quietly, whispering the news to Audata, who sat next to her. The little Strider glowered, furious that her plan had been foiled. She was already scrambling towards the tech supply table she'd set up here in the attic, fiddling with various instruments and radios that Harlow didn't understand. Obviously, she was trying to figure out what was wrong, but as she didn't have answers, Harlow turned her attention back to Max.

"Audata's trying to figure it out," she replied. Sam handed her a pad of paper and a pencil so she could write down whatever Max said next.

"We have a problem..." A crackle interrupted the Ventyr. Harlow caught one last fragment of his news, "...two swarms, not one..." a high pitched whine filled Harlow's ears. "...locate one queen though... not with... guard..." Static took over and then a series of muffled buzzes and clicks.

Harlow frowned at Sam, shaking her head. She'd been trying to listen and write down what Max was saying. "He's gone." Sam removed the headphones from her ears and the buzzing grew louder, overwhelming in volume.

Tomyris peeked out the window now, quickly returning. "There's got to be two swarms. Max is right. This is bad."

Audata shook her head, pushing one of her radios hard in frustration. "The noise they're making. It interferes with the signal. We won't be able to communicate with the ground forces that way."

Tomyris stood. "We're going to have to shift sooner, trap their focus."

Audata nodded. "I'll get the messengers ready. See if you can give us some cover to make up time."

Harlow followed Sam and Tomyris to the roof. Once all the Striders shifted into their Feriant forms, the group would be able to communicate telepathically. They wouldn't need the walkies, but it had been a good way to coordinate their defenses, and a more covert approach with the ground forces.

Sam winced as they climbed onto the roof. "Hope that noise they're making doesn't block our abilities."

Tomyris' mouth twisted with worry. She didn't respond. Sam and Harlow shifted at the same time. There was no time like the present to try it out.

*Can you hear me?* Sam asked.

*Yes,* Harlow answered, relieved that one thing was going as planned.

The other Striders checked in as they shifted, all but Mirai, which was understandable. They'd gone behind enemy lines, and it was tough to say what was happening. Harlow said a swift prayer to Akatei for their safety, and then poised herself to launch when commanded.

Vespae drones approached slowly, crawling out of the wooded mountains surrounding Sanctum on all fours. Behind them, the more elite queensguard walked upright, surrounding a queen. Unlike some of the other queens Harlow had encountered, this one's wings were in more than decent shape—they were beautiful.

When another queen joined her, stepping out of the woods to take the first queen's hand, Harlow frowned. The drones surrounded the village, but did not begin the attack. Harlow used her enhanced Feriant vision to hone in on the queens. The second queen's wings, like the first, were in good shape.

Harlow wondered, briefly, if it might indicate that they were younger. There was not another way to tell with the Vespae, as far as Harlow knew. But, of course, they knew so little about them. It was impossible to even tell how many had surged from the breach in Nea Sterlis. The release of magic when the Vascularity collapsed had spit them out into the world in such a way that had obscured all but the fact that they were there.

Not that anyone could miss that fact. They'd barely waited three days before systematically attacking every village, town and city in their way. They'd appeared everywhere, in every nation, all over the planet. If the Illuminated knew how they were doing it, how many there were, or anything that would help the people of Okairos, they never said. They just locked themselves in their cities, and kept the lights firmly turned off for everyone else. The message was clear: *ab ordine libertas*. From Order comes freedom. Submit to the Illuminated Order, or stay victim to an increasingly dangerous world.

This dangerous world, where innocent people would die today, all because people like Connor McKay needed to have all the power. Harlow clucked her giant raptor's tongue, agitated by the thought as she watched the queens, who appeared to be talking to one another, assessing something about the village itself. The second queen scanned the rooftops, looking at each of the Legion in turn. When she came to Harlow, she pointed, making a high-pitched noise.

"What in seventeen hells is she pointing at Harlow for?" Tomyris muttered.

Sam trilled in response. There was no need to translate; Harlow understood. She didn't like it either.

The Vespae still didn't approach. The second queen walked through the drones, and they parted for her, making a pathway towards the village. The queen made direct eye contact with Tomyris—apparently she'd identified her as the leader, which Harlow couldn't blame her for. While Tomy wasn't the largest of the Ventyr present, she carried an aura of absolute authority.

The queen spoke, making a series of buzzes and clicking noises. Of course, no one could understand her as she pointed over and over at Harlow. Finally, obviously frustrated, she threw her long, pale hands in the air. She was graceful as a dancer, and just as beautiful, her long, white hair plaited in a complex braid that used more than three strands. The first queen hissed, a low menacing sound in response. The second hissed back, and then turned to try again.

Tomyris stepped forward, holding up a hand before calling out. "I am sorry we cannot understand you. But your interest in Harlow Krane must go unsatisfied. There is no circumstance in which we'd allow you to take her, or any of our people."

*Sam*, Harlow insisted. *Tell Tomy I can go with them, if it will stop them from attacking the village.*

There was a long pause, while Sam relayed the information.

Tomyris placed her hand on Harlow's wing. "No," she murmured. "We don't know the terms, so you stay."

Across the telepathic link, the rest of the Legion agreed. Even Peyton, who'd been one of Harlow's least favorite people for the past few months, was absolute in her stance. Something about that surety that she belonged with them soothed her, afraid as she was.

The first queen hissed again, and the noise rippled through the drones. The second queen's brow furrowed, and while Harlow knew little about the Vespae, she recognized frustration easily enough. The second queen looked directly at Harlow, then made a low noise. One that sounded like a plea.

She was cut off by one of the drones that stood, yanking on her arm, dragging her back to the first queen, who struck her across the face. The blow was brutal in force, her taloned fingers dragging across the second queen's face and sending her to her knees. The gashes were deep; the first queen hadn't held back in the slightest.

Harlow had the sinking feeling that whatever they couldn't

understand had been the second queen's attempt at something she *could*—she'd tried to find a way to do things differently—and now she was being punished for it. Harlow shifted back into her humanoid form without thinking.

"Stop," she cried. "Stop hurting her."

The first queen turned towards Harlow, then let out an ear splitting screech. As the drones raced forward, Harlow caught sight of the second queen's face as her own people dragged her back into the forest. Though her alien features made it difficult for Harlow to know for certain, she thought she saw regret on the second queen's face.

Around her, the Legion was launching into the air. Harlow had no choice but to shift and follow. The Firestarters in the ground forces, a combination of sorcières and humans with a talent for the fire element, moved their hands in coordinated motion, pulling threads so rapidly Harlow couldn't track them. Dozens of sigils flamed to life. These were Sanctum's secondary wards, a series of tangible, magical barriers. White-hot flame shot into the air as the sigils connected to one another, creating a wall of fire that the drones simply ran through. Some caught fire and died, nearly instantly, but others streamed through the holes their dying comrades made.

Harlow dove with the other Feriant, using the force of their giant wings to skim through the waves of Vespae surging forward, sending dozens to the ground with each subsequent plunge into the fray. Behind them, the Ventyr used celestial fire to burn the fallen before they could rise. It was an effective strategy and if there had been more of them, it might have stopped the Vespae's attack—but there were almost two thousand drones, and only nine pairs of Striders and Ventyr in the air, and Harlow.

They weren't holding them back. The ground forces were making progress, with magic and weapons alike, but they were only slowing the Vespae down, not stopping them. Fighting had moved into the village. The most terrible, wonderful noise Harlow had ever heard—Cian's roar—rose above the sounds of battle, drowning out the Vespae's buzzing. No, not drowning it out, *stopping* it. The Vespae froze, in some kind of vestigial fear, as though some ancient instinct reminded them that firedrakes were their enemies.

Tomyris didn't miss a beat. She headed straight for the queen, who was the only one not affected by the sound of Cian's draconic fury. The queen was pulling threads rapidly, her hands glowing with some power that was neither celestial, nor aethereal in nature. Harlow could hear the wards around the Lodge weakening. This was how they managed it in other places—how they'd gotten past the last barrier in the breach under Nea Sterlis. The Vespae were ward-breakers.

Sam and Harlow plummeted low, ahead of Tomyris, to clear the way of drones. Quickly, they shifted into their humanoid forms to engage with the queensguard, who were less affected by Cian than the drones, but who were sluggish as they fought. Above them, Cian had risen in the air and was now clearing the perimeter of the village of approaching Vespae, with long sweeps of white-hot flame, very similar to what the Firestarters used.

The queen snarled in frustration, but only momentarily, as Tomyris wasted no time: her sword of celestial fire pierced the queen's rib cage, jamming through her back as Tomyris twisted her head in one nearly effortless-looking motion, breaking her neck, then slicing her head off completely as soon as she freed her sword. As the Council had assumed, this created chaos in both the remaining queensguard and the drone ranks.

Harlow shifted back into her Feriant form, tearing the guards who tried to escape apart with her talons and beak. Swiftly, she shifted back into her humanoid form to use her shadows to pick off the drones, now fleeing the village with arrows. She was running through her energy stores like water, but they had one chance to quell the attack. Slowing down meant death, not just for herself, but for everyone she cared for.

She, Sam and the other Striders got as many as they could with their shadow arrows, while the Ventyr of the Feriant Legion followed the ones escaping into the forest. A shout went up in the village, then a horn sounded. It was the signal that they'd turned the tide—to go after the ones escaping, rather than press back towards the Lodge.

Harlow followed her fellow Striders into the air, combing the forest for stragglers. They worked for a solid hour, coordinating kill after kill. No one could find the second queen though, the one the first queen had injured. They'd proven for certain that killing the queen meant disabling the coordination of the drones. It wasn't wise to let the stray queen go—she'd only find another swarm to lead.

Finally after nearly ninety minutes of searching, with snow beginning to fall in heavy sheets, Harlow and Sam shifted in a clearing to talk with Tomyris, who'd just returned from the village. The rest of the Legion was headed back to help the cleanup and medical crews, and they were to find Max and Mirai, and try to hunt the final queen down. Apparently, the Council didn't think finding her was a "true priority," according to Audata. Their mission was finding Max and Mirai.

Sam sat down on the forest floor, closing her eyes. She took one of Harlow's hands, and one of Tomyris', searching the threads for signs of their friends. She was nearly out of energy, like the rest of them. Harlow and Tomyris lent her as much power as they could spare. When her eyes fluttered open, she pointed into the trees. "They're that way—Max is injured. I can't communicate with them, but I think Mirai is with him."

Tomyris nodded. "She was probably stung. Vespae poison has to be some kind of blocker."

Harlow helped Sam up, and then followed her and Tomyris into the thick forest. They moved quietly, not knowing if there were still lingering Vespae hiding, and not daring to shift forms or teleport now. They'd all used too much magic, and if they weren't careful they might not be able to fight off any stray drones. Max and Mirai weren't calling out for help, and there was no telling why they might not be. Exercising caution was best now.

Sam pointed to two sets of footsteps that appeared in front of them. "They went that way."

Snow fell in heavy sheets now, almost like rain, dampening the sounds of the surrounding forest. When Tomyris turned, pushing both Harlow and Samira behind a tree, she clamped a hand to each of their mouths, shaking her head.

Unlike Samira and Harlow, Tomyris' eyesight was supernaturally enhanced, made more so because she stayed in her Ventyr body at all times. When Harlow and Samira both nodded, indicating they understood, Tomyris released them, peeking around the tree again. She made several hand signals, requesting that Harlow and Sam follow her closely, but quietly. They skirted a path through the trees, heading towards a clearing Harlow could see in the distance.

She spotted Max and Mirai, crouched behind an enormous spruce. Both glanced back at the same time. Max motioned for them to join the two of them, his wings flexing, full of tension. He held a gash in his side, which was bleeding through a makeshift bandage that wasn't even coming close to covering the mortal wound. If he didn't get help immediately, Max would die.

"There's Vespae in a cave ahead—and they have someone captive," he whispered as they approached, not addressing his wound, or need for aid.

"How many?" Tomyris asked, keeping her voice quiet.

Tomy and Max conversed softly, while Sam and Harlow looked Mirai over for injury. She was obviously in shock.

Mirai's eyes were wide with fear. "I'm fine—I was stung, but I'm fine," she whispered to Harlow. "Help him, *please.*"

Harlow glanced at Max who nodded, taking Mirai's hand.

"Okay," Harlow whispered. She didn't even bother to glance at Sam, who tensed at Mirai's plea. There was no way that she'd ask her to do this, not in front of Tomy. This would be an extraordinarily intimate moment, and if she could manage it, it would save Max's life, but she couldn't imagine doing something of the sort in front of Finn, even though he'd understand it completely.

Just as she could use Tomyris' venom to heal herself, she could heal Max with hers, since Mirai's link to the aether was incapacitated by the Vespae poison. The Claim was fueled not by magic, but the aether itself. This wouldn't be easy, but it could work. Harlow squeezed Mirai's hands, feeling the bonds between the Strider and Max, her partner. Their Claim was strong, and it stirred deep, jealous feelings in Harlow.

The threads between them sung with their love for one another, which made her ache for Finn. The deeper she fell into their bond, the more agitated she became by their Claim. Her fangs protruded, somewhat reluctantly, but she honed in on Mirai's deep love for Max, her desperation at his injury. Still, no venom came.

Harlow brought Mirai's hands around her waist, turning so she stood in the other woman's arms, then guided her forward. Perhaps she needed to feel Mirai's desire for Max to do this, needed to channel their connection to make it work. It was harder for Striders to force their venom than it was for the Ventyr. She didn't look at Max, as her body pressed against his, but beyond him, focusing only on Mirai as her fangs slowly cooperated.

One of Mirai's hands spread over Harlow's abdomen, pinning her to her chest. This was easier if Harlow focused on her, not Max. The Strider's lips grazed her ear. "Thank you," Mirai purred, her hand pressing harder into Harlow's abdomen.

In another life, one without Finn, Harlow thought she would have been interested in Mirai, which made this easier, but also more confusing. It took some sort of attraction to elicit a Strider's venom, but not necessarily romantic feelings. Mirai was trying to help her along, but it wasn't working.

And then it hit her: she cared for these two. Despite their reluctance to let her in all the way, they'd never hesitated to help her look for Finn and Larkin. They'd always been as kind as they could manage, while protecting themselves. This moment wasn't about any kind of romantic attraction. It was about love and community. Whether they were sure about her or not, these were her people, and she could help save them.

Venom hit Harlow's tongue and she struck quickly, biting Max in the neck as Mirai breathed a ragged sigh of relief. He winced beneath her, but when she drew back, he looked better. Mirai hadn't let go of her—she sobbed softly against her shoulder now.

Harlow turned, placing both her hands on the girl's face. "I'm sorry," she mouthed, worried that the other Strider might be angry with her for having bitten her Claimed. Even though it was the only way to save him, even though she'd had their consent, Harlow still worried. Mirai shook her head as all of the intensity of the moment drained away.

"Thank you," she whispered, hugging Harlow tightly. "You saved him."

When she released her, Harlow stepped away, letting Max go about the business of biting Mirai himself. She didn't look back at the two of them, knowing they must need any privacy the rest of them could give. Sam took her hand, drawing Harlow into a hug.

"You're a good friend, you know that?" Sam whispered in her ear.

Tomyris patted her cheeks, nodding as she unfastened her med kit from the pack strapped to her massive left thigh. "That was a hard thing to do."

Tomyris was one of the Legion's field medics, and she left Sam and Harlow to look both Max and Mirai over. Harlow took a few deep breaths. The day had been dizzying so far, and they still had to deal with the Vespae in the cave.

# CHAPTER EIGHT

When Tomyris was sure that both Max and Mirai could manage another fight, they moved quickly towards the cave they'd mentioned, about a half a mile away. They stayed hidden and quiet as they approached on foot, but there were no sentries in the forest.

Huge boulders surrounded the cave, so they had significant cover to take stock of the situation. Tomyris took a sharp breath in, pulling Harlow to her side.

"Is that your sister?" she murmured, nearly silently against Harlow's ear. The quiver of both fear and hope reverberated in her ear.

Harlow couldn't see what everyone else was looking at; the cave was too far for her to make out clearly. Harlow tried her best to engage her Feriant vision, but she hadn't mastered the ability to shift parts of her without the whole yet, so she pushed her second sight through the clearing and into the cave, looking for her connection to Larkin in the threads of aether.

Two Vespae guards held a humanoid figure between them as a Vespae queen stung her, shoving her wretched spine into her prisoner's neck. To Harlow's surprise, it wasn't the queen that had tried to communicate with them in the field, but another. *They'd had a third queen with them?*

Harlow winnowed her focus, but couldn't sense the identity of the Vespae's prisoner until the girl screamed. The Vespae poison could block their connection, as it did with most aethereal power, but it couldn't mask what twenty years of jump scares and tickle fights had etched into her mind and heart: the sound of Larkin's voice.

Harlow didn't think, didn't ask permission, didn't stop to make a plan. She simply shifted, shooting into the air above the treeline. Mirai and Samira were right behind her, their dark wings mirroring hers as she dove towards the cave.

*You take the queen, Harlow,* Samira said.

*We'll get the guards and Max and Tomyris will pull Larkin out,* Mirai added.

Neither scolded her for acting rashly. The Feriant Legion had little hierarchy among them, and they often acted on instinct, rather than constructing meticulous plans. Harlow felt no guilt for launching into action. It was Larkin, after all.

In a matter of moments, her talons sunk into the Vespae queen's flesh, ripping her wings from her back as she howled in pain. But she released Larkin, who fell to the ground in a limp heap. Harlow tore the queen's head from her shoulders in one clean bite, as Mirai and Sam made short work of the guards and Tomyris and Max spirited Larkin away.

*That was too easy.* Mirai said, her raptorial eyes blinking as her head tilted to the side, examining the cave. *Why didn't they guard the queen better?*

Harlow picked at the queen's body with her talons, and Sam's giant head dipped, cocking to and fro as she took in the body. *She wasn't their queen. That's why they didn't try harder—either the one they dragged away, or the one we killed must've been their queen.*

*Then what was this all about?* Harlow asked.

*Maybe they left her here to guard your sister?* Mirai mused.

*Another swarm—smaller this time— is flooding the village. The queen that got away is leading them.* Samira replied. *Tomyris got a call on the walkie—the signal's working again. The wards are down, but Cian's doing a lot of damage. We'll win, but they need reinforcements.*

*Go.* Harlow insisted. She wouldn't dream of letting the Rogues fight without the rest of them. *I'll get there as soon as I'm sure she's stable.*

Sam bumped her raptor's head against Harlow's, showing her a vision of where Larkin lay unconscious, but safe. She bobbed her giant head once, showing that she understood. Communicating in her Feriant form was much simpler than as a humanoid. Sam and Mirai took off, disappearing into the storm.

Harlow followed, but dove for the tree where her sister lay unconscious. She'd barely shifted as she fell to the ground, immediately examining Larkin for broken bones and other serious injuries. The urge to squeeze Larkin was hard to resist, but until she regained consciousness, she should move her as little as possible.

Still, Larkin was *here*. After months of looking, and their family's despair at losing her, she was here. Her baby sister. She refused to think about Finn. She wouldn't until she knew Larkin was going to be okay. A tear fell onto Larkin's face, splashing onto her little sister's cheek.

"Harlow?" Larkin asked. Her eyes were heavy, and her movements shaky as she wiped Harlow's tear off her face. Her forehead wrinkled in confusion, but then she'd been stung. She was likely groggy from the poison.

"It's me. How hurt are you?"

Larkin shook her head, trying to sit up. She touched the wound at her neck, wincing a little. It was already knitting together, but slowly. "Other than my neck, I'm okay. Where is Vivia?"

"Vivia? Vivia Woolf?" Her sister struggled to sit up. Harlow pressed a hand to her shoulder as her mind spun. Why was Larkin talking about Rakul Kimaris' wife? "Rest for me."

"Yes, Vivia Woolf. I was traveling with her. Where is she?" Larkin's eyes watered, full of fear. Harlow shoved aside the stab of pain ricocheting through her chest. Larkin didn't seem all that happy to see her after all this time.

"There was no one else in the cave with you," Harlow explained, wondering how Larkin came to be traveling with the Argent who'd been the battery for the Illuminated's Vascularity spell in Nea Sterlis.

All new reports from Nuva Troi indicated that Rakul had returned to the Dominavus—that he still commanded them—and yet Larkin acted like Vivia was a friend. It was true that the firedrake had tried to stop her husband from cutting her down, but still. If Rakul had gone back to the Dominavus, how could they trust Vivia?

"Look for her. Please. She was injured. The queen took her first..." Whatever Larkin said next was obscured by her sobs.

"We'll figure it out."

There was no way she could leave Larkin here alone to look for, of all people, a potential enemy, but Larkin was crying so hard she was afraid of what might happen if she didn't. She pulled the pistol the Feriant Legion were required to carry from her shoulder holster. "Take this," Harlow said, pressing the gun into Larkin's hands. "It's loaded with adamantine bullets. Shoot any Vespae who comes near and then run like your life depends on it, okay?"

Larkin's fingers closed around the gun, but her chest still shook with sobs. She was likely in shock and hysterical.

"It won't kill them, but it will slow them down enough to buy you some time 'til I get back."

The promise that she was coming back calmed her little sister. Larkin dragged herself off the ground, into a seated position, with her back resting against the trunk of the pine tree. "I lost track of her about a half a mile back, to the north."

Harlow raised her eyebrows. Her little sister had never been outdoorsy, or any good with directions. Neither had she, for that matter, but the past months with the Feriant Legion had changed things.

"Vivia taught me how to navigate," Larkin said, her voice soft. "Please find her. She's saved me so many times since Finn and I were separated."

Harlow's heart beat out of her chest. "Is he alive?"

Larkin nodded. "The last I saw him, he was. Another swarm got him, though. They didn't kill him..."

Though Larkin trailed off, Harlow guessed what she was thinking. If she'd been out here in the Falcyran wilderness, she knew what the Rogue Order did: the Vespae didn't take prisoners. The fact that they'd taken Finn rather than kill him outright was strange—as strange as the Vespae queen's obvious interest in her—but she didn't have time to think of that now. Her chest constricted as her mind raced towards hope.

Harlow pressed a kiss to Larkin's forehead, calming herself as much as her sister. There was no need to get ahead of themselves, or for Larkin to upset herself more than was necessary. "Tell me about it when I get back, pal."

"Okay," Larkin whispered. "I'll be fine by myself."

The wind shifted, and so did Harlow, launching herself into the sky. She flew north, the blizzard obscuring her view of the ground. As she flew, she found the threads that connected her to Larkin, though the connection was muddied—obscured. *Could the Vespae poison, in blocking access to the aether, also be blocking her connection to Larkin?*

That might explain why Thea hadn't been able to find either of them. A cloud hit Harlow in the face, surprising her. She refocused her attention on the ground, looking for any evidence of

Vivia Woolf. She flew for miles, circling back in an expanding grid, but came up short.

Snow fell harder now, and Harlow worried Larkin might not be warm enough. Getting her back to the village was a priority. Just as she was about to turn back, the faintest whiff of something metallic scented the wind. Her raptor's sense of smell was keen for a few things, and the scent of fresh blood was one. Somewhere nearby, someone was bleeding profusely.

Her enhanced vision helped her to find the scuffs in the snow below that were quickly disappearing under the accumulation of snow pouring from the sky. Someone had tried to cover their tracks. Harlow dove, flying above the treeline, her hearing honing in on the ground below. Whoever was down there was attempting to muffle the sound of their breathing, probably with their hands. Their inhalations were ragged and as Harlow drifted closer, looking for a place to land in the trees, she heard their heartbeat, erratic and weak.

Whether it was Vivia or not, whoever was down there was hurt and scared. Harlow shifted, using her shadows to slow her fall. She was still learning the ins and outs of using pure aethereal power, rather than manipulating threads the way most sorcière did, and her last step to the ground fell short, causing her to tumble a little as she met the ground.

A soft chuckle rang out from under the tree where she'd sensed the wounded party. Harlow looked up to find a silver-haired Argent, with a beauty so otherworldly it was breathtaking, clutching her side as she laughed. A mass of pale hair fell around her sharply planed face as she doubled over in pain.

Vivia winced as she shifted positions. "You've almost got a handle on your power now, don't you? It won't be long 'til you've mastered it. Your kind are so adaptable."

Harlow squared her shoulders. It was high praise, considering this woman was, in some ways, the reason she had the power she did. She'd likely seen her own granddaughter go through the same learning process with her powers. Harlow was grateful to the firedrake for helping her sister, and she certainly respected her position in history, but she couldn't trust her on Larkin's word alone, especially given Rakul's position with the Illuminated. "Why didn't you shift?"

Vivia shook her head, wincing. "You're smart to ask. I can't shift—not yet anyway—powering the Vascularity left my ability to connect to the aether damaged."

Harlow nodded; though she'd have to have Enzo confirm that for her, it sounded logical. "And why aren't you with Rakul? Or were you taking my sister to him?"

Vivia gritted her teeth, her narrow eyes closing for a brief moment, tempting Harlow to ask if she was all right. Her hands glowed slightly with the same dark light that Harlow's shadows sometimes had. *Did she have the ability to heal herself?*

From the little Cian had told her about Heraldic's power, Harlow knew that while they couldn't do spells or work threads like sorcière, they were capable of some things that more mundane shifters could not accomplish. Cian had been secretive about it, and Harlow respected their privacy, but now she wished she'd pushed harder.

A bit of the pain on Vivia's face receded. "The Illuminated think I'm healing at our villa on Santos Island. Rakul's gone back to them—to win their trust—and I set out to find Finn and Larkin."

"To win their trust?" Harlow asked, suspicious.

Vivia nodded. "Yes. The Dominavus are the Illuminated's best weapon. If we can divide them, we can break the Illuminated from within. We're trying to help you."

Harlow's mind raced. In Nea Sterlis, Vivia had not wanted to be cut down; she'd begged Rakul not to go through with his plan. And for his part, Rakul Kimaris had seemed genuinely sorry to have created this situation. It was plausible that they'd try to help now, but Harlow couldn't make that decision. The

Council would have to decide. For once, she was glad to let them take control, not to have to do this on her own. Their purpose clarified for her in that moment. They made the awful decisions by vote, so individuals didn't have to.

A spot of relief came over Harlow. "Larkin says you kept her safe. How did you find her?"

The Argent struggled to her feet. She was a little unsteady, but the scent of blood was fading. She wasn't bleeding any longer. "I may not be able to shift, but I am the oldest firedrake on this planet, Harlow Krane. I am descended from *queens*." The statement sent a chill through Harlow. Vivia Woolf was the Empress Lofrata's daughter. If Okairos still had a monarchy, she would be Empress now. "I can do things with aether you've never dreamed of—or I could before the Vascularity. Suffice to say, I was able to find your sister, and I've done my best to help her learn to survive as we made our way to you."

"All right." Harlow was willing to accept that she could trust Vivia Woolf. All she said made sense, and certainly the firedrake had reason to oppose the Illuminated. They killed her *entire* family. "You healed yourself. Can you heal others?"

Vivia nodded. "Was Larkin harmed?"

"She's okay, but she needs your help." Harlow sighed, hating what she was going to say next. "I'll carry you to her, hop on." She shifted before she could think too long on the indignity of being ridden like a horse. Harlow would do anything to help her sister, including this.

# CHAPTER NINE

V ivia was able to finish healing Larkin quickly, and once that was done, Harlow carried them both to one of the Rogue's safehouses just outside the village. She didn't want to leave her sister so quickly—she wanted to smother her with attention, to hear every word of what had happened since she'd lost her in Nea Sterlis—but there was a strange distance between them.

Larkin stood near Vivia, closer than she usually did with people outside their family. They'd obviously been through a lot together, but it made Harlow feel self-conscious about being too affectionate toward Larkin. She tried to brush it off. Larkin had only been back for an hour, and she was likely in shock from the attack. The best thing to do was give her space to calm down, and *then* Harlow could hover like the busybody she was tempted to transform into right now.

The safehouse had been one of a few private cabins the former resort had maintained for staff. An auburn-haired human named Piper Winslow, the Education Councillor, was there with a mix of human and immortal children. The Councillor was about the same age as Harlow, and though she was friendly with many of the Warbirds, she'd always behaved with cold indifference towards Harlow.

Today, as the wiry human's eyes ran over Harlow's body, there was clear disgust in her eyes. Harlow didn't remember the last time she'd felt so *disliked*. Many of the Rogues reacted to her with wariness, but most weren't unkind. Piper's expression softened as they entered the safehouse, as she looked at the children. She was a fierce kind of person, older-seeming at times than she actually was because of how much responsibility she'd taken on. Today was one such example; being out here with a group of Sanctum's littlings had to have been tremendously frightening. Harlow couldn't blame her for being on edge.

The main room's furniture had been pushed to the periphery in favor of a complicated pillow and blanket fort at the center. The children ran haphazardly around the big room. Their energy was buoyant, despite the situation. Unfortunately, they were accompanied by half a dozen shifter ghasts, who were all changing into gruesome creatures to make the children scream with laughter. Harlow shuddered at the sight of them playing together. Why were children *like this?*

"We were on a hike to see the early morning aurorae when the call came over the radio," Piper said, interrupting Harlow's train of thought. Her voice was curt and she avoided eye contact with Harlow. "I brought the children here. The Vespae have never gotten so close before..."

Harlow squeezed Larkin's hand, steering her away from a ghast of a rabbit shifter, whose ribs and entrails were showing as it hopped across the common space of the cabin. Three children followed it, shrieking with delight at the horrific thing. Harlow felt Piper's eyes on her. She was clearly confused by Harlow's reaction to the ghasts. It was odd for sorcière to be disturbed by the spirits, and humans often found it curious that Harlow was repelled by them.

She spoke first, hoping to move things along quickly.

Though she was confident the Warbirds didn't need her to triumph over the second wave of Vespae attacking the village, she needed to get back all the same. "We'll take care of it. This is my sister, Larkin, and Vivia Woolf. She has news for the Council."

Larkin smiled at the human, offering her hand. "So nice to meet you. Can Vivia and I help you strengthen the wards?"

Piper nodded—though it was clear she wanted to say no. When she spotted Vivia she inclined her head in a show of respect, and there was relief and reverence in her green eyes. "Your Majesty."

Vivia hugged the human, to Harlow's surprise. "There are no more queens, dear child. No more of my kind. I am only here to help, the best way I know how."

Harlow thought the prickly Education Councillor would react with disdain, as she was so suspicious of outsiders. But she underestimated the power of Vivia's heritage. Piper Winslow's eyes widened with reverence.

"The way you always have," Piper whispered. "We have our stories about you, about the sacrifices you and your ancestors made for us."

Vivia kissed Piper's forehead. "It was our duty, as it is mine now, to help the Rogue Order. I'm no one's empress, no one's queen. Just a woman who needs to make things right."

Harlow glanced at Larkin, whose eyes shone with pride. Jealousy stirred in her, but she got it. Vivia was impressive, beautiful, regal, and so genuinely humble it made Harlow's head spin. She radiated the kind of goodness that was hard to deny, inspiring the kind of deep trust that only came from training. As Lofrata's daughter, she'd likely spent her entire life learning to serve Okairos on a level the Illuminated would never understand. Of course, Larkin was having major hero worship. If Harlow weren't so jealous that she was taking Larkin's attention, she probably would be too.

"Just wait til you get to know her," Larkin whispered. "Vivia is *amazing*."

That was big praise from Larkin. Harlow squeezed her hand. Despite her mixed feelings, she was happy her little sister was safe. And the veneration Piper Winslow showed for the Argent made sense. If history had gone differently, Vivia would be her ultimate protector, the humans' leader, though not their ruler. Before the Illuminated came, there had been democratic governments for that, and this was what the Rogue Order proposed they return to now. That the Immortal Orders shift into protective roles, rather than extractive ones, with elected governments to work everything else out.

It had sounded like a dream to Harlow since she'd learned of it, one too good to be true at first; but now, watching the objectively untrusting Piper Winslow talk with Vivia Woolf, she couldn't help but feel inspired. Okairos had been different once, with immortals and humans working together in everyone's best interests. It could happen again, if the Illuminated would just loosen their hold on power—and if they could find a way to deal with the Vespae.

Piper turned away from Vivia, who bent to talk to a sorcière child about the picture she was drawing. The human took Larkin's arm, gesturing towards some children who were busy drawing pictures and reading in the cabin's living room. "Thank you for your offer to help with the wards. I didn't want to ask the children to help, though some of them have an aptitude for magic... I didn't want to frighten them."

Harlow was pleased that Piper's attitude towards Larkin had warmed, but when she smiled at her, the human's freckled face tightened. Harlow averted her eyes immediately, the smile dropping from her face. Inwardly, she cringed. *How had she offended this human so easily?* Sometimes it felt like everyone knew a set of rules she didn't. For fear that the horde of ghasts would turn their attention towards her, Harlow worked on calming herself.

The four adults watched another group of three children chase a ghost-rabbit into a wall, where it disappeared, eliciting even more shrieks of delight. Piper had done an excellent job of keeping them from being frightened. None of them comprehended what was outside their door right now. Harlow had to get back to the fight—she couldn't stall here any longer. She squeezed Larkin's hand again and let go.

Larkin brushed a kiss to Harlow's cheek. "Be careful. We'll help keep them safe."

Harlow watched with ambivalence, as a look passed between her sister and Vivia. They were obviously used to working together, and there was a great deal of trust between them. Still, she was reluctant to leave Larkin alone.

"Okay, I'll see you in a bit," Harlow said, kissing Larkin's forehead.

Harlow shivered as she passed through Larkin's strengthening wards. Maybe Vivia being here would change things for the Rogue Order. They could certainly use a win.

The trip back to the village was quick, her mind racing with new information. Harlow dropped out of the sky as soon as she reached the continued battle for Sanctum. The ground squads were holding the last of the swarm off well enough, but another soldier wouldn't hurt. Harlow joined Sam and Mirai in sweeping through, dragging their razor sharp talons through the second wave of soldier-drones.

*Your sister okay?* Mirai asked as they made a second pass, using their wings to knock the drones down for their Ventyr counterparts again. It was almost too easy now. Either someone had already killed the queen, or these drones weren't bonded with her, because they lacked the coordinated viciousness that typically made the Vespae so dangerous.

*Yes. Vivia Woolf was helping her, she wants to join us. Piper Winslow was at the safehouse with some kids—she had a weird reaction to seeing her.*

Sam did a fancy loop-de-loop. They were just playing now. The battle was all but won. *Humans have a lot of respect for the Argent. It's why they're not more suspicious of you, Harls. They love Cian.*

Harlow would have laughed if she were in her humanoid form. It sure *felt* like everyone was suspicious of her. But perhaps "felt" was the key word. Maybe she was being too sensitive. She turned her attention back to the task at hand. They'd almost subdued the last of the Vespae.

*Shit*, Sam swore. *Three are getting away.*

*There's another group headed towards the Lodge*, Mirai called.

*I'll get the stragglers, you go for the others*, Harlow replied. Mirai and Sam headed the opposite direction, with only a quick goodbye.

The escapees headed back into the forest, booking it back over the mountain. They were far enough ahead that she had to increase her speed in order to catch up to them, and that was a push for Harlow. She was nearing the end of her energy. They were headed vaguely in the direction of the safehouse and Harlow could stop them before they got there.

The creatures changed course slightly. They would miss the safehouse by half a mile. Harlow lost track of time as she pursued the stray Vespae, flying faster than she'd ever tried to go before. Her mind and body both strained under the effort. Several times, she lost sight of the Vespae through the trees. She took a moment to look around, and was surprised to find she'd entered territory she didn't recognize.

In her humanoid form, that might not be obvious, but her Feriant perception marked landscapes quite differently. Audata had been right: it wasn't possible they'd seen all of this part of the mountain range. Not that Harlow had doubted her, but here was hard evidence. Below her, the Vespae crested a sharp ridge.

Harlow followed, quite suddenly pulled by some unknown

force that carried her over the ridge. It felt like being sent through a tiny hole with a slingshot. She paused, banking hard to come about—almost impossibly, she'd gotten ahead of the Vespae. Behind her, the Vespae were still heading in the direction she'd already come. Strange magic pulsed around her, almost as though it were pushing her away from the ridge: more evidence the Vespae might be warding experts.

Audata had warned the Council several times not to think of them as "creatures" because they moved and acted differently than Okairons. To manipulate aether so purposefully, you needed a hard grasp on reason, on logic. Underestimating the Vespae had been a mistake, one Harlow hoped they wouldn't continue making now that there was evidence of their abilities.

Harlow rose higher, soaring into the cloud cover of the storm. She swept in and out of the clouds, observing the little farm below. It was overrun with Vespae, more than she'd ever seen gathered, but she was too tired to get an accurate count. Her energy was flagging severely. She wouldn't be able to maintain her Feriant form for much longer.

*What were these Vespae doing here?* Her Feriant body carried her upward, as she swept back towards the scouts she'd followed. She needed to take care of them before reporting back about this place. They were headed straight for the farm, no doubt to reveal Sanctum's location, if the Vespae weren't already aware of it. While it was possible the farm was the origin of the swarm that attacked, she couldn't know.

She hesitated, watching the scouts move closer to the farm, thinking of the queen who'd tried to communicate. It didn't ever feel *right* to kill the Vespae, but she had little choice. If she let these two return to the farm, they'd be fighting Vespae again in mere days. They'd done well this time, but Cian's presence had been a surprise, one they wouldn't get a second time. Sanctum had been compromised, but killing these two might give them more time to figure out what to do next. Harlow dove into the trees to stop the scouts before they got any closer to the farm.

Once she'd dropped the bodies into a crevasse, she let the storm do the work of hiding their trail. She turned back toward Sanctum, flying fast as she could manage with diminishing energy. As she went, she both saw and felt the wards she'd passed through before, that alien, repellant feeling again. It reminded her a little of the iridium they'd found on the Vespae bodies.

Once on the other side of the wards, she tried to find any remarkable feature in the landscape to mark for return with the rest of the Warbirds. There were none. The sameness of this place was menacing; everywhere she turned, the view was the same as the last. The magic of the wards, combined with her low energy, clouded her head. She couldn't hold her Feriant form for much longer.

Harlow dropped to the ground to avoid losing her grip on her alternae in midair, shifting as she went. She walked back in the direction she'd come, and found the wards easily enough, though she could not pass through them in her humanoid form. Trying gave her a little shock, a warning that going through would likely result in a bigger shock.

This farm was so close to Sanctum it turned her stomach. As she examined the wards, she began to understand how they'd missed it on routine patrols. The ward itself repelled her, which was usual for warding, though this was stronger than she was used to. The repulsion instilled fear—and then an extra layer of confusion and a strong desire to forget she'd ever seen this place.

It reminded her of having a nightmare. *You wake, and your mind's first instinct is to forget the horror of the dream—to distance yourself from it.* This was the same, her mind scrambling desperately to forget she'd seen the Vespae. She wasn't as good at discerning spellwork as Thea or Enzo, but she was almost positive that if she turned around now and flew away, she might actually forget the farm was here.

Snow fell heavier and faster now, and the magic of the strange wards pressed on her, making her sleepy and slow. The feeling was familiar, but she couldn't put her finger on it. All she wanted to do was lay down, forget all of this and sleep. Harlow shook her head. She had to get away from here, but not before she made sure she could get back. Harlow was exhausted, but she fumbled with the zipper to her jacket, fishing out the phone inside.

It felt like forever since she'd used a phone, but Nox and Indigo had ensured before they left that each member of patrols had one, charged by generator, that hacked into a satellite that provided detailed geo-location services. The phones were only to be turned on in a dire emergency.

Harlow switched hers on now, and as it flared to life she pulled up the geolocator and noted her exact coordinates, sending them over encrypted text back to base with a note about what she'd found. Audata replied instantly. *Recorded. Vespae threat eliminated. Return to Haven. Developments in Nytra to report*. Harlow replied with her acquiescence, and shut off the phone. She stumbled away from the wards, feeling better the further away she got.

# CHAPTER TEN

Harlow rushed into the Dairy upon return, expecting to find a debriefing happening, and hopefully information on where Larkin and Vivia were, as they weren't at the medical station. Larkin was nowhere to be found, but Vivia stood at the center of the Warbirds' attention, their eyes alight with interest as they asked her questions.

Much like with Piper, the Warbirds were eager to talk to Vivia, and while they were obviously watching what they said, they were enthusiastic about the Argent. The ache in her chest was nearly unbearable. Part loneliness, part jealousy, it was all ugly.

"You okay?" Audata asked, having appeared out of nowhere.

"Why is it so easy for them to like everyone but me?" The words were out before she could think about the wisdom of them. She was too tired to hide her real feelings.

Audata stared at the Warbirds for a long moment before answering. "Besides the obvious reasons?"

Harlow nodded, even though she wasn't sure she wanted to hear what Audata had to say. The Strider was brutally honest, and Harlow didn't know if she could stand the truth right now.

"Look at Vivia, she's probably exhausted, but she's over there talking to people like she's a beauty queen at a mixer." Audata's expression was even, as she glanced up at Harlow. "You don't make things easy for people. They can tell you're feeling things, even when you try to hide it. You're unpredictable for them."

Harlow swallowed hard. She wasn't sure how to respond, but that wasn't what she'd expected Audata to say.

"You make people uncomfortable—just like I do, because I don't show enough feelings. Most people like a happy medium, and we're too much and not enough."

Harlow looked down into Audata's brown eyes, and though the Strider's expression didn't change, Harlow felt the truth in her words. They both felt too much—felt everything, but expressed it differently.

"You don't make *everyone* uncomfortable," Harlow replied. If Audata liked to be touched, she would take her hand, but she didn't, so Harlow stayed still but for a slight flex of her hands.

A small smile curled at the corners of Audata's mouth as her eyes tracked the movement of Harlow's fingers. "Neither do you."

Harlow was overcome with gratitude for Audata's mere existence. Lately, she'd felt far too edgy, as though her ability to navigate social situations had evaporated, but Audata never appeared to care about any of that. It wasn't that she didn't care about any social mores—the lone Strider hated when people lied, or were cruel—but Harlow's rough edges, that typically frustrated others, didn't faze Audata.

"Did you get the coordinates for the farm plotted? There were so many of them, Aud. If we could take them by surprise, we might make a dent in this mess."

Audata hummed, a quiet noise she made when she was busy thinking or overwhelmed. "I found it. Once the team finishes their hellos, we'll get started on a plan. Kate and Cian are coming as well. They should be here any minute."

Harlow nodded. "Have you told my parents that Larkin is home?"

The Strider nodded. "Yes. She's with them now." Audata paused, her eyes narrowing. "I apologize. I don't believe I explained the way things are between you and your parents very well."

Harlow didn't bother to ask what she'd told Larkin. Thea would catch their little sister up soon enough. "Larkin is very perceptive. She knows me better than anyone—except maybe Thea."

"And me," Cian's voice purred at her shoulder. "I just hugged our girl. I'm so proud of you for finding her, my dar—" Harlow looked back at her friend, who was now staring at Vivia, mouth open, silver eyes full of tears.

"Vivia!" Cian rushed towards the other Argent. She opened her arms, smiling wide.

They exchanged quick words, Vivia explaining the same things she'd told Harlow, about Rakul and the Dominavus. Cian nodded, believing it all so easily. Harlow was immediately frustrated, and far more jealous over Cian's acceptance of the firedrake than she had been about the Warbirds.

In her irritation, she engaged her second sight, searching the threads between Vivia and Cian to find out why the usually shrewd Argent was acting like there was nothing to worry about with Vivia. There were literally hundreds of threads connecting the two of them, ones that spoke of friendship, family, and shared culture. Ones Harlow didn't even have the ability to understand, they ran so deep.

Harlow felt as though she'd pushed too far, in that moment, intruding on things that were Cian's private business. She pulled her awareness of the threads back, and though she could still sense the connection between them, the finer points were less obvious now. Refining her boundaries around her talent might prove to be more complicated than she'd first assumed.

Audata sighed, the noise edged with her own frustration, though her face remained smooth and emotionless. "We may have to continue the debriefing later."

Harlow was tempted to protest that they needed to make a plan for how to deal with the farm full of Vespae. But it was obvious that no one was going to get much done. The Warbirds crowded around Cian and Vivia, talking with the two of them excitedly about the battle, each person trying to impress the fire-drakes with their prowess. Vivia was an exciting distraction—but weren't there priorities?

A glint of annoyance flashed in Audata's eyes as she watched her meeting end without her say-so. The tiny Strider finally shrugged and walked out of the Dairy, pulling her jacket off a hook by the door as she went. Harlow followed close behind, the frigid air hitting her face with an unpleasant bite.

"Can we go talk out our plan?" Harlow asked Audata as Tomyris and Sam sidled up alongside them. "There were more Vespae than I've ever seen at that place. Something big is going on there."

Tomyris took her hand and squeezed. "We should wait til we're all together and work things out. Besides, maybe Cian can help Vivia with her shifting—maybe they know something we don't about how to help her. We should let them talk."

That made sense, but it was still frustrating. Harlow's fists clenched as she wrapped her arms tightly around her body.

"Tell us what you saw," Audata said as she latched the Dairy's garden gate and walked towards the village proper. "We should begin research on the abnormal wards tonight."

Tomyris rolled her eyes. "Research. Ugh. I need a nap."

Sam kissed her lover's cheek as they walked through the village of stone houses. Snow was piling up in the cobblestone streets, covering the mess of the fight. The Vespae had made it all the way into the village, though the ground forces had fought them back.

The thought was chilling, seeping deep into Harlow's bone marrow. The Vespae had broken through their wards, and could do it again. There was no precedent for any settlement or town surviving an attack like the one that occurred here, and nobody knew what the implications of this were. Uncertainty hung in the air.

The village wasn't quiet as they walked—there was too much going on for silence—but there was a deeply unsettling lack of voices. The usual sounds of gossip and friendly chatting in the streets was notably absent, people's faces gray with fear. Audata noticed this as well, and pulled Harlow into an alley, Samira and Tomyris following close behind. The four of them huddled together, out of the wind.

"Tell us what you saw," Audata commanded.

It felt a little like a clandestine meeting, here in the narrow alleyway, shadows already falling as the sun sank below the horizon. The stone of the village buildings, which was normally cozy and friendly, suddenly gave off an air of menace. Harlow kept her voice low as she recounted what she'd seen and felt following the Vespae, a warm feeling of belonging buzzing through her as her friends listened.

These *were* her friends, she realized as they nodded thoughtfully at her story. Was it really so important that everyone like her, if people like Audata, Tomy and Sam did? If her family loved her, messy as that was. If Finn loved her, wherever he might be... Did it actually matter that some people thought she wasn't trustworthy?

Harlow didn't quite register that Audata, Sam and Tomy had started discussing what she'd seen in the mountains. Her discovery felt profound, monumental, despite the smallness of it in comparison to what was happening in their community at large.

It was okay for people to misunderstand her. It was okay for them not to like her, or even trust her—so long as she wasn't doing things to directly cause that distrust. The only thing she needed to concern herself with was doing her best to live in alignment with her values, and to be open to hearing she was wrong, when someone gifted her with the knowledge she'd done something out of line. She couldn't *actually* spend her life trying to anticipate everyone's reactions to her. That was an enormous waste of time and energy.

"I have things I'd like to look up," Audata replied, interrupting Harlow's epiphany. "Samira, will you come with me?"

Sam nodded. "Yes, are you wondering about the possibility that the Vespae use threads differently?"

Audata nodded as Tomyris yawned. "I'm going to go get a snack and take a nap. Sounds like tomorrow is going to be a big day." She kissed Harlow's cheek as they departed. None of them asked her to come along, or for her help, *and it was all right.* They hadn't abandoned her. Very likely, they expected that she'd want to see Larkin now. That she'd be *excited* to see her youngest sister.

*And shouldn't she be?*

The thought brought an unexpected weight pressing down over the buoyancy of her epiphany. The all-too-familiar dull numbness of the past few months descended over her like a heavy curtain, falling slowly. Soon she'd be covered in it, all her emotions smothered but the barest hint of despair that could never quite be banished. The hopelessness would set in next, the thoughts she tried to block, the ones that whispered that she'd never feel joy or happiness again.

Harlow tried to shake it off. Larkin was back. She would go to Selene's to see her. Now. But Aurelia would be there—and she *couldn't.* Her breath came in short gasps, and she clutched her chest. Panic. That's what this was. She was emotionally and physically spent, and now she was having some kind of panic attack.

"Slow, breathe slow."

*Kate. Where had she come from?* She did as the vampire asked though, breathing in and out slowly until the blood roaring in her veins calmed. It had been a wretched day, despite their win. Despite getting Larkin back, which she couldn't seem to face at the moment. Her emotions felt as though they were on a horrific roller-coaster she couldn't control.

"I'm fine," Harlow said as her breath returned to a normal pace.

"Clearly not," Kate said as she led Harlow out of the alley, towards a group of people who were restacking a pile of fire-wood that must have been knocked asunder during the attack on the village. She handed Harlow a pair of gloves and they joined in the efforts. Despite what Tomy had said, it seemed wise to do something with herself, at least until she pulled herself together.

"So, Audata says you found Larkin?" Kate's voice was tentative. After their last encounter, Harlow couldn't really blame her.

"Yes," she answered, trying to keep things short and focus on stacking the wood. Kate meant well, trying to help her, but the gap between them was too wide. Harlow didn't know how to close it.

They stacked wood in silence for a long while. Harlow was surprised when the job was done. As people moved on to find other things to do, Kate simply stood staring at her. She was dressed like an average human, wearing a sweater and a pair of thick leggings and snow boots, her short hair pushed back from her pretty face.

"You can't stay mad forever, Lo." The use of the nickname hurt. "Does it help to be angry with all of us?"

"Shut up," Harlow snapped, showing her anger exactly as it

was. She barely felt the cold, she was so hot with the fury bubbling out of her.

She'd spent months convincing herself she was dispassionate. That she simply didn't trust Kate anymore. The truth was that she *was* angry, and it *did* help. Staying mad staved off the void inside her since she lost Finn. The deep insecurity that she'd let herself get so lost in a partner that she didn't feel whole without him.

The vampire sighed so deeply that Harlow felt Kate's exasperation in her own chest. Everyone wanted her to stop being angry, to forgive and forget, but she *couldn't*. She didn't blame the people she loved for wanting better for her, nor could she tame the rage inside her, or make it smaller for their comfort, no matter how much she wanted to. For a moment, it looked like Kate might walk away in the face of Harlow's open fury. It was what nearly everyone else had done, and it was what Harlow expected now.

Instead, Kate stepped forward and wrapped her arms around Harlow, pulling her head down to her shoulder. It brought Harlow back into the moment, back into her body as Kate spoke. "Be mad then. Don't keep shutting us out."

Harlow felt the eyes on them, people watching to see what they'd both do next, and it reminded her of Nuva Troi, of Section Seven. As much as she wanted her earlier epiphany to have changed the way she'd act in this moment, that wasn't how it worked. It would take time, and right now she was angry. She took a few steps away from Kate and the people nearby, her boots crunching on the snow. "Petra told you to come talk to me, didn't she?"

Kate followed, steering Harlow towards a more private part of the street. "What if she did? She loves you, and she knows something about being estranged from the people you love."

That hurt. Harlow had been a terrible friend, avoiding Petra because she was with Kate. The roller coaster of emotions stopped abruptly, crashing to a halt as the last of Harlow's energy drained from her. Not even the heat of her anger kept her going now—she was empty, bereft. How had she missed all of these important truths about herself? About *life?*

She sunk down into a crouch, then plopped down on a bench. Snow fell in big fluffy flakes, as she buried her face in her hands. "Oh, I fucked this all up."

Kate sat next to her. "That's the way to do it."

Harlow peeked out at her. "What?"

Kate leaned back on the bench, stretching her legs out in front of her, her usual careless smile gracing her face. "You're as bad as Finn. Why don't the two of you ever get it? Life is a series of fuckups, and then you die... Or, if you're us, you don't."

Harlow raised an eyebrow incredulously, but she couldn't stop the smile pulling at the corner of her mouth. Kate opened her mouth, stuck out her tongue and a huge snowflake landed on it. Harlow couldn't help but smile.

"Made you smile," Kate said, bumping her shoulder to Harlow's.

Harlow tipped her head back to watch the flakes floating out of the sky. They were clumping together now, resembling pixies from her favorite faery stories. "That snowflake was a paid actor."

Kate snorted. "Seriously, Lo, life is all about mistakes. If we don't learn from them, then what's the point of immortality?"

Vampires thought a lot more about "the point" of immortality than the rest of the Orders, who simply took it for granted. This was the first time Harlow had really felt the depth of the idea. What *was* the point of immortality, if they just kept doing harm?

Harlow let out a frustrated sigh. "I don't know, Kate. You tell me." Her words carried more sting than she'd intended, but she was tired of all this. Tired of feeling bad, tired of being lonely and scared. Tired of pretending like she was anything but mad all the time.

"Well, I sure as hells don't think carrying all this outrage around helps anything. Your family owns a bookstore. Don't you know better than this?"

Harlow face contorted. "What's that supposed to mean?"

"All this anger. Seems like a perfect villain's origin story to me." Kate's voice was light. She was making fun of her.

Harlow groaned. "You are the *worst*." But when she met Kate's wide eyes, her perception altered. Kate wasn't making fun of her, she was teasing her—teasing her back to a reality where Harlow didn't take every single thing so seriously.

That was a reality she knew Finn would want her to live in. It struck her that this was not what Finn had ever wanted for her. When he'd left her, messy as that had been, he'd always felt he was doing it in service of her happiness. He'd wanted her to have a good life, even if he wasn't there to enjoy it with her.

Harlow took a few deep breaths, the frigid air brightening her outlook and cooling her temper some. Maybe she could let some of this anger go. Kate spoke again. "You have to work things out with your parents at some point. Or are you going to spend eternity being pissed at Aurelia?"

Harlow's anger returned at full force—a wave of dry, crackling heat that scorched the back of her throat. Couldn't Kate be happy that she'd warmed to the idea of moving past her anger at her?

"Maybe I will," Harlow growled. "She lied."

"So did I," Kate pleaded.

"And I'm mad at you too." Harlow's voice was shrill, nearly a wail. Heads turned on the street, so she lowered her volume to a harsh whisper. "I hate all of you. Don't you understand? I hate you for coming out of this unscathed after you deceived everyone. And now you get everything you want while I'm alone again." The words came out in a tumble, and like always, Harlow wasn't sure how much of it she actually meant.

"You're alone because you're *choosing* to be alone," Kate shot back, her voice low and cool. "We've all tried to be there for you, but you're shutting everyone out again. When are you going to grow the fuck up?"

Kate's words hung between them. Sharp barbs played on the tip of Harlow's tongue. There were so many things she could say to hurt Kate right now, so many buttons she knew exactly how to push, and if she did, they'd be screaming at one another like poltergeists, here in full hearing of the whole village.

*Nothing is as draining as staying mad.* The thought appeared as if from nowhere, but she knew from working with both Enzo and Riley that this was the process of healing, even in deep grief. Progress was slow, and she moved backwards as often as she did forwards, but maybe after weeks of feeling like she was in perpetual reverse, she was finally allowed to advance again.

Harlow surprised herself when she spoke. "You're right."

The truth was hard; she didn't know if she'd ever see Finn again. But she was lucky: her entire family was alive and safe. Everyone she loved had made it out, except him. Thousands, maybe millions, of families across Okairos couldn't say the same right now. She'd lost one man, and it hurt more than she could bear, but Kate was right: she wasn't alone.

"I am?" Kate asked.

Harlow laughed, tears streaming down her face now that she let her grip on her rage loosen. "Yeah."

"Wow, that's a new one," Kate muttered, awe in her voice. "I'm right."

Harlow pulled her ex in for a hug. "You shouldn't have started a relationship with Petra if you wanted to be right much," she said as she hugged Kate.

A snort was her answer, and a hug so tight Harlow gasped as Kate asked, "Will you go see your parents now?"

Harlow nodded. "Yeah. I'll go. You go see Lou, okay?"

Kate looked confused. "Why?"

Harlow took her hand for a brief moment. "Because we're lucky, Katie. We're so fucking lucky to be here."

Kate's eyes widened, watery around the edges. Kate rarely cried, but something in Harlow's tone must have reached her. "*Fuck, Lo*," she muttered over her shoulder as she turned towards her sire's house.

Harlow turned in the opposite direction, heading towards Selene's home. Her heart was still heavy with missing Finn, with the grief over the possibility of never seeing him again, but she had no intention of giving up. She was afraid of what Larkin might tell her about him—that she might be wrong to hope—but it was time to find out.

# CHAPTER ELEVEN

Selene's tiny cottage was blessedly warm when Harlow walked in. A fire blazed in the hearth, and she heard the sounds of Thea and Larkin talking in the kitchen. Selene was probably in there as well: the delightful scent of pumpkin pasties baking drifted in, filling her nostrils. At home, Selene rarely had time to cook much, with her full social calendar, but she was an excellent chef.

Harlow discarded her boots and hung her coat up on one of the wood pegs in the entryway. When she turned, Aurelia stood behind her, silver hair tucked behind her ears, a pair of glasses pushed back onto the top of her head. She wore a rumpled wool sweater and a pair of ill-fitting jeans. Her usually stylish mother, quite frankly, looked a mess. Her eyes were rimmed red from crying, and her gaze held sheer terror.

In fact, she looked to be frozen in place, staring at Harlow. Aurelia was afraid of *her*. Of what she might say. When they'd first arrived in Sanctum, Harlow had said a lot—things she now wished she would have tempered better. They were all true, but as she got older, she'd realized that perhaps every true thing didn't need to be said. Selene had been angry as well, but Harlow knew that in the past month Aurelia had been sleeping here. And if she was, then the two of them were on their way back to themselves.

If Selene could forgive Aurelia, could she? Harlow wasn't sure if she could. Not if Finn never came back. But in this moment, looking at her terrified mother, she knew she would never stop loving her. Harlow believed Aurelia thought she'd been doing the right things, keeping her family safe. And she knew beyond a shadow of a doubt that Aurelia was sorry for all the pain she'd caused her family. Maybe that was a start.

"Hi," she said, not knowing what else to say.

The fear in Aurelia's eyes receded to mere wariness. "Hello, my darling."

Conversation in the kitchen stopped. They knew she was here. Harlow closed her eyes and remembered dozens of winter weekends at the lake, so similar to this one. There were two brief years after the twins left for college, but Larkin wasn't yet out of secondary, when only she and Thea came home for winter holidays and it had been the five of them. Harlow loved the twins, beyond all measure, but those had been special times.

Her bottom lip quivered as she opened her eyes. Aurelia stood in front of her now. Tentatively, she took Harlow's hands. Harlow didn't draw back. "Thank you for bringing her home, Harlow. I am sorry. So, so sorry for everything else."

Aurelia's head dipped in shame. Selene stepped into the back hallway, and Harlow gave Mama a small, reassuring smile. She was ready to defend Aurelia, that much was clear. But Harlow had no intention of attacking. This hurt so much, and she had no words to reply to that, so she drew Aurelia into her arms and said the only thing she knew in her heart. "I love you, Mommy."

Selene had always been and would always be Mama to her girls, but Aurelia had turned into Mother when the girls got older. She'd always been so elegant and self-assured—so in control—it had fit her better. Here, at what felt like the end of the world, Harlow wanted her Mommy.

Aurelia clung to her, shoulders shaking. "I love you too."

Selene's hands flew over her face as she suppressed a sob. Larkin and Thea both wrapped their arms around her from behind. Harlow dragged Aurelia down the hall and into the embrace of the rest of her family. For long moments everyone cried, holding each other so tightly Harlow thought they might break their hands from clutching onto one another so hard.

When they finally let go, Aurelia's hands cupped her face. "From the moment you were born, and for all eternity, you will always be my darling girl."

Harlow sniffled as Selene pulled a hanky from her pocket, wiping her eyes and nose like she was a toddler. "I know... I said things—"

Aurelia shook her head. "I let you all down."

Selene sniffled now, her forehead wrinkling. Thea and Larkin leaned on one another. Harlow hugged Aurelia again. "I suppose it had to happen sometime."

Aurelia laughed through her tears, gazing lovingly at Selene. They shared a private thought between them. Selene squeezed Harlow's hand. "It's hard to grow up and find out your parents are people, isn't it?"

That was exactly what it was. Aurelia had always been up on such a pedestal for her that she'd never seen it that way before. The maters were people, like anyone else. They made mistakes, just like she did, and would continue to do so.

"The pasties are done, Mama," Thea said, sniffing the air. "If you leave them in for much longer, they'll burn."

Selene bustled about as everyone else worked in quiet tandem to put pasties onto plates and pour mugs of tea. The Kranes piled onto the overstuffed linen-covered couches in the cottage's living room and ate quietly. Harlow was torn. She wanted to ask Larkin about Finn, but Larkin had already told her what she knew, and Harlow didn't know how to push for more information.

She didn't realize she wasn't eating until Larkin's hand brushed hers. "I wish I had more to tell you about Finn." Larkin's eyes glossed with tears.

Harlow took Larkin's hand and squeezed hard. "It's enough to know he was alive the last time you saw him."

Selene glanced between her girls. The look she gave Harlow was clear: *That's enough.* Harlow's head inclined slightly, a subtle acknowledgement that she understood that Larkin needed rest and time with her family to recover. When Aurelia pulled a puzzle out from a stack of games under the coffee table, each of the Kranes fell into a familiar routine. Larkin turned the puzzle pieces over, as Aurelia sought out the edges, while Thea and Selene began matching middle pieces.

Harlow spread out onto the couch, waiting for her turn at the puzzle. She and the twins typically had the job of grappling with the pieces that seemed like they were in the wrong puzzle. Conversation started up, slowly, focusing on catching Larkin up with the dynamics of Sanctum's social ecosystem. Stories and memories from childhood snuck in, everyone sticking to comfortable topics and family jokes.

When Selene and Larkin got into an intense discussion of how to wash vintage wool, Aurelia moved Harlow's feet. Her touch was ginger at first, but Harlow drew her feet back slowly, smiling at her mother. Like Aurelia, her feelings were still raw, but she craved something normal, despite the feeling that even in this good moment, something was *wrong*.

When Aurelia was settled, Harlow shifted direction on the couch, piling pillows up next to Aurelia so that their heads were close together.

"What's going on in your busy head, darling?"

It was a question Aurelia asked her thousands of times in her life. Harlow smiled as she felt her mother's long fingers rake through strands of her tangled hair. The feeling was so familiar, she hated to ruin it. "Nothing."

"Liar," Aurelia chided.

The admonition felt *good*. It was such a blessing to be known. To be understood when she lied to make others comfortable. For someone to know her, without all her awkward ways of trying to fit.

"I keep having these doom-y feelings," Harlow explained. "Any time things are good, I'm tense, waiting for something to go wrong. I feel ridiculous."

Aurelia's fingers paused, and Harlow glanced up at her mother, who wore a pensive look. "Have you considered that perhaps it's not ridiculous, but perfectly logical?"

Harlow shrugged. Enzo and Riley had said something similar before. Lots of bad things had happened—and Finn *was* still missing. It was natural that she'd expect for things to go wrong.

"I guess. I wish I could feel a little less desperate about things."

Aurelia's eyes narrowed slightly. "That's not exactly what I meant, love. I meant your Strider's talent for sensing connections between people—"

Aurelia was interrupted by Larkin's wide yawn, accompanied by a stretch that morphed into the youngest Krane wedging her body between Aurelia and Harlow. "I'm exhausted," she said as she yawned again.

Aurelia and Selene cleared the plates from their meal as Thea joined her sisters on the couch, taking Aurelia's place. The three of them wound around one another, an inextricably linked pile of limbs and sleepy comfort. Larkin's eyes fell closed nearly as soon as her body relaxed.

On the other side of her, Thea too was falling asleep, pulling

Larkin into her lap. A million questions spun in Harlow's head, but as Aurelia covered them with blankets they floated away. The comfortable sounds of the maters washing dishes and talking softly in the kitchen was a balm for her battered heart. There was so much to work out still, but tonight, she could have this.

# CHAPTER TWELVE

Harlow woke to Larkin pulling the blanket off her, or so she thought, until she fully opened her eyes. Larkin was sitting up with her eyes open, but she clearly wasn't awake. Harlow glanced at the clock above the fireplace—it was past midnight and the cottage was quiet. She shook Thea awake, pressing a finger to her sister's mouth, gesturing to their little sister, who was now perched on the edge of the couch. Larkin's eyes were wide and unfocused, back ramrod straight.

"How long has she been like that?" Thea asked.

Harlow shook her head. "Not long, I don't think. She woke me, moving."

Thea got up, stealing upstairs to the maters' bedroom. Harlow moved to sit on the heavy rustic coffee table. An ember in the fireplace popped, and Harlow realized she was chilly. She got up, adding another log to the fire, stoking it until it crackled to life.

When she turned back, Larkin was still staring straight ahead, and Thea came downstairs grimacing. "They were...."

Harlow rolled her eyes. "Please don't say it."

Thea shook her head. "I couldn't even if I wanted to."

She sat next to Harlow on the coffee table. "Should we shake her?"

Harlow shrugged. "Wait and see what the maters say, I guess."

Aurelia came down first, wearing a silk robe that was obviously Selene's. "Don't wake her," Aurelia said, after checking Larkin's vital signs. "I believe she's walking the spirit paths. We need to wait for her to return." She pushed her youngest back onto the couch very gently, covering her with the discarded blanket. "I'm going to make some coffee."

Harlow and Thea both nodded, still staring at Larkin.

"The two of you can move," Selene said from the stairs. "It might take her a while to return. You might as well get comfortable."

Thea pulled Harlow into one of the oversized chairs that flanked the couch. "She's kind of creepy like that," Thea whispered.

Harlow glanced back at her, giggling. "Are you ten?"

Thea smiled. "It kind of feels like it tonight." She wrapped her arms around Harlow, pulling her younger sister back against her chest.

Harlow settled against Thea's sharp angular body. "You're so bony," she complained.

"Are *you* ten?" Thea's laugh cut short. She stared at Larkin. "Look at her eyes."

Larkin's eyes darted to and fro in such rapid succession that it looked like it might hurt. Harlow took her youngest sister's wrist into her hands, pressing to feel her pulse. "Her heart is beating really fast."

Aurelia peeked out of the kitchen. "Is something wrong?"

Thea's face twisted with worry. "Come look at her."

Aurelia rushed into the living room. "Something's not

right." She glanced at Harlow. "You've traveled to the paths before... To Nihil."

Harlow nodded. "I have. But never on purpose."

Larkin shivered, making a small whimpering noise, her eyes moving faster now, as though she was watching something distressing. Harlow took her hands, focusing on the threads that flowed between them, their affinity shining in her mind's eye with golden light. She traced Larkin's threads, the magic that made her littlest sister *her*. And then she spotted the threads that went to the same tiny eye in her own heart, straight into the limen.

She wasn't ever able to explain with words how it felt to sense the threads with her second sight. It was both like seeing things with her eyes, and completely unlike it at the same time. Harlow followed the slender bundle of threads through that eye, stringing a path back out for herself and Larkin as she went. Outside of her second sight, she felt Thea's fingers lace through hers, grounding her to the waking world.

Beyond that, she felt Aurelia and Selene both. She was anchored, solid in her family's perfectly-imperfect love. They would make it out, she was sure of it. That surety wobbled slightly as she was cast into Nihil, the limen crystallizing around her, more real now that she was no longer following the threads.

Harlow found herself in the chamber where she'd first seen Ashbourne and the generals, the wardens of Nihil, over the summer. Instead of the quiet pulse of the limen's heart, the room was in chaos. Not one of the generals were in their stasis chambers. The heart of the aether boomed erratically, shaking the room.

Someone bumped into her astral body, pushing her hard, though she wasn't sure how that was possible. She turned to find Ashbourne, his heavy brow furrowed with concern.

"You should not be here," he said. "Go home."

"I followed Larkin here," she explained as he took hold of her elbow.

"Larkin?" It was both question and answer. He dragged her now and she moved her spirit body's feet, desperate to keep up. They traveled down what appeared to be a long glass hallway. The clear walls were ornately carved, and beyond them, aether swirled, lit by the storm at the heart of the limen. Harlow could make out shapes in the aether—hundreds, maybe thousands, of screaming faces. She recognized some as humanoid, others creatures she could hardly imagine.

"What is happening here?" Harlow slowed down, unwilling to go further until she understood the situation better.

Ashbourne slowed, but continued to drag her forward. "The Ravagers have escaped."

"Escaped?" Harlow repeated, the idea too big for her to process all at once.

She knew one Ravager had escaped before, and that was the reason for Morgaine Yarlo's visit to Okairos. The creature was wreaking havoc on the human girl's planet, and she'd been sent to try and stop its progress. If the other two Ravagers were loose, what did that mean? Harlow's throat went dry, but she shouldn't be aware of physical sensations here. Not like this. She yanked hard on Ashbourne's arm to get him to stop.

The tall Ventyr turned and the frustrated concern on his face reminded her that he was Finn's uncle. They were so similar, and yet very different at the same time. Ashbourne was, no doubt, more handsome—though Harlow wasn't sure how that was possible. But while Finn's eyes always held warm humor behind the darkness that lurked there, Ashbourne was only cold power, ancient and fierce. "Someone let them out."

Harlow stumbled, though she wasn't sure how it was possible to be clumsy in her spirit body—something in the limen had gone off balance. What Ashbourne said made no sense. Letting the Ravagers loose was unthinkable. Their uncontrolled elemental energy had nearly destroyed worlds before. Harlow's mind spun out, her perception blurring.

Ashbourne dragged her up again, pulling her along. "Stay focused. You must not lose yourself here."

"Who would do something like that?" Harlow asked.

Ashbourne turned. His jaw clenched tightly, his brow creased into deep furrows. "I don't know. The Ravagers cannot be allowed free reign..." His deep voice broke a little then hardened once more. "Please, you must find Larkin and go."

He felt protective over her sister. Cared for her in some way, that was clear. But that care was not something she recognized. Even Connor McKay had emotions she understood. Whoever— whatever—Ashbourne the Warden had become after an eternity in this prison, she could not comprehend it.

And yet, he'd stopped, his grip on her arm gentling. It hadn't hurt her spirit body, but even so, he realized how hard he'd been holding onto her and his face softened a measure.

"Where did the Ravagers go?"

Ash didn't answer her question. His eyes narrowed in intensity. "You must get out, *now*. The structure that holds Nihil together is disintegrating."

Harlow pointed to the screaming faces in the aether. "And that?"

Ash didn't answer, but began walking again. He didn't run, but his stride was quick and purposeful. "Come this way—there is a place your sister often meets me outside Nihil." They turned a corner and the walls became thicker and more textured, like stone.

Ash glanced back as they descended into darkness, a ball of light illuminating in front of him. "Step carefully. This part of Nihil is not an aethereal construction. It is real, and you too shall become more real here."

The metaphysical mechanics of that were baffling, but

Harlow didn't have time to think. They'd entered a maze of some kind. "What is this place?"

"The Labyrinth," Ash said. "It has always been here. Like much of the limen, it is but an echo of a real place. But it is... more corporeally inclined. Your sister often appears here. Come."

Harlow looked back, remembering the long glass hallway and the screaming faces. Ashbourne's mouth pressed into a grim line, as though annoyed she'd remembered.

"Do you know so little of the aether? Of what made the Ravagers?" His voice was curt.

Harlow shrugged. "I'm sure you can imagine that Connor and the rest of your kind haven't made that kind of information readily available."

Ashbourne snorted, something nearing a laugh as he moved on, walking quickly through turn by turn of the Labyrinth. "I should have considered that." His face smoothed into thoughtfulness. "There are two kinds of power that allow magic to be used. You understand this, yes?"

Harlow nodded, following Ashbourne. This place was dizzying in its complexity. The Ventyr's steps were sure, but she wondered how she'd ever find her way out. In the distance, there were sounds of something breaking apart, erratic crashes and otherworldly screams.

Ashbourne was trying to keep her calm by talking to her. Harlow recognized the strategy immediately, and appreciated it. Fear had her heart in its cold vice-grip, and she needed to stay moving and sharp. She wouldn't lose Larkin again. "Celestial and aethereal, right? The glowing light—your people use that, rather than aether, right?"

Ashbourne made a "hmm" noise, tilting his head in a raptorial fashion that reminded her of the Feriant. "Not 'rather than.' I would say primarily. Celestial power comes from the universe itself, from all that is outward, while aether comes from within.

The Ventyr use both, but we fare better with celestial power." He held out the glowing golden orb in front of him for emphasis. "Aether, because of its nature, is more sentient than starfire. It is prone to individuation—which makes it dangerous."

Harlow had no idea what Ashbourne might mean by that. Somewhere ahead of them, she heard a voice calling out for help. "That's Larkin!"

"Yes," Ash replied, grabbing her hand and rushing them forward. Harlow allowed herself to be dragged.

When she spotted Larkin, she broke free of the Ventyr and ran to her sister's side. Larkin's eyes were unfocused, her expression disoriented. She fell into Harlow's arms. "Harlow?"

"It's me," Harlow answered. "Let's get you out of here."

Ashbourne placed a hand on Larkin's back. "I am so glad you are all right, littling," he said softly.

Harlow glanced up, and finally understood why the ancient immortal had been so interested in her sister. Though there were no threads here, something was missing. Some*one* was missing, and Larkin reminded him of that someone.

"You have a sister," she guessed.

The ancient being—in all ways that counted, a god—bowed his head. "Yes. Thalia was much like Larkin."

There was great sadness in the past tense of the statement. Despite the Ventyr's long lives, Harlow knew immediately that Thalia was gone, and Ashbourne had treated Larkin like his own ever since she was a child. In the distance, something rumbled and creaked. The shrieking increased now, making Harlow want to cover her ears.

"The prison is coming apart," Ashbourne said. "Go. Now."

But Harlow didn't know how. He'd been right. She was more real here, less connected to the aether, and that made all the difference. "Before, when I was here, you sent me back. Can you do that now?"

Ash nodded. "Be careful, little bird. The Ravager you spoke

to knows you. It speaks of you often. I fear it will find you when it makes its way to your world."

In the din of Nihil breaking apart, everything stopped for Harlow. Her ears rung with the reality of Ashbourne's words. What he was saying couldn't be true. It just *couldn't*. She hadn't *meant* to draw the creature's attention when she'd first traveled to Nihil. Was this her fault?

Next to her, Larkin stilled. "They've escaped?"

Harlow wouldn't accept this. It was too much. Her world had endured enough. "*No.*"

"Yes." Ashbourne's reply was fierce, unyielding as adamantine.

Beyond the Labyrinth, the hideous creaking noise dissolved into an infernal groan. Small stones came loose from the Labyrinth walls, floating in the air, suspended.

"And the other?" Harlow was stalling, trying to wrap her mind around yet another unsolvable problem, one she feared she might have caused.

Ashbourne shook his head. "The other I must follow to Sirin, which is where I believe it has gone. It is the worst of the two—and I must find it, and bring it back."

So he would not help them. Next to her, Larkin's body tensed. She was as scared as Harlow was.

"What about the one that's gone to Okairos?" Harlow's voice came out in a high-pitched shriek.

"You must find a way to vanquish it, or bring it back here." Ashbourne said it so simply that for a moment it sounded *possible*. But how could it be? How could they vanquish it on their own?

More stones came loose from the Labyrinth. The whole thing pitched, like an unstable ship upon a roiling sea.

"Your brethren," Harlow gripped Larkin's arm, trying to steady them both. It felt as though the limen itself might break apart, but if she'd caused this problem, she had to try to solve it. "The generals. Will they help us?"

Ashbourne laughed, the sound dry and bitter. Unlike Larkin and Harlow, he had no trouble keeping his balance. The world-between-worlds was breaking apart and he was steady as a rock. "The generals will not come to our aid."

"But... I have to..." Harlow couldn't find the words to express what she needed to say. That she couldn't be the cause of this, and return to Okairos with no solution.

He sensed the source of her struggle. "There is nothing you could have done differently. Some things are woven into the tapestry, and cannot be unraveled. This is one such thing." The Ventyr's dark eyes were solemn. "You must go."

"Come with us," Harlow begged, as she and Larkin stumbled into one another again. Larkin ducked to avoid a stone from the Labyrinth hitting her in the head. "We'll need your help."

Ashbourne shook his head. "You have my brother to help you. He was there at the beginning."

Harlow wanted to scream. They didn't have time for this conversation anymore, but he was seriously out of touch if he thought Connor would help them. Ashbourne pushed a loose stone the size of a boulder away from them. At least the Labyrinth was breaking apart slowly, though the noises that came from Nihil increased in pitch and frequency.

"And my nephew. I must do my duty elsewhere, and you must go home." Ash pressed fingers to Larkin and Harlow's foreheads, respectively, and before Harlow could ask another question, she felt her body lose its modicum of corporeality and slide back along the threads so fast it was dizzying. When she opened her eyes, she was in the cottage once more, staring into Larkin's eyes.

# CHAPTER THIRTEEN

Aurelia, Selene, and Thea sat frozen for a fraction of a second, before launching themselves at Larkin and Harlow. When hugs and assurances were given that they were both all right, Larkin announced, "The Ravagers are loose. Nihil has been destroyed."

"What?" Aurelia gasped. "How?"

Harlow shook her head. "We didn't have time to find out. Ash sent us back."

"What were you doing there to begin with, bun?" Aurelia's words were slow and careful.

Larkin sighed. "I wanted to see how Ash was doing. It was never safe enough with Vivia to dream-walk."

Everyone was silent. No one wanted to get into a fight about safety on Larkin's first night back, but it was obvious from the identical tight-lipped expressions on Selene, Aurelia, and Thea's faces they were suppressing the urge to chide. Harlow hid a smile. It was no wonder the twins had thousands of nicknames for Thea that all indicated that she was their third mother.

Finally Selene spoke. "Where have they gone? Did Ash know?"

Larkin glanced at Harlow. "He thought the one that was interested in Harlow might come here. He's gone after the other."

Harlow's cheeks flushed. The creature's interest in her elicited shame. A log in the fireplace popped, sending sparks everywhere. Everyone jumped.

Aurelia put a hand on Harlow's arm. "It is not your fault, darling. We don't even know if it's here."

Harlow wasn't so sure about that, even after all that nonsense Ash had spouted in Nihil about the tapestry not being unraveled.

"What about the other Wardens?" Thea asked. "Won't they come here?"

A hysterical laugh bubbled up from Harlow's belly. "They're gone. No one is coming to help us. Ash says we have Connor to help us. And Finn." Her voice shuddered around Finn's name, her hands fluttering around her face.

"Slow down," Aurelia urged, her tone gentle. "We'll figure this out."

But Harlow couldn't see how. The doom-feeling was coming true. War with the Illuminated was imminent, on the horizon. The Vespae had overrun the planet. They were a rag-tag group of refugees, hiding in desolation, and Finn was *still* missing. How, *how* did anyone expect her to slow her thinking down or figure anything out?

The scream Harlow had been repressing since Nihil burbled out of her in a feral noise. "It never stops," she cried, strangled desperation breaking over her in waves. "Why can't we catch a break?"

*Why can't I catch a break?*

"We have," Selene said, her voice steady and calm. "We got Larkin back. *You* got Larkin back."

Everyone was silent for a long moment. Harlow saw the panic in the maters' eyes. She inhaled slowly, Thea's fingers still wound around hers, and she gripped them tighter for support. Thea squeezed back, a silent reassurance that she understood, that she wasn't going anywhere.

"I'm sorry," Harlow whispered, her eyes falling into her lap.

Selene stroked her cheek. "There's no need for apologies. Sometimes when situations are at their worst, we can't see the progress we're making."

Aurelia nodded, gazing at her wife. "When the hits keep coming, and it feels like they won't stop, it's hard to remember that we keep getting up." Her eyes slid to Harlow's. "We underestimate the strength it takes to rise."

Harlow wanted desperately to feel comfort in her mother's words, but she could not. But she wouldn't add to anyone else's troubles.

Larkin's head tilted. "There was something else, before, when Finn and I were in the limen with Morgaine... The Ravagers can't function in corporeal realms easily. They need a body. A human body. Morgaine said she doesn't know if immortals make good hosts..."

"So it will inhabit a human?" Thea asked.

From the look on Thea's face, it was clear her question was for herself, not the group, but Larkin answered anyway. "I think so."

The Kranes sat in silence, letting both the depth and breadth of the problems closing in on them sink in. Harlow waited for someone to say something. For a brilliant solution to pop out of one of their mouths, but nothing came. Every moment of respite came paired with something terrible—some new twist of fate that made everything worse. *How were people meant to bear the weight of so much going wrong?*

The front door banged open, cold air flooding the living room of the cottage, a burst of snow swirling in with the wind. Alaric stepped inside, pulling the door hard against the howling storm raging outside. As he pushed his hood back,

Thea stood, her movements sharp in reaction to her bond-mate's emotions.

Alaric's dark eyes were wide with panic until he counted them. He didn't bother to take off his boots and coat, but strode across the room, pulling Thea into his side, tucking her beneath his arm, as though protecting her from something. For a moment, he hesitated. When he spoke, Harlow could tell he was making every attempt to keep his voice even and calm. "The Vespae broke the wards. They took Petra. You're needed at Kate's."

The air in the room went from heavy desperation to outright panic in the space of a moment. Everyone moved quickly, going for their coats and boots, talking at once, as was the way with the Kranes in a crisis.

"The Vespae don't take prisoners," Thea murmured.

"They do," Larkin replied, searching for her socks under the coffee table. "They took Finn. They didn't kill him. They *took* him. I watched it happen." Larkin turned to Harlow. "In the attack, before you found me, didn't they act like they wanted you?"

Harlow nodded. Pieces of the puzzle were starting to take shape in her mind, but she didn't know what the picture was. *Why hadn't they come here? Why hadn't they come after her, if they'd wanted her?* She glanced at Alaric. "When did they take her?"

Alaric met her eyes, his shrewd sense of duty in a crisis narrowing in on her. "About twenty minutes ago."

Nihil. They'd been in Nihil twenty minutes ago. Not their bodies, but their spirits. *Had that kept the Vespae from finding her, or had they simply not wanted her anymore?*

Larkin's jaw clenched as she thought. "It's like they're looking for something specific."

Harlow nodded as she slid into her jacket. "They are. Audata's put it together. They're looking for a building, an observatory. But I don't know what that would have to do with Finn, or me—or Petra, for that matter."

"An *observatory*?" Aurelia's skin went white, all blood draining from her face. "Let's go."

"What is it, darling?" Selene asked.

Aurelia had never looked so grim. "I know why they're taking them. Let's go."

Unreasonable hope bloomed in Harlow's chest. She took Aurelia's hand, clasping it hard. She didn't know what her mother had put together, but she had to ask. "Could *these* Vespae—the ones who took Petra—have Finn?"

Aurelia's hands went to Harlow's cheeks. "I don't know, love. They might."

Harlow fought to keep her thoughts linear, but didn't succeed. Her mind raced. She'd been right there, at that farm, and he might have been below—needing her. She couldn't think of that now. One thing at a time. They didn't know anything more than they had before, not really, but the hope blossoming in her chest didn't absorb the reason she tried to impose on it. It opened in hundreds of tiny buds—buds that if Harlow could pull them from inside her, she knew would be shaped like lilacs.

Harlow closed her eyes against the tears that threatened, pushing thoughts of Finn deep down inside her, until she could breathe again. When she opened them, Thea's boots were on, but she had lost her coat. When she turned, Alaric was holding it open for her, his face grave. Harlow knew where the glint of protectiveness in her brother-in-law's eyes came from. If the Vespae were attacking and taking people, his priorities were with Thea, no matter how much he loved Petra.

Harlow's heart swelled. Alaric glanced her way, and she nodded at him, and he at her. They understood one another. Thea and the twins she carried would be protected at all costs. Harlow wondered how long she had left with her eldest sister. They couldn't stay here—not if the Vespae knew where they were and were able to break through the village's wards so easily. She and Larkin dressed quickly for the cold and their little party set out into the cold night, towards Kate's house.

～

KATE'S COTTAGE WAS NO BIGGER THAN SELENE'S AND decorated in nearly identical linen-colored furniture. It was packed so full of people they were spilling out into the garden. All the top Rogue officials were here. At the center of everything, Kate sat on the couch, head in her hands, rocking back and forth. Lou was next to her, trying and failing to comfort her daughter.

Harlow went to Lou's side. Lou had already been in her seventies when she was turned, and though the transformation had smoothed some of her wrinkles, she still wore more age than most vampires. Her salt and pepper hair was short and she was a stout woman with pale skin and a hard face, with gentle eyes. Those eyes were worried now. Kate did not lose control. *Ever.*

So Kate wasn't dallying with Petra; she was deeply in love with her. Harlow knew they'd fallen hard for one another, but this was news to her. *Maybe it wouldn't be if you'd been talking to your friends*, a nasty voice in the back of her head chided.

Enzo and Riley rushed in from the storm, leaving snowshoes at the door, as Harlow touched Lou's shoulder. "Let me try?"

Lou nodded, rising. "Help her, Harlow. We need her to tell us what happened. All I got out of her was that they took her."

"Get everyone out of here," Harlow replied. "Aurelia has something to tell us—something important."

Lou nodded and cleared the cottage of all but the most important Rogue officials. When only a few were left, they went into the dining room, leaving Harlow alone with Kate.

Harlow wondered if it wouldn't have been better for Enzo or Riley to help. They were both empaths and could probably do a better job than her. But as she sat, Kate reached for her hand, pressing it to her chest. "I can't breathe without her," she gasped.

Terror gripped Kate Spencer like nothing Harlow had ever seen. She squeezed Kate's hand. "I know."

"You don't!" Kate screamed in her face.

Harlow gripped Kate's hand harder, so hard it probably hurt. "I *do*," she hissed, then softer, "Katie—I do."

Kate's eyes widened and she slowed her rocking. She breathed deeper. "Oh," she said, her bottom lip shaking. "You do."

Harlow nodded again. "Tell me what happened. Was she out when you and I were stacking wood?"

Kate nodded. "Yes, yes... She was burning the bodies... But they were waiting when we got back tonight... Waiting here.... I tried to stop them, Lo."

Kate wheezed between words, her panic rising again. "Breathe," Harlow said, keeping her voice low and soothing. She touched her friend's face. "Breathe and tell me what happened so we can help her."

"They didn't attack like before. They just took her and left. They were so fast... I tried to follow, but... I.... I got lost."

Harlow nodded. "I know you did. It's okay."

"No!" Kate insisted. "It's not. I didn't have my emergency phone. I can't track it back."

"Kate," Harlow said firmly. "It's okay. I know where they took her, and when you're ready, Aurelia says she knows why."

Kate's eyes lost some of the wild panic and she drew breath after shuddering breath. "Okay," she said, after a long pause. Kate's fists clenched tightly as she regained control of herself. "I'm ready."

Harlow took Kate's arm and led her into the dining room, where almost two dozen people were crowded into chairs and corners. The room wasn't big enough for this kind of thing, but it didn't really matter at this point. They were all together.

Kate's arm wound tightly around hers. Something about it made her proud. After everything they'd been through, they were still friends. Right now, her friend wasn't the Rogue Queen, she was a woman whose heart was in pieces. Harlow helped her to sit, and spoke. "Kate says that when she and Petra got home, the Vespae were waiting. They took Petra and left—"

"Why are you telling us this?" a human asked. "Why isn't Kate telling us?"

Harlow's heart sank to see the compact frame and auburn hair of Piper Winslow, the Education Councillor.

"*Please*," Kate managed to say, her voice shaking.

The human woman's eyes narrowed at Kate, and then Harlow. Vivia was sitting next to Piper, and she put a hand on her arm. "I believe Harlow has some pertinent information about what's happened here, don't you, Harlow?"

Harlow nodded, looking around for Cian—she saw them standing towards the back with Alaric and Thea. None of them would typically be allowed in a meeting like this—maybe Cian, but not the rest of them.

Harlow felt like an outsider and a bit of an imposter, but she nodded and continued. "When Kate tried to follow the Vespae, she found the same thing I did earlier today—they've taken over a small farm. There's thousands of them gathered there, and they have some unique warding. It's nearly invisible, hiding the farm entirely..."

"We have that kind of warding here. How is that unique?" Piper interrupted. The way she looked at Harlow felt resentful, and personal. Though Harlow had tried to dismiss her attitude in the past, tonight it was clear that whatever issue Piper had with her, it was more than being wary of her close relationship with Finn.

Harlow took a deep breath, thinking of Finn, and the way

she'd watched him navigate thorny moments like this early on during their summer in Nea Sterlis, with various important people in the lower Orders. He always stayed calm and empathetic, rather than impatient.

"Right," she said after she'd collected herself. Piper looked vaguely surprised to be agreed with. *Had she been expecting Harlow to fight with her?* "We do, you're right. But these were different. They made it hard to think as I passed through them— and I *could* pass through, but only in my Feriant form."

Vivia nodded now, her face thoughtful. Harlow would bet money she had a theory working—all of her sisters made the exact same face when they puzzled something together. Her resentment towards the Argent dissipated a little more. It wasn't Vivia's fault that people automatically liked her, and not Harlow.

She turned her attention back to explaining herself, feeling calmer. "After breaking the wards in my alternae, I started to feel excessively confused when I dropped into my humanoid form. So I marked the geolocation and sent it back to base." Harlow glanced at Kate, who still clung to her. "The exact same thing happened to Kate when she tried to follow Petra's captors."

Piper looked to Aurelia. "You said you know something."

*How had the Education Councillor defaulted to running this meeting?* Harlow wondered. *Shouldn't Lou be running it, if Kate can't? She's the former queen after all.*

Aurelia bowed her head respectfully to the human. "I have a guess as to why they're taking certain prisoners."

Piper Winslow's face didn't move a muscle, she simply made an imperious gesture with her hand for Aurelia to continue. The atmosphere in the room was tense. Many of the eyes on Aurelia were suspicious, wary. Harlow wasn't the only outsider; it felt like her whole family was intruding on something that wasn't meant for them.

*Because it wasn't.* The Rogue Order wasn't made for them.

It was made for people who could not function in the Orders and the world they'd built—and they'd all done so fairly easily, always. Kate squeezed her hand and when their eyes met, the vampire nodded. Kate always had an uncanny way of following Harlow's trains of thought without her having to say much.

Aurelia cleared her throat as all eyes focused on her. Harlow's heart hurt to see her mother move so uncomfortably in her chair. Apparently she sensed the same discomfort Harlow did, but she steeled herself quickly and spoke. "It's possible these Vespae have Finn McKay, and it's likely he knows where the observatory they are searching for is."

Audata, who sat next to Piper, sat up straight. "Why would he know that?"

Aurelia took a deep breath. "The Illuminated have secret caches of information all over Okairos. Mostly in remote areas. We know they're constantly watching us, but we're not all they're watching. They also monitor the stars closely, and the occurrence of the portals. They track them."

Most of the people around the table nodded. While they hadn't known this explicitly, theories about secret locations of Illuminated information had been posited a number of times.

Aurelia spoke again. "I believe they think Petra and Finn have knowledge of the observatory."

Piper pursed her lips momentarily, then her eyebrows lifted above the frames of her glasses. "They know he's Connor's child... And Petra, well she would have as much of a chance of knowing where the observatory was as he would, wouldn't she?"

Aurelia nodded as the human woman trailed off.

"Why are they interested in Harlow, then?" Piper asked. It came out like a challenge, raising Harlow's hackles, but Aurelia didn't miss a beat.

"As all of you know, I've been privy to many of the Illuminated's secrets over the years. I assume they believe she might know things that I do."

Whispers spun about the room, weaving webs of discord. People weren't sure what to think, or if they could trust what Aurelia said. Harlow heard whispered questions about why they hadn't tried to take Thea, or even Larkin.

"Why wouldn't they just take *you* then?" Piper asked, her voice rising above the quiet chaos. "Why do they want these children?"

Vivia cleared her throat. "If I may, Piper?"

The human nodded, her expression morphing into pleasantness. She looked younger at that moment, more like she was Harlow's age than she had for the whole conversation. The responsibility of her role, whatever it actually was, obviously weighed heavily on Piper Winslow. Harlow didn't believe for a moment that the human was only the Education Councillor.

Vivia spoke, and the room fell completely silent. "It's my belief that Aurelia is onto something pertinent. However, I also believe we should keep an open mind here. The Vespae tried to talk with us, for the first time *ever*, before they attacked us."

Someone, Harlow didn't see who, spoke up from the crowd. "They still tried to wipe us out."

Vivia nodded. "Yes. They are brutal in their methods. But they have an aim of some kind, and I believe we'd be wise to find out what that is. It might help us solve things between our people with less bloodshed."

The room erupted into loud conversation. Not even Vivia Woolf, with her iconic status among the Rogues, could suggest such a thing without evoking controversy. Vivia ran a hand through her long, silver hair, which caught the light with a silken sheen. The firedrake waited, as though thinking deeply, before holding a hand up to silence the room. It only served to give her words more gravitas. Vivia Woolf knew *exactly* how to work a crowd. "Before the Illuminated came, we had a theory that they attacked so viciously because they were very territorial, like wasps..."

"Thus the name..." Piper murmured appreciatively.

Vivia nodded, obviously pleased that Piper had mentioned it. "Yes, exactly. My point is only that we should avoid thinking of their motivations as though they are Okairons. My mother used to say that though their actions were difficult to understand, she didn't believe they were evil..."

More whispers filled the room at the mention of the ancient Empress—the one the Illuminated had eventually overthrown after they helped to rid Okairos of the Vespae originally. It was a reminder of how dire the situation truly was.

"They've killed so many," Cian mused. They were likely the only person who would dare counter Vivia's point.

"I don't suggest that their actions are excusable, or that we should not fight them. Only that measuring evil by Okairos' standards might not be the best way to understand their motivations." The ancient firedrake didn't falter for a moment. This was what immortality could look like if it weren't spent in pursuit of power over others.

Vivia stood. "The best thing we can do now is get our people back and work on fortifying our wards, but of course we'll leave this to a vote." She looked at Cian then, and the rest of Harlow's family in turn. "Come, let's allow the Council some room to talk without the rest of us."

Kate hugged Harlow. "Thank you."

"We'll get her back, okay?" Harlow promised.

"Finn too," Kate replied, her chin quivering a little. "We'll get them both back."

They hugged again, before Lou pulled Kate into a conversation with a few of the Council members and Vivia Woolf. Harlow slipped out the front door, looking for her family. People filed out of the cottage, going their separate ways in small whispering groups. The storm had stopped, for the time being. Harlow's family huddled around Aurelia and Selene, watching the crowd disperse.

Harlow joined them, as Cian took one of Aurelia's hands. "Do you really think it's possible that the Vespae who took Petra have Finn too?"

Aurelia nodded at the firedrake. "I do." She turned to Alaric. "What about the caches in Nuva Troi? Do you know where they are?"

Harlow understood why Aurelia hadn't brought this up in the meeting. She glanced at the cottage. The Council was gathering around the dining room table again. She noticed that while Vivia had said "they" should let the Council speak, that she herself had stayed. This was how power worked; even wonderful people like Vivia worked to have more of it.

Alaric ushered the family along, to keep them moving away from the crowd. When they reached the maters' yard, he moved quickly and quietly, wrapping his own coat around Thea as they all settled into chairs. Everyone was waiting for him to speak, but his focus was on his bondmate.

Harlow hid a smile. Thea was annoyed with the attention. She pulled her handsome husband towards her. "I'm fine," she muttered. "Tell them about the caches."

Alaric rolled his eyes slightly at Thea's admonition. Harlow was glad to see he wasn't offended by her sister's grumpiness. "There's a cache in Nuva Troi. In Connor's office, beneath the Illuminated Order's building. There's one in every major city on the planet—the Knights have been trying to get into one for years."

Cian nodded, rubbing their hands together to warm them. "We've never had any luck. The one in Nuva Troi is the most heavily guarded. But if this observatory is here in Falcyra... That might be a different story. Do you know where it is, Alaric?"

"No," he answered. "I'm sorry."

Thea shivered. Alaric gestured towards the house they shared with the maters. "Could we head inside? Thea is cold."

Selene's keen eyes darted between Thea and Alaric. Aurelia

watched her wife, then watched the direction of Selene's gaze. The two of them made eye contact, hope and careful joy lighting their eyes. Despite the difficult nature of the past months, they were connected as they ever were, it seemed.

"Yes," Selene said, standing to take her eldest's arm, dragging her up from her chair. "Let's get you inside."

Thea rolled her eyes. "Don't start treating me like a fragile thing. I won't have it."

Larkin's mouth twisted into a little knot. "What does everyone know that I don't?"

The entire family huddled together as they walked inside, filling Larkin in on the good news that she was about to be an auntie. The aching void inside Harlow's chest shrunk a tiny bit as the cold air stung her cheeks.

# Chapter Fourteen

arlow spent an hour with her family, before she and
Cian joined the rest of the Warbirds at the Dairy,
which was abuzz with activity as they arrived. Vivia,
who'd apparently left the Council meeting, broke away from
gear prep to hug Cian. Harlow listened while they spoke, but
apparently she'd left shortly after they had. Nothing had been
decided yet, but she was optimistic that they'd approve a rescue
mission.

Harlow went about setting her gear up. None of them
would dress until it was time to go; their fighting gear was too
well-insulated to wear inside. Enzo had designed it carefully,
weaving spells into the seams that made it warmer and more
protective.

There wasn't a lot left to do to prepare. Until the Council
officially approved their mission, all they could do was rest.
Harlow joined the majority of the Warbirds in finding a place to
nap until word came through. Tomyris and Sam made room for
her on one of the big couches and she soon dozed off.

She woke to Audata's return from the Council meeting.
They had approved what Audata called "fast, exploratory

action." The Warbirds were sanctioned to rescue Petra, and anyone else they could find, in a targeted, quick attack that would be focused on rescue and information gathering, and nothing else.

The Warbirds spurred into action with this news. Claimed partners ran through drills as they geared up, while Sam and Tomyris were sent on a surveillance mission to get a better idea of the farm itself. Yet another blizzard had fallen over the area overnight, and the day was dark and gloomy, with low visibility. Harlow was sipping a big mug of bone broth with Cian when Sam and Tomyris returned. Once they'd dried off, they joined Harlow and the others on the floor in the training room to finalize the plan.

"There's a big farmhouse," Sam explained as the Warbirds stretched their muscles in a circle around Sam and Tomyris. "Looks like that's where the queen is staying with her guard. They don't let anyone in there."

Tomyris nodded. "And there's a bunch of outbuildings and sheds, but the barn is where they're keeping Petra."

Harlow reached for Cian's hand, her heart beating so hard it hurt. "You saw her?"

Sam's smile was grim. "Yes. She was knocked out, and they were moving her from the farmhouse to the barn. Looks like they had their queen dose her."

Murmurs spread through the room. Audata had a theory that a swarm's queen might be more poisonous than her drones. If she was right, Petra would be incapable of doing much to help when they got her out.

Sam sketched a map of the farm on a piece of paper, while Tomyris continued. "We also saw them carry in more food than was necessary for one person, though it was hard to tell how much they had. It looks like at least one other person is being kept in the barn."

Harlow's heart thumped so hard she thought it might bruise

her ribcage. Was Finn there? A few of the Warbirds glanced her way. Mirai and Peyton both shot her sympathetic looks. If anyone could understand how she felt right now, it was this group of people.

Audata looked at the map Sam drew first, then handed it to Vivia to look over. Apparently, the firedrake was being treated as one of their leaders now. Harlow was grateful. The Argent had more experience with Vespae than any of them did. Her knowledge was invaluable.

The Warbirds crouched together, watching as Vivia explained the plan. "The blizzard gives us some cover, but our strongest ally is speed. We need to do this in under ten minutes, if possible."

Everyone nodded along as she explained their flight path, and the formation they'd surround the barn in. Cian would cover them from above, but would stay hidden for as long as possible. "Sam, Tomy—I want you to go in with Harlow and get the prisoners. Teleport them out immediately, and if there are more prisoners than just Petra, pull anyone off the line that you need to help you, okay?"

Sam and Tomyris nodded. Harlow had questions though. "Do *you* think there's more than just Petra at the farm?"

Vivia's silver eyes met hers. "You're asking me if I think Finn's there?" The Dairy went so silent that the wind's howling outside filled Harlow's ears. "I don't know, Harlow. But whoever they've taken, we have to get them back and find out what's been going on at that farm."

Harlow nodded, but Cian spoke. "Of course, I think we should rescue whoever's there...What do you think they're doing to the prisoners? They can't talk to them, right?"

The look of utter helplessness on Vivia's face sent a visible chill through everyone in the room, and her words did nothing to reassure anyone. "In all the time I've been dealing with the Vespae, no one has ever been able to communicate with them.

Until the other day, I've never even seen an attempt to talk to us. Not *ever*. And they weren't successful, were they? They can't speak as we do."

Vivia stared at the ceiling for a long time. Her silver hair was braided into two thick braids, like the rest of the Warbirds, and she played with the ends of one as her face scrunched up in thought. Finally she spoke. "I think we have to come to terms with the idea that it's possible someone else is helping the Vespae. Someone who could potentially talk to their prisoners."

Audata's eyes widened in a way that Harlow knew meant that she had a theory. "Someone could be using them as a weapon."

Vivia shrugged. "That's certainly a possibility, but we won't know until we get whoever is there out. It's our best chance to gain vital intelligence on their motivations."

A dry, hollow laugh rasped through Harlow's lungs. "That's why we get to rescue them, isn't it?"

Audata and Vivia exchanged a look. Vivia sighed, her eyes falling closed. "I don't know what you want us to say, Harlow."

Cian answered for her. "The truth."

Audata turned to Harlow, sliding the map to Vivia. "Yes, that's why they're approving the mission. They don't care about rescuing Petra, but they did care about the possibility that the Vespae might have Finn."

Harlow pushed up off the floor, anger filling her. "But not because they trust him, or *us*, right?"

Each of the Warbirds tensed.

Audata's face didn't move, nor did her tone turn conciliatory. "Correct. They want Finn to give information about Connor, and the cache of information in Nuva Troi. That is the reason we're being allowed to go."

Peyton was the first to speak, surprising Harlow with her words. "That's fucked up. He's her Claimed. One of *us*." The Ventyr woman made eye contact with her partner, Vance, a tall redheaded Strider. He nodded, his freckled face clouding with regret.

Peyton turned to Harlow. "I know we've given you a hard time." Many of the Warbirds nodded; it was obvious they'd talked about this. "A lot of us have baggage about the McKays. They've gone after a lot of our families over the years."

Harlow couldn't look up as tears threatened to fall on her cheeks. She knew how bad it felt to have Connor and Aislin McKay come after your family. Peyton cleared her throat. "But you and Finn both are different. You're ours now."

Harlow glanced around as Peyton stood, pulling her to her feet as the rest of the Warbirds, and Cian, did the same thing. "You're one of us, Krane. And whatever the Council's intentions, ours are to get our people home safe."

"Thank you," Harlow whispered.

Peyton dragged her into a hug and a cheer went up. "Let's go get your man."

# Chapter Fifteen

The group broke up to make their final preparations for the mission. Cian hugged Harlow hard, followed by Sam, Tomyris and each of the Warbirds in turn. The show of affection calmed her wild heartbeat, but only slightly. It was good to finally have the Warbirds' full support, and feel as though she belonged, but as it lessened the anger and frustration she'd been carrying with her, it made way for fear.

Harlow busied herself with tying up a pair of insulated knee-high boots. Enzo had been working with Audata to create thicker gear that the Vespae's poisonous stingers wouldn't be able to penetrate so quickly. The new clothing wasn't as flexible as the old had been, but the loss of a tiny bit of mobility would be worth it, if it stopped the Vespae from being able to incapacitate their magical abilities.

As Harlow was finishing gearing up, Audata handed her a small round device that looked a little like a black elevator button. She'd been passing them out to everyone, clipping them onto their gear somewhere prominent. When she stepped aside she explained to the group. "Nox developed these before she left, and I've finished them the best I could." Audata's mouth twisted in unusual uncertainty. "I'm not sure if they'll work, but Nox thought she'd found a frequency that might disorient the Vespae. Use these when they close in to give yourselves a way out. Since we haven't tested them—"

Tomyris clapped a hand on the solemn Strider's shoulder. "We know, love. It's a risk, you don't know if they'll work." The Ventyr's words were gentle.

Samira smiled at Audata. "They'll work."

Audata's eyes slid to Harlow's. Harlow only shrugged. She had no idea what would work and what wouldn't, and Audata wanted honesty. "We're bringing them home, regardless."

"Hells yes, we are," Max agreed.

When Harlow looked around the circle, she saw nothing but reassurance. Every face reflected the same confidence. No one was holding anything back. They'd rescue Petra, and Finn if he was there.

"Thank you," Harlow said, bowing her head in gratitude. There was nothing else for her to say.

∼

THE FERIANT CROSSED THE WARDS WITH THEIR Ventyr partners on their backs. Harlow carried Vivia, who used a momentary shielding that mimicked the Feriants' biofrequency for a short amount of time. "I'm all right," Vivia called to Harlow as soon as they crossed the ward. "It worked."

Through their telepathic link, they checked in with the other pairs. All were well. Four pairs broke off with Cian, who carried Audata. The six of them would try to bring down the Vespae's odd wards so that everyone could teleport out, if need be. The Ventyr flew on their own now, moving into formation now that they were past the wards.

When the Warbirds broke through the cloud cover above the farm, there were Vespae in the barnyard, huddled together in small clumps against the storm. The vast numbers Harlow had seen before weren't present now. A quick survey revealed two or three dozen in the barnyard.

*Where are the rest of them?* Sam asked.

*I don't know,* Harlow answered. *Wherever it is, it can't be good.*

*Let's make this fast and we won't have to find out,* Mirai added as their formation tightened up, dropping to the ground around the barn in a dive so fast it happened almost without notice.

The Vespae appeared mildly sedated, almost hibernating. They didn't immediately react to the Warbirds' arrival, and Harlow wondered if they hadn't seen them. The Warbirds surrounded the barn, staying close to one another, covering Harlow and Sam as they shifted.

Now the Vespae woke, buzzing between themselves. Tomyris pushed Harlow and Sam toward the barn door. "I think the queen is elsewhere, maybe with the rest of them. This is what they were like at Sanctum when we killed the queen."

Tomyris turned away from the Vespae to open the heavy barn door in one hard shove, and as expected it made a loud creaking noise. The rest of the Vespae in the yard turned their attention to the Warbirds. Their buzzing grew louder. Tomyris shouted, "Get going. We need to get this done even faster—we caught a lucky break. I'll cover you."

"Ten minutes," Samira whispered as she and Harlow slipped inside. "That's all we've got."

Harlow nodded, mirroring Sam as she formed long daggers from her shadows. Outside, the Vespae in the yard sprang to action, clashing with the Warbirds guarding the barn. Harlow's eyes took a moment to adjust to the dim light inside. It didn't smell as though animals lived here, which Harlow found to be a comforting scent. Instead, it smelled like bodily refuse and rotting food. Harlow tried her best not to gag as Samira tensed next to her.

A low groan sounded in a stall to their left. Samira and Harlow crouched in defense, but none of their enemy's strange, pale forms sprung at them from the darkness. There were no Vespae here—not in this part of the barn, anyway. They moved cautiously toward the stall, where they found Petra, bound and groggy on the dirt floor.

Samira untied her, while Harlow began to search what seemed like endless dark, narrow stalls. There was no one else so far, just junk, covered in dust and cobwebs. When she glanced back at Sam, Petra was slumped against her. "Sorry," the Ventyr murmured as she drifted off. "Don't think I'm going to be much... help..."

Outside, the sounds from the fight between the Vespae and the Warbirds were intensifying. They didn't have long to find Finn, if he was here. Harlow resisted the urge to grit her teeth, and kept searching. Her breath came in short, shallow gasps as she moved, acutely aware that they were running out of time.

"Returning scouts," Tomyris shouted from the barn door. A heavy thud accompanied Tomy's growl as she fought off an incoming drone. "The rest of them aren't back yet, but the scouts turned tail."

They'd gone back to report to the larger force. And if they were already mobilized, then they had even less time to find Finn. Harlow fought the urge to rush, forcing her attention to focus on her search. She couldn't afford to make a mistake. Not if there was even the slightest possibility Finn might be here.

The stalls were deep and narrow, stuffed full of old furniture and appliances, covered in threadbare blankets. She had to remove each blanket to look for Finn, worrying he'd been hidden somewhere.

"You're okay," Samira reassured Petra, dragging her towards the barn door. Harlow shot a look down the center of the barn just in time to see Tomyris sweep out the barn door, clearing the way of encroaching Vespae with a violent swipe of celestial fire.

They had a path out, which meant Harlow needed to move faster. Her ears rung slightly with the rush of her blood. Every moment was painfully slow, her awareness that she was failing pounding with every beat of her heart.

"She can't fight or fly," Sam said, pushing Petra toward Tomyris. "Get her out."

Harlow searched another stall. She could feel herself getting careless as the bloom of hope she'd felt before waned. So careless, she almost missed the figure huddled in the corner of the stall she searched. It moved, and she rushed forward, pulling the blanket off it.

Her heart dropped out of her chest. The figure was as tall as Finn, and similarly built, but blonde. A bruised face lifted to hers. "Jareth?"

The vampire nodded. It was one of the Humanist leaders, Jareth Sanvier. The one they'd seen on the video of the Governor's Mansion over the summer. She didn't have time to wonder what he was doing here, or how they'd hit him hard enough that he'd stayed wounded; she had to keep looking.

Harlow stepped out of the stall. "Sam, come here. It's Jareth."

Samira retrieved the vampire, who like Petra was barely conscious. "We've gotta go, Harlow. It's bad out there. Time's almost up."

Harlow's chest ached as she searched another stall and another. Tomyris called to her. "Harlow, he's not here. Come *on*." She adjusted her hold on Petra, who muttered something indistinguishable.

Harlow stilled, standing in the middle of the barn, refusing to take another step until she was sure. There was nowhere else to look, but it was obvious Petra was trying to tell them something. "What did she say?"

Tomyris shrugged, tossing Petra over her shoulder. "Doesn't matter. We're going."

"Finn!" Petra screeched, her voice shrill over the din of the battle outside. Her eyes flew open, panicked. "Don't leave him."

Time slowed as Harlow watched Petra's hand fling out, towards the back of the barn. She'd searched back there already. But then she saw it: the flimsy rope ladder that led to the hayloft. Before anyone could tell her no, Harlow was scrambling up into the hayloft, hoping the rope would hold her weight..

It was darker up here than it had been below. There were no windows in this part of the barn, and she had to adjust to the lack of light again. She blinked desperately, trying to hurry her vision along, but it would not cooperate. Time slowed as her brain processed the lump of solid darkness in front of her. Her hands shook as she stepped forward, acknowledging the terrible reality inside her mind: part of her had given up, the pain of hoping to see him again almost too much to bear.

And now... *Now...* Now Finbar McKay sat slumped in the corner of the hayloft, not even bound. His face was sliced open in several places, his body obviously battered, but whole. As his storm blue eyes opened, he cracked a grin, his half-healed bottom lip splitting open, blood trickling out.

"Hey, Harls." He grinned that lopsided, wicked grin that she loved and her heart flipped twenty times in a mere second. *He was really here.* "Come to play?"

It was an odd thing to say. Time rushed forward, and so did she, hauling his heavy body up off the floor. He didn't help.

"Oh," he laughed. "So it's an escape day?"

"Yeah," she said, playing along, though she didn't know what he meant. It didn't matter. He was here, in her arms, and she'd go along with any silliness he wanted to engage in to keep him calm. It was obvious he'd been dosed with Vespae poison, likely the queen's. "Time to escape."

"Sounds good, babygirl." He laughed again, throwing his

body against the wall, away from her. "You wanna tussle again? Like last time, or the time before?"

Now he was resisting her? They didn't have time for this. Harlow tried to grab him, but he was surprisingly quick, given how injured he'd appeared a moment ago.

Finn shook his head, wagging his finger at her like she was a naughty child. "I'll give it to you, you're getting better at this. How'd you manage to smell like her? You even got the Claim right." His face darkened dangerously. "Is she here? Do you have her?"

*What in seventeen hells was he talking about?* "I'm right here," she soothed.

He lunged at her, using his full strength to pin her against the wall, his hand around her neck. "I'll fucking kill you if you laid a hand on her."

Harlow struggled, not understanding who Finn thought she was. She had to act fast, so she kneed him hard in the groin, wincing in anticipation of his pain. His grip on her slipped, and she concentrated as hard as she could, pressing herself against him, making full body contact in an attempt to engage the Claim's connection through the haze of Vespae poison lingering in his blood.

The poison. That was it. The Vespae poison blocked their connection, but *their* venom would revive it. Finn's body reacted to hers, as if by instinct, and though he still groaned in pain, she felt his arms tighten around her as she wrapped her legs around him, letting her mouth graze his neck.

This wasn't the time she'd have chosen for an arousing reunification, but he needed to *feel* the Claim, to heal and come back to himself. She'd seen it work dozens of times with the other Claimed pairs in the Warbirds. So she focused on his hard, warm body, heaving against hers in violent, confused frustration. Her hips tilted against his and she felt his cock stir.

"You are evil, you know that?" His face turned towards hers. "But you smell so godsdamn good. Fuck it."

His mouth crashed into hers as he slammed her against the wall, his hands sliding up her body. She tasted his blood in her mouth and her own body sprang to life, warmth flooding her abdomen, pooling between her legs as her fangs protracted.

As much as she wanted this moment to last, past any sense of reason, sounds of fighting reached her ears, someone calling her name. It was time to go. She pulled back from Finn's kiss, and struck hard, clamping her mouth around his neck, her fangs sinking deep into him as her venom dripped into his bloodstream. His body went slack against hers, affixing her to the wall.

For a moment, she wondered if something had gone wrong. Then he sprang away from her, his face healing quickly, the split in his lip almost disappearing. His eyes filled with tears. "It's *you.*"

Harlow had no idea what Finn had been through. Whatever it was, it had obviously taken its toll. "Of course it is, McKay."

Finn's mouth fell open and he stepped forward, incredulously reaching for her. He stopped, hearing the fight below. "We've gotta get out of here."

"Let's go home," she said, her voice husky with unshed tears.

Finn nodded, looking around at the hayloft as though seeing it for the first time. "There's a rope ladder," she said.

Finn grinned that wicked grin again, but the smile didn't reach his eyes. He swept her into his arms, shifting as he took three long strides towards the open loft. They were on the ground safely before Harlow could think, running for the front of the barn, where Tomyris, Sam, and Jareth fought nearly a dozen of the queensguard who had pushed their way inside. They were alone, which meant everyone else was overwhelmed outside.

So the queen had returned. These elite Vespae soldiers weren't like the rest of the hive drones. They were better fighters, stronger, more independent. And they had their friends cornered.

Finn was like nothing she'd ever seen, cutting through them with the grace of a dancer and the strength of a lyon. He fought with precise, feline grace and she followed his moves, the shadow to the glow of his celestial force. There was no sign of his imprisonment in his body's movements, but when he glanced back to check on her, there was exhaustion in his eyes. He didn't have long to fight at this level; he was giving it everything he had.

Harlow was paying too much attention to Finn. One of the drones' stingers grazed her cheek as she ducked its attack, rolling away as she sent long shadow darts through its eyes. The thing fell, but its poison wove through her, even through the tiniest scratch.

Harlow decapitated the last of the queensguard coming at her and then the way cleared as they pushed outside, moving into tight formation with the rest of the Warbirds, who'd clustered around the barn door.

Tomyris nodded once to Finn. "Good to meet you, McKay." She hauled Petra, who'd passed out, over her shoulder again. "You know the best way out of here?"

More drones descended on them. The Warbirds were holding on, but they were losing ground quickly as the Vespae's numbers increased.

Finn nodded. "I do. Can you call your forces back? Unless you've got another wave coming, we can't fight them all."

"This is all of us," Harlow explained. She made eye contact with Sam. "Did we get the wards?"

"Yeah, but we've only a got a minute or two. It's time." Sam grabbed Jareth's arm, causing him to wince. "We're going to teleport in a second. Hold on tight."

They hit the little buttons Audata had given them. A high-pitched shriek filled the air. Harlow could barely hear it, but she felt it deep in her bones. Around her, the rest of the Warbirds hit their own devices, both the sound and the feeling increasing pitch and intensity. The Vespae screamed, falling to the ground —it had worked better than Audata thought it might.

The Warbirds blinked out, almost at once. When they did, Harlow knew the Vespae sting had done its work, dulling her ability to teleport enough to keep her from leaving with Finn. She could still shift though, and fly back.

A logical voice in her head told her to let him bite her, to let the Claim heal her. But the exhaustion in his eyes, the slump of his shoulders, kept her from asking him. He'd been healed by her bite, but he'd been dosed for Akatei knew how long. The Claim was an exchange of energy, and he had none to share with her. He couldn't take her with him either.

She felt sure she could shift. *This wasn't a problem. They'd both make it out, she'd just be a little slower.* "There's a little village, south of here, on a fjord. Do you know it?"

"The haunted ski resort from that old documentary?" Finn asked, incredulous. Of course he knew about a decades-old documentary about Sanctum's fake destruction. That was Finn.

Harlow nodded, wishing she had a moment more to appreciate that he was still *him*. They'd have time for that later. "Go," she insisted. "I'll be right behind you."

"You all right?" he asked, a frown wrinkling his brow.

"Yep," she said, pulling a small explosive device from a pack at her thigh. "It's my job to set this though, so you go on." It was half true, she had been tasked with setting the bomb, but she could have done it already. He didn't need to know that though.

Finn brushed a kiss to her lips as he vanished, his words echoing as he disappeared. "See you there."

Harlow closed her eyes to follow, tracking the threads that connected them. It would be easy to follow him now, to make sure he got there all right. She gathered her strength. Cian would be here any minute to sweep the battlefield with draconic fire; they must be waiting for her to set the bomb. Harlow had to get out before the fallen Vespae came around, but her body wasn't cooperating. She couldn't shift.

"Hey there, dollface." A chill slipped down Harlow's spine. She turned to face Mark Easton. He grinned at her, sending her into a sick panic. Bile rose in her throat and the world spun as he stepped towards her, that evil smile reaching into the deepest parts of her. Something wasn't right. Mark had been deranged at the end, corrupted by jealousy and Olivia Sanvier's motivations, but he'd never looked like this. He'd been bad, but the thing before her was something else. Something much, much worse.

Whatever the thing that stalked towards her now was, it wasn't Mark. She was sure of it as it spoke. "It's been so long, darling girl. I'd almost forgotten how sweet you smell."

Mark had never spoken to her like that in his life, but this feeling was all too familiar. The fuzziness in her head, the emotions she couldn't affect or control, rising up in her. Now she understood Finn's confusion completely. Her feet, which had felt frozen a moment ago, moved now. "Why are you doing this, Alain?"

The incubus shot forward. "You killed my son. You and McKay."

Harlow was still stuck. Mark's father was using his power as an incubus to make her think she couldn't move. If she could focus, she could break his hold on her, but she needed to buy time. "I did, but only because he tried to kill me first."

Alain's appearance changed, melting into Aurelia. "He wasn't trying to kill you, you fool. He tried to elevate you. Make you more than this filthy *thing* you've become."

"Fine," Harlow agreed. Her toes wiggled in her boots. If she could just eke out a bit more time, she'd be able to move. "I get why you want to kill us. But why are you with the Vespae?"

Alain's Aurelia-face darkened. "You killed my child, Harlow. I have nothing left to live for."

Harlow's feet tingled. Just one more moment and she'd have it. "So the entire world has to pay?"

"This is not a good world. It could use remaking." Before her eyes, the vision of Mark blurred, and cleared into a mirror image of herself. "I had such a good time with your boy," Alain hissed, sounding just like her. Cold dread pooled in her belly. "And I'll have an even better time with you."

"Eat shit," Harlow spat at the incubus. She was back in control, and shoved the bomb in her hand at him—hard. The movement engaged it as Harlow's body cooperated.

She wished she had time to rip Alain Easton apart for hurting Finn, but she knew when the risks were too high. As she shifted, leaping into the air, she spotted him throwing the bomb away from himself as it exploded. Cian would be here soon to clear the battlefield. It was too much to wish for—she knew that —but Harlow hoped the firedrake's flame burned Alain Easton to a crisp.

# CHAPTER SIXTEEN

The flight home was long, and rather than feeling jubilant at finding Finn, Harlow felt mixed up in her mind, twisted by Alain Easton's horrific influence. He was stronger than Mark had ever been. The sickness he'd wrought in her in just a few moments made her nauseous.

To calm herself, she felt into the threads, and when she was finally able to find Finn, a little of Easton's influence drained away. Harlow landed in the village, a few blocks away from where he'd ended up. She needed a moment to breathe—she couldn't face Finn like this, a shaking mess.

People crowded the streets, rushing to meet the returning Warbirds. Harlow ducked into an alleyway and dropped into crouch, burying her head in her hands. The tight, thick fabric of her gear stretched uncomfortably against her skin as she curled into herself. Harlow unzipped the high funnel neck of her jacket, which now felt as though it was choking her. Her breath came in sharp gasps as tears streamed down her face.

"Harlow?" a voice called out from the end of the alley. "What are you doing back here? Finn's this way!"

It was Thea, and she sounded so damn *happy*. *Why could*

*Thea feel happy and she couldn't?* Harlow tucked her head further into her chest, covering her ringing ears. The vision of Mark—no, Alain—shifting into *her*, played over and over in her mind. How had *that* happened? She knew incubi could affect your emotions, but he'd done something like shapeshifting. And what was he doing with the Vespae?

Her skin prickled, heat flushing through her. She heard voices at the end of the alley, and prayed they'd leave. *Couldn't everyone leave her alone?*

"Babygirl." *Finn.*

Harlow couldn't look up. He shouldn't have to see her crying like this. Not when he just got back. She took several quick deep breaths, wiped her face and stood quickly. So quickly she ran into a wall of muscle. Her face smoothed as an eerie calm came over her.

"Hey," she said, looking up. "Teleported in wrong and got kind of sick to my stomach. Just needed a second to recover."

Finn's stormy eyes narrowed, then his face smoothed too as he called down the alleyway. "She's fine. Just a little portal-sickness."

He knew she was lying, and he'd covered for her. That tiny fact seeped into her. Finn knew her by heart. Her hand slipped into his, her fingers lacing through his, as she blinked back tears.

Thea nodded, waving. "We'll give the two of you some space." Her sister winked, calling out to whoever had been following her that Finn and Harlow found one another. She disappeared into the crowd that was gathering in the street.

"Is everyone okay?" Harlow asked, trying to keep her voice light. Finn's hand tightened around hers.

"Everyone else is fine," he said. "You're not."

Harlow couldn't look up. She couldn't burden him with this. He hadn't been back for even a minute, and what Alain had done to her was nothing in comparison with what he'd obviously been doing to Finn.

Cool fingers gripped her chin, tipping her head up until her eyes met his. They were glowing with rage. "You saw him. *Alain*. He fucked with you."

Harlow's eyes fell. "Yes."

"Please look at me," he pleaded.

She would give him anything, painful as it was to make eye contact with him. Her gaze dragged up his body as she tried to ignore the terrible shape his clothes were in. Desperately, she tried to keep her breath even. He would *not* comfort her right now. She wouldn't allow it.

"You lied about being able to teleport," he said. His voice was flat. Not even, not calm. Devoid of emotion.

She nodded. His grip on her chin loosened as his hand swept over her face, his palm grazing her cheek as he stroked her skin. Harlow's eyes fell closed. This was unreal. Finn was *here*. "I saw how tired you were."

"Please don't lie to me." His head lowered towards hers and she could feel the heat of his body as he stepped closer to her, his hands tentative as they slid around her waist. "Please, Harlow."

The plea in his voice broke her. He'd been lied to, manipulated, and then the first thing she'd done was trick him. It had been for all the right reasons, and she knew he knew it. But she couldn't, *wouldn't* do it again.

"I'm sorry," she said, lifting her eyes. A true smile crept onto her lips. "You're *here*."

Her words woke the reality of the moment in them both. Whatever else had happened, they were finally together again. They crashed towards each other, clinging to one another as their breath ripped through them, hearts beating out of their chests. Neither cried, though she felt their desperation coursing through the threads that bound them. That would come later.

Now there was no room for anything but this deep need to hold onto one another. To hold on hard enough to make up for a tiny fraction of every time they'd missed each other. For every moment either of them had given up hope. When they finally loosened their grip on one another, both their hands shook as they clasped them together.

"So," Harlow said, trying to sound halfway normal. "Do you want to take advantage of some alone time?"

Finn caught onto her game and nodded, speaking in an exaggeratedly calm tone that he often called "broadcast journalism voice." "That would be great."

Harlow couldn't help but snicker as she leaned against him. He was making jokes. Here, in the village, making jokes. She almost hated to hide away with him. Part of her wanted to shove him in front of everyone, yelling, "Look here. It's Finn fucking-McKay!"

But only he would laugh at that, because it's what she used to say when they were teenagers and he got too big for his britches, thinking he was cooler than he was. She'd look up at him and sneer, laying the snark on thick. "Look here. It's Finn fucking-McKay," she'd say and he'd calm right down, going back to being his sweet, goofy self again.

His hand tightened around hers as they made their way out of the alley. They slipped by the crowds that were gathering at the center of the village to hear what had happened at the farm. They walked in silence, which was comfortable at first. But as they got further away from the crowds, Harlow wasn't sure what to say to Finn. She'd been imagining this moment for months, and now that it was here, she was lost.

Finally, when they were about a block away from home, he stopped. The street was empty. "I'm not going to break, Harls."

She turned to face him. "I just don't know where to start."

He took a deep breath. "Let's start with this: I'm happy to see you."

A shuddery breath shook her chest. "I'm happy to see you too... But that doesn't seem like enough for this moment." He stepped towards her and she let her forehead crash against his chest as he drew her in. "I'm fucking this up."

A low laugh rumbled through him, sending comforting vibrations through her. He scooped her up into his arms, lifting her a few inches off the ground. "*Fuck me up forever.* That's what you said in Nea Sterlis, remember?"

Harlow nodded. The feeling of his body against hers, the ease with which he held her aloft, the smell of him, even unwashed as he was, it was all exactly what she wanted. "I remember."

"You can't mess this up, babygirl," he murmured against her mouth as his lips met hers. The kiss was sweet, almost chaste in its gentleness. She couldn't tell if he was being gentle for her sake or his, but she matched his energy, giving him only what he gave her. When he lowered her to the ground there was a warm glow on his skin. He looked a little less tired than he had in the barnyard.

"Come on," she insisted, suddenly wanting to be inside with him, away from any prying eyes. "We're almost there."

They stepped forward, holding hands and leaning against one another. She felt him thinking, but neither of them spoke. They'd been apart for too long, and that was too big to talk about right now. They just needed to *be* for a little while. When the cottage came into sight, Axel was in the front window, napping.

"There's my boy," Finn murmured.

Even a half a block away, Axel heard him. The cat's eyes flew open, and he stood, scratching wildly at the window, howling for his dad. Finn laughed, but it sounded more like a sob and the two of them jogged forward, using the last of their energy to get into the cottage, where they were bombarded by cat purrs. Axel attached himself to his cat-dad, as Finn pulled Harlow into his side.

And then he fell to his knees, clinging to them both, sobs

finally shaking through them both. His mouth met hers and their tears combined. Axel purred between them. The kiss was long and slow, but no heat built between them as they fulfilled their longing for one another, slowly as thick honey pouring from a jug. Axel jumped down, rubbing against Finn, yowling with indignation over his abandonment.

Harlow stood slowly, feeling old as time as she held her hand out to Finn so she could drag him off the foyer floor. "I think you're going to have to prove you know where the food is. Reassert yourself as the cat dad extraordinaire."

Finn nodded, his eyes watery but noble as he stretched an arm toward the kitchen. "Show me to the bin."

He followed her through the cottage to the kitchen, where she pointed to the metal bin where they kept Axel's food. Finn scooped a heaping bit out into the food bowl, which was obviously placed near a larger bowl of water. The black cat purred loudly as he ate, looking back at Finn every few moments to make sure he was still there.

Finn turned to Harlow, searching her for signs of injury. When he found none, he lifted her onto the tiled kitchen counter, fitting himself between her legs. His eyes roamed over every bit of her, hungrily now, lingering on her thick, muscular thighs, and the subtle bulge in her arms. For a brief moment, the old Harlow panicked, wondering if the way she took up more space would matter—if it would make him want her less. The worry was fleeting, gone before she had time to consider it too deeply.

"I've been training," she explained, flexing as he squeezed her bicep. "A lot. Everything kind of got... bigger."

"I noticed," he said, his chest heaving with increasing desire. Finn's breath caressed her ear as he bent slowly toward her, his hands sliding down her sides and under her seat. He lifted her off the counter for a moment, squeezing her ass cheeks hard. "It's fucking phenomenal."

Harlow's breath hitched as the motion brought the core of her in contact with the hard length growing in his pants. Finn's mouth crashed into hers, his tongue caressing hers slowly, with the kind of intensity and pressure that made promises. His fingers closed around one of her braids, then the other, and he pulled her head back, looking into her eyes.

"Should we talk?" Harlow asked, without much conviction.

"We can talk later." He lifted her, then walked towards the stairs.

"I'm covered in Vespae blood," she warned. "It's gross."

Finn cleared the staircase in a flash of Ventyr speed. "Then I'll bathe you."

Heat whipped through her as her heartbeat raced in anticipation, but she laughed. "Someone has to turn on the water heater. This place is *vintage*."

Finn set her down, a wicked sparkle in his eye. "Where is it?"

She told him and he disappeared, returning quickly. Harlow had never been so grateful for Illuminated speed. "Now," he said, "Where were we?"

Harlow lowered her voice to a mock-sexy purr. "Thinking about cleaning me up. I'm *dirty*."

She felt Finn's laugh in her bones as he kicked the bathroom door open. "I'm counting on it, babygirl."

Inside the bathroom, they got to work tearing each other's clothes off while the water heater filled. Harlow pushed the pile of their dirty things outside the door. Neither of them smelled very good, and he was coated in a layer of grime that was unusual for him. Whatever had happened in the weeks he'd been captured, they hadn't allowed him to bathe.

Though she hungered for him, they needed to take this slowly. Harlow paused to turn the water on. She wasn't sure how Finn had been hurt, or how the Vespae or Alain Easton had messed with him. She unraveled her braids, stepping into the shower, which was unusually luxurious with its double showerheads. But of course, this had been a posh resort once, so features like this in the otherwise humble cottages were the norm.

She stepped under one shower head, and he the other. Layers of dirt washed off him as he rinsed, his cock growing with every passing second that he watched her. His eyes took in every curve of her belly, drinking in the heavy swell of her breasts, and the hard muscle she'd gained. She held out her hand, trying to draw him closer now.

"Let me look at you," he murmured. His eyes were feverish with desire, and his cock was at full attention, but his voice was hesitant. "I just..." His smile was watery. "I wasn't sure I'd ever see you again. Please, can I just watch you?"

Harlow nodded, letting the water flow over her skin. She washed her hair slowly, rinsing it and then moved onto her body. As evidence of the fight slid off them both, his muscles relaxed. He washed, never taking his eyes off her as he cleaned every inch of himself.

Harlow slid one hand down her abdomen as he spread soap over his chest. Her breath quickened to a pant as the slide of her hand against her slick skin dipped lower. Finn rinsed, watching her, his lips parting as her fingers reached between her legs.

He leaned forward, one hand moving to the tile wall behind her. He was close, but not yet touching her, as she stroked slow, deliberate circles, teasing herself. Their eyes locked as his free hand traced her spine. His lips met hers, though his body stayed maddeningly far from her own.

He deepened the kiss, and then he was kissing her neck, sucking and licking her wet skin as she teased herself, refusing to dip her fingers inside, or to rub the throbbing bundle of nerves that begged for attention. Finn's mouth traced her collarbones, between her breasts, and then lower, licking the curves of her belly, then back up to capture each of her nipples. His mouth was the only thing touching her, aside from the hand that steadied her back.

He knelt, both hands gripping her ass as she spread her legs for him. Harlow's breath caught as she ran fingers through Finn's wet hair, tipping his head back so his eyes met hers. "You're here," she whispered.

Finn's smile was bittersweet. "I am."

The hurt of their time apart showed, but he needed this. She needed it too. Maybe it was the Claim that drove them, or the trauma of the past months, but they needed this now, not words and explanations.

Finn's eyes dragged away from hers as he pressed his face into her. His mouth met her clit in a long, slow kiss. Harlow spread her legs wider as he buried his face between her thighs. He squeezed her cheeks hard as he licked and sucked, moaning against her as she braced herself against the tile wall.

"I need you inside me," she begged.

He slid up her body, their wet skin finally making contact as he pinned her against the cold tile of the shower wall. Steam curled around them as she wrapped her legs around his waist. The head of his cock nudged at her entrance, sliding in easily.

As he entered her, he gazed into her eyes. "I love you."

"I love you," she replied.

It wasn't an elegant speech, but it was everything either of them needed. They were here, together, now. Later, there would be talking—so much talking—but now there were those three words, and their bodies moving against one another.

She gasped as he thrust harder, filling her completely. At the same time, he shifted into his true form, the base of his cock vibrating slightly as he moved slowly in her. Water from both shower heads cooled. The hot water heater had run its course.

"It's going to get downright frigid in here, in just a second," Harlow said, hating to interrupt.

Finn gripped her with one hand, turning one shower head off, while she did the other. "Bedroom?" he asked.

She nodded. He tried to move, but they were stuck. Harlow laughed. His wings and his true form had wedged them into the small space. "You're too big."

He grinned wickedly. "Say it again."

Harlow moved her hips, rocking against him, so her clit ground against his pelvic bone. "You're too big."

He shifted, setting her down momentarily so she could step out of the shower. He wrapped her in a towel and then scooped her into his arms. "Bedroom."

Harlow pointed, and a moment later he deposited her onto her bed, pulling the towel from her as he spread her legs. In the dim light of the blizzard that still raged on outside, his eyes glowed as his fingers spread her open, caressing her clit, before dipping deep inside her.

He lowered himself next to her as he fingered her, pulling her tight against his body as his mouth closed over her nipples, sucking each into stiff peaks as his fingers thrust into her. Her hips bucked against his hands, her orgasm mounting as his mouth and body slid lower and lower. When his mouth closed around her clit, his fingers thrusting deep inside her, she saw light.

Immediately, she pulled him upwards, dragging his body over hers until his cock slid easily into her. He shifted again, his true form filling her nearly to the point of pain, he was so large. He moved slowly at first, kissing her, whispering how much he'd missed her, how much he needed her, as she moaned.

Her hips moved against his, encouraging him to move faster, harder. He obliged, as if by instinct, feeling her soak his cock with her desire. Above her, his fangs protracted.

"Yes," she cried, pulling his head to her neck.

When his fangs pierced her skin, there was a brief moment of pain, and then euphoria, lighting every nerve in her with celestial fire. Harlow's orgasm burst from her in waves of light and shadow, as she clenched around his cock. She pushed his shoulders, using her legs to guide him, flipping them over. His wings spread out under him on the bed, his hands moving from her hips to her breasts as she rode him, leaning backwards to guide his cock to the place inside her that was most sensitive, as she rubbed her clit.

He rose into a seated position, his wings creating a cocoon of warmth and light around them as she writhed against him, rubbing every part of her against him in a fever of wet heat and long kisses. When her own fangs appeared, she pulled his head back, digging her fingers into his hair.

"Bite me, babygirl" he said. "Claim me."

The heat that roared through her at his words was all the encouragement she needed. Her fangs sunk into his neck, her venom sliding down her throat with his blood as she sucked his neck. Deep inside her, his cock moved slower, but harder now as he came, roaring her name as he gripped her.

Golden light and dark shadow intertwined, writhing as their bodies did. When their movement slowed, drowsiness overtook her. Her eyes flickered to Finn's, which watched her carefully. "I love you," she murmured, barely able to stay awake.

His eyes drooped as well, his exhaustion taking over as he shifted positions. There was the mess of their encounter to clean up, but Harlow could hardly function. He slipped from the bed, returning with a warm, wet cloth and new sheets. As he washed her, she protested, "I should be taking care of you."

His smile was sleepy, but happy. "I need to do normal things. Please."

It was true that he was typically in charge of their aftercare, but he'd been imprisoned. She had no idea what he'd endured these past months. Shouldn't she be the one to care for him right now?

"Stop thinking so much, and sleep," he murmured as he

lifted her, easily as if she were a feather to change the sheets beneath her. "Just sleep."

Her body took over, the comedown from the stress of battle coupled with the heady rush of re-engaging the Claim taking over. By the time he crawled into bed next to her, his wings creating a canopy of warmth in the chilly cottage bedroom, Harlow was fast asleep.

# CHAPTER SEVENTEEN

When Harlow woke, it was dark still, the house silent save for the tiny feline snores by her head. Axel was tucked under the covers, sharing her pillow. The heavy weight of Finn's arm around her waist reminded her of the beautiful new reality she lived in. *Finn.*

Behind Axel's small symphony of sleep, there was the deep, even rhythm of Finn's breath, and beyond that, his heart, beating soft and slow. Part of her wanted to stay here, revel in this feeling of safety for as long as possible. But as she was already awake, the perpetual feeling of being late immediately overtook her. She'd imagined this would disappear when she got Finn back, but here it was. They were buried under an almost unimaginable load of problems that continued to compound by the moment.

A flicker of opalescent light distracted her from her thoughts. "You're thinking so loud you could wake the dead," Finn murmured, sleep still lacing the deep timbre of his voice.

She rotated to face him, wrapping her arms around his neck. He pulled her closer, one hand darting out behind her head to scratch Axel's ear. "This feels like a dream come true."

Harlow wasn't sure what to say, and hated herself a little for it. He always knew how to comfort her, but her mind just wouldn't work fast enough. The only thing she could think to ask was, "Are you okay?"

Finn answered with a long, rumbling noise. "Physically, yes.... Otherwise..." He paused, and Harlow didn't rush to finish his sentence, or prompt him. She just breathed against him, slow and steady, sending waves of love through the dozens of threads between them. "That is amazing," he breathed. "I bet you have all kinds of new tricks."

Before, that statement would have opened up a wave of lust between them, but now that the fervor had abated, they felt something quieter. Desire, yes. But also the deep comfort of simply being together. This moment was peaceful, filled with love and room for whatever he needed. Harlow let his need guide them, hugging him tightly for a moment, then relaxing gently as they both sunk deeper into the bed. His wings lit with a soft glow around them.

"There you are," she said with a smile. Her fingers traced over the harsher lines of his face in its true form. He was still her Finn, still immediately recognizable, but more rugged and beautiful at the same time.

"I know we need to talk about what happened..." he trailed off. "And I can give you the basics. I need to be debriefed." Finn, always the dutiful leader.

He quieted, but she felt there was more. "You need time to process the feelings though," she said, tipping his chin so his eyes met hers.

Finn nodded. "Yes, can you give me a little time?"

Harlow answered with a kiss. "All the time in the world."

Finn and Axel looked up at the same time, both hearing a noise downstairs. "Enzo's trying to sneak in," he murmured, before calling out, "We're awake."

There were footsteps on the stairs and then a soft knock at

the door. "I know you're probably both all wrapped up in reunification bliss. I just wanted to bring Finn some clothes. They're outside the door. No rush."

Harlow pulled the blanket around her and sat up. "Thank you."

"We'll be down in a few minutes," Finn added. "You can tell Riley they can come in the house."

Enzo laughed. "All right. I think Cian would like to see you as well." Footsteps disappeared back downstairs, followed by the comfortable sounds of Enzo and Riley moving around in the kitchen.

Finn looked at the ceiling, as though he could see the firedrake above. "Cian is *flying*."

Harlow smiled. "That they are. Gloriously so, in fact. How did you know?"

Finn hopped up from bed, moving quickly as he picked up the clothes Enzo had left outside the door. "It feels like all my senses are working better."

Harlow grinned, watching him slip into a pair of thick joggers and a heavy sweater. "It's the Claim. The longer we're together, the stronger both our natural talents will become. It's what happened with the other pairs in the Warbirds. Some can even share their magic."

He glanced up at her, grinning as he pulled on a thick pair of socks. His hair fell into his face. *Stupid, floppy hair*, Harlow thought to herself, remembering how angry she'd been last spring when she'd discovered he was back in Nuva Troi. That felt like it was worlds away now, but she still loved that hair, and it had grown even longer now with the months apart.

She got up from bed, as he sat in the little chair next to the window. Axel hopped onto his lap. They didn't speak as she dressed, but the quiet was cozy, rather than tense. She looked up from pulling on a pair of leggings and a long v-neck sweater to see him smiling.

"How do you get more beautiful by the minute?"

She leaned over the chair, pressing a kiss to his lips. The fact that he was here, asking her silly questions, watching her dress—was surreal. His expression shifted to something like fear, though she wasn't sure. He was trying to hide it, but he looked at her like she might disappear.

Her head tilted slightly as she pulled away. There was distress written in the way his shoulders hunched, and his brow furrowed. She didn't want to push, but she needed to know before they talked to anyone else, so she could protect him from probing questions, if need be. "Did Alain torture you?"

Finn looked beyond her and his voice dropped deeper and flatter, sending a chilling rumble through her. He stared at some point on the wall behind her. "I'm not sure it qualifies as torture, if you can't even manage Connor's cruelty."

Harlow's heart nearly shattered. Connor McKay was a monster, and while she knew he'd exposed Finn to all kinds of awful things as a child and teenager, she hadn't known he'd actually tortured him. Her jaw clenched hard, and her shadows billowed around her hands, her fingers staining inky midnight blue almost immediately.

Finn's eyes softened, and he took one of her balled fists in his much larger hand, unfurling her fingers with the other. "Stand down, soldier," he murmured, kissing her palm. "My time with Alain was short. Confusing, yes, but not so bad in the scheme of things. Mostly the Vespae just left me alone."

Harlow let out a shudder of a breath. "Are you saying that to make me feel better?"

He looked up at her, his eyes filling with love. "No. Being taken by the Vespae and then getting stuck with Alain was unpleasant. But the real torment was not knowing if I would see you again. The long, lonely hours of fretting were the real torture."

"What is he doing with them?" Harlow asked, not able to keep her curiosity at bay any longer.

Finn shook his head. "I don't know, but it can't be good. They respect him." His stomach growled loudly before she had to think about it further.

"Let's get you some breakfast," Harlow said, relieved not to have to think of what to say next.

Axel jumped down at the word "breakfast" and meowed plaintively at the bedroom door. The three of them made their way downstairs to the sound of family in the kitchen. When Axel ran ahead of them, the chatter stopped. The entire family was crowded into the cottage's tiny kitchen. Harlow couldn't help it, she burst into tears, turning to bury her face in Finn's sweater. He hugged her tightly, his heart making erratic little thumps that let her know how moved he was.

"Hi," he said, his voice shaking a little.

Larkin ran forward, and he scooped her into a hug, pressing her against Harlow's side. Cian was next, and soon Harlow and Finn were surrounded by nearly everyone they loved, weeping softly. No one had words for what the past few months had been like or what they were feeling in the moment, but if it was anything like the riot of emotions in Harlow's heart, it was happiness and bittersweet grief, all at once.

Joy for the fact that they were together again, grief for all they lost getting here. Nothing would ever be the same. But for the first time since she'd lost Finn, Harlow thought that might be a good thing. That they might all be able to move forward, grounded in a kind of integrity that she hadn't known was missing until she found it in this moment.

From the outer edge of the circle, Riley said, "We have coffee and sausage rolls ready to go, but we need to be at the Dairy in ten."

The family drifted apart, everyone putting on coats and boots and gathering up breakfast and to-go mugs from the kitchen. Harlow caught sight of Aurelia murmuring something that looked like an apology to Finn, who interrupted her with a giant hug. She made eye contact with Harlow over his shoulder, tears streaming down her face again. Harlow couldn't help it—sobs wracked her chest. She continued to dress for the cold, but could not stop crying.

The floodgates of everything she'd been suppressing were open, and now she was a mess. Ghasts gathered in the living room and kitchen, too many to count. Harlow squeezed her eyes shut against them as Finn watched, helpless against them as they moved through him and the others to get to Harlow. It had to be a disturbing sight, watching them swarm her. The more that approached, the more distraught Harlow became.

"What's happening to her?" Larkin asked.

Aurelia tried to explain, while Selene murmured softly in Harlow's ear. "Calm down, dearest, and they'll leave you alone. You know how it works."

When she didn't calm, Selene sighed. "Harlow, stop this now."

The admonition didn't help. Harlow was overwhelmed. Finn pushed through her sisters and the maters, kneeling in front of her. He glanced back at Riley, who nodded immediately.

"We'll meet the rest of you there," Riley said as Enzo ushered everyone but Finn out.

Enzo bent down next to Finn, taking Harlow's hands. She felt his gentle presence in her mind. He didn't try to stop the tidal wave of emotion rolling over her, instead riding it alongside her. "You have to let more of this out," he whispered. "You can't keep it all in."

She nodded, but even as the tears slowed more ghasts gathered around her, pressing towards her, their ghostly fingers feeling more corporeal by the moment. When she looked down, the rotting hand that clasped her shoulder was real, bruising her shoulder with its intensity.

"What's happening?" Finn asked, trying desperately to pry the ghost's hand from her shoulder, to no avail.

Enzo crouched down next to Harlow, murmuring a few words, his hands moving rapidly in the air pulling the threads. An aethereal sigil appeared and the ghost's now-corporeal hand faded first into incorporeality, and then disappeared altogether. He and Riley shared one of their private looks.

"Harlow's emotions seem to be drawing the ghosts to her, which is not uncommon for Striders," Enzo explained. "All sorcière are limenal creatures, but Striders especially, who are more connected to the limen, where most ghosts come from."

Harlow groaned, a soft noise, under her breath. This was the absolute last thing she needed right now. Ghosts being attracted to her—becoming corporeal—*and* having to listen to long explanations about it.

Enzo expressed his exasperation with her attitude by flicking her softly on the forehead. "Hush. I'm trying to explain."

She flicked him back, causing him to snicker. Riley and Finn exchanged a look that clearly said they didn't understand the dynamic. But this was how it had been since they were children. Enzo was as much Harlow's sibling as any of her sisters, and sometimes their interactions devolved into this kind of behavior.

"*Anyway,*" Enzo said, drawing the word's syllables out for emphasis. "But this corporeality thing—it's unusual."

Enzo glanced at Riley who sighed before speaking. "After Harlow showed me The Warden, there wasn't much I could do with the text. We have some records here, but our digital archives aren't accessible. But I started talking to some of the human elders. Especially the Falcyrans."

Riley's voice dropped to nearly a whisper. It was clear they'd uncovered something they found disturbing. "The Falcyrans have an old tale about creatures that sound very similar to the

Ravagers. There is a winter tale about ghasts crossing the limen —becoming real—when the Ravagers return."

Finn nodded. "I remember a story like that from the Knights' archive. I don't think it's the same one. Maybe from Avignonne?"

"We could ask Kate and Lou..." Harlow murmured. "See what they know."

"We'll handle it," Riley assured Harlow. "You two focus on what's next with the Warbirds."

Enzo rose, smiling as he pressed a kiss to the top of Harlow's head. "Riley's right. We'll figure out this *ghastly* problem."

Harlow's face flushed as she broke into hysterical laughter at the same time Enzo did. They were still laughing as they walked out the front door. Axel followed them, weaving between their legs as they walked through the village, heading towards the Dairy.

Finn shook his head, offering Riley his arm as they walked over a slick spot on the cobbled street. "I never get punny humor."

Riley snickered, which sent Enzo and Harlow into further peals of laughter.

"What?" Finn asked as the three of them leaned against one another for support.

"*Punny* humor?" Harlow said, raising her eyebrows. "As in 'that's punny.'"

Finn shrugged, clearly lost. He picked Axel up, pressing a kiss to the cat's forehead, before the creature squirmed out of his arms, and ran towards the Dairy, chasing shadows. Harlow hugged Finn, whispering, "Punny rhymes with funny."

When she pulled away he smiled, and then laughed. "Oh," he said simply, taking her hand. It wasn't his usual witty banter, but she'd take it.

Riley and Enzo walked ahead of them. The air was cold, but the clouds that threatened more snow kept it from being utterly frigid. Harlow had learned that a sunny day in this part of Falcyra meant terrifyingly low temperatures, not warmth. The clouds were gloomy, but she feared the cold.

Finn was quiet as they walked through the village, which appeared to be sleeping in this morning. Hardly anyone was about. As Riley and Enzo disappeared inside the Dairy with Axel, who'd been waiting at the door, Finn paused, pulling gently on Harlow's arm.

"My dad..." His face crumpled into a deep frown.

Harlow waited. Sometimes it took Finn a little while to talk about his parents. Even though everyone was expecting them, she wouldn't rush him.

"The torture. It wasn't to be cruel."

Harlow waited, biting back all the words she wanted to say about how much she hated Connor—how there was no excuse for torturing a child.

Finn looked at his feet, rather than her face. "I'm not excusing it. My father's parenting philosophy was...terrible. But he didn't do any of it for pleasure."

Harlow opened her mouth to interrupt, but Finn shook his head. Those blue-gray eyes widened, begging her to hear him out. Her mouth closed and she nodded.

"I admit freely, there are things he does for pleasure that are cruel. But the way he raised me was because he was afraid, Harlow. Afraid of his own people coming here, finding us. Afraid of what they might do to not only me, but this whole planet. I'm not saying he's good, or even right. But he isn't evil. He's *scared*."

Harlow's eyes fell closed. She believed what Finn said, but still couldn't make sense of it. "Fine," she finally said. "I can believe that. But it doesn't make the power-hoarding any better."

Finn sighed. "Of course it doesn't. I just want you to understand that horrific as it was, it made me able to do things now that I might not be able to otherwise. It's fucked up. I spent years talking to James Quinn about this shit, and I still don't have it worked out."

Harlow nodded. "What about your mom?" He never talked about Aislin's role in his childhood.

Finn shrugged. "There's nothing to say about Aislin. She wasn't there. Either she was drunk, gone, or arguing with Connor. Mostly, she wasn't there."

His words unlocked a memory for Harlow. Aurelia had been interviewed by a human lifestyle magazine when she was in primary school. The interviewer had asked what she and Selene did to give themselves a break from their "brood of children." Aurelia's answer had been, "Immortals are children for so little time in comparison to the span of their lives, Selene and I choose not to miss a moment of it."

The maters hadn't been perfect parents, not by a long shot, but they'd been there, cherishing their children every step of the way, and Harlow had to appreciate that. She threw her arms around Finn, hugging him so tightly she felt his lungs expand in reaction to her.

"Thank you for telling me," she whispered as he lifted her off the ground an inch or two, returning her embrace.

"Thank you for being the person I can tell."

He grabbed her hand, and Harlow led him into the Dairy. "Prepare yourself," she warned. "They're a lot."

# Chapter Eighteen

I nside the Dairy, the couple was immediately surrounded by both the Feriant Legion and several Council representatives, Piper Winslow included, who talked all at once. Harlow wasn't sure how Finn was handling things so well, but he'd simply taken a long, even breath and responded calmly, guiding the group towards the seating area and Audata's string board. Questions peppered him from all sides, and Harlow could barely keep track of who'd asked.

"How long were you with the Vespae?" someone asked.

"I'm not sure. I'd have to look at a calendar, but Larkin and I were only together outside the breach for four days... after that I was with them the whole time."

"Do you have any idea what they're searching for?"

"No, no clue."

Finn sat, which caused everyone to try to find seats of their own. There was no room for Harlow, so she stood behind the group, as near to Finn as she could get. She was happy to see that they were responding to him differently than they had to her.

Her happiness, in itself, was a relief. She wasn't resentful in the slightest that the Warbirds' acceptance of her and Finn both

on to the Council as well, though Piper stood with her
s crossed tightly across her chest and a sour expression as
everyone else pelted Finn with questions.

"Do they have language?"

"I think so. But they don't seem to need it because of the—"

"Hive mind." That was Audata, who'd come to stand next
to Harlow.

The group asked about a dozen other questions about the
structure of the hive, but Finn's answers were all things they'd
already known. It was confirmation at least that the Vespae had a
complex social hierarchy based on their relationship with the
queen, and that they had some sort of communication rooted in
shared knowledge.

When the questions finally slowed, Finn noticed the string
board. As the group talked over what he'd found, versus what
they knew, he wandered over to it. Harlow and Audata followed.
Mirai and Max brought out food then, which lent a more conge-
nial air to the debriefing as everyone dug into the various loaves
of bread and wheels of cheese.

"Where did you find all this?" Finn asked Audata.

"On the Vespae," Audata explained. "We believe they're
searching for that building in the middle."

Harlow had already tracked Finn's gaze; he'd barely looked at
the other items, but was zeroed in on the figure of the observatory. He tapped it and said, "Do you know where this is?"

Audata shook her head. "No, do you?"

Everyone quieted, sensing Finn was about to say something
important. He turned to the group. "Yes, that's ORAIS."

"That's a strange name," Max said, mouth full of bread.

Finn picked up a marker and went to the giant pad of paper
on the easel next to Audata's board. "May I?" he asked.

She nodded. "Of course."

He wrote the name he'd just said on it, but it wasn't a word, as

Harlow had assumed, but an acronym. Behind each capital letter he wrote a word: Organization for Research in Alien Intelligence and Societies. He turned, then tapped the words he'd written slowly. "This is what you're looking for, and if you have a topographical map of this area, I can probably show you where it is."

A slow, amazed smile spread over Harlow's face. He'd been back less than a day, and he was already solving problems. This was what he was good at, bringing threads of information, and people, together. She'd missed his easy ability to figure this kind of thing out. Harlow was the emotional compass. He was the ship that brought everyone to where they needed to be. They were finally back in their element.

Several people moved quickly, searching for the right maps. Mirai brought several to Finn; he discarded three or four, then nodded at one. Vivia spread the one he chose out on the coffee table, which had been cleared. She weighed it down with plates and empty mugs. Finn pointed to the fjord, and the valley where Sanctum sat. "We're here, right?"

Audata nodded as Finn traced his fingers along the map, over several high peaks in the mountain range. "ORAIS is around here, above this fjord."

A few of the Legion exchanged looks with one another. "When you were a kid, did your dad teleport you in?" Max asked.

Finn's laugh was sardonic as he sat back on the couch, his arm going around Harlow's shoulders. "No, of course not. We hiked through the mountains. It was training."

Max and Mirai both nodded. "You're dad's an asshole," Mirai said. "But there was a reason for the hike."

Tomyris groaned. "Gale Alley."

Sam leaned forward to look at the map. "Shit, that's right."

Finn glanced at Harlow, a question in his eyes.

Vero, who'd grown up in Falcyra, answered. "Gale Alley is

where the wind buffets the peaks so hard that you can't fly through. You also can't teleport in the area at all."

"Because of the iridium," Audata said. "Of course. Why didn't I think of Gale Alley?"

Vero shrugged. "I mean, I think most people figured it was a legend. It's so remote and the weather's so terrible. It's a good location for a secret facility. Nobody goes the other way into that valley either, because of all the stories about the Gate of Lithraea."

"Connor definitely made us do the hike," Finn said. "Even my mom. Which is wild when I think of it now."

Vero grimaced. "It's wild for *all* of us to think of your mom hiking, Finn." Everyone laughed at Vero's easy way of talking, and Aislin McKay's incredible reputation for being prissy. Vero was one of the Warbirds Harlow had especially hoped would like her eventually, so it was nice that she was being friendly now. "Seriously though, there's a lot of legends about the Gate. About creatures called vvyk in the forest, and an old human ritual. Real weird stuff."

"I'd like to know more about that," Finn replied with his signature focused seriousness that made people feel like they were the center of the world. "Hiking in is unpleasant. It feels wrong. Repellent."

"Like the Vespae's wards," Audata mused.

Finn nodded. "Yeah. You think they're amplifying iridium?"

Audata wore her thinking face. "Mmm, they might be. More likely they're mimicking it."

Finn glanced at Harlow, concern forming in the wrinkle between his eyes. She squeezed his hand, a silent reassurance that Audata wasn't being dismissive, or offended. He clearly worried he'd offended her, as she walked off without another word.

"She's just thinking over what you said," Harlow explained.

Finn's smile was tentative as he watched the tiny Strider walk away. "Okay," he said finally, the cloud of worry clearing.

They turned back toward the group, who were having an animated discussion about Gale Alley. Vivia shifted her weight a little, adjusting the very full cup of tea she held in her lap so it wouldn't spill. "So if we want to get to ORAIS, we'll have to hike in."

"Why would we want to get there?" Mirai asked. "I mean, I get that the Vespae are looking for it. But what is it?"

Everyone looked to Finn. "It's both an observatory and an archive of information the elder Illuminated, from the original envoy, have on what's beyond Okairos."

"Beyond Okairos?" Max asked. "I mean, I know we came from elsewhere, my parents made that clear, but does anyone actually know much about where the Ventyr are from?"

Each of the Ventyr in the room shook their heads. Finn was quiet for a long moment, making eye contact with Cian, and then Harlow, an apology on his face. "I know a little. Not a name, or anything like that, but only that where our parents came from there was endless war, royal families fighting with one another, but also... Conquering whole planets for resources."

"Resources..." Audata's eyes widened as she drifted back towards the group.

"Yes," Finn said. "People, unfortunately, were counted as resources by our ancestors."

"They still are," Mirai replied, though she took Max's hand when she said it.

"That's true," Finn said. "And I don't claim that the Illuminated treat the people of this planet well... But it is still better than what they left behind."

The room was silent for a long while. Sam finally spoke up. "So ORAIS was used to monitor what, then? It's an observatory."

Finn shrugged. "I don't really know. I was a teenager the last time I was there. But I know what I'd use the equipment there for *now*, if I were given access to it." The room was so quiet it seemed no one was so much as breathing, waiting for Finn to continue. "I'd be watching for evidence that the Ventyr have found us, especially now that technology here has advanced so much. We would be a valuable commodity for the empire now, much more valuable than when the envoy originally arrived."

Harlow shivered, her body going cold just thinking about what it would be like for more Ventyr to be on Okairos, when the small number of them that had lived here for two thousand years were so powerful.

"I think it would be worth the hike to see what information ORAIS holds, though it may be a dangerous trip to get there, especially if the Vespae are honing in on the location," Audata said after a long pause. "We need to know what they're looking for, and why they think that the children of the original Ventyr envoy will help them find it."

"But it wasn't just the Ventyr that they took," Max reasoned. "They also took Jareth Sanvier. Or did all that have to do with the fact that Alain was angry with him for making that video at the end of summer?"

Finn shrugged. "I'm not sure. We didn't have much of a chance to talk in there. Where is he now?"

"Being debriefed by the rest of Council," Piper replied. "We'll convene later to discuss what to do with you all."

Vivia sat next to the human. The firedrake pulled a strand of her silver hair, twisting it tight around her tiny fingers, then let it go, a thoughtful look on her face. "The Vespae took Jareth, Petra and Finn, and they tried to take Larkin..." she trailed off her brow furrowing further.

Cian leaned toward her. "What are you thinking?"

Vivia gazed at Cian appraisingly. Their relationship had developed in an odd way, as she obviously thought of them as a littling in comparison to herself. It was as if she might be seeing them as more now. Harlow glanced at Finn whose eyebrows had raised in awe or amusement—maybe both. Cian had always seemed so wise to both of them. To see them treated as something of a novice was disorienting.

After a pause that felt awkwardly long for everyone but Vivia and Cian, Vivia explained. "All the people they've taken are children of the leaders of the Immortal Orders."

"Right," Harlow interjected. "Jareth is Berith's natural son." Nearly everyone in the room cringed visibly at the terrible faux pas of Berith having given his child a rhyming name. Harlow ignored them. "Aurelia thought it was because they believed they might have knowledge of the information caches…"

Vivia sat forward, looking hard at both Finn and Harlow, as though trying to discern what was so special about them. "Yes, and it might be that, but in the same vein, your parents all had knowledge of how to create the Vascularity that imprisoned them."

Harlow had leaned towards Vivia as she spoke, and now she fell backwards, into the crook of Finn's arm. He played absently with her hair, both of them thinking hard. "Let's say that was part of it," Finn said, his voice so soft and slow at first it was almost a whisper, as though he were thinking aloud. "Why would they want to know about that? They were eager to enter our world."

"It's their home," Max reasoned. "Why wouldn't they want to come back?"

No one had an answer for that at first. But then Sam turned to Vivia. "*Are* the Vespae actually from here?"

Vivia locked eyes with Cian. "Shortly before my mother was executed, she told me that she wondered if perhaps the Vespae had come to us the way the Illuminated had. She was terrified, grieving the terrible loss of our way of life. I didn't think much of it at the time, but it certainly seems possible they could be from somewhere else. They weren't always a problem—" The Argent's eyes misted, and she seemed unable to continue.

Cian took over. "The theory had been that they had simply

outgrown whatever remote territory they originated in. The world was very different back then. There were places we'd never seen, never even imagined existed."

Several people nodded, and the group fell silent once more. Between the Ravagers, the Vespae, and the Illuminated, their problems became more unmanageable by the minute.

Audata turned to the rest of the Council members. "This gives us all a lot to think about. Finn, will you come with us? It might make things easier if you could answer some questions in real time."

Finn looked to Harlow. "I'd like it if Harlow could come too."

Piper Winslow looked ready to argue. Harlow shook her head, meeting the human's eyes with steely grace. "No, love. It will go easier if it's just you."

Finn looked between the two women, saw the tension between them and wisely nodded. "All right." He stood, kissing her deeply before following Audata and the Council out of the Dairy.

A few of the Warbirds let out low whistles of approval as Harlow blushed, gathering around with questions of their own about how their first night back together had gone. Harlow watched as Finn paused by the door, an odd feeling overcoming her as the Warbirds gossiped around her. It was a combination of hope, belonging, and new confidence that she wasn't quite sure she'd ever felt. It was okay that he was going to his meeting, and she was staying here to chat with her friends.

He blew her a kiss as he disappeared out the door, and Harlow turned to the Warbirds. There were questions she had about levitating in intimate moments that needed answers, and she finally had a group of people to ask. She wasn't about to let this moment go to waste.

# CHAPTER NINETEEN

The days after Finn's return were full—sometimes wonderful, and sometimes hard. Each morning when Harlow woke up next to him, she had to fight to believe he was real. She could tell he was struggling with what he'd been through, and though she tried to let him know she was there for him, she couldn't quite manage to break through.

They trained with the Warbirds each day, keeping busy, and that was gratifying. Finn was in his element with fellow warriors, exchanging knowledge and techniques that pushed the entire Legion into what felt like a renaissance of learning about their abilities, and what they could do together as Claimed pairs. Harlow was proud of Finn—he was a born leader and teacher, and he seemed in his element.

But when they were alone, he was quiet. Too quiet sometimes, and Harlow worried about the growing distance between them. Nothing was bad, exactly—they got along well—but there was space between them she hadn't expected. Space he'd asked for, she reminded herself, though she wasn't sure she was giving it the right way. He needed rest, and so did she, but knowing that didn't stop her from worrying she'd made the wrong choice.

Harlow hated being worried all the time. She'd thought it would stop when she got him back, but here were her anxieties about *everything*, smacking her in the face, over and over. She frequently realized that a lot of what she thought she perceived was just that, her *thoughts*. But it wasn't so easy to shut off the worrying she'd grown used to in Finn and Larkin's absence.

A week after Finn's rescue, on the day after the Humanist delegation arrived in Sanctum, he was so quiet at breakfast with Cian, Enzo and Riley that she became truly concerned. When he washed his dishes without speaking to anyone and disappeared out the back door, she scrambled to get her boots on.

"I'll speak with him," Cian said, setting their coffee down. The worry in her heart echoed in every thread that connected Cian and Finn. "You stay here."

Cian left so fast Harlow didn't have time to object. Riley poured her another cup of tea, while Enzo frothed milk with a whisk. "He's just processing," Riley said.

Harlow watched Enzo pour the frothed milk into her black tea, making a little design on the top, just like in a cafe. Her best friend smiled at her. "How are things going with him and the Warbirds?"

"Really well," Harlow replied. "He's in his element with them. But at home—with me..." she trailed off, trying not to feel sorry for herself. A ghost peeped out at her from behind the refrigerator, looking as though someone had called its name. It was so excited to do something gruesome that it struck Harlow as funny. She burst into laughter, which must have offended it, because it disappeared instantly.

"They are not to be laughed at, apparently," Enzo said with a grin.

Harlow shook her head. "It just looked so silly. Like, *hello, are you going to cry about it?*" She laughed again with Enzo, but it didn't seem as funny when her worry for Finn crept back in.

"It really is just him adjusting," Riley said as the laughter died down. "I get the sense he's not ready to talk yet. Give him some time."

Enzo nodded as he slid onto the bench seat where Riley was curled up with Axel. "He knows you're there for him when he's ready. You just have to be patient."

That was reassuring to hear, but Harlow couldn't say she actually felt better. "Turn the radio on," she said, settling into her chair. "The meeting's about to start."

Riley turned their battery-powered radio on, and the announcement portion of the meeting was already in progress. Lou Spencer explained that the leaders of the Humanist movement had not known their silent investor was Alain Easton. Nor had they any idea that Easton was working with the Vespae. No additional information had been uncovered about that.

It sounded like the vampire was reading from something she'd written and Harlow's mind drifted while Lou explained that the Humanists also had not carried out the terrorist attacks in Nuva Troi over the summer. Apparently, the working theory was that the Illuminated had faked them to generate hatred for the Humanists. It was a clever idea, but Harlow's mind wouldn't focus.

Larkin slipped in the back door. "Hi," she mouthed, taking a seat next to Harlow after pouring herself a cup of coffee. "Finn and Cian went to Vivia's place for the announcement," she whispered to Harlow. "I saw them on my way over here."

Harlow nodded, pretending like she was listening. A stab of disappointment went through her. She hated to feel clingy, and she knew that without the convenience of their phones that there was little reason to expect to be informed about a casual change of plans like this one. But the fact that he'd just walked off and left her for the morning rankled.

Lou spoke now about the Humanist leaders being very amenable to allying with the Rogue Order. Harlow turned her attention to the radio.

"...have generously offered to help us move our population to their compound north of here, called the Grove. We will begin organizing for this move in the next few weeks. With the Vespae having breached our location, it is only a matter of time before a larger problem arises.

"You will receive household instructions on your move, along with any organizations you are affiliated with. After the conclusion of these announcements, we ask that everyone report into their org leaders for more information..."

Lou continued speaking—about how great the Humanists appeared to be, something about them actually having found a white ash grove, how that would be an asset for the inevitable fight with the Illuminated's forces. The certainty that there would never be an end to this conflict took root in Harlow's gut. The War of the Orders had lasted for years, and they hadn't been dealing with the Vespae or Ravagers. It had only been a few months and Harlow felt as though she'd aged decades.

Next to her, Larkin sighed with relief. "Good. I hope Thea and Alaric will get to go, don't you?"

It took Harlow a moment to comprehend that Larkin was speaking to her. She'd spaced out completely, unable to focus on anything, her anxiety about what was going on with Finn at a fever-pitch with this new twist in the path ahead of them. A few deep breaths brought her back into the moment. "Yeah, I hope Thea will agree to go."

Larkin searched her face, obviously using her sisterly instinct to try and detect what was wrong. "You'll go wherever the Warbirds go, won't you?"

Harlow glanced at Enzo and Riley, who wore matching expressions, both filled with the ache in Larkin's eyes. "Yeah, I guess Finn and I will have to."

Larkin nodded, then turned to Enzo and Riley. "What about you?"

Enzo smiled. "We're not aligned with any particular organization..." He looked to Riley, who took his hand as they answered Larkin. "We'll be headed to the Grove with the rest of Sanctum."

Larkin nodded slowly, thinking things over. "Will Cian go with the Warbirds?"

"Probably," Harlow answered.

"What about Axel?"

"If we go somewhere else with the Warbirds, he'll go with the maters, or Enzo and Riley." Harlow watched closely as Larkin nodded, swiping a bacon and cheddar scone off the plate at the center of the kitchen table. Her sister was perseverating on something. "You've got a lot of questions, pal. Everything okay?"

Larkin shrugged. "I hate being apart. And I'm tired of *resting*."

Everyone laughed, relief edging the threads that bound them to one another. It was such a typical Larkin thing to say. Unlike Finn, she seemed more or less back to herself after her experience through the limen and traveling with Vivia. After several discussions with the maters, Larkin revealed that her adventure had been mostly limited to actually traveling through the limen itself, and the day she'd been rescued. As she'd put it, "Everything else was hiking."

Harlow glanced at the clock on the wall in the kitchen. "I need to get to the Dairy. We're probably meeting about what's next. Wanna come with, Larkin?"

The youngest Krane nodded, getting up to find her jacket. Riley and Enzo stayed put. Harlow felt uneasy at the upcoming changes. "You're sure you'll go to the Grove?"

Riley nodded. "Yes, they'll need empaths. The more refugees we take in, the more counselors are needed, and there just aren't enough."

"Okay," Harlow said, pulling on her boots. "I'm guessing we're not coming with you, not at first anyway."

They'd been lucky so far, given that they were voluntarily

separated from the twins and the Wraiths. But this felt bigger. Some of them might not make it to the Grove, and there was every possibility that if the Warbirds were going into combat, she and Finn might not return.

Enzo took her hand. "We have time. You heard what Lou said. We're not saying goodbye today."

"Right," Harlow replied. She knew that, but her brain skipped ahead in moments like these, preparing for the worst immediately. It was all she knew how to do. Larkin handed her coat to her and she zipped herself in, planting a quick kiss on Axel's head. It would be torture to leave him.

Riley looked up at her. "Stay present, Harlow. It will help."

She tried for a smile, even knowing that Riley would see right through it, then followed Larkin out into the brisk morning air. The sky was clear today, the kind of crystalline blue that didn't occur in Nuva Troi, which meant it was so cold that Harlow felt the tiny hairs in her nose freeze.

Larkin shivered, hugging Harlow's arm for extra warmth as they walked through the village. "I feel like I'll never be warm again."

People were bustling about after the announcement. Harlow watched the crowd for Finn and Cian, but didn't see them until they were halfway to the Dairy. Strangely, they were headed in the opposite direction.

Finn pressed a kiss to Harlow's forehead as he tugged on Larkin's ponytail. "Hey, kiddo," he said.

"Yo-ho, buddy-boy," Larkin replied.

Finn raised an eyebrow at her. Larkin shrugged. "If you're going to call me kiddo, I'm insisting on calling you some truly weird shit back."

Harlow snickered, while Finn just nodded. "Fair."

"Where are you two headed?" Harlow asked.

"The meeting's in the bathhouse," Cian said, grinning wickedly.

Larkin raised an eyebrow, as Cian and Finn turned them back in the direction they'd come from.

"You were just complaining about the cold," Harlow said.

Larkin shrugged. "It's fine with me. It just doesn't seem like a very *professional* place for a meeting."

Cian took her arm as they turned the corner that led to the bathhouse. "We're not running a corporation, silly."

They entered the bathhouse through an inconspicuous wooden door in an alley, walking down several flights of stone stairs. Soothing harp music floated up towards them. The geothermal heat that made building a village in such a remote location possible was combined here with an underground mineral spring, and the original owners of the resort had converted the space into a gorgeous spa.

There were several more public pools, but Harlow knew the private one Audata had procured for the meeting. She'd done this before when she thought the Warbirds needed to relax and recharge. The vampire working the front desk smiled at Harlow and Cian, then blushed when she caught sight of Finn.

Harlow kept her smile to herself. This had been happening a lot and she found it strangely adorable. Denizens of Nuva Troi were perpetually cool about their celebrity worship, but here in Sanctum, people were from everywhere. Some people had harbored crushes on Finn since they were teenagers, as he'd always been in the news, gossips and on socials. Meeting him in person was often overwhelming for some of them.

"Your party is in the D'vor pool, Ms. Krane," the vampire said.

"Thank you, Clara," Harlow replied, motioning for the others to follow her. They walked around the edge of the public pools to the softly lit changing rooms, which were full of wooden lockers to store clothes in. The four of them found lockers next to one another and undressed. The textured lime-stone floors were deliciously heated beneath their feet and

Harlow relished the warmth as she waited for everyone else outside the changing area, watching the people doing laps in the exercise pool.

The water in the pools appeared to be a dark blue in the low light of the public area. Witchlights danced on the ceiling, which was painted like the night sky, reflecting in the six public pools. Steam rose from the more heated of the group, and immortals sat chatting amiably, drinking tea in the warmer pools. This was a common place to socialize and warm up.

Not many humans frequented the bathhouses, as human culture had a different view of nudity that confused many immortals. Privately, Harlow thought it prudish, but humans had many ideas about sexual attraction that she didn't always understand. To her, and to most immortals, bodies of all shapes and sizes were simply art to adorn with more art. But to humans, nudity often embarrassed them, making them think immediately of sex.

Once everyone was undressed and had towels, Harlow showed them to the D'vor room, named after one of the vampires that had originally owned the resort. At the center of the room was one long, extra heated pool. The gilt on the domed ceiling made the water appear to be molten gold. Steam clouded the room, which was full of naked Warbirds, splashing in the water and chatting amiably.

On one of the wide steps that surrounded the pool, Piper Winslow sat wrapped up tight in a towel. Next to her, Audata reclined on a cushion, naked as the day she was born, a look of supreme serenity on her face. When her eyes met Harlow's, they sparkled. The little Strider had endured many hours of Piper's prickly company since Finn's return, and Harlow had a feeling this was her subtle revenge.

Larkin stepped into the water, grinning as she sunk into its heated depths. "This is bliss," she said, slapping Harlow's shoulder. "Why haven't we been here every day?"

Harlow flicked water at her sister as Finn immersed himself next to her. When his body brushed hers under the water she empathized with Piper's discomfort. It *was* hard not to think about sex sometimes. But, for her, the only body arousing her was Finn's, his arms going around her waist as he pulled her into the depths of the pool.

Cian, Vivia, and Larkin sat near Sam and Tomy. Vivia poured them tea from a large pitcher as they chatted. Relaxation emanated through the threads in the room. There was a subtle green floral scent in the air that combined with a hint of something woody. As Finn hugged her close, she leaned back against his chest.

"I'm sorry I walked out this morning," he said softly, his mouth against her ear. "Most of the time I feel okay, but some mornings, I wake up and I can't stop worrying that someone will take you from me. That I might lose you."

They weren't alone, and the amount of preternatural hearing in the room meant that this wasn't the place to have this conversation, but everyone was busy with themselves. Even Piper looked like she was relaxing, sipping tea with Audata and chatting somewhat amiably.

"You can talk to me," Harlow replied, keeping things simple.

"I know," he murmured. "I just don't know what to tell you. I don't want to relive the things Alain tricked me into seeing, and the rest of it was just me in my head, worrying about all of you. But especially you."

Harlow didn't much care who heard or saw them at that point. She turned in Finn's arms, wrapping her legs around his waist. Yes, she understood full well why Piper might be uncomfortable now. Pressed against Finn's body, the soft water causing them to slip deliciously against one another, she could think of nothing but having him inside her. Not that she would, but it might be fun to talk about later.

"That's a wicked look," he murmured in her ear as he pulled her closer.

"I love you." She kissed his cheeks. "I was just so anxious while you were gone. I lost myself in grief."

He pushed damp hair from her face, his eyes glowing with love. "And that's what *I* worried about most."

Floating here, facing him, it felt like they were alone. But soft snippets of others' conversations reached her ears, perfectly clear. She felt the relaxed expression slide off her face, locking her gaze on Finn's. He'd done this on purpose. Talked with her about this in front of the others so they'd hear them, empathize more deeply with them as a couple. The evidence was in the shrewd glint in his eyes, combined with his love for her.

Nothing about what they'd said had been false. That was the beauty of it. She just wasn't sure she liked the way he'd maneuvered them into this conversation here, for strategy. His brows pulled together slightly, his expression begging her to understand. This was who he was, a strategist, always thinking a few moves ahead. Steam clouded around them, hiding their faces from the others.

Harlow shook her head once, closing her eyes and leaning back in the water, letting herself float. She would take this slightly confusing moment any day over what she'd endured while he was away. From across the pool, Audata called them in. The Warbirds quieted down, gathering around Audata and Piper to listen.

When the noise died down, Audata nodded to the human. "Piper is joining us to talk about a special mission, but first, I'm sure some of you may already have guessed what we'll be doing next."

"Guard duty!" Rian shouted from the back of the pool. The big Ventyr grinned, their dimples making their dark face even cuter than usual. Their partner Eliana grinned along with them, splashing them.

Audata smiled at the Warbirds' resident goofs as she slid into the water. "Essentially. We'll be partnering with the Humanists' envoy of soldiers to accompany the civilian population to the Grove."

"The usual teams?" Tomyris asked, winking at Harlow and Finn.

"For the most part—" Audata started to say.

Piper pulled her towel around her more tightly as she interrupted. "The Humanists have some issues working with the Knights of Serpens."

The Warbirds fell silent. To their credit, every single face wore some version of the same grim look. They'd accepted Finn and the Knights, and resented that the Council and the Humanists hadn't followed suit.

Finn sighed as he pushed out of the pool. Water dripped down every gorgeous nook and cranny of his abdomen. "I'm sorry. It's me, isn't it?"

Piper Winslow stared at him as he grabbed a towel, her eyes going wide as saucers before she looked quickly away, scowling. "Don't be so fucking dramatic, McKay. *We've* barely finished vetting the Knights, you can't blame them for being worried. They don't want any of you coming and going." She glared at Harlow. "Your sister and her bondmate are welcome at the Grove, but they'll stay put until we're sure of the rest of you."

Tomyris leaned back against the edge of the pool, water beading on her graceful collarbones as she flexed her muscles, her wings stretching out behind her. She saw what Finn had done, and now she obviously wanted in on the fun. She too had abs to show off. "So what's that mean for Harlow and Finn? You want to lock them up at the Grove?" The Ventyr's eyes sparkled dangerously as Piper's eyes went wide again.

Audata stepped in front of Tomyris, a look of vague annoyance crossing her face. Her brood was messing with the poor human more than she'd intended. "No. They're only asking that Alaric and Thea stay put and not leave—"

"And that Finn and Harlow not be a part of the accompaniment," Piper interrupted. She'd obviously lost ground though.

Harlow bit the inside of her cheek to avoid smiling. She felt sorry for Piper until the human spoke again, her confidence returned, apparently. "But fear not, we have another mission for the two of you."

Finn looked up from the glass of tea he'd just poured. "You want us to go to ORAIS, right?"

Piper shot a finger at him. "Ding, ding, ding. You got it, McKay."

The cringe that rippled through the pool was practically audible. The human's tone was discomfiting. Harlow hadn't spent much around the Education Councillor, so she wasn't sure how to take this kind of behavior. Every muscle in Audata's body was tense, as though Piper's performance made her incredibly uncomfortable.

Larkin moved to stand next to Harlow in the pool, nudging her first, then covering her mouth to whisper. "What's up with her?"

Harlow didn't answer, or move a muscle. Piper was looking straight at them, as though she'd heard Larkin perfectly, which was impossible for a human. The woman had a preternatural sense that others were talking about her, apparently.

"The mission to ORAIS is too dangerous to send a large team. You can choose two others to accompany you," Piper continued. "But no one we find vital to our mission to align closely with the Humanists will be given clearance, nor will anyone we need for vital missions elsewhere."

There it was. They'd tipped their hat. The Council was sending them because it was dangerous, and they didn't much care what happened to Finn and Harlow. They didn't hate them, but if they were killed, it wouldn't matter to their overall goals. On the other hand, if they brought back valuable information, it would be a bonus. They'd prioritized aligning with the Humanists, which frankly, made all the sense in the world.

Harlow glanced at Finn, who wore his best diplomat face. She'd seen him use it dozens of times over the summer in Nea Sterlis. He'd assessed the situation the same way she had, then. "Great. I'd like to call Arebos Flynn back to join us. Will that be a problem?"

His tone wasn't challenging in the slightest, but Harlow sensed the misstep immediately. He should have *asked* the human if he could take Ari, not *told* her that he wanted to. Finn didn't seem to see the mistake.

Piper's jaw clenched tightly. "I suppose not. Take anyone from your own team you like, except Cian. They're with us."

Cian visibly tensed. They didn't like being ordered about any better than Finn did. For his part, Finn's forehead crinkled. Harlow knew Cian would have been his first pick, but that he could recognize the Argent was in high demand. Still, he wasn't used to being thwarted like this, and though the others might not see it, Harlow knew he was seething, ever so slightly.

Harlow jumped in before his arrogant mouth could dig them a deeper hole. "That's okay. We'll be good with Ari, and maybe one other person."

Piper shook her head, laughing. The sound was dry and just as arrogant as any noise Finbar McKay could produce. "Let me know when you decide. I'll need a full briefing on your plans before you go. I'm your Council contact point and I'll approve or deny any move you make on the Fifth Order's behalf."

It was the first time Harlow had heard anyone use the term for the combined group of the Rogues and Humanists. Despite the fact that the tension was thick as claggy, over-baked cake, she was pleased to hear it used. Finn had no such reaction. She didn't need to look at him to feel him carefully considering his next words.

"We'll be happy to let you know our plans," Harlow said, before Finn could speak again. "Let us talk about who else might be best on the mission and we'll meet soon."

Piper nodded, obviously curt, but the vitality had gone out of her attitude. "Great. Let me know as soon as possible."

The human woman stood, turning on her heel to stalk out of the pool. Everyone was silent as she went. When the door closed, everyone was silent for long moments. Everyone waited for Piper to reappear, like a monster in a horror film. They always had one more jump scare in them, but apparently Piper did not.

Rian stuck a tongue out at the door, and Eliana raised their brows. "What a bit—"

Eliana's curse was cut off by Audata shaking her finger. "None of that, please. Piper was elected as one of the team leaders for the missions ahead."

"She's the *Education* Councillor," Harlow said, unable to stop herself. "What qualifies her for something like this?" Surely someone could explain what in seventeen hells was so special about the woman.

Vivia stood, gliding out of the pool like a nymph from a faery story. "Enough. The Council has made their decisions. We don't need to know more. Audata, you get everyone here briefed on their teams. Finn, Harlow, you're with us. We'll meet you in the tea room."

Cian followed, and the two of them exited the D'vor lounge. Harlow turned to Larkin. "I'll come over to the maters' later, okay?"

Larkin grabbed her arm. "I want to come to ORAIS with you."

"No!" she and Finn said in unison. A few of the Warbirds looked their way.

Larkin spoke quietly, averting her eyes from the rest of the group. "Can you just let me come talk before you say no?"

"Fine," Finn said, as though his word was final.

Harlow glared at him. "No, pal. Go home. There's nothing you can say that will change *my* mind. And if my mind can't be changed, what do you think Selene and Aurelia are going to say?"

Finn's voice was even and quiet. "She's not a child."

Harlow didn't want to make a scene. "Let's talk privately."

Larkin grinned, making a beeline out of the pool. Harlow followed Finn outside of the lounge, then grabbed his arm when they were outside the heavy doors. "She's not coming with us, Finn. I won't have it."

They stood alone in the hallway outside the private lounge. Finn looked down at where she gripped his arm. "Harlow."

The way he said her name rolled over her, cold as a plunge in an iced over lake. She stepped back, her emotions roiling under the surface of her skin.

Finn's head cocked slightly. "I said she could *talk to us* about why she thinks she needs to go, not that she could come." His arms folded over his chest. "Do you really want to create an environment where Larkin feels as though she can't come to us about her thoughts and feelings?"

Harlow's cheeks flushed hot and her eyes fell to the floor. "No, of course not, but..."

"Then let her talk, for Raia's sake. It won't hurt you to listen to her."

He was exasperated with her, that much was clear, and before she said things that went too far, she needed space. "I need some air," she murmured as she took several big steps away from the staircase. "You can talk without me."

# CHAPTER TWENTY

O utside the bathhouse, the sunny day had turned cloudy. Weather was moving in as Harlow broke into a slow jog. She didn't want to talk to Enzo and Riley, or any of the Warbirds. What Harlow wanted right now was her parents. A block away from the maters' house, she nearly ran into them. They were both dressed nicely and coming from the direction of the Council house. They'd probably been to pick up their orders.

Harlow stopped quickly, trying not to knock either of her parents over. "They're sending us to find ORAIS." Selene and Aurelia glanced at one another. Of course, they already knew this. "Larkin wants to go."

"Oh dear," Selene said. "Why don't you come back to the cottage and have a cup of tea with us."

"Yes," Aurelia added. "Have some tea and we can talk about this."

Harlow drew back. "You're not thinking of *letting her go*, are you?"

Selene's mouth drew downward as her eyes widened. "Darling, she's an adult. If she wants to go, and Finn thinks she'd be an asset to the mission, who are we to tell her no?"

It felt as though all the air had been knocked out of her lungs. "Are you kidding?"

Aurelia's shoulders hunched, whether from the cold or emotion, Harlow couldn't tell. "We aren't in the habit of telling our adult children what they can and cannot do with their lives."

Harlow backed away. "Well, maybe if you did every once in a while, we wouldn't end up in such a mess all the time."

The maters protested, but Harlow had already turned, jogging again, but this time she wasn't sure where to go. If no one saw what she did, that Larkin didn't belong on a mission like this—that even after the months of training she had, *she* barely belonged on a mission like this—then what use was there in talking to anyone?

Without thinking about it, she'd jogged up the biggest hill in the village. At the top, there was an excellent view of what had been a park when Sanctum was a resort. Now, they used it for various group activities, including defense classes for civilians. At this time of day, the experienced fighters should be teaching a group of children the basics of escaping a hold and working in groups to subvert enemies larger than themselves. It was gruesome training, but given their circumstances, it was the best way to ensure the children had their best chances of survival.

But the kids were nowhere to be seen. Instead, strangers—Humanists—filled the field, running through a set of drills. They started with a set of postures that reminded Harlow of the mind-body practices Cian had tried to educate her in last summer. But these were different, more obviously aligned with preparing the body for fighting.

There was something about the quality of movements that felt familiar to her. She was so entranced watching the Humanists begin their training that she didn't notice Jareth Sanvier's approach. "You want to join us?" he asked.

She looked down at the fighters moving in unison. They were repeating the same set of movements several times before moving onto a new set. She wasn't sure she could keep up, but unlike the methods Cian had tried to teach her that required a great deal of flexibility and coordination, these were more succinct. Utilitarian.

Harlow nodded, curious, despite the fact that apparently the Humanists didn't trust her. She followed Jareth to the field, finding places in the back of the group. He stood behind her as she watched the people in front of her and then began to move, mimicking the motions of their bodies as best she could. Jareth spoke quietly behind her, instructing her, like a teacher in an exercise class might. His words made sense to her, and she caught on quickly.

With Jareth's help, she realized that there were just a few sets of movements and the fighters cycled through them several times. She was surprised by how quickly she picked up the sequences, how natural they felt to her. Something shifted below her, undulating in time with the movements. Her shadows. They'd emerged.

She nearly stopped, but behind her, Jareth murmured. "There's nothing wrong. You're moving with the aether. That's what these postures are meant to do, align us more closely with aethereal power."

Harlow used her second sight then, pushing it out into the threads. In her mind's eye, the threads danced along with the fighters on the field. They were a surreal picture, thousands of infinitesimal threads of dark-light flowing around them in a sea of coordinated waves.

Her eyes closed, so she could better feel the movement of the magic within the threads, her shadows moving in time with the threads themselves. When they opened, she stood on the spirit paths. She was in the limen. Faint echoes of the people on the field surrounded her.

She walked around, looking at them from all angles. They were here, but they weren't. It was like the vision she'd seen with Ashbourne, of the women on other worlds, the night Connor beat Finn in Nea Sterlis. But she had seen those women's faces and figures clearly. These were mere impressions.

*Your people are fascinating,* a terrible voice said.

Cold fear gripped her. There was no mistaking who that voice belonged to—the Ravager she'd spoken to last summer. She spun around, but there was no giant entity anywhere. Only the echoes of the people on the field, and the clouds of aether at her feet.

*Oh, I am not here,* the creature said. *I suppose that's not quite accurate. I am here, but not here.*

Was it talking to her, or itself?

*I have no interest in harming you, little bird. Right now, I am only watching.*

"Watching?"

*Yes, watching. My brethren spent their imprisonment plotting the havoc they wished to wreak when set loose. I have never been much of a planner.*

Harlow wasn't sure what to say. If she knew how to run, how to escape, she might. But she wasn't sure that was wise. She wasn't sure of anything at all. "So, you're just watching us?"

*No, not* just *watching. But yes, watching.*

Maybe it was best to keep it talking. "What else are you doing?"

The creature, the Ravager, laughed. Or at least Harlow thought it did. The sound was more like shrieking, and Harlow wanted to cover her ears, except that wouldn't help. The Ravager's voice was in her head, whatever that meant in her incorporeal state.

Something brushed against her legs, both in the real world, and here in the limen. She looked down to find the auburn cat

Axel made friends with over the summer—Morgaine Yarlo's cat. Larkin said his name was Bayun, and that he was incredible.

"Hello," she whispered, crouching to speak to the cat. Bayun was in his corporeal body. "Better get out of here."

*Not without you*, said another voice in her mind. This voice was different from the Ravager's. Imperious, and distinctly feline.

"Did you just *talk*?" Harlow tried to pet the cat. She wasn't sure if that was possible in her incorporeal form, but his fur was so fluffy and soft, it was worth a try.

The cat lifted his chin to be rubbed, his throat vibrating with purrs. *It is dangerous for you here*, Bayun said. *It is not safe. Not with* them *afoot.*

*Who are you talking to, little bird?* The Ravager demanded, its terrible voice raising to the pitch of thousands of Vespae buzzing. *Why can't I see you any longer?*

*Follow me.* The cat beckoned. *Quickly.*

Harlow did as the cat asked. There wasn't time for questions. The aether surrounded them in thick clouds. Within it, there were echoes of voices and strange shapes that looked like faces. As soon as one took shape, and she began to make out its features, it disappeared.

*Don't fall behind*, the cat commanded.

"What is wrong with the aether?"

The cat looked over its shoulder. *The aether is troubled here.*

"Troubled how?" Harlow asked. Aether was thought to be semi-sentient, but neutral.

*Once, someone drew too much power from this place. Misused it. Are disturbed entities on your side?*

"Yes," Harlow said, thinking of the ghasts.

*When aether is disturbed, its ways of knowing are troubled. It attempts to understand what has happened, which causes it to individuate. Once it does, the result is rarely anything good.*

The clouds of pure aether pressed into her body. She felt

hands pulling at her hair. Not to harm, but too curious, too invasive all the same. The huge feline hissed and the aether backed off. Harlow looked down at her hands. They were real. She was corporeal.

"Am I really here?"

*Yes, unfortunately so. The aether had pulled you in, but just up here, you should be able to return the way you came.*

"The way I came?" Harlow asked, feeling utterly confused. The aether cleared, forming more normally. She saw the vague outline of the Dairy, the loft, in particular. Cian, Vivia, Larkin and Finn sat talking, though she couldn't hear what they were saying.

*Through the portal within.*

"Within?"

*Perhaps you think of it as being located in your heart. I believe my girl has mentioned this valve is significant to your kind.*

His girl. Echo. Morgaine's Echo. Harlow bent down. "Did Morgaine get home okay? Did she find Echo? Are they together again?"

*You are a good person, Harlow Krane,* the cat said. *Much like my Echo. Perhaps a bit less... violent.* The cat seemed amused now, as though thinking about his violent human friend pleased him. *We do not have time to tarry, though I would like to speak with you more. Get her home. Now!*

Harlow wasn't sure who the cat was speaking to, but his tone had turned urgent. Bayun bumped her once with his head, and the contact pushed her back into herself, where she had the sense she was being sucked inward. Deeper and deeper she went, into the inner place she called her heart, where she found the tiny pinprick of reality beyond this place. Without really knowing how she was doing it, operating on pure instinct, Harlow dove into the pinprick, guided by some unknown force.

The only way to describe the sensation was that it was as though she'd turned herself inside out, and then back right again. She hit the floor hard. "Oof," she groaned, picking herself up off the hardwood. Her head spun wildly. Hardwood? She'd been on the field before. Axel nudged her face with his, purring loudly. Where had he come from?

"Harlow?" Larkin shouted, panicked for some reason.

Harlow's vision was blurry, and she felt as though she might vomit. She had the vague impression that Finn was sitting next to her, steadying her against his chest. "Breathe, babygirl," he said. "Just try to breathe."

"Where is the cat?" she asked, rubbing her eyes. Her vision was improving, and she felt slightly less like she might lose her breakfast, but she was utterly confused about where she was and how she'd gotten here.

"Axel's right here, darling." That was Cian.

"No, not Axel. Bayun. Where did he go?" Harlow was nearly frantic with worry now.

Finn's arms tightened around her. "Bayun's not here, Harlow. You and Axel just appeared out of nowhere."

Harlow's vision cleared, just as Axel climbed on top of her, purring loudly. She was in one of the private tea rooms, above the bathhouse. She rested against Finn's chest, his arms caging her.

"Hey," he said as she blinked several times.

"Hey," she replied. Her mind swirled, trying to make sense of what happened. There were footsteps on the stairs, which Cian stopped.

"Have any of you seen Harlow?" It was Jareth Sanvier. "She was hanging out with us at the field, and she walked off. I lost track of her, but she was acting kind of strange."

Finn pulled Harlow to her feet, giving her a look that she interpreted to mean, "Follow my lead." She nodded, setting Axel on the floor in front of her.

"She's here," Finn said, stepping forward, motioning behind his back for her to follow.

Harlow peeked around Finn's shoulder. "Hi!" she said, a flush coming to her cheeks.

Jareth looked genuinely concerned. "You're okay."

She smiled, taking Finn's hand. He squeezed hard, once in what she'd consider a quick, staccato note, if it were a noise. *Keep your answers short.* "I'm fine."

Everyone stepped back to allow Jareth into the lofted room. Each of the private tea rooms at the bathhouse looked over the main pools, though they were curtained and most had privacy sigils that could be activated upon arrival. There was an awkward split second of silence. Jareth's eyes narrowed slightly. Harlow spoke. "Sorry to worry you. Axel got out of the house."

"And came to a bathhouse?" Jareth asked, obviously incredulous.

Harlow gestured to Larkin, who now held the cat.

Jareth's eyes softened immediately when he saw Axel. "Can I pet him?"

Harlow was surprised by the reaction, but she couldn't see what the harm was. "Of course."

Larkin let Axel down, and he wound around Harlow's legs, allowing Jareth to crouch down to pet him. As he did, he said casually, "Sometimes people struggle with the energetic aspects of raotham—some have reported strange experiences. You didn't have anything like that happen, did you?"

"Raotham?" Larkin asked from the couch, where she'd folded herself back up. It was a clear deterrent, meant to give Harlow time to think of what to say.

Jareth glanced up. "A mind-body alignment practice that the humans in our organization have practiced for hundreds of years. Some consider it a lost art, as the civilization that it originated from, near present-day Avignonne, simply disappeared without a trace."

The story reminded Harlow of the Alabaster Spire, which had similarly disappeared from Nea Sterlis. It was an odd connection, one that seemed mysteriously tied up with all of this. Jareth looked to Harlow, his pointed expression indicating that he expected an answer to his original question.

"Nothing weird happened with me. Axel just came to find me."

"And you came here, rather than taking him home?" Jareth asked.

*He knew.* He *knew* she hadn't chased after Axel, and that something else had happened. But they knew so little about what the Humanists' goals were. The Rogue Order might trust them, but this was something more, and she wasn't sure she was even willing to have the Feriant Legion know about it yet.

Harlow shrugged. "I needed to get to this meeting anyway, there was no reason he couldn't come."

Jareth stood. "Look, I get it. You don't know if you can trust me. But know when you're ready to talk about the limen—the aether—and the Ravagers, I'm here."

Finn was perfectly still. Harlow wasn't even sure he was breathing. He looked like Axel, right before he pounced on a bug. Focused, and deadly. Jareth noted this as well, apparently, because he threw his hands up in the air, in a mock-defensive position.

Jareth's tone was light, but his words were serious as he backed towards the stairs. "It's a good faith offer, and I won't push or tell anyone else what I think might have happened out there."

No one said a word, or moved a muscle. Harlow held up a hand. Jareth paused, waiting for her to speak. "Why should we trust you, when your people so clearly don't trust us?" She gestured to herself and Finn. "*Specifically* us."

Finn moved then, crossing his arms and shifting his stance. Something in Harlow swelled. He was intimidating as a god, beautiful and stalwart. Maybe Jareth Sanvier saw a brutal temper, or a spoiled bad boy, but all she saw was a hero. When he spoke, she was even prouder. "You know they're sending us on what's likely a deadly, impossible mission because your higher ups don't like me."

Jareth nodded. "I do. I offered to go with you. They said no, but I'll offer you the same, bring me with you to ORAIS. You get to pick your team. Pick me."

Larkin snorted softly, a delicate noise. Everyone turned her way. She shrugged. "Kinda desperate, that's all."

Harlow raised an eyebrow at her little sister. "And what are *you* up here doing?"

Larkin rolled her eyes. "It's not the same. I've proven to be an essential part of ill-advised, very likely deadly missions in the past. What's *he* done?"

Jareth scoffed, then pulled a face at Larkin. "*I* burned down the governor's mansion. Heard you have some experience watching houses burn, little witch."

There wasn't a trace of malice in Jareth's words. The banter felt familiar, even fun. Like he'd fit right in with all of them. Harlow hated that she liked him so well, so quickly. Larkin snickered. "I like him. Let him come, McKay."

Finn and Cian both rolled their eyes. "We'll think about it," Cian said.

Jareth nodded. "That's all I ask. Thanks."

He left then, whistling an old Falcyran folk song as he went down the stairs two at a time.

Cian turned to her. "Come sit, and tell us everything that happened."

Harlow joined her people on the couch, where Larkin activated the privacy sigil so they could strategize in private.

# CHAPTER TWENTY-ONE

Harlow felt certain she would scream if she had to consider another minor detail. They talked over Harlow's experience in the limen, and who to choose to go to ORAIS, from an infuriating number of angles. For three days, they talked it over, again and again. This was all made more complicated by the fact that Ari returned from Nuva Troi with a detailed report, which he'd spent the morning giving to the Council, and now Harlow and Finn. There had been rumors, and news from refugees of the outside world, but not a lot of specific information about Nuva Troi until Ari arrived.

The Wraith lay flat on his back in front of the fire, claiming he'd never get warm again, much as Larkin often did. Axel climbed onto his chest, purring happily and making biscuits on Ari's muscled chest while he talked. Apparently, the Illuminated's wards were holding against the Vespae. It had taken them time to get them up, and much of the city had been damaged in the initial onslaught of the Vespae. Harlow listened in horror as Ari described all the places she loved that had been destroyed. She might never see the city she loved again—because it might not ever exist that way again.

Finn was none too happy that the Council had Ari's report before he did, but they were still determined to shut the Knights of Serpens out. The Fifth Order might be progressive in many ways, but just like most of Okairon society, they held grudges deeply. Finn and Alaric's proximity to their parents made them permanently untrustworthy, though it did seem the Council had finally acknowledged that the Knights were not a danger to them. They just didn't want them as a part of their governing body.

Someone knocked at the front door. Harlow got up to answer it, leaving Finn and Ari to talk. A teenage griffyn shifter stood outside, just shifting back into their humanoid form, a lanky young person with a puff of short curly hair and luminous golden eyes.

"Piper wants to see you in her office," they said before turning fast and shifting on the run, a streak of gold fur disappearing out the front gate at full speed.

"Do we know that child?" Finn asked from behind her, laughing.

"That's Kym," Harlow replied. "Their claim is that they're the fastest shifter in the village, and they take every chance they can to prove it."

Finn went to let Ari know that they were going to the Lodge, but he was already asleep. He and Harlow dressed for the cold without talking, then made their way out into yet another frigid day. Harlow was well and truly sick of winter.

Finn was chatty, apparently, now that they'd left the house. "Why don't they fly? Kym, I mean."

"Their wings aren't developed enough to carry them aloft. The Heraldic mature very slowly. Cian is only considered to be *nearing* middle age now," Harlow explained. Finn hadn't had the benefit of learning more about the Heraldic, as she had in the past months.

Everything about Finn lit with interest. Like many of the

Ventyr, he could be acquisICIONal in nature, but what Finn loved to collect most was knowledge—knowing things relaxed him. The cogs turned in his mind, as he pieced together all he did know about the rare shifters. The moment his thoughts turned to the task at hand, his body tensed again. "She's going to ask who we're taking."

Harlow wanted to groan, but that wouldn't help things. They were still locked in a perpetual argument about this. Larkin desperately wanted to come to ORAIS with them, so much so that she'd had Vivia vouch for her survival skills and stamina.

"What do you think about Jareth?" Harlow asked. It was easier than trying to tackle the Larkin issue first.

"I think we should take him," Finn replied.

Harlow nodded, slipping her hand into his. "I agree. Even if it's just to watch him—to learn more about the Humanists. I think we'd be smart to suss them out a bit more."

"Agreed," he said, his tone going curt. His hand tensed around hers.

"You still think we should let Larkin come?"

Finn sighed. "I don't want to argue about this."

Harlow was so tempted to fight. To give all her reasons that Larkin shouldn't come again. But she remembered something Aurelia had said—about not clipping the Krane girls' wings when they were ready to fly. She wasn't the boss of her sisters. As much as she wanted to keep them all safe, she knew that wasn't possible. They were all going into danger, and there was no stopping that.

She'd prefer Larkin go to the Grove with the rest of the civilians, but she wasn't really a civilian anymore. Harlow hated that she was about to agree to this, but if it was what her sister wanted, she didn't see how she could stand in her way. "Fine, she can come. But she has to carry Axel. Just for being a brat about the whole thing."

Finn stopped short. "Wait, who said Axel was coming?"

Harlow threw her hands in the air. "Where do you suppose he's going to go? I'd planned to have Larkin take him to the Grove."

Finn grabbed her arm. His grip was loose, but insistent. "Harlow. We can't bring a *cat* with us to ORAIS. Do you have any idea how ridiculous that sounds?"

She stared at him. They'd been doing so well and now he was getting imperious with her? *Where the fuck did he get off? He was getting his way. She'd said yes to Larkin coming.* "I guess you should have thought of that before you agreed to let my baby sister come on another potentially deadly mission. Now we have to take our cat too." She stomped forward, pushing past him. They'd nearly reached the Council building. "Plan better next time," she called over her shoulder.

He caught up to her, fury radiating off him. "We're not bringing Axel, Harlow. Someone else can take him. Petra—we don't know where she's off to yet, do we?"

Harlow sighed, drawing the noise out into a groan. She was being purposely aggravating—she wasn't lying to herself about it. Of course they weren't going to take their cat on a dangerous mission to a secret Illuminated compound that the Vespae were desperate to find. Her anxiety would never recover from that kind of bullshit. But she felt like he hadn't listened to her about why she didn't want Larkin coming along, acting like she was trying to exclude her, rather than keep her safe. And now, rather than being an adult about the whole thing, she was being petty.

"Just tell Piper that we're bringing Larkin, Jareth, Ari, her, and our cat. She'll understand."

They stood in front of the Council office doors now. Finn looked mad enough to shoot fire from his ears, like a dragon. And then he stomped his foot, like a small child. Tears gathered in the corners of his eyes. "Please," he choked out.

*Fuck.* She was being shitty, and instead of just irritating him, it had actually made him upset. Harlow's eyes fell closed, her shadows dancing around her fingers in a soothing fashion. She took a long, deep breath, banishing her frustration as best she could.

"I'm sorry," she said, feeling every syllable of her apology in her bones. "We'll find somewhere else for him to go." Finn started to nod, and it just slipped out of her mouth, without a thought: "*Of course.*"

Inwardly, she cringed at her tone. Why did she have to add that?

His eyes widened, and his jaw clenched. "Did you actually say all that just to piss me off? I *love* that fucking cat."

"Because you are being such a fucking dick about this Larkin thing."

They were lucky no one was in the square. The two of them were shouting now.

"She's an adult." Finn shook his fists in the air to punctuate each word. It would be comical if she weren't so mad at him.

"The two of you *disappeared*, Finbar. You haven't asked me once how it was for me when you were gone. When the two of you vanished through a breach in reality that I couldn't follow you through."

"I asked," he insisted. "You were vague."

He had asked, and she had been vague. But they were on an epic roll now, both of them stubbornly not backing down. "You could have asked again."

"You could have followed us," he spit out. "You just didn't."

Her mouth fell open. She'd thought they were blowing off steam, but that was below the belt. Harlow was too shocked to cry, and that was saying something. The silence that filled the space between them was pregnant with regret. They stared at one another, both of them obviously fighting with their pride.

Just as she was about to apologize, he reached for her,

pulling her towards him, but not quite embracing her. "I'm so fucking sorry. I didn't mean that."

Harlow stared up at him. They'd pushed each other too far. Her eyes fell to her boots. "We can't do this," she murmured. "We can't fight like this. I don't want this to be how we solve things."

He hugged her then, so tight she could hardly speak, but she apologized anyway. "I'm sorry too."

Finn's fingers stroked her hair. "I should have talked to you about why you didn't want Larkin to come."

Harlow nodded, taking in the smell of him. "I shouldn't have screwed with you about Axel."

They'd apologized, and she believed they both meant it sincerely, but she didn't feel better. In fact, all she wanted to do was crawl in bed for a week with Thea and cry. With ice cream. And *Pretty Little Firestarters* reruns. But that was all a lifetime away from the present reality. Now *she* wanted to stomp her foot.

Instead, she drew in a sharp breath and tried to compose herself. "We need to go in. We're in agreement about who's coming?"

He nodded, his face as solemn and exhausted as she felt. They were all so tired these days. "Let's go then."

$\sim$

PIPER'S OFFICE WAS TINY, CROWDED WITH FURNITURE, and a lot of books. Novels from what Harlow could tell, and an odd variety, including a wide range of comics. Piper caught Harlow's confused look as she dragged a finger over a stack of vintage romance novels, mixed with books about ancient history and biographies of famous immortals. Most of it was popular stuff, fluff, not the kinds of books she'd recommend to anyone who was serious about history, and not what she'd expect the Education Councillor to be reading.

"I like a wide range of genres," Piper said, snatching the stack away from Harlow.

"Of course. *The Parapsych Triad* was very good. I liked it a lot."

Piper looked at her like she'd said she thought cats might fly. She had no idea what Harlow was talking about, which was strange, since it was the most famous series in the pile Piper had just defended. Perhaps she'd forgotten she had it, or maybe she was one of those people who stubbornly didn't keep up with things like trendy books. If so, that was another point against her. Harlow hated reading snobs.

Finn cut to the chase, explaining who they'd like to have come along to ORAIS. Piper nodded absently. She was obviously distracted. Finn shot a glance at Harlow. It was clear neither of them knew what to say, or how to even attempt to handle the human.

"Are you sure you want to meet today, Councillor?" Finn asked, his tone cautious. "We can come back another time."

"I'll be fine," Piper snapped. "You're not taking Sanvier, though. His higher-ups said no. *Again.*"

Finn tried to explain why it would be a good idea, but Piper shook her head. "The Humanists were clear with both of you, Sanvier isn't going to ORAIS."

Finn glanced at Harlow, who nodded. "Okay," he said. "That's fine, I guess. Do you want us to replace him? We know he's a good fighter. We might need someone like him along."

Piper began writing on a notepad. "No, you have Arebos Flynn. That will be good enough. You'll leave in three days, so you'd best get about your preparations."

"I'll let Sanvier know then," Finn said.

"Focus your attention on preparing for your journey, McKay. Sanvier is a big boy. He's been told he's not going. The two of you don't need to be colluding behind your superiors' backs. If you make us look bad in all this, I promise I'll make things difficult for you."

Harlow tensed, waiting for Finn to argue again, but he didn't. He just nodded, his jaw clenching as he stood. Piper raised her eyebrows at Finn, daring him to speak again. When he didn't, she continued writing on her notepad.

Harlow recognized the dismissal and stood to leave as well, but Piper spoke as she stood. "I'd like a word with you, Krane."

Finn's eyes widened nearly imperceptibly, but Harlow noted the frustration winding through his shoulders as they tensed. "I'll wait for you outside."

When he'd gone, Piper continued staring at Harlow for an uncomfortably long few moments. "The two of you really don't remember me, do you?"

A shiver of anxiety slipped down Harlow's throat, settling low in her belly until it felt a lot like dread. She did not remember ever having met the human before. All she could do was shake her head in embarrassment. "I'm sorry, I don't."

The human's resulting laugh was entirely without humor. "Of course you don't. I sat next to you or behind you in a total of eight classes in secondary, ten for Finn."

The dread in Harlow's stomach curdled. She struggled to find words. When she came up with nothing, she apologized. "I am so sorry I don't remember you, Piper. Secondary was a difficult time in my life."

There was that humorless laugh again. "Right. What with the rich and powerful immortal parents who adored you, and a group of equally rich and powerful friends. It must have been *terrible* for you."

Indignation rose in Harlow's throat. "We don't know each other, Piper, so I can't compare our lives. But make no mistake, things have not been easy for me—especially not lately."

Piper rolled her eyes. "You're serious, aren't you? A little trouble with a boyfriend and a few tussles through the gossips, and you're sure you've got it bad."

"That doesn't seem fair," Harlow replied, trying hard to keep the whine that edged her voice to a minimum. "I *am* sorry I don't remember you from school, but my life hasn't been as easy as you seem to believe it to be."

The human sat back in her chair, her eyes narrowing. "Have you ever had to work for any of the opportunities you've had, Krane? You bought a fucking *penthouse* when Easton kicked you out, for fuck's sake. Do you know where I lived when my shitty ex did the same?"

Of course she didn't. The puzzle of why Piper had been so unfriendly to both she and Finn made sense now, but she didn't like knowing she was at fault.

"A tiny attic room I rented from a vampire who expected a 'donation' weekly, as part of my rent. That wasn't made clear until I'd moved in, and by that time, I'd spent my entire savings on the security deposit. I had no influence, no network to fall back on. No one to ask for help."

The contrast, which was so obvious to Piper, and had been less so to Harlow, slammed into her. It wasn't that she didn't know that she was more fortunate than most humans—she did. But it wasn't usually brought to her attention in such sharp relief to her own experience.

Harlow wasn't sure what to say. Her mind raced, as her sense of empathy reframed her entire life through this human's perspective. Every muscle in her body contracted painfully. It was impossible to close her mouth, which gaped open as she struggled to find the right words.

When she saw herself the way that Piper must... The Monas and the maters, hundreds of thousands of followers on socials she barely used, money—even if it had been a paltry amount to her. She'd always had everything she needed, even if she'd refused to access the help that was *always* offered to her. This human, and most humans, didn't automatically have that kind of support.

"That's fucked up, Piper," she said, finally. "Nothing like that should ever happen—to anyone."

Piper made a little snorting noise, derisive, but affirmative. "You know all the right things to say, don't you?" The human sat forward, leaning on her desk as she made intense eye contact with Harlow. "But do you know how to *do* the right thing? When it counts, are you going to be able to step aside and let the people who've always been vulnerable take the lead? Is Finn?"

"I—" Harlow was interrupted by the door to Piper's office opening. Harlow glanced back. Finn. He'd been listening on the other side of the door.

For the first time since he'd returned, his eyes were free of burden. Clear, unwavering purpose shone there. "When all of this is over—or as soon as I can get access to my accounts—I will sign over my personal fortune to the Fifth Order. If my parents are killed in the coming days, I will sign over everything they have to you as soon as I inherit. The Fifth Order will be funded by the greatest fortune on Okairos."

Piper's eyebrows raised slightly. "In return for what? A seat on the Council?"

Finn's face went smooth as a becalmed sea, his shoulder squaring. "In return for nothing."

The human shook her head. "Not even our trust?"

Finn crossed his arms, smirking. "I don't believe for one second I could buy your trust, Councillor. Not yours or any other human's. You asked if we would do what's right, didn't you?"

Piper nodded. Finn looked down at Harlow. "Do you agree with me—that this is what we should do? You won't be bonding with rich, powerful Finn McKay; you'll lose everything too."

Harlow stood, taking Finn's hand in her own. "I won't lose

anything. Give it all away." She looked down at Piper, waiting for a response.

Though Piper's laugh was curt as she stood, Harlow swore she felt the human open up a little. "The two of you are still assholes, but this is a step in the right direction. I'll let the rest of the Council know."

Finn turned to go, leading Harlow out of the office. Once they were in the hallway, he paused, stepping back inside the door for a moment. "I do actually have a request."

Piper looked up from the piece of paper she was writing on. "What is it?"

"That we'll be allowed to live in safety when this is over. That you won't enact violent punishments for immortals who've wronged you."

Piper slammed her pen down hard, crossing her arms tightly over her chest. "We're not like the Illuminated, Finbar McKay. That was never even a consideration. Agreements about reparative justice will be made when things are settled."

He bowed his head. "And for that, I am grateful. Thank you."

Finn turned, blocking Harlow's view of Piper's office as he led her out of the building. They didn't speak the entire way home, but he held Harlow's hand so tightly she thought it might be crushed, and there was new determination in every line of his body. Whatever else had happened in that office, Finn had dramatically changed the course of the Fifth Order. If their efforts were successful, the world would finally transform.

# CHAPTER TWENTY-TWO

A whirlwind of activity took over their lives, leaving little time for Harlow to worry about the journey ahead. Their little group would teleport as close to ORAIS's location as they could, then make the rest of the journey on foot. As such, Harlow and Larkin began research on the Gate of Lithraea, and Lithraea's Way. They were lucky enough to have a whole host of Falcyran humans in the village to talk to, which Larkin loved.

It was odd to talk to elderly humans, who'd aged so much more than their parents, and yet were younger by hundreds of years than most of the people they knew. Taking the time to hear their stories was special, more than just research. For Harlow, it further shaped her new understanding of the ways simply being immortal had changed everything about her life. It wasn't that she'd never spent time with humans. She'd spent two years with human friends, Mark's friends. But they'd all been the same age as her, and some were even wealthier than her family.

These people were different, and while Harlow was careful not to treat them like means to an end, she understood that they were giving her so much more than an expanded understanding of archaic lore. The lore itself was disturbing though. Stories about Lithraea and her helpers, the vvyk, were varied. She was a trickster goddess, like Voltos, and her role in every story obscured her motives. The takeaway was that their route wouldn't be easy, but it was the fastest way to ORAIS.

Harlow and Finn barely had a moment alone together, let alone time to talk about what had happened in Piper's office. They fell into bed each night exhausted, both physically and emotionally. On their last day in Sanctum, Harlow rolled over in bed, tired upon waking, to find Finn already wide awake.

"What time is it?" she mumbled.

Finn illuminated the witchlights that hung over their bed with celestial fire, dim enough to be pleasant, not so bright as to be harsh. Neither of them seemed able to tolerate harsh lighting these days. Cian had been staying over in Vivia's extra room a lot, after talking late into the night. They were alone in the bedroom. "It's not even five."

"What's wrong?" Harlow asked, moving Axel from his position in the exact center of the bed so she could cuddle up to Finn.

His head fell back against the headboard. "Did I make the right choice? Giving up the money?"

Harlow rolled onto her back. "I think so. Why are you worried?"

He shook his head. "Not about the reality of living without it."

He didn't elaborate, but every muscle in his face and neck were taught, so she curled back into him, hoping to distract him from the storm of worry raging inside him. "Do you ever picture what our lives will be like when all this is over? When we get to start living again, I mean?"

Though Harlow couldn't see Finn's face, she felt his eyes on her. The pause was long—too long. She swallowed hard, fear pooling in her chest. There had been a subtle push and pull between them since he got back that she wasn't used to. They'd always bantered back and forth, disagreeing with one another, but this was different. Harlow struggled to figure out if it was natural, given the stress they were under, or if something was actually wrong.

"No," he said finally. "I don't."

His tone was flat, devoid of any emotion. Harlow recoiled, shame blooming through her, though she couldn't understand *why*. When she drummed up the courage to drag her eyes to his, there was an icy distance coursing through his entire demeanor that pushed her out of bed.

"Oh," she replied, not knowing what else to say. She was tempted to simply start her morning routine, to shut him out the way he was shutting her out. Her mind raced through a series of catastrophic thoughts, immobilizing her.

Finn wasn't looking at her anymore. He was staring at a spot on the wall, just behind her head, and to the untrained eye it would probably seem like he was looking right at her. He'd looked beyond her that way before. A long, long time ago—when they were just seventeen.

And when they'd been seventeen, she'd taken that very personally. After all, it had been directed *at her*. It made all the sense in the world for her to walk away as a teenager, to put her armor on, rather than risk getting even more vulnerable than she already felt. But as an adult—one who was trying to trust that he loved her—she had to risk it.

"What's going on?"

His gaze slid from the wall to meet her eyes. Something almost imperceptible shifted from that icy chill to a softer, fearfulness. His jaw twitched as he held eye contact with her, and he clutched the blankets so hard his knuckles turned white. "I'm having a hard time imagining that things will ever be okay again—that we'll make it out of this."

*Why hadn't she just asked him what was going on before?* Her fear of rejection was a powerful thing, and the more it was allowed to fester the more it grew. She'd taken his request for time to process too literally.

Harlow's attention snapped back to Finn as he buried his face in his hands, shoulders heaving. She scrambled onto the bed, straddling his lap, pulling him into her arms. His arms went around her as he wept against the thin sweater she'd worn to bed.

"Shit," he swore, clinging to her. "I promised myself I wouldn't make this your problem. I'm just so fucking scared that this will all end the way the War of the Orders did. That we'll end up like the last Feriant Legion did."

They'd been separated by the Illuminated. Tortured. Executed. And then the Striders had been exterminated. It was a legitimate fear, especially since they were about to leave the safety Sanctum had provided them. Once they left, the risk of the Dominavus finding them would increase exponentially.

She hugged him tighter, but he pushed her away, holding her at arms' length. "I get it. Why Rakul did what he did in the catacombs. Why he went to so much trouble to save Vivia."

For a moment, Harlow was confused about what this had to do with anything. But then she saw the steel in his eyes. The hard warrior's face she'd seen dozens of times over the summer. "I'd ruin the world for you. If this goes sideways—if they take you —*nothing* will stop me from getting you back."

The shake in his voice was gone now, ironclad conviction replacing it. *Finn McKay would burn worlds down to get to her.* She remembered thinking that months ago. Why she'd doubted it for even a second was beyond her.

"I wish I could be as good as you are, babygirl," he whispered, stroking a piece of hair away from her face, his fingers tracing her softly curved jawline as his eyes fell.

"Good as *me*?" Harlow said, pulling his chin up so his eyes met hers. "You're the one who's given up their fortune and power, for a group of people who don't have much respect for us —because it's the right thing to do. Some would demand that respect, or at least a show of it, in exchange for doing the right thing. I wish I was as good as *you*."

"I had to do it," he murmured. "The resources my parents amassed. No one should have that much while others suffer."

"No," she agreed. "They shouldn't. You *are* a good man."

Heat flared between them, Finn's skin warming against hers, emitting a faint glow. She was acutely aware that she'd only worn a slouchy sweater to bed—one that barely covered her ass—and nothing else. Finn noticed this at the same time she did, the heat intensifying between her legs. His soft pajama pants were thin, doing nothing to disguise the fact that his body had already responded to hers, his erection pressing hard against her.

Finn pulled her closer, his tone deepening as his fingers gripped her hips. "You make me want to be less ruthless than the men who came before me, but I'd throw all semblance of 'good' away if anyone took you from me."

As he spoke, his grip tightened, both their breathing quickening to short, shallow pants. Harlow's hips swiveled, leaning into his hard length, growing thicker by the second beneath the soft, wet core of her. She reached between her legs, yanking his pajama pants down to expose his cock.

She eased him into her now-dripping core, Finn groaning softly as he watched her work. His fingers wound into the hair at the base of her neck. "I will destroy anyone who takes you from me. Do you understand?"

Harlow froze. Fear lanced through her, unbidden and unwanted. She knew what he was trying to say, but someone had wanted to keep her too close before, and it had ended badly. She tried to banish thoughts of Mark, but it wasn't so easy.

His eyes met hers. Love warmed them to a glow. "Unless you *wanted* to go."

A little smile pulled at her lips. He understood. He understood how to make sure the parts of her mind that were trying to protect her didn't scramble his words, or make them into something they weren't, without her permission. They were back in sync, on solid ground.

Finn pulled her body against his, as he looked into her eyes. "I will never cage you, Harlow. You are always free to fly away. But I will *never* let anyone hurt you again."

A little moan unfurled from her lips. *Away?* There was nowhere she wanted to be but here. She pushed down on him, pulling him deeper into her, the movement smooth and torturously slow.

Harlow rolled her hips, taking him deeper and harder with each thrust. He pushed her sweater up, exposing her breasts to the frigid air in the bedroom. His hands slid to cup her breasts, his thumbs swirling around her pebbled nipples.

"Yes," she urged him on, her back arching as he captured one nipple in his mouth, sucking on it as he thrust harder into her, their bodies grinding together where they met in a slippery friction.

This was all she needed, this promise that he would never abandon her. There was no fortune waiting for them on the other side of this war, no castle awaiting their victorious return. If all they had was this, it was all she needed.

Finn's mouth left her breast, in what felt like utter betrayal. "Shhh," he whispered. "You don't want to wake Riley and Enzo, do you?"

She shook her head, and his hands slid to her ass and he pulled her off him, another cruel betrayal of her pleasure. He pulled her close, sliding his cock against her, teasing her as he whispered into the shell of her ear. "Turn around for me."

She did so immediately, turning onto all fours, then backing up into his lap, where he pulled her up so her back rested against his chest as he slowly entered her. He shifted at the same time, his cock growing longer and thicker as they moved. She rested her head against his shoulder, lifting her face to be kissed.

Finn's mouth captured hers as his hands roamed over her, one cupping her face as his tongue slid against hers, the other playing with her nipples. Despite facing away from him, the position made her feel exposed. There was nowhere for her to shy away from his hands that explored every roll and curve of her body.

To her surprise, this heightened the sensation of every touch. Her back arched at the thought of being completely vulnerable to Finn, letting him have her body and trust. Trust that he was here for good. That they would die together before living apart ever again.

His wings wrapped around them, trapping the wet heat they gave off. Finn broke their kiss, dragging his mouth along her jaw, then behind her ear, every breath stimulating the sensitive shell of her ear as the hand that had cupped her face wrapped gently around her neck, applying light pressure to her throat that elicited a primal sound from deep inside her.

This pleased him. "You feel so damn good." The hand that played with her nipples strayed lower, stroking her belly as his cock drove deeper inside her.

"*Fuck.*" His fingers gripped her soft flesh as he growled, "I need you."

Harlow whimpered with pleasure as the pressure of his hand on her curved stomach increased the pleasure of his cock inside her. She clenched hard around him, wanting *more*.

She brought her fingers between her legs. Within moments, her vision went blank, her body exploding in a rush of wet heat. The hand around her neck went over her mouth, his second hand pressing even harder on her belly, causing his cock to hit the spot inside her that sent her so far over the edge that her shadows flooded the cocoon of his wings.

As her orgasm seemed just about to peak, his fangs sunk into her neck, sending her into new heights of pleasure. The hand on her belly slid lower now, replacing her own on her clit as he moved his wrist into her mouth.

"I need you inside me," he whispered into her ear. His words were a plea, a deep need begging to be filled. Her fangs protracted and she sunk them into his wrist, pulling his blood into her mouth, the taste of it sweet and thick as it mixed with her venom.

"Yes," he hissed.

Golden light twined with her shadows as light bloomed behind her eyes. Everything clenched hard for a moment. She fell to all fours and he met her on her knees, thrusting hard into her as she came apart around him, burying her face in a pillow as she silently screamed. All was undone and remade as he came inside her, their magic twisting in time with their bodies—singing for the moment of pure grace their love wrought in the darkness.

Finn's body fell against hers, his arms tightening around her, even as he pulled out. She rotated in his arms, tangling her legs with his. They stayed like that for a while, dozing until Axel woke them, wanting breakfast. Finn went to feed him and turn on the water heater while Harlow packed the last of their clothes. They were traveling light.

Harlow dug in her dresser until she found *The Warden*, tucked underneath some sweaters she was giving back to the community. Finn's arms snaked around her waist after setting a steaming cup of coffee on the dresser for her.

"*The Warden*?" he asked.

"I think we should take it to ORAIS. If we can access the archive there, maybe we can learn more about it."

He kissed the top of her head. "It's a good idea. Bring it."

Harlow set the book on top of the rest of their clothes, only to find Axel snuggled between the scant piles of items they were bringing. The black cat looked up at her, purring loudly, blinking several times in slow succession at both Harlow and Finn.

"What are we going to do with him?" Harlow asked.

"You take a shower," Finn suggested. "I'll have it worked out by the time you're out, I promise."

Harlow started to protest, but he was already gone, the water already running. She kissed the top of the cat's head and took advantage of the last hot shower she could expect for a while.

~

When Harlow came downstairs, Petra was waiting in the living room. She hugged Harlow as soon as she entered the room. The past few days had been hard. Since they were the ones leaving first, they had to say goodbye to everyone they loved. Petra had been in talks about where she was going for nearly two straight days, and this was the first time Harlow had seen her.

As she had in each of her goodbyes, Harlow tried hard not to think about what might happen when the people she considered her family were separated. Instead, she clung to Petra, breathing her in. How she smelled expensive when she hadn't had access to perfume in months baffled Harlow, but maybe Petra was just made from different stuff than other people—perhaps her flesh was cut from couture. For some reason, that thought grew a lump in Harlow's throat.

They sat on the couch together. Finn excused himself to make tea. "Lou, Kate and I are going to Castel des Rêves," Petra explained. The little island nation was located south of Nea Sterlis and was considered wine country. "Lou's sire was from there, you know?"

Harlow hadn't known that, but it wasn't too surprising, given her experience with vineyards.

"Anyway, the Council wants to see if we can get the vampires there to align with us."

Castel des Rêves was largely populated by vampires and humans with a hands-off Illuminated governor, Nephele Ostralios. Unlike Falcyra, they'd lived together in near-perfect harmony for hundreds of years. Harlow had heard whispered rumors about Castel des Rêves, and the mythic levels of peaceful coexistence there, since coming to Sanctum. It made sense to see if they would help, but the Castel des Rêves vampires were notoriously avoidant regarding Illuminated politics, preferring to stay on their island, in peace.

"Have the Vespae made it to Castel des Rêves?" Harlow asked. If they had, it might be the only reason the vampires would help.

Petra shook her head. "Not yet, they got their wards up sooner than other nations, and they've held. We know it's a long shot, but the Council thinks it's worth it to ask before we decide when to make our next move. I've been friends with Nephele for years. She hates the Illuminated—it's why she vied for the position. I think I can convince her and the other Ventyr there to help us, even if the vampires won't."

"Makes sense. When do you go?"

"This afternoon, in an hour, actually... How do you feel about Audata?"

It was a strange question. Harlow wasn't sure why Petra asked. "I love her. Why?"

Pink flushed in Petra's cheeks. "She's coming with us too. I just wondered if you liked her."

Harlow narrowed her eyes. "Why? Do *you* like her?"

Petra fingers fluttered. She clasped them together. "I... I mean. Of course. She's so smart... And pretty."

Harlow giggled. "Being pretty is a real asset in a dangerous mission."

Petra sighed. "I've never been in a position like this before."

"What does Kate say?"

The flush in Petra's cheeks deepened. "She likes her too."

Harlow smiled, but something pulled on her heart. "Be careful, Petra. Audata is a sensitive person, and she hasn't found her Claimed yet."

Petra nodded. "I take that really seriously, and Kate and I have discussed it. We're not trying to force anything. Promise."

"Okay," Harlow said. "Well, for what it's worth, I love her."

Petra let out a giddy breath. "Thank you. One last thing, can I take Axel with me? He'll be safe in Castel des Rêves."

Relief washed over Harlow. "You have somewhere to stay where he'll be welcome?"

Petra nodded. As though summoned, Axel jumped onto Petra's lap. He stood, rubbing his face against hers, then flopped down to take a bath. The cat loved Petra more than just about anyone other than Larkin, Finn, and Harlow, primarily because she loved him so much in return. If Larkin couldn't take him, then this was the perfect solution.

"Thank you," Harlow whispered. Petra glanced at her watch. "You have to go now, don't you?"

"Yes," Petra said, her chin wobbling.

"Don't," Harlow whispered. "If you cry, I will too."

Petra blinked hard a few times, averting her eyes. "We'll be together again soon," she murmured.

"We will," Harlow promised.

Finn came in, holding Axel's backpack. He picked the black cat up and held him close, kissing his head before handing him to Harlow. Her throat closed, watching him turn away, his shoulders shaking with tears. She knew he wasn't ashamed, but was trying not to set her off.

"I love you, buddy," she whispered, big teardrops splashing on his fur. He purred, nuzzling her. "You'll be safe with Petra, and I'll see you again soon."

Something in the threads between them crackled. She'd

never thought to make a connection like this with the cat before. For the briefest moment, she thought she heard a voice in her head, the same as she had with Morgaine's cat, Bayun.

*We'll be together again soon.*

Harlow stared at Axel, wondering, her heart beating fast, but the crackle disappeared, and no more words came through in her head. He jumped into his backpack with not even a peep of resistance.

"See you soon," she said, hugging Petra one more time.

"Love you both," Petra said as she squeezed Finn's hands one last time.

After they left, Harlow sat on the couch, trying not to think about the way her chest felt hollow, as though someone had scooped her out like a squash for roasting. Enzo and Riley would be home soon, and she needed to pack, but every part of her ached.

"Why don't you go over to the maters?" Finn said, interrupting her angst-fueled reverie. "Send Larkin over here with her stuff, and Ari and I'll finish the packing. We can have a late dinner with Enzo and Riley. I invited Sam and Tomy too, so you don't have to try to catch them."

Harlow nodded, grateful for his foresight. But he'd done this type of thing before, sent people he loved on missions they might not come back from, parted ways with the ones he cared for too many times.

"Thank you," she said, as she dressed for the cold. "I'll be back."

$\sim$

THE WALK ACROSS THE VILLAGE WAS A BLUR OF people stopping her to hug and say goodbye. Harlow was surprised by how many people were genuinely sad to see her go. After years of being practically shunned by the sorcières in Nuva

Troi, as well as this summer in Nea Sterlis, this was a different feeling. She was a little overwhelmed by the time she got to the maters, and found they were all out back in the garden, a little bonfire going in their firepit.

Aurelia met her at the garden gate. "Hello, love, we were about to send Larkin to get you and Finn. Join us by the bonfire?"

It was a little cold for a bonfire, but it sounded festive, and Aurelia was holding a fuzzy blanket. Harlow smiled. "I'd love to."

Aurelia stepped aside, revealing that the backyard was full of Finn and Harlow's family and friends. "Surprise," Aurelia said softly.

Fingers closed around hers, and Harlow leaned into Finn's steady bulk as he whispered in her ear. "I thought you needed at least half a day with your people."

"What about the packing?"

Finn's arms went around her waist, pulling her tightly against him. "It's handled, nothing to worry about but enjoying yourself." He pushed her towards the little crowd of people, then sped past her to hug Cian and Vivia both.

The next few hours were a pleasant haze of hugging and chatting. She argued with Thea and Alaric about baby names, and listened to Riley and Enzo tell stories about their adventures in domesticity, all with the satisfaction of knowing that the people she loved were cared for. She had no idea what the future held, if all of them would make it through this safely, but knowing they loved one another this deeply helped ease that anxiety.

A sinking sadness crept over her as she thought about the twins and Nox. As if by instinct, Ari was at her side. The shifter loomed over her, his jet-black hair falling into his eyes. "Nox gave this to me, to give to you. I shared one with your parents, as well as Thea and Larkin."

He passed her a nearly paper-thin tablet, which she switched on with a swipe up. There was only one file icon on the home screen. She tapped it and a video filled the screen, showing Indigo, Meline, and Nox. The three of them smiled and waved. They looked phenomenal, happy. Nox's sweet face brightened as she kissed Indi's cheek and then popped out of frame, leaving just the twins.

Indi's dark hair was cut short, just below her chin, in a sleek bob, and Meline's honey-blonde hair was thrown into her signature messy bun. Both wore eyeglasses, though Meline's were more classically "fashion," while Indi's were heavy black, horn-rimmed frames. They didn't look alike anymore, but in all the ways that counted, they were exactly the same as they'd ever been.

"Hi sissy," Meli said. "We can't say much..."

"Except that we love you," Indi finished.

"And that we're doing okay," Meline continued.

Indigo leaned on Meline, and there were tears in both her sisters' eyes as Indi said, "We'll be together again before you know it."

Meli looked about to burst into tears, but she smiled, nodding furiously. The video ended, and Harlow's heart had the feeling of a nearly-healed bruise being knocked about. The video was meant to make her feel better, but it didn't. Until everyone was safe, nothing would be better.

Sam and Tomyris walked in, just in time to distract her from spiraling into worry. "We just came off patrol," Sam said, after brushing a kiss to Harlow's cheek.

"But we wanted to stop by, before we head to Samira's aunties' gathering," Tomyris explained.

Sam and Tomyris both had far more experience with this kind of thing than she did. Tomyris' parents were in Castel des Rêves, and while some of Sam's family was here, a lot were gone, though Harlow didn't know where, as the Strider was extremely private about her family.

The Ventyr's eyes narrowed, assessing Harlow. "Are you doing okay?"

Harlow nodded.

"Good," Sam said. "We can do this. We'll see each other again soon."

All over the village, Harlow assumed similar gatherings were taking place.

She surprised herself by wondering where Piper was—whether the human had family to go to, or friends. A part of her resented the woman, but mostly, she regretted not knowing more about her, or a way to make things right between them. They'd have time enough for that, she supposed. She rejoined the party, wearing herself out on all the love she could take in.

When most everyone had gone home, or inside to use their two hours of generator power for the evening to watch an old movie, Harlow joined the maters and Thea by the fire. Inside the house, Larkin was talking animatedly, moving her hands as she explained something to Ari, who laughed with his whole body.

Thea hugged her from behind; her baby bump was just starting to appear. The bruised feeling in Harlow's heart intensified. She had no idea how long it would be before she saw Thea again. Their mission to ORAIS was open-ended; everything about where they went after depended on what they found. Harlow hated the uncertainty, but they might be gone for days, or even months.

"Let's just be us for the rest of the night," Thea murmured, pulling Harlow towards the circle of chairs around the fire.

Harlow sunk into a chair, her entire body going limp as Selene tucked a blanket around her knees. She fetched Harlow a mug of hot chocolate from the thermos by her own chair, and then sat back down. Thea and Aurelia chatted casually for a while about a novel they'd both been reading, a literary retelling of an old faery story.

"Is that the one about the courts in the labyrinth?" Selene asked.

Aurelia nodded. "Yes, it's a brilliant retelling. The labyrinth and the challenges are a symbol for the main character's inner turmoil."

Harlow smiled at Thea, both of them listening to their parents debate about whether or not it was effective to use folkloric elements as symbols. If Harlow closed her eyes, she could imagine she was back in the Monas, shelving books while Selene and Aurelia debated the merit of literary tropes. She could practically smell the books. Her ache for home filled her the longer Selene and Aurelia talked.

The story itself wasn't one Harlow remembered well, but it was about a character she did, Rhiannon, a warrior-queen of the faery, whose companions could shift into birds. She smiled, wondering if she'd liked stories about Rhiannon so much as a child because of who she was.

"Do you think stories about Rhiannon are actually about Striders?" Harlow interrupted, though she kept her voice low. Thea had dozed off in her chair, her hands resting on her bump.

Aurelia sipped her hot chocolate, smiling first at Thea, then at Selene. "You thought the same once, didn't you, love?"

Selene nodded. "Yes, because of my grandmother, I wondered if stories about Rhiannon were actually ways to talk about the Feriant. I researched the issue thoroughly in my youth —to my family's great surprise."

Selene and Aurelia rarely talked about their families. Unlike most sorcière families, whose many generations were alive and well, theirs had both fallen prey to many tragedies, and as a result, the Kranes had grown up without grandparents, aunties, uncles or cousins. Harlow had always thought that was why

Selene and Aurelia wanted so many children, to make up for the tragic loss of both their families.

"Why was it a surprise to your family?" Harlow asked, her curiosity piqued.

Aurelia grinned. "Because your mother was near constant trouble until she met me."

Selene grinned back, a wicked glint in her eye. "And then I got into an entirely different kind of trouble."

Harlow made a silent gagging motion, enjoying feeling like a child for the moment. Adult concerns were looming. For the rest of tonight, she wanted to pretend. "Please move on. What did you find out about Rhiannon?"

Selene reached out and took Aurelia's hand, pressing a kiss to her wife's palm. Harlow was fairly sure she saw her use tongue and rolled her eyes. When Selene tucked Aurelia's hand back into her jacket pocket, Harlow's heart warmed. They always took care of one another.

"That the origin of the Rhiannon stories predated the Immortal Orders entirely. They were human folklore long before the Illuminated arrived. The Books of the Fey were all derived from ancient human lore. The story of the courts and the labyrinth is one of the oldest."

"I've never read it," Harlow said, hoping Selene would tell it to her. She had a wonderful memory for stories, and as children she'd often told tales from memory before bed.

But Selene merely shrugged. "It's been a while since I read it. You girls loved the Violet book best when you were little, and I think it was in the Red. What's it about, love?"

Aurelia sighed. "The idea that the faery courts gather each century for a battle of wits and prowess in a giant labyrinth. Rhiannon is the hero, of course."

"Why?" Harlow asked. When Aurelia raised her brows, she clarified, "Why did they have 'a battle for wits and prowess' in a big maze? What was the point?"

It was Aurelia's turn to shrug. "Honor, I believe. Most of the stories about Rhiannon are about her proving her honor, aren't they?"

Selene launched into a lecture about how Aurelia was confusing Rhiannon with stories of Aphora's consort Pallas, and that they were similar characters in mythological tales, but not the same. Harlow closed her eyes, drifting off to the lovely sound of her parents debating and flames crackling in the background. When Finn came to carry her home, she faintly heard Aurelia say, "Take good care of our girl, Finbar. I believe the past year has worn her out entirely."

"With my last breath," Finn promised. Vaguely, Harlow thought he sounded like one of the chevaliers from faery stories before drifting off to sleep in his arms.

# CHAPTER TWENTY-THREE

The next day, Harlow and Finn said one last round of goodbyes. They'd promised to keep things short, and the sun was just coming up when they met Ari at the Lodge, where he'd been staying in guest quarters. Larkin was running a little late, as usual. The three of them were dressed for extremely cold weather with a compact pack strapped to their back. As a part of their gear, each person had a light block of adamantine for Harlow to form into skis, crampons, or snow-shoes as the situation called for.

They would make three carefully plotted teleports before reaching Gale Alley, where they would have to hike the rest of the way to ORAIS. The route to get there was treacherous at best, and Harlow had been doing her best not to think about it. As they waited for Larkin, Harlow noticed that she'd lost the scarf she'd tucked into the strap of her pack on the walk over. She'd been too hot after her shower and hadn't needed it, but she certainly would in a little while.

She looked around and didn't see it. "Hey," she said softly to Finn, who was going over charts with Ari one last time. "I dropped my scarf on the way over. I'm going to track back and look for it."

He nodded. Ari was asleep on the couch next to him, snoring lightly, his feet in Finn's lap. Finn looked as though he might drop into a nap as well. Harlow left them to it with a small smile. She was glad it would be just them—just family—on this trip.

The village was bustling with activity and Harlow wound through the streets until she spotted her scarf, just outside one of the popular bakeries, stuck to a snow-covered bush. She grabbed it, wishing she had time to wait in the long line forming outside for something else to eat.

As she turned back towards the Lodge, someone stepped out of line to greet her. She smiled at Jareth Sanvier as he fell into stride next to her. "You'll lose your place in line."

He grinned. "Maurice has a special spot in his heart for me."

Maurice was the lead baker, and Harlow imagined he *did* have a special spot in his heart for Jareth. She'd seen the two of them making eyes at one another. Again, she smiled, wishing a little that Jareth, with all his charm, was coming along with them. He would have made a good addition to the team.

"Hey," Jareth's tone was hesitant, as he paused in the street. "I should have explained my motives better. I'm sorry."

Harlow frowned. "What do you mean?"

Jareth sighed. "I'm not always very good at explaining myself and I wish I'd tried a little harder to get Finn to like me."

Harlow was completely confused. She stopped in the street, just outside the Lodge. "Finn likes you just fine."

Now Jareth frowned in confusion. "Then why doesn't he want me to come on this mission?"

Harlow's heart skipped a beat. "He did. We requested that you come with us."

Jareth stepped back, his mouth opening and closing, before he glanced at the Lodge, and then around for anyone in their proximity. Harlow did the same. People were filling the square as the village's day got started. With so many people leaving, it was busy. Anyone might hear them. Jareth shook his head once, and Harlow understood. They were likely being watched.

He gripped her arm, pressing gently, but firmly. His voice lowered to an almost inaudible decibel, his lips barely moving. "Something's off with the Council."

Jareth really was far, far too charming to be trusted. Harlow wasn't sure what to say, or how to say it, so she kept it simple. "What?"

"The Education Councillor, in particular. Something's off about her."

Harlow's heart stilled. Since meeting the woman, she'd thought the same thing. Something was *strange* about her. Harlow pulled Jareth into an archway that led to the Lodge gardens. The little tunnel was likely lovely in the summer, covered as it was in thorny wild roses. They would be somewhat hidden here. She did her best with a muffling spell, though they were not her specialty and her shadows begged to be let out. But if someone saw them, they'd know she was doing magic, and she didn't want to draw attention.

"We still have to be very quiet," she whispered when the threads finally snapped into place for her spell. "I'm not very good at working magic this way."

Jareth nodded. "I overheard my superior officer talking to one of the other Council members a few days ago. The human that helped Finn and Larkin make it through the limen, Morgaine Yarlo, did you know her?"

A lump rose in Harlow's throat at the thought of the human, and losing Finn and Larkin in Nea Sterlis. "Yes."

"When she was with the Council, apparently she brought up some of the signs of someone being possessed by a Ravager."

Every muscle in Harlow's body stilled, her lungs stopped

moving, and it felt as though her head might be crushed with the weight of her fear.

"It starts with them acting erratic, out of character and even forgetting things, then moves on to hallucinations and paranoia. Apparently, Morgaine actually talked to the one on her world a few times—and get this—the Ravagers choose someone in power to inhabit."

He raised his eyebrows, and Harlow had to admit that the theory sort of fit. Piper did have an odd amount of power for being the Education Councillor.

"What happens after the hallucinations and paranoia?"

Jareth lowered his voice even further. "I only caught part of what was said. Something about the Ravager *ascending*."

Harlow was certain she didn't want to know what that meant. "That doesn't sound good."

"It really doesn't."

Harlow took a deep breath. "But it also doesn't mean that Piper is the Ravager's host."

Jareth sighed. "I just keep thinking that it doesn't make sense. There's something really off about her."

There *had* been times when Piper had behaved erratically, like the way she was ignorant of the bestselling Wesley Arden series in her office. No one hadn't heard of those books—they'd been made into shows, movies, everything. Literally millions of people had read them. For a moment, Harlow let her imagination run away with her. *Could* the human be the host for the elemental? And if she was possessed, did that mean that the real Piper didn't hate her?

Rational thought crashed back in: they had no evidence, and Jareth's theory seemed far-fetched, even though Harlow was inclined to trust that what he said about Morgaine was true. What reason would he have to lie? Neither of them knew the human well enough to make such a claim against her. Harlow could just imagine how approaching the Council with an accusation that the Education Councillor had been possessed by an elemental being hellsbent on destroying the world would go. It would be a bloodbath, and she would be the loser.

Jareth was still speaking. "I don't have a lick of proof, Harlow. But I have a bad feeling about Piper Winslow. Why did she lie about me not coming with you to us both? I was told you didn't want me along."

Harlow let out a puff of air. This was a lot, right before they were supposed to leave. "We asked for you to come. She said your people denied us."

He shook his head, seeming to come down off the high of his own theory. "Listen, I don't want to jump to conclusions. It's just as likely that the Rogue Council doesn't want the Humanists allying too closely with the Knights. That's the most obvious answer."

It was. It was an incredibly logical answer. Her spell was wearing thin. If she put too much more energy into it, she'd be tired before teleporting and that wasn't ideal. She grabbed Jareth's hands. "Go to my sister Thea about this. Tell no one else. She'll know if any of this sounds like it might hold water."

"She'll tell Cian and Alaric," Jareth reasoned, looking concerned.

Harlow nodded as the muffling spell dissipated. "She will. And that's a *good* thing."

Jareth nodded as they walked in silence back towards the square, but Harlow couldn't help but notice that he seemed disappointed. It occurred to her that it was possible that Piper Winslow just didn't like Jareth, and that was probably something he wasn't used to. The woman had an irritating way about her, but she was also rightfully frustrated with immortals' incredible lack of self-awareness. Harlow wasn't foolish enough to dismiss the vampire's ideas outright, but this theory was far-fetched at best, and outright offensive to Piper in many ways.

There was a brief awkward moment, and then the vampire's

arms were around her. He was a good hugger, and the feeling that wrapped around her heart reminded her of how she felt when she was with Enzo. Jareth could be a good friend. Maybe they'd get that chance someday.

"Be careful, Harlow," he said as he pulled away. "I want you to show me the sights of Antiquity Row when all this is over."

The muscles in her throat tensed. "It's a date."

They walked away from each other, Harlow's mind scrambling to put the pieces of all Jareth had said together, and in truth, she didn't come up with much that made her believe he was right. It did worry her that she didn't have the time to follow up on this, but Thea could more than handle it. Harlow smiled to herself as she entered the Lodge; the mystery of it all would give Thea something to distract her from the worry that she was being treated like an incubator.

Larkin had arrived while she was fetching her scarf. Likely, it was better to talk about what Jareth had said after they'd made the necessary jumps for the day. She didn't want any of them distracted.

"So, who's jumping with who?" Ari asked as Harlow joined the group.

"Larkin and I are together. Ari, you're with Finn." Harlow explained.

Finn tapped the map open on the coffee table. They'd all seen it dozens of times now, but it was a good reminder to help them get the location fixed in their minds. "We'll jump to this location first—it's a Humanist safehouse about thirty miles north of here. Then we'll break, patrol, and make our next jump."

Larkin's face scrunched together. "I still wish we could do it all at once."

Ari shook his head. "I know. But it's safer to do it in three parts so no one gets overly tired."

Larkin hugged Ari's arm. It was sweet how close they were. "I know, buddy. I'm just scared."

The big shifter shot her a serious look. "Me too. We can do this though."

Harlow took a deep breath, trying to banish all worries about being immediately tracked by the Vespae, or worse, the Dominavus.

They geared up. Finn checked all their packs, making sure they were safely closed and that they'd brought all they needed to. He examined Harlow's last, pressing a kiss to her lips. "See you at the safehouse."

She nodded, then turned to Larkin. "You're good?"

Her sister nodded. "I am. I got lots of practice teleporting with Vivia. I'm good at it. *Promise.*"

Harlow knew her sister was good. Vivia had spent hours in the last few days going over what Larkin was capable of after their travels together, and the list of what Vivia had to teach was impressive. She wished she'd gotten to spend more time with the firedrake.

Finn pulled Harlow aside to adjust the adamantine block on her pack again. It wasn't necessary, they both knew that, but he clearly needed an extra moment with her. "You remember the alternate for jump two if anything goes wrong?"

Harlow nodded, knowing she wasn't supposed to say it. There were protocols around this kind of thing, even here, among people they assumed were friends. The Knights took even more precautions than the Feriant Legion did. All three jumps had alternate locations that had never been spoken about aloud.

Finn and Ari threw their arms around one another in a dramatic hug, laughing, and Harlow took Larkin's hands. There was no going back now. She was terrified to take her little sister out into the unknown, but this was what she wanted. Harlow had to try to trust that it would be okay. A little tug on her shadows indicated that Larkin's magic was merging with hers, making their power to teleport stronger.

When it hit a crescendo, Larkin nodded to Finn, who murmured, "Now."

They jumped. The teleportation process always took a beat longer with someone in tow, and even with Larkin helping, the drag was longer than Harlow had ever experienced. They tumbled out of the between-space involved in teleportation. Harlow was nauseous, but she didn't throw up.

An acrid scent filled her nose as her blurred vision clarified. The safehouse was on fire. Part of Finn's plan had been to be open about the first jump, and slightly more secretive about the second two, while keeping the alternates completely locked down. While they'd anticipated there was a possibility they'd be followed when they left, no one had thought *this* was possible.

Someone had eliminated their first resting spot. Immediately, Harlow thought of Piper Winslow and Jareth's accusations. The Education Councillor was one of the few people who'd known they would stop here. Harlow hadn't put much stock in what Jareth had said before, but now... Finn shouted, breaking her train of thought. "Alternate two. *Now.*"

Harlow swiveled, checking that Larkin was all right. Her younger sister's eyes were wide with fear. She'd been terrified of fire since the night of the Solstice Gala, when Finn and Harlow's home had been burned to the ground.

"You okay?" Harlow shouted, stepping towards Larkin.

Larkin didn't answer. She'd frozen, staring at the fire. They didn't have time for this. Finn grabbed Larkin and sandwiched her between himself and Ari. Ari held her sister tight, pressing his cheek to hers for closer contact, nodding once to Harlow as they blinked out.

He was making sure she had enough power to get to the alternate location, farther away. Harlow tried to jump, but her magic sputtered, not connecting her to the between—movement distracted her. She couldn't catch sight of whatever was lurking, but it was moving fast, towards her.

It was now or never. Harlow jumped smoothly to the second alternate location, then fell to her knees on a black sand beach, her entire body retching as it tried to expel the stress of the teleportation. Larkin sat next to her, shaking and pale, but in one piece.

Columns of rock protruded from the angry gray ocean, taking a beating from the enormous waves. The scent of salt air hit her face, combining with something metallic and wet. Finn pulled Ari and Larkin back, further ashore. He shouted something, but Harlow couldn't hear what he said over the sound of the crashing waves. Finn appeared before her, panic in his eyes as he grabbed her.

They blinked out, appearing further up the beach, away from the dark water, just in time to see the biggest wave she'd ever seen crashing onto the exact spot Harlow had been standing moments before. Everyone watched as the waves compounded onto one another, getting closer and closer with each increase in size. Harlow had never seen the sea look so sinister, not even in Nea Sterlis' hurricane season, or Nuva Troi's depressing winters. Something about the combination of the dark rocks and sand with the monster waves gave Harlow the impression of looming menace.

"We have to move further in," Ari shouted above the noise of the water. "A storm is brewing at sea. This beach won't be safe for long."

Larkin raised her voice. "Why don't we go to our next location?"

Harlow glanced at Finn, who shook his head. "We can't," she yelled back. "Everyone has to rest first."

There was fear in Larkin's eyes, but she nodded, rather than arguing further. They started picking through the steep rocky shoreline, climbing ever higher. It was a touch warmer here than it had been inland, but not by much. The Apennine Mountain range ended here at this shore, and its jagged peaks crested above them, casting long shadows onto the cold beach.

Finn took last in line, making sure that no one fell behind, while Ari tracked a path through the treacherous rocks. Everything was coated in ice. Harlow winced every time her feet almost slipped. The wind whipped through them, feeling as though it lashed every inch of exposed skin.

Every second in this environment was painful, which was why Finn chose it. Everyone knew this location was one of the most dangerous in Falcyra—unpredictable waves, avalanche-prone mountains, and predatory shades that were only found in the darkest of regions. When evening came, they would have to be careful not to step beyond the light of their fire.

It wasn't an ideal place to rest, but if they were going to make the last jump to Lithraea's Gate tomorrow, they would have to make it through the night.

# CHAPTER TWENTY-FOUR

Ari found a tiny cave safely above the water. He and Finn both worked to gather wood for a fire, while Harlow tended to Larkin, who was still not saying much. When she had Larkin wrapped in her blanket, sipping water, Harlow crouched in front of her.

"Hey, pal. You okay?"

Larkin nodded, but her eyes were still wide with fear. "I shouldn't have come. I'm sorry. I'm the reason we can't jump again."

It was true, and it wasn't. Taking both Larkin and Ari had drained Finn too much to safely make another jump, but emphasizing that wouldn't be helpful. Besides, Larkin didn't need to hear any of that right now. She needed to think about why she was here, and if she wanted to stay. "Do you want to go back?"

Larkin's eyes met Harlow's. "To Sanctum?"

Harlow nodded. "I could take you back. You could go to Nuva Troi with the maters."

Larkin shook her head, then sighed. "Maybe you *should* take me back."

"Why do you want to be here so much?" Larkin hadn't ever really explained what this was all about to Harlow. She'd talked to Finn, but Harlow hadn't pressed him for answers, knowing her little sister had spoken to him in confidence.

Harlow kept hold of Larkin's hand as she snuggled closer to her, tucking herself into her sister's blanket cocoon. Ari and Finn both disappeared to find firewood.

"I wasn't sure why I felt like I needed to come at first," Larkin explained. "But I started having dreams about ORAIS shortly after I arrived in Sanctum."

"Why didn't you tell me?" Harlow asked.

Larkin leaned against Harlow, snuggling into the crook of her arm, like she had when she was small. "I didn't know that's what they were at first, until I talked to Finn. And by the time I knew, you were so against the whole thing... I just..."

"Didn't feel like you could talk to me." Finn had tried to warn her that this was the environment she was creating, but she hadn't listened.

"I know you just want me to be safe. I also know I'm meant to be here. There's a room inside ORAIS that appears in all my dreams."

Harlow was about to ask Larkin to describe it to her, but Larkin started coughing. Harlow slipped out of the blanket's warmth to fetch her sister more water. Finn and Ari returned with wood. Soon, they had a small fire going. Finn sat down next to Harlow, while Ari brought a few energy bars out of his bag, unwrapping them and passing them out. They were terrible, but packed with calories, and Harlow felt better almost immediately.

"Who burned the safehouse?" Harlow finally asked, when the last of the sticky goo of the energy bar was rinsed from her teeth.

Finn shook his head. "There was no time to investigate."

"Something came at me when I was on my way out. It was moving fast."

Ari sipped his water thoughtfully. "Could have been one of the Dominavus, or another Illuminated."

"Or a vampire," Larkin added.

Finn nodded. "Or an incubus."

That was a possibility. Alain Easton would have the ability to move as quickly as one of the Illuminated or a vampire. And he was almost certainly still looking for them. And unfortunately those weren't the only options.

"Jareth Sanvier had a theory that Piper might be the Ravager's host."

Everyone looked up, as though startled. Harlow stared at the little fire, stretching her fingers toward it. "He heard his commander talking about the signs of a Ravager possession, and thought it fit. I didn't believe him, but she knew where we were going."

Finn's eyebrows raised so high he looked like one of those wrinkly face dogs for a brief second. "That's a big accusation." He glanced at Ari. "Arebos here got his hands on the same intel."

"It was all Nox," Ari said with a faint smile for his sister. "But yeah, we've seen it. Doesn't track with the Education Councillor though..."

As the Wraith trailed off, Finn picked up his train of thought. "Unless the Council just wants us dead. Nobody had to be possessed by an elemental for that to be the case."

Harlow's heart fluttered erratically. *Her family.*

Finn caught her expression and grabbed her hand. "I don't actually think it's them, babygirl."

Ari lay back on his pack. "Finn's right. More likely, it's the Dominavus or Easton. From a tactical standpoint, they have a vested interest in us and they'd wait until we separated from the larger group to pick us off. Too much risk with so many elite fighters at Sanctum, and I'm not convinced the Illuminated can even find the place. If I hadn't had the exact coordinates, I wouldn't have been able to."

Oddly, that did make Harlow feel better, awful as it was that there were so many possibilities for who might want to kill them.

"We have too many enemies," Larkin said, with a sad little laugh that didn't make it to her eyes.

Harlow hated the way the past months had changed her sweet little sister into someone who'd experienced more trauma in a few short months than anyone should in a lifetime. She shouldn't have to laugh shit like this off.

Finn grimaced at Larkin. "Everything really does just keep getting worse, doesn't it?"

Larkin laughed, wagging her eyebrows. "Like a psychological thriller. The twists and turns just keep coming."

"You'd better hope not," Ari said with a smirk. "You don't have 'final girl' chops."

Larkin gasped dramatically. "How dare you say that? I do. And that's for horror, I'm the heroine of a *thriller*, Arebos."

The two of them bantered back and forth as Finn scooted behind Harlow, pulling her body between his legs to wrap her in his warmth. The cave was small enough to hold some heat, and Harlow was grateful it wasn't the start to some awful tunnel that subterranean horrors could crawl out of at night. Ari and Larkin's discussion of horror films wasn't helping her frame of mind.

Still, the cave wasn't exactly cozy and Finn's body heat comforted her. "What will happen when night comes?"

Rekyvaar had been plastered all over socials for years as "the most dangerous beach in Falcyra." In some ways, it was iconic, as much for the deadly waves as the shades that haunted the black sand shores.

Larkin's voice was soft. "We'll die."

Harlow smacked her sister's leg. This was no time to joke. Larkin glanced at her, grimacing. "I'm not kidding. Shades kill people here every year. We don't have enough wood to keep a fire going. We *could* die here."

Ari shifted uncomfortably, making eye contact with Finn. "She's right, man. This wasn't ever supposed to be an overnight stop, and there's no more wood out there unless we head toward the forest..."

"Which we're not doing," Finn replied.

The forest at the base of the mountains was the source of the aberrant shades. It was nowhere any breathing creature should be past sunset.

Finn checked his watch. "We have six hours 'til sunset. Ari, can you keep watch? The three of us need to sleep if we're going to make the jump to the next spot before dark."

Ari stretched his legs. "I've got this."

Finn nodded once, then lay down, pulling Harlow into the crook of his arm. Behind her, Larkin snuggled up so they were back to back.

"Wake us in five hours, all right?" Finn said.

Harlow didn't even hear Ari's answer—sleep took her immediately.

∿

HARLOW WOKE TO PITCH-DARKNESS, BUT FOR THE dying embers of the fire. She sat straight up. Finn was next to her, fast asleep, as was Larkin. Night had fallen and outside the moons had risen, sending silver light through the mouth of the cave.

*Where was Ari?*

The air was cold and still; all was silent. She shook Finn's shoulder, but he didn't wake. She knew better than to make noise. That would only draw shades. She shook Finn again, harder this time, but he still didn't wake. She tried Larkin, who didn't wake either.

Whatever was happening, it wasn't natural sleep. Finn was one of the lightest sleepers she knew. Harlow didn't want to leave Finn and Larkin, but Ari was nowhere to be seen. She crept silently to the front of the cave and found him slumped just outside the mouth, his head sticky with blood. Someone had hit him. He was breathing, and when she felt for his heartbeat, it was strong.

She shook him gently, and his eyes fluttered open. He winced when he saw her. Harlow pressed her finger to his lips. He saw the moons, and Harlow read the panic in his face. They were supposed to be long gone by now.

His eyes were unfocused and drooping, so she dragged him back towards Finn and the others. Ari squeezed her hand hard, shaking his head. He didn't know what had happened. Then he went deadly still, staring at something behind her.

Harlow felt the shade first: she was already cold, but it felt as though someone dragged an icicle down her spine. She turned to the front of the cave, slowly, pushing Ari behind her. He was injured and she was not.

Shades weren't like ghosts, or even poltergeists, both of which could affect the corporeal world only in small ways. Instead, shades were violent, predatory spirits, prone to killing people. This one was tall and shrouded in darkness, but it had been a sorcière in life. Its eyes glowed with telltale dark aethereal light.

Harlow wasn't sure what she was going to do, but she was the only one capable of protecting the group, so she'd do whatever it took. It was strange that it hadn't killed them already, though. From everything she knew about shades, they killed quickly, feeding on the life force of their victims. She summoned her shadows and stepped forward. When she opened her mouth to ask what it wanted, futile though that might be, she found she couldn't speak.

The shade sent inky, aethereal power flowing into her mouth, silencing her. This was another danger with Shades—they could siphon magic—and this one was using hers.

*Silence*, the shade cautioned inside her head. *You are being hunted.*

Harlow couldn't believe the shade could communicate with her. She took another step forward, trying to make out its features. At first, she thought it wore a cloak of feathers, but now that she was closer, she practically gasped. The "cloak" was the shade's wings. It had dark, feathered wings that sprung from its back. And they looked familiar, like her own wings in her Feriant form.

A shade's manifestation could be odd; they didn't always appear as they did in life. Sometimes they morphed into strange hybrid creatures, like this one had done.

*Were you like me in life?* she tried asking it. *A Strider?*

*No, child*, the shade answered, its eyes glowing with that aethereal light once more. *I was a Feriant.*

Rakul and Vivia's child Inasa had been, as Cian said, "pure shadow, a creature of the limen." If this shade were Inasa's spirit, it might explain why it was helping them. *Inasa Kimaris? Were you Inasa in life?*

Inside her head, Harlow heard laughter. *No, I told you, I am a Feriant. Inasa Kimaris was a witch. Sleep now. I'll keep watch.*

The shade's logic made no sense. The Feriant was a Strider's alternae, a side effect of Striders being a combination of sorcière, Illuminated and draconic heritage, through Vivia, Rakul, and their many progeny. A Feriant was a part of a witch, not something independent. The shade waved a hand, and Harlow stumbled into Ari, who helped her to the ground. Sleep took over almost instantly. Harlow tried her best to fight it, but could not keep her eyes open.

# CHAPTER TWENTY-FIVE

"... It seemed like the shade was *speaking* to her, and we both fell back asleep."

Harlow opened her eyes slowly. Ari and Finn were huddled together by the fire, whispering. She sat up. "Where's Larkin?"

Finn held out a hand to her, pulling her into a seated position. "Doing her business. Right outside the cave." He grimaced, letting her know that he could hear Larkin perfectly well. "Ari says a shade got to us last night. What happened?"

Harlow didn't know. That was the problem. "It was the spirit of a Feriant, or at least that's what it said." She looked to Ari for confirmation.

The Wraith shook his head. "I didn't hear a word it said. I could barely make out its shape."

Larkin stepped into the mouth of the cave. It was obvious she'd been listening, but she didn't comment as she sat down next to Harlow.

"The shade was the spirit of a Feriant," Harlow repeated. "But it didn't appear as any of the Striders I've ever met. It had wings, but retained humanoid attributes..."

"Like the Ventyr?" Larkin asked.

Harlow ran a hand over one of her braids, and finding it messy, began the work of unraveling it as she spoke. "Sort of, except it had bird wings."

"And you're sure it was a shade?" Finn asked.

Ari nodded vigorously. "Yes, the creature had all the hallmarks of a shade. It was able to use magic, appeared to be intact, unlike ghasts, and it was capable of complex thought and speech."

"It wasn't violent or angry though..." Larkin's words came out somewhere between a statement and a question, as she rummaged through her pack for breakfast. "But of course, shades don't actually have to be violent or angry."

She found the energy bars she'd been searching for and handed them out. "It's just that they usually are. They have to have a strong motivation for being here, and things like anger and revenge are the typical motivators."

"Then what was this Strider's motivation?" Finn asked.

Harlow cleared her throat, needing to clarify. "Actually, the shade was very specific that it wasn't a Strider. It said it wasn't a witch."

Larkin's eyes widened. "Was it Inasa Kimaris?"

Harlow shook her head. "It said it wasn't. It also said we were being hunted, and then put me back to sleep."

Finn and Ari exchanged a look. Harlow glared pointedly at them until Finn spoke. "There's evidence of that outside. Footprints. They circle around the entire area, then head south. But they never came close to the cave."

Harlow's skin prickled and her hands felt clammy. Nausea rose in her throat. She handed her energy bar back to Larkin. "I think I'm going to skip breakfast, until after we've teleported."

Larkin nodded solemnly. "Makes sense."

Harlow stood, needing to stretch her legs. "Are we sticking with the plan and making three jumps?"

Finn shook his head. "Seems pointless now. We know we're being tracked. We might as well get on with things."

"So, straight to the Gate of Lithraea?" Larkin asked.

Ari scrunched his face at the sound of the name. "Seventeen hells, is that what it's called?"

Harlow nodded as she repacked her blanket. "Yes, the Gate's name is an old human word."

Now Ari was curious, which wasn't a surprise. Ari was always curious. "For what?"

Harlow looked up. "Not what. *Who*. Lithraea was a human goddess of death and poison, in this part of the world." She glanced at Finn. "Before the Ventyr came." Finn looked as though he might apologize, but Harlow kept speaking. "The Gate was built by an ancient human society as an entrance to the 'rocks of Lithraea,' which are a deep canyon that was once the bottom of an ocean. The cult of Lithraea believed the ritual of traveling through them was a rite of passage."

"I've never heard of Lithraea," Ari murmured. Shifters were notoriously more religious than other immortals, and Ari was obviously disturbed there were deities he hadn't heard of.

"Then you haven't heard of her nasty little servants, the vvyk," Harlow added. She and Finn had talked about their path once, and only once, because while it was technically safe, it would not be pleasant. "They're said to put travelers through an existential crisis. It's what made getting through the Gate a ritual."

Ari's glared at Finn. "That's what you were talking about? When you mentioned the possibility of hallucinations?" Finn nodded as Ari's mouth fell open. Harlow saw it coming—the adventure junkie in Ari had taken over. The shifter loved a challenge. "How have I never heard of this place?"

Larkin glanced at him, then shot an apologetic look to Finn. "You wouldn't have. It's all human lore. The Illuminated would have most people believe humans were without culture before their arrival."

Finn shrugged. "Hopefully, that's all going to change when the Fifth Order can get Connor and Pasiphae to sit down and talk."

"Does anyone really think that's gonna work?" Ari asked.

"Don't start this again," Finn cautioned. "I can't today, Arebos."

The Wraith nodded, but Harlow sensed this was a sore subject between them. Finn tended to believe his father was more inclined towards peaceful resolutions than almost anyone else. Harlow didn't argue with him over it. "We should go."

"I'm going to pee real quick," Ari said.

How Harlow had missed her body screaming to relieve herself, she didn't know, but she did actually have to go. "Me too," Harlow and Larkin said in unison.

"You just went," Harlow chided, pushing Larkin toward the cave's opening.

"I have to go again," Larkin whined, sounding like she was ten.

Finn made an "ick" face when they all walked out together. It wasn't as though they were watching each other, but it felt safer to go together now that they'd confirmed that someone had tracked them to this location. When Harlow was finished, she waited for Larkin. The sound of the waves on the shoreline below filled Harlow's ears. The wind was so cold all of her appendages had gone numb.

She only heard Larkin's footsteps when she was nearly upon her, which signaled to her just how careful they needed to be. Harlow looked around, carefully feeling through the threads for any signs of disturbance. It wasn't her talent to track aethereal power that way, but Sam had given her a few hints. She found Ari easily, but only their connection, not how near or far he might be. Trying to find anyone who might be watching them, or worse, hunting them, would likely be impossible at this juncture. She tucked her arm in Larkin's as they waited for Ari.

When he rounded the corner he'd disappeared behind, there was an intense look in his eyes Harlow could not identify. As he approached, his voice was low. "Laugh at what I'm saying and continue moving back towards the cave. We're being watched."

Larkin laughed, and Harlow thought she looked completely natural. Harlow did her best to smile, but thoughts of the burning safehouse invaded her ability to pretend. Whoever, or whatever, was following them had certainly tracked them now that they'd all left the cave. They were in danger now, perhaps more than they'd been overnight, with the shade's unlikely protection.

When they returned to the cave, Ari whispered what he'd tracked to Finn, who nodded. They huddled close to him, listening carefully as he explained the jump they'd have to make to get to the Gates of Lithraea at the same time.

"We'll be tracked," he explained. "I don't see how we can get around that."

Larkin's face pulled together into an unpleasant knot. She was thinking, not unhappy. "How does one track teleportation? Does the jump itself leave a signature?"

Harlow wasn't sure what her sister was getting at, but it was an excellent question. Finn appeared to be thinking along the same lines, because instead of blowing past the question, he paused to give it thought. "Yes, and no. You'd have to be aware that someone had teleported and be well versed in recognizing teleportation signatures. It's not exactly easy to do, but not hard or rare either."

Larkin nodded thoughtfully. "So, if say, you didn't have a clear line of sight on the people you were trying to follow, you might not immediately know they'd jumped."

A slow smile came over Finn's face. "Exactly. And the trail gets harder to follow by the minute, after the jump is made."

Vivia had been correct—Larkin was skilled as both a strate-gist and an adventurer. Harlow asked, "So we trick whoever's watching into thinking we're still here?" She looked to the back of the cave, where several small boulders stood away from the wall, and walked towards them, thoughtful. Finn followed close behind.

"Could you move these?" she asked.

"Easily," he answered.

"Then sit," she ordered. "I need a model to work with and some cover at the front of the cave."

Larkin and Ari both moved, piling the last of their wood onto the dying embers from the previous night's fire. Harlow's shadows danced around her fingers, thrilled to be put to work. She transformed the first boulder to look like Finn. It wasn't perfect, but from a few steps away, it was a good approximation. The fire was roaring now and each of the members of the party took their turn posing for Harlow as she created stone versions of them.

Finn moved each around the fire, and they surveyed their handiwork from the back of the cave.

Larkin laughed, her shoulders shaking giddily. "I think it might work... but..." She frowned a little, her pretty face scrunching unpleasantly again. "What about the sound? It will be silent here when we leave."

An air of apprehension clouded Finn's countenance. "I can help with that." Swiftly, his fingers moved, glowing with celestial light as he pulled threads.

Harlow had no idea he could weave illusions. The Illumi-nated had the capability, of course, to work with threads as sorcière did, but the fact was that they typically *didn't*. They had so much power otherwise that it was atypical to see them actu-ally do magic of any kind, unless it was violent.

When Finn's fingers stilled, she understood why. For all intents and purposes, it sounded as though a lively conversation was happening around the fire about human folklore. A continuation of what they'd talked about before. The effect was nearly flawless. If people knew the Illuminated could do such spells, they'd never trust them again.

"We should go now," Finn murmured, picking up his pack. He avoided Harlow's questioning eyes. "It will loop in about five minutes. I'm not sure how obvious it will be. I've never woven something quite so complex."

Harlow's heart felt as though it would skip a beat. She grabbed Finn's arm. "I didn't know you could do that."

Under her fingers, the muscles in his forearm tensed. "I know. It's not easy to do, Harlow. And I have a knack for it, but I rarely use the skill. It's a struggle to maintain."

There was a film of sweat beading on his forehead as he spoke. He was already struggling to maintain it. She felt guilty, but her first reaction was relief. The Ventyr were powerful enough without being capable of effortless illusion.

After adjusting her pack, Larkin pulled a few threads. Harlow's second sight revealed the spell itself as she worked. Larkin was adding to Finn's work, adjusting it little by little, giving it strength as she went. She was making it so he didn't have to work so hard to maintain it, but also something else.

When her fingers stilled, she smiled. "Now when it loops, it will do so with variation. If someone is paying close attention to what's being said, it will sound like we're going over old ground, circling back to old topics, so to speak."

Ari chuckled. "Typical sorcière and Illuminated."

Larkin snorted her agreement, taking her place at the center of the tight knot Finn and Harlow made. Ari joined her, his arms wrapping tightly around Larkin's waist as Finn and Harlow joined hands, pressing their bodies close to Larkin and Ari's. This was the safest way to assure they arrived at the Gate at the exact same time. They'd leave a stronger trail, but with the illusion, it might buy them some time.

The jump was quicker than the previous had been. Combining their power made it smoother, as well. When they were assured everyone was all right, Finn urged them on. It was a shame they were in such a hurry; the Gate of Lithraea was situated in the heart of a primeval forest of trees so tall the sky was nearly obscured in their evergreen canopy. Snow dusted the ground here, in places, showing evidence of winter, but it was barely enough for them to leave footprints behind.

A breeze blew a few snowflakes into Harlow's hair, carrying the scent of pine in the abnormally warm air. The whole place would be pleasant, if not for the eerie silence. A forest like this should be full of birdsong and squirrels chattering at one another, but there was nothing. It was as though the forest had swallowed sound itself. And the air was so warm. Too warm— Harlow unzipped her jacket a bit.

Ari bent down to press his palm to the ground. "It's *hot*."

Larkin looked back at him. "There are hot springs here, just beneath the ground. Lithraea's Way will be even warmer."

Finn fished a compass from his pack and then nodded once he got his bearings. Without another word, the group tightened their formation, Larkin and Harlow at the center, Ari taking rear guard.

The tiny hairs on the back of Harlow's neck raised as a pall of foreboding seeped deep into her bones. All around them, she felt eyes boring into her from the shadows.

Finn glanced back at her, nodding once. *You feel it?*

*Yes*, she replied. *We're not alone here.*

*This is why Dad didn't come this way before*, he added as he faced forward. *Even he had the sense to be afraid of this place.*

*Finn*, she called out to him in her mind. *Do you know what the vvyk are?*

His head turned slightly, and she saw the grim line of his mouth, the intense glow of focus in his eyes as his free hand reached back for hers. He squeezed it once, but didn't answer her, shaking his head just once.

Next to her, Larkin had gone pale, her skin turning a sickly gray that made the light sprinkle of freckles across her nose appear as a livid rash. "They're *here*. The vvyk." Larkin's voice shook as she spoke the gnarled, guttural word. Her eyes went wide and vacant, words tumbling from her lips in a mesmerizing rhythm:

"Boughs above and flame below
*(silent are the watchers' moans)*
No currency, no seed to sow
*(writhing beasts ne'er overthrown.)*


WALK SOFTLY ON THE FOREST FLOOR
*(secret songs no longer known)*
Lest thou stay here evermore
*(though together, still alone.)*"


THEY'D ALL STOPPED TO LISTEN TO LARKIN'S eldritch words, weirdly entranced by the soft cadence of the awkward verses. Ari snapped out of the fog first, clapping a hand over Larkin's mouth. The movement brought the rest of the group around.

Larkin blinked, then pushed Ari's hand away. "What in seventeen hells was that?"

There was real fear in Finn's eyes. "The vvyk. They influence your mind."

"But what *are* they?" Ari insisted. "How do we fight them?"

Finn's answer confirmed what Harlow had suspected. "We don't. No one's ever seen the vvyk and lived to tell about it. We need to move quickly. They won't follow through the Gate."

"No, they won't. Even *they* are afraid of that path." Larkin blinked a few times, shaking her head. "What are we going to do?

Harlow was solemn. "We're going to go as fast as we can through the canyon. The vvyk will whisper all through the Way —the path through the Gate. There's no preparing for it, no trick out of it. There's only getting through it as fast as we can."

Larkin's dreamy look returned. "The verses are the warning. The vvyk capture those unworthy to enter the Gate, and their whispers... They're the test."

Harlow tried to ignore that whatever the eldritch creatures were, they were sending information through her sister.

Ari frowned. "And we don't know what happens after? There have to be accounts of people who've made it through."

"There are," Harlow replied, thankful that she had this much information from talking with the human elders. "But no one is able to speak of it afterwards... *Though together, still alone.*"

Larkin bit her bottom lip. "That's *one* interpretation."

"We don't have time to discuss interpretations," Finn spit, panic filling his eyes. "They vvyk—"

"Are the least of our worries," Ari interrupted. "Our pursuers are here."

Everyone fell silent, but Harlow heard nothing amiss. The forest was still eerily silent. Finn, however, nodded, lowering his voice to barely a whisper. "They must've guessed where we'd go —but they're off course. We've got to move, now."

Harlow's hands shook as they jogged forward, keeping their feet as quiet on the forest floor as they could. Giving into fear wasn't an option, and she'd assumed this journey would be dangerous, but she hadn't known what they'd be up against.

Somewhere, deep in the forest behind them, a sharp scream pierced the silence. "Run," Ari commanded as they entered a clearing.

Ahead, the Gate of Lithraea loomed. It was an arch carved

into the stone outcropping that rose out of the forest floor, likely a hundred feet high and intricately sculpted with writhing shapes. As they approached, Harlow's eyes ran over the carvings. If the creatures depicted were meant to be representations of the vvyk or their whispers, she deeply regretted their choice of paths. The scenes depicted on the Gate were terrifying, depraved, and beyond anything Harlow could have previously imagined.

"We are so fucked," Larkin murmured as they passed through the Gate.

No one answered, but Harlow was glad to hear her sounding more like herself. Once inside the Gate, the carvings gave way to a narrow, twisting path. It was easy to believe this had once been a deep oceanic canyon, an abyss at the bottom of the sea.

Deep grooves were worn into the rock walls that towered above them. Once, an underwater current had carved this path out over millennia. The Way was dark, narrow, and twisting. Sometimes they could walk two or three across, and others the path narrowed to such a tight space that they had to go single file, turning to the side to squeeze their way through.

Finn set a punishing pace, and for a while, Harlow wondered if the only thing threatening them here was their fear. Perhaps that was the secret of Lithraea's Way. Fear of the unknown, stoked to a fever-pitch by rumor, surrounded by a forest full of unseen horrors.

Harlow glanced at a narrow sliver of sky, and wondered briefly if she could shift and fly above the canyon, but already the winds of Gale Alley howled above them, sending alien echoes skittering through the rocky corridors below. Those echoes combined with the soft sound of moving water, though Harlow could not see a river or stream.

For a while, no one spoke. The little group seemed lost in their thoughts and the echoes of the Way. Harlow's thoughts drowned in the whisper of water. She became sure, after a time, that a river must run parallel to the canyon they traversed.

Several times, she opened her lips to ask what the others thought or if they heard it too, but could not seem to form words. This, she chalked up to exhaustion, and the wicked pace that Finn set for them. Ari still drove them from behind. Any time one of them slowed, he gently pushed them forward, saying nothing.

When Harlow glanced back at him, his eyes were as glassy as she imagined her own were. She tried to speak to him, but the words formed in her mind and died on her tongue before she could get them out. There was nothing for it; this place was an enigma.

*An enigma that had to be governed by magic.*

Harlow engaged her second sight, trying to see into the threads that made up Lithraea's Way. Much like when she'd tried to see into the waters of the Pyriphle, the magical river that flowed through Okairos' underworld, she found no threads in these rocks—only pure aethereal power made up the canyon.

The water she heard was the Pyriphle. She was sure of it now. This canyon had been cut by the river of dark power that ran through the deep vaults of the world, and into the limen, the world between. No wonder that they could not speak, that they could do little but forge ahead. The way the canyon walls rose above them would only amplify the aethereal river that flowed beneath them, around them, and perhaps, now, through them.

Harlow closed her eyes, attempting to use only her second sight to navigate. What she found was very like the limen itself. There was the canyon, and the dim glow of the others around her, but she also saw *more*. In her second sight, she saw the Pyriphle's true form. Not a river of water, but of pure aether, flowing like liquid rather than its usual mists or clouds. Her shadows sang at the sight, longing to join with it.

In her corporeal form, she moved with the group, regulating her breath, putting one foot in front of the other. In her aethereal form, she was freer. She rose above her body, above the mouth of the narrow canyon, trying to see beyond the Gate.

Deep within the ancient forest, there were disturbances. Something fought with the vvyk, unseen as the creatures themselves, obscured by the trees.

Their pursuers had not yet entered the canyon, and at this point, had lost nearly an hour of travel time. Harlow calmed at the thought and pulled back towards her corporeal form, though she did not engage her primary sight. Movement to her left caught her attention. A figure materialized in Harlow's second sight—it was the shade from the previous night.

Harlow's mouth still wouldn't form words, so she tried speaking with her mind, as she did with Finn. *Can you hear me?*

The sound the shade made sounded like laughter. *Yes, I suppose you'd call it that.*

*What are you doing here?* Harlow asked, trying to get a better look at the shade in the daylight. The shade was tall and shapely, with wide curvaceous hips and broad shoulders, across which a pair of giant wings hung like a mantle. Its face was sharply planed, with high cheekbones, an aquiline nose and generous mouth that curved into a smile.

Its features were both familiar and alien. Something about the proportions of its body was different from Okairon humanoids, and even the Ventyr. Harlow could not quite lay a finger on it until she saw the shade's ears, visible in front of its long plaited hair. They were very similar to Ari and Nox's arched ears, but more dramatically pointed. Like the Ventyr, its limbs were longer than the typical Okairon, and its movements graceful and fluid, as though it were made of nothing at all. Like all shades, its entire form was the same midnight blue as the aether.

*Rhiannon?* Harlow whispered in her mind. The shade looked a bit like the illustrations from her favorite faery lore.

Again, the shade laughed. *I have heard that name before, but it is not my own. I don't remember if I've ever had one.*

*How do you know you're not Rhiannon then?* Harlow figured

if she was going to hallucinate, for this was certainly what was happening, she might as well ask questions. Their proximity to the Pyriphle and the canyon's ability to amplify the supernatural would likely cause hallucinations, which aligned perfectly with the ancient human practice of using the canyon as a coming of age ritual. Combined with the fear of the forest, and the vvyk, it would be a powerful spiritual experience.

*An interesting question*, the shade mused. *I suppose I do not know if I am or am not for certain, but those names are not familiar to me.*

*But you know you are a Feriant?* Harlow asked, trying to tease apart what her unconscious mind was trying to tell her.

*Of course*, the shade answered. *That is not something I could forget.* Its wings flexed, and in Harlow's second sight they caught the light, their feathers iridescent as an oil slick.

Harlow tried another tack. There was some logic here her mind wanted to impart, some collection of information just at the precipice of revelation. *What is a Feriant then?*

The shade's smile turned devious. *You think this is a game, child. A conjure of your mind, due to the river or the canyon. Make no mistake, Harlow Krane, I am real as you are.*

The shade's form began to dissolve. Harlow reached out, though she knew it was futile to try to touch a shade, or a figment of her imagination. To her surprise, her fingers closed around flesh and bone. The shade's luminous eyes widened, its lips parting to reveal a set of wickedly sharp canines.

*How interesting you are. Seek the truth of this world and your place in it and perhaps I shall enlighten you.* The creature slipped out of her grip, dissolving into nothing more than shadow. Harlow shook her head as her second sight receded, her primary sight returning to show the canyon widening ahead.

# CHAPTER TWENTY-SIX

A head of her, Finn broke into a jog. They'd been walking quickly, and now Harlow caught sight of the state her companions were in. Each was in a state of confusion and disarray, their eyes clouded and their lips moving, though no sound came out. When Finn ran, they ran, and Harlow followed.

The canyon widened further, the dark rocks opening to a snowy scene. Outside the canyon, a cyclone of snow raged, limiting visibility severely. Finn skidded to a halt, throwing his arms out wide to stop Harlow and the others from passing him. Larkin's feet slid, and she let out a panicked shriek, but Ari pulled her back before she fell.

A sudden change of the wind's direction revealed what Larkin had seen when she slipped. The canyon had abruptly opened onto the edge of a gouge in the earth. Harlow's mind tried to make sense of what she saw amidst the snow, but it took Larkin's shuddering words to clarify it for her. "Would we call that a crevasse?"

"It's more of a ravine, I think," Ari said, his usual humor returning now that he had Larkin righted and secure.

Finn's head tilted to the side as he appraised. "Seems like a gorge to me."

"What in seventeen hells is wrong with all of you?" Harlow sputtered. They'd nearly ran straight off the edge of what very much looked like a cliff.

Larkin raised her eyebrows. "I forgot. Harlow is scared of heights."

Her little sister said it like it explained a hissy fit, rather than a completely natural reaction to finding oneself unexpectedly at the edge of a cliff in a storm, while being pursued by an unknown enemy through dangerous territory. And she wasn't scared of heights. Not technically, anyway, especially not since she gained the ability to shift forms.

What Harlow *was* afraid of was her humanoid body's natural proclivity towards clumsiness. That she would step wrong and fall to her death. After slipping on the Ledge of Wishes beneath the Order of Mysteries as a child, it was a reasonable fear, despite her new ability to turn into a giant bird. Harlow let her gaze follow Larkin's, only to find a nightmare waiting for her.

"I'm sorry, Harls," Finn murmured as he moved to stand by her side. He stared across a narrow stone bridge that crossed the ravine. It was ancient, without side rails or handholds of any kind, and looked to be falling apart. Harlow watched as he looked in every direction, knowing his Ventyr eyes saw more than hers. He was looking for another way. The instant he came to the conclusion that this was the only way across, he spoke. "I could carry you."

She did want him to, but the looks on both Larkin and Ari's faces deterred her, different as they were. Ari's eyes were full of pity. The graceful shifter had probably never been afraid of something like an old bridge in his whole life. He was utterly fearless. She hated the idea of Ari thinking she was so weak that she couldn't make it across the bridge. Harlow knew very well that he didn't think her fear was shameful, but both he and Finn would think about her differently if she couldn't master it.

Larkin, on the other hand, looked hopeful. Hopeful that her sister would make her proud. Harlow couldn't let her down. "No," she said, her words firm and steady. "I can do this."

"Okay." Finn pulled his hunk of adamantine from his pack. "Harlow, can you form crampons for us? We'll need them now."

*To keep from slipping to our deaths,* a voice inside her warned. She ignored it, letting her shadows loose to reform each hunk of metal to form the correct size crampon for each of her companions' boots. When they'd affixed the spiky contraptions to their feet, Finn went first.

"Step slowly and carefully," he warned.

The bridge wasn't so narrow that most people would be truly afraid. Of course, the drop was harrowing. But even at its narrowest, the structure was at least two to three feet wide. The trouble was that as soon as Harlow thought about how easy it would be to slip over the edge, the more unsteady she felt.

Despite her growing fear, she dutifully put one foot in front of the other, staring a few feet ahead, refusing to let her eyes wander right or left. They made good progress, and ahead of her, Finn, and Larkin had all finished the crossing when a low rumble sounded behind her. Harlow startled, and her crampon skidded off the rock directly beneath her next step. She fell to her knees, her body freezing with fear.

Behind her, Ari called out. "It's just a rock slide below. You okay, Harlow?"

She nodded, but couldn't speak. Ari didn't get closer, but he spoke in low and soothing tones, trying to help her get up. "Just clear your mind," the shifter soothed. "You can do this."

But she couldn't *just clear her mind.* She'd never been able to manage such a feat. That was the problem.

"Harlow," Larkin called. "You have to try to get up."

Did she think Harlow didn't know that? Did she really think

that every single bit of her wasn't battling to rise and keep going? But her sister kept yelling, and Finn joined her, along with Ari. They were trying to cheer her on, cajole her into just being fine. But that had never worked for Harlow. She'd always needed a little more time, a bit more patience, and had a steeper learning curve than everyone else.

Every shouted word made her flinch, and every flinch shifted her closer to the edge of the bridge as the wind picked up, buffeting her about. In her peripheral vision, she saw Finn making motions to shut everyone up. His silence was the worst, his clear calculation of how he was going to save her showing in every move he made. A part of her mind, that nasty part that had always been with her, whispered terrible things.

Things that tortured her late at night about the mistakes she'd made. The waste of space and talent she obviously was. Deeper and deeper her shame went, until she was at the bottom of the abyss. In her mind's eye, she stood alone at the back door of an apartment building in Nuva Troi, the only being that loved her being taken away from her, while she beat uselessly at the door.

Useless. That was a good word. *Useless.* Why was she even here? Tears pricked the corners of her eyes as her skin flushed, and that word repeated over and over, an erratic, panicked beat.

*Useless.*

*Useless.*

*Useless.*

A dark presence appeared next to her. The words slowed as the shade appeared. *What are you doing, little witch?*

"Baking a tart," she murmured.

*Humor,* it replied. *So you are not so far gone.*

It made a certain kind of sense. Her companions were silent, still figuring out what to do with her, she assumed, while she hallucinated.

*Useless.*

*No more of that,* the shade pleaded. *You are making my head hurt with your misery. The last thing you need is to draw the ghasts. The ones in these mountains are hideous.*

Again, it made a point. Harlow would hate for the last thing she saw before she tumbled to her death to be a ghast. The shade crouched down in front of her, craning its oddly beautiful face so that it looked straight into her own. *Why do you not use your wings?*

A gust of wind howled through the ravine, sending snowflakes flying. "Shifting now would be suicide," she murmured. "I would just get blown into the rocks."

*It is not required that you shift the entire way,* the shade explained, gesturing to its own magnificent feathers. *Manifest your wings, and use them to keep you balanced.*

Again, this figment of her imagination made sense, and if she could do it, she would. Harlow choked on a sob. "I don't know how to do that. I've only ever shifted fully."

*Is that so?* Its tone was less incredulous, and more probing.

Because of course, the thing was her, and she was it, and it knew what she did. When she'd made contact with the Pyriphle in Nea Sterlis, she'd partially shifted. That was before she'd made the Claim and initiated her Feriant side. She'd been able to do it then, albeit without her control, but if she could do it then, why couldn't she do it now? The truth was, she'd never tried.

"I'm different from you," Harlow argued, afraid of trying and failing, being stuck here forever, or falling.

*Yes,* the shade argued back. *But we are also much the same. Would it hurt to try?*

All Harlow ever did was try. She tried and failed. Over and over... until things worked. *Until they worked.* Yes, that was it. Harlow wasn't the kind of person who got things right on the first try, and she often struggled, but she stuck with things—and when she did, she excelled.

Harlow closed her eyes and thought about how she made

the shift the first few times after the Claim. She concentrated on only her wings. Nothing happened. She opened her eyes to ask the shade what it thought she should do, but the creature had disappeared, which startled Harlow further. Just like a figment of her imagination to disappear when she needed the advice most. She appreciated her brain's addled attempt to help her, but she wished it wouldn't be quite so jarring in its efforts.

Still. She could try again. Perhaps something was wrong with what she'd done before. A slight pressure on her back reminded her that her pack was there. That shouldn't matter, but at the back of Harlow's mind, a list of the things she'd lose in the pack if she simply shifted wings through it played like a ticker-tape.

Harlow closed her eyes and slipped out of her pack, moving it slowly to the front of her body. Then she searched out the rest of the worries she had about this idea, letting them all gather in front of her, rather than trying to tamp them down.

Her body wasn't technically engineered to have wings, as it was. It wasn't anatomically possible. But that's where science met magic, because it definitely wasn't anatomically possible for her body parts to turn into a giant bird's body parts. So maybe she could manifest her wings now. She would have to hold them tight to her body at first, until she gauged the direction of the wind.

But that too would be easier with her wings. Their feathers were sensitive, sending messages to her brain about her surroundings in the air in her Feriant form. It would be the same in this form, in this way. Her wings belonged to her, no matter if she kept her humanoid form, or shifted fully into the Feriant.

One by one, her doubts and logical concerns rose and then floated away, acknowledged, validated and addressed. It wasn't the quickest way to go about things, but it was her way. Thinking things through if she had to, even if it was frustrating and annoying. *That* was what worked for her.

A loud rip and a rush of cold wind on her back told Harlow

*something* was happening. Soft feathers brushed the skin of her cheek. She opened her eyes; her wings had appeared. There was no pain, no drama. Just her wings, cradling her in their safety as she stood, perfectly balanced for the first time in her life. Each step she took forward was subtly steadier than any step she'd ever taken in her humanoid form.

Harlow didn't realize how off-balance she often was until this very moment. Her wings flexed and contracted with the wind, moving by instinct, just as they did in her Feriant form. Before she knew it, her feet were on a wider path and steps later she was in Finn's arms.

He kissed her hard, clinging to her. "I knew you could figure it out."

When he pulled away, Ari was standing behind them. "The shade," he breathed. "She helped you."

Harlow's breath caught in her lungs. "What?"

Finn frowned. "Didn't you see the winged woman talking to you?"

Harlow searched his face, then Larkin and Ari's. It was obvious they'd all seen the shade. "You saw her too?"

Larkin nodded. "Very clearly. Why wouldn't we?"

Harlow's heart beat faster. "Did you see her in the Way?"

Larkin spoke up first. "I think we were all lost in our own... thoughts. I wasn't aware any of you even existed."

Finn stroked her cheek, concerned. "You saw her there too?"

Harlow nodded. "But I assumed she was a hallucination, a part of the magic of the place. What did the rest of you see?"

No one answered. Their eyes averted. Whatever they'd seen and heard, it was like the legends. They couldn't talk about it. They'd experienced something she hadn't. The wind howled louder now, the cyclone in the ravine worsening by the minute. Across the ravine, four tall figures exited the Way.

"Can you make them out?" Ari asked Finn, all talk of the

shade and Harlow's crossing forgotten. He had to raise his voice above the storm.

"No," Finn shouted, grabbing Harlow's hand. "I'm sorry," he said softly.

Before she could ask what for, his arm stretched out in front of him, glowing with both aethereal and celestial light. The ground beneath them shook, the tremor radiating towards the narrow pathway they'd just crossed. Harlow felt her wings disappear, and saw the stone bridge crumble with their pursuers on it as her vision went completely black.

∾

Her eyes opened to the world upside down. Finn carried her, thrown over his shoulders like a sack of flour. She looked around—they were on a rocky path, snow swirling wildly around them. Someone had wrapped her in a blanket so she couldn't move.

"Finn?" she shouted, after calling his name in a normal tone didn't yield results. The wind was very loud, after all.

"We're almost there," he shouted. "Just let me carry you the rest of the way."

Behind them, Ari grinned, waving at her through the quickly drifting snow. She'd never live it down if Ari knew she'd let Finn carry her after waking.

"Put me *down*!" she yelled, squirming wildly.

Finn obliged, simply letting her fall into the bank of snow in front of him. Harlow spluttered, breaking free of her blanket. When she manifested her wings again, it was easier—they sprung free from her back, casting the blanket into the screaming storm.

"Thanks," Finn yelled. "That was *my* blanket."

He was smiling though, and pointing to the reason why it didn't really matter. Harlow turned. Rising above them was the observatory, and just a few feet ahead of them, at the base of the mountain, was a gondola lift. Ari ran towards the little shed at the base of the lift. As the rest of them trudged through the snow, the cars began to move, one making its way towards them. They'd made it to ORAIS.

# CHAPTER TWENTY-SEVEN

T hough it had hardly been two days since they left Sanctum, it *felt* like years since Harlow had been indoors. She hadn't realized how much the sound of the wind's incessant howling had plagued her until it went silent. The ride in the gondola had been a pleasant break, but being inside the actual observatory was blissfully quiet.

They'd entered ORAIS through the glass front doors, which popped open with a simple scan of Finn's left retina. Now, he and Larkin were standing in front of a podium at the center of an enormous atrium, arguing about the logic of code breaking, which was yet another of Larkin's hidden talents. When Harlow expressed surprise at how much she knew about the subject, she'd just shrugged and said it felt like reading music.

The podium at the center of the room, which Finn kept calling a "terminal," housed a computer that could be used to open the facility. Though the retinal scan had remained the same as the last time Finn had been here, the code to enter the building itself had changed. Granted, being out of the wind and snow was a blessing, but every door out of the atrium of ORAIS was locked, and the room was nearly as cold as it was outside—

and Finn and Larkin's argument echoed off the glass walls and marble floors. Worse, when Ari had volunteered to run a perimeter patrol, more to escape Finn and Larkin's argument than anything else, they'd found they were now also locked *inside* the foyer.

Harlow and Ari considered setting up their tents. "We'd be warmer inside them, I think," Ari reasoned.

Harlow agreed, looking around the atrium. "We'll be warmer if we try to insulate them." She pointed to the cushions on half a dozen upholstered benches. "If we set up the tent, then build a cushion fort around it, it'll insulate the tent. Maybe we should put some on the floor beneath the tent as well?"

"For cush?" Ari asked, a sparkle in his eye. "Your old bones are tired after the hike?"

Harlow snickered. "For cush—and extra insulation. These floors are like ice."

"Let's do it. Let's build a pillow fort." Ari waved his hand in front of his body dramatically, deepening his voice. "The most epic pillow fort on Okairos."

"The pillow fort at the end of the world," Harlow added.

It was amazing how much Ari felt like family and how good it felt to be joking right now. There was something comforting about the fact that they'd had a harrowing two days, and yet they were still making jokes about pillow forts. If this really was the end of the world for them, at least she'd die laughing.

"Come on. If we get this done quickly, we have a delicious dinner of...." Harlow pointed to Larkin, who'd glanced over at them, a little look of jealousy creeping into her eyes at the fun Harlow and Ari had been having.

"Energy bars!" Larkin chimed in, smiling now.

"Energy bars," Harlow repeated as she collected cushions. "Yes, we have another delicious dinner of energy bars to look forward to."

"But not too many," Ari called from across the room.

"Because we are running dangerously low on food."

Finn had gone quiet, watching them gather cushions. He was somewhere else entirely, lost in thought. Suddenly, his eyes lit up, and he typed something else into the terminal. The crystal chandeliers above them lit, but slowly, like they were on a dimmer. Inside the observatory, more lights came on, as the sound of mechanical humming purred through the building. The unmistakable sound of doors unlocking surrounded them.

Ari threw down the pillows he carried and rushed to the doors that led outside. He pulled them, found they opened, and then closed each of them in turn, bolting the manual lock as he went.

"No need for anyone to follow us inside," he murmured to Larkin as she helped.

The four of them gathered their packs, leaving the bench cushions and the unassembled tent on the floor. Finn reached out for the double doors that opened onto the main entryway to the observatory. As he did, a voice spoke. "Welcome back, Finbar."

"Hello, Stella," Finn replied as he walked into the front hall. He turned, spinning easily on the beautiful marble floors. "Aren't you coming?"

"Who, exactly, was that?" Ari asked.

Finn looked around. "Oh, that's Stella, the AI that runs the observatory. If you get lost or need help, you can just ask her."

Everyone just stared at Finn, not moving a muscle to enter the building.

"Like in a science fiction movie?" Larkin asked.

Finn shrugged. "I guess. Except Stella is real. Stella, meet Larkin and Harlow Krane and Arebos Flynn."

"Welcome, friends of Finbar," the disembodied voice said.

Finn cringed at the use of his full name. "Stella, my dad isn't here. Can you just call me Finn?"

The voice answered. "If Connor McKay is not here, then I

may do as you ask, Finn."

Finn smiled at the group. "She can't hear you unless you say her name. It's not as creepy as it seems, I promise."

"How do you know?" Larkin asked, stepping gingerly inside the lobby.

"Know what?" Finn asked as everyone followed him down the front hallway and into a lounge with a panoramic view of the storm outside. If the sky ever cleared, the window would provide a gorgeous view of the mountaintops surrounding them.

"That she's stopped listening," Larkin explained as she peeled off her coat. It was warming up inside the lounge. Finn picked up a tablet off a long, rustic wooden console table that stretched across the back of a tailored beige sectional that faced the semi-circle of floor to ceiling windows. The room was beautiful, with a vaulted wood ceiling that peaked at the center of the circular room. A long rectangular dining table, heavily built with clean lines and surrounded by upholstered white chairs, sat at the opposite end of the room.

The center of the room was sunken, a fireplace at its center, surrounded by a circular couch, covered in plush cream-colored cushions and throw blankets. A bar at the back of the room lit up as Finn tapped several buttons on the tablet he'd picked up. Next, the fireplace lit, crackling merrily. Everything was done in a luxurious style that had been popular about seventy years ago, with clean lines and what architects and designers of the time had called a "modern" style. Now, it was charmingly retro, preserved beautifully, as all things ruled by the Illuminated were.

Finn set the tablet down momentarily to take off his jacket. "Might as well get comfortable. It will take Stella a bit to procure food for us, but we can make coffee now, if you'd like."

Harlow's mouth fell open as her eyes fell on the espresso machine at the bar. She suddenly wanted a latte more than anything in the entire world.

"But there's no milk, of course," she whispered, unzipping her jacket. She left it on one of the stools in front of the bar, with her pack. "Stella," she whispered. "You don't have milk for the espresso bar, do you? Or coffee beans for that matter?"

"Yes, Harlow Krane. I do," the voice replied. "You will find beans in the cabinet next to the espresso machine, and I will retrieve milk for you now."

Harlow found the beans, exactly where Stella said they would be, and went about grinding them and preparing the espresso machine. It appeared to be in working order as she busied herself making her first shot. When she opened the door to the stainless steel refrigerator, she found exactly one glass bottle of milk inside, and nothing more. The expiration date on the bottle was ten days from the current day.

"Stella," she asked, her mind reeling. "Where did you get this milk?"

"I made it," the voice replied. "I regret that it is a plant milk, but it has been calibrated to steam well for your latte, Harlow Krane."

"Just Harlow, Stella," Harlow murmured, taking a small sip of the milk. It was perfectly fresh. "You can just call me Harlow."

"As you wish, Harlow."

The work of making the perfect latte distracted her from what felt like a surreal change. They'd gone from burning safe houses to extreme weather to haunted forests and crumbling bridges. Now *this*. Some kind of retro-futuristic resort the Illuminated had created to—what? Hang out in? She'd thought ORAIS would be more like a lab, spare and utilitarian.

As she took the first sip of her latte, she wasn't sure why she was surprised. She stared at the luxurious wood that paneled the walls. It was a rare variety, a rich and creamy pale shade that made her chest ache with nostalgia for something she'd never seen, a time she'd never lived through, but seen in photos of the maters before they'd decided to have children.

"Are you staring at the wall, Harls?" Finn asked from the bar.

Harlow turned slowly, taking the lounge in again. The others were gathered in the center of the room, drinking water from tall glasses and popping popcorn in foil bubbles in the fireplace. It could be Yule, as festive as it was. Light jazz played quietly from a speaker as the afternoon sun dimmed in the sky. Lamps cast glowing pools of light on the marble floors.

"Why didn't you explain that it was like this?" Harlow asked, keeping her voice low.

Finn shrugged. "I wasn't sure what it would be like now. Turns out, it's exactly like it was when I was a kid."

Harlow couldn't muster words. She was too tired.

"I also didn't want to get any of our hopes up that there might be conveniences like food and beds here. For all I knew, my father had this place torn apart."

"Did you say *beds*?" Harlow asked. "If there are showers, I will die happy."

Finn smiled. "There's all of that and more." He called down to the others. "Come take a little tour of ORAIS with me, everyone."

They followed him back through the front entryway through a large archway and into a smaller vestibule, where two long hallways forked into two diverging paths.

Finn pointed left. "Down there are the living quarters. Every room is essentially the same, so pick anywhere. For now, let me show you the observatory and the offices and labs."

They took the right-hand passage, a glass skyway that led to another building entirely. The domed observatory was visible from this angle, as was the steep drop down the mountainside. Harlow's wings had disappeared, leaving her back open to the cool air of the skyway. She'd have to see if there were extra clothes anywhere here later on.

They saw the observatory first, which was home to an enormous telescope and a veritable command center of computers.

"Stella won't be able to fire this up for another day or two, probably," Finn explained. He'd been telling them about the way ORAIS's generator worked in the kind of detail that had Harlow thinking about other things.

"Stella," Finn prompted. "What's the progress on the perimeter wards?"

"It is ninety-two percent complete, Finn. I will inform you upon completion, as you asked," the AI replied.

They followed Finn out of the observatory and into another atrium, decorated similarly to the one they'd entered through. Finn pointed to three hallways in succession. "Offices and archives that way, another kitchen and lounge, and then the labs. I think we probably all need some rest. We can get started going through things tomorrow."

Everyone was quiet as they moved back towards the lounge. Finn explained that the fridge should be filling up with the food he'd asked for, and what they could expect from Stella's capabilities. She was a combination of state-of-the-art tech and magic, with the ability to replicate nearly any food, though some things took longer and her generators were still charging.

Harlow hoped she could find a replacement for her sweater. There hadn't been room in the packs for extra clothes, and Harlow would be cranky if she had to darn her damaged sweater herself. Of course, she'd use magic to do it, but still, it was a tedious idea and would take nearly the same amount of time doing it by hand would, since she wasn't talented with textiles like Enzo was.

She missed him and Riley intensely. They'd have loved to see ORAIS. Enzo had made Harlow watch every vintage spy movie they could get their hands on as kids, and there was an Auvray DeVille classic where the titular spy came to an observatory much like this one, only to find the villain was training an army of lingerie models to be super soldiers.

Auvray had seduced at least three of them before the film

was over, of course. She *was* an international super-spy, after all. Harlow laughed softly thinking about it. They'd reached the lounge once more, the sun having set quickly below the jagged mountains that encircled the observatory. Ari and Larkin were busy asking Stella about the different kinds of foods she could provide. They played off one another's suggestions in a comfortable way that made it feel like being home.

"I need a new sweater," Harlow told Finn, catching his arm. "And I think I need to lay down before I eat, if that's okay."

One hand curved over the back of her head, tender as he searched her face. "You need some alone time? Or would you rather talk about what happened today?"

Harlow definitely did not want to talk. "I need to fix my sweater and lay down."

He nodded. "You remember the way to the bedrooms?"

It was her turn to nod. "I do."

He pressed a kiss to her forehead. "I know I said they were essentially all the same, but the last door on the left has my favorite view. There should be extra clothes in the closet at the end of the hall. My mom always kept extra stuff in there. Or there's ORAIS sweaters in the front hall."

Harlow narrowed her eyes at Finn, suspiciously. "Who made those?"

Finn shrugged. "Aislin, I guess. She had an idea that this would be a world-class scientific research station someday, but you know Connor…"

There was no doubt in Harlow's mind that whatever Connor McKay's vision for the future of ORAIS had been, he'd had no issue disappointing his wife. It was hard to understand how the two of them had stayed together for so long or how they maintained the fiction of an aligned relationship when in private they were almost permanently at odds. She kissed Finn quickly, grateful for the fact that they would not end up in a similar position.

# CHAPTER TWENTY-EIGHT

T he ORAIS sweaters were unsurprisingly done in good taste. Aislin had an excellent sense of style, and they had a kind of timeless quality to them that made the slightly retro look eternal. But the crewneck on them was unworkable for Harlow. Just looking at the neck made her feel as though she was being choked.

The closet in the sleeping quarters was Harlow's next stop. She'd had no expectations when Finn mentioned "the closet"— but this was a whole godsdamned *room*. It rivaled the editor's closet at *Ordinas* magazine, which she, like everyone else in Nuva Troi, had seen dozens of videos of over the years. When she and Enzo were estranged, she'd enjoyed the cameos he'd made on the magazine's web series called "The *Ordinas* Closet."

This closet would blow her best friend's mind. Not only for its size, which was impressive, but for its curation. The closet was a meticulously organized study of couture ski and après-ski fashion throughout the past six or seven decades. Harlow marveled at the selection of items, almost fearing to touch any of it; every piece was such high quality. The room itself was illumi-nated softly from lights positioned behind the racks and racks of sweaters, snowsuits, and various leggings. As she moved toward the back of the room, she found a wall of boots and an enormous freestanding dresser that contained undergarments and gloves.

"What *is* this place?"

Harlow recognized Larkin's voice, and stuck her head out from the back to let her sister know where she was. "Hi, I'm back here."

Larkin's mouth was slightly open as she wandered through the closet. Harlow had begun trying on sweaters after finding a section of folded items that turned out to be a collection of half-zips. She'd gathered a small wardrobe's worth of items that would fit her when Larkin arrived.

"This is excessive," Larkin announced when she reached Harlow's pile of clothes.

Harlow cast her eyes down at her pile. "I don't think anyone else here wears the same size as me—"

"I didn't mean your selection," Larkin interrupted. Her tone was curt, which was unusual. Sometimes Larkin got cranky when she was tired and overstimulated, though—all the Kranes did. Harlow tried not to read too much into it, especially as Larkin continued in a much gentler tone, "I meant this entire place. What is this all *for*?"

Harlow had been wondering the same thing. "I don't know. It's not what I was expecting."

"It's not?" Larkin's eyebrows raised, but the look in her eyes was hopeful, as though she were relieved to find she wasn't the only one astounded by ORAIS's ostentatious luxury. Of all the Kranes, she'd spent the least amount of time with the Illuminated.

"No, I expected it to be nice. I've seen Finn's parents' house in Nuva Troi... But I wasn't expecting—" she gestured to the whole place. "Whatever this is."

Finn had appeared in the doorway. "This is all Aislin," he

explained. "She used to come here for her 'little escapes' when I was a child." He lifted Harlow's enormous pile of clothes with little effort, allowing her to stack three pairs of boots onto the top before disappearing without another word.

Larkin's eyebrows raised again. "What's he gonna do with your clothes, pal?"

Harlow laughed. "He's going to go organize it all. Like, in a really, really anal way that will include color-coding."

"That's so Finn," Larkin said, smiling.

In that one sentence, Harlow heard all the ways Finn had become Larkin's family too. She was so proud of Larkin, and who she'd become. It had been terrifying to think of taking her on this mission, but it all made sense now.

"So, does this place feel familiar?" Harlow asked. "Have you seen the room from your dreams?"

Larkin shook her head as she ran a finger along a row of puffy snow boots that had surged in popularity in the last few years after being thought of as old-fashioned for a while. "No, not yet." She selected a bright red pair and sat next to Harlow to try them on. "I keep thinking about Piper being the Ravager's host."

"Yeah," Harlow said, watching her sister pull the boots on. "Me too. It seems less likely to me the more I think of it."

Larkin stuck her feet out, admiring the boots. "Really? The more I think about it the more likely it seems."

"Really?" Harlow asked. "Why?"

A sigh hissed from Larkin's lips. "So many people seem to like her, which makes me think at some point, she must have been really nice. But to us... or you and Finn, I guess, she's been awful. The way she acted in the bathhouse was gross."

Harlow wasn't sure she'd call it "gross," but it hadn't been Piper's best moment. Usually she and Larkin had similar takes on people, but they obviously disagreed about this. "She's

human, we're immortal, and that dynamic is a lot more complicated than I ever imagined."

Larkin shrugged, rolling her eyes a bit. "It seems more
personal than that, and the Ravager was super interested in you,
wasn't it? She seems weirdly obsessed with being mean to you."

Harlow wanted to hug her sister for being so defensive of
her. "I think the more likely explanation is that Finn and I were
rude to her in secondary, without meaning to be, and that experience wasn't unique for her. But we're the only people she went
to school with at Sanctum, so it *looks* like she's singling us out."

Harlow sighed, as Larkin grimaced at her. She couldn't
believe she was defending Piper Winslow this staunchly either.
"With everything the way it is... I think she's just really angry
with us. There's going to be war, and she's responsible for a lot."

Larkin wore a distant look Harlow had seen on her face
several times in the past few days. "Humans live such short lives.
So many won't see this resolved."

That wasn't something she hadn't considered. The long life
she'd been blessed with meant that she had time to see the world
change. Her urgency to get things solved was lessened by that
factor, as well as the ones Piper had pointed out to her. The
defensiveness she'd felt in the Education Councillor's office,
which lingered still, dissipated. The humans' resentment of the
lower Orders was warranted. What Harlow had read as Piper's
rudeness was actually exhaustion, fear, and the knowledge that
she—and her people—would bear the brunt of every mistake
immortals made trying to solve things. Just like they always had.

Just like everyone on Okairos had when Connor McKay and
the convoy leaders had decided to stay on the planet and rule as
they saw fit. The pieces of how they'd conquered, even after the
battles were over, spun around in her head.

For the first time in her entire life, Harlow thought about
the fact that sorcière were part human. Of course, this was something she knew—everyone learned it in school. But she'd never

really taken the time to *think* about the fact that the lower Orders had all been human at one time. In fact, she'd never thought about the fact that most vampires had been human in their lifetimes.

"Look," Harlow said softly. "I don't know how we fix this, but I know once we do our part here, we keep following Finn's example. We let the humans lead. They know more than we do about what they need."

Larkin's eyebrows shot up. "You really believe that?"

"Don't you?" Harlow asked, getting up.

"Yeah," Larkin said softly. "I do, but it surprises me a little that you do."

Harlow sighed, more from needing a breath than frustration. "I know I can be pretty focused on myself sometimes, but I do think about the wider world."

Larkin glanced up, shaking her head, as though shaking something off. "That's not... I mean... I know you care about things."

Harlow brushed a kiss on her sister's cheek. "It's okay, pal. I get it. You've always been so much further ahead on stuff like this than me. I'll make you proud. Promise."

Larkin grabbed her hand. "I'm already proud of you, Harlow."

In that moment, Larkin sounded ancient, as though she'd been waiting eons to hear Harlow admit all that. She wished she'd talked about these things sooner. Larkin was so savvy about all this, and probably could have helped Harlow see her way through the spots she'd been missing sooner. But there was time now—the door was open and Harlow wouldn't lose these types of opportunities again.

"Goodnight," she said as she crossed the closet.

"Nighty-night," Larkin replied.

Her sister's tone struck a dissonant note. Harlow spun to look at her, but Larkin was happily sorting through sweaters, touching the cashmere with a reverence Harlow deeply related to. Part of her wanted to be left alone with the closet for the evening, but the day was catching up to her and she needed to rest.

Across the hall, she found the door to the bedroom Finn preferred standing open. It wasn't even really a bedroom, but more of a suite. Rich woods graced the vaulted ceiling, with another panoramic view of the mountains. All Harlow saw now was darkness and snow, of course. She sank into a chair in front of the delightfully retro, conically shaped fireplace, her mind racing.

Somewhere, in the recesses of the room, the soft sound of Finn hanging clothes comforted her, reminding her of the few brief weeks of peace they'd had last spring. It stung to think of the house he'd built for her, especially after the fire, but what stung more now was that while she'd been amazed that he'd gone to such lengths for her, the fact that he'd been able to do so was not a surprise.

It had been special because it was done for her, not because the finishes of the house had been particularly out of the ordinary. A deep crease formed in Harlow's forehead as more of her life sharpened within the context of her recent realizations. Deeper and deeper she went, examining facets of her life she rarely considered. The sound of Finn's footsteps and the soft whoosh of the door shutting brought her back to herself. He sank into the chair next to her, a contrast of dark and light, his tousled hair shadowy against his pale skin.

When he smiled at her, offering his hand, she took it, allowing herself to be pulled from her own chair, into his lap. "You're thinking hard," he said, stroking her hair.

"How much time have you spent thinking about how differently humans live than we do?"

The hitch in his breath startled her. "A lot," he said after a long pause. "Last year, while we were finishing key aspects of the

Haven Project, I spent about six months just interviewing humans about what they needed."

Harlow sensed he would say more, so she didn't respond, or ask questions. She let her arms slide around his neck, digging her fingers into his silky soft hair as he spoke.

"It was a humbling experience to come to terms with the fact that I am not, in fact, a relatable person whatsoever."

A low laugh escaped Harlow's lips. "No. You really aren't."

He looked up at her. "Do you hate it?"

"What? The fact that you're not relatable?"

He nodded, gesturing to their surroundings. "All this is just a tiny portion of what I grew up with. When I look at it in comparison to what the humans at Sanctum had before they came to the Rogue Order..."

Harlow finished for him, "It makes you a little ill."

He nodded. "It does. It's why I offered to sign it all away. I don't think I can live in the shadow of what Connor's done any longer."

Harlow hugged him tightly, not knowing what to say next, but letting the words come anyway. "We still have a lot to learn about the way the world actually works, don't we?"

Finn's eyes were sad when they met hers. "We do—in some ways. But in others, we probably know far too much."

# CHAPTER TWENTY-NINE

Over the next few days, Harlow and Ari worked to sort through the offices they could get into, while Larkin and Finn worked on unlocking Connor's office and the command center in the observatory. Ari, Finn, and Harlow took turns patrolling as well, though Stella's perimeter surveillance was one of the first things they were able to restore, and was reassuringly boring to watch. Periodically, the cameras caught sight of wildlife, but even that was rare in these windy climes.

Perhaps the best thing about ORAIS though was that because there was so little to do outside of searching the station, there was time to rest. Furthermore, because Harlow finally had Finn and Larkin back, her mind began to recover from the stress of the past few months. She was fully rested for the first time in months, and she'd never felt more mentally agile. If only they could get into Connor's office; she was sure it held some sort of information that would tie together the central problems Okairos faced.

On the eighth day at ORAIS, as Harlow woke from her afternoon nap to yet another blizzard outside, movement in the corner of the bedroom caught her eye. Sleepily, she turned over, reaching for Finn.

"Come here," she called, barely opening her eyes. "Come kiss me."

*I don't think we have reached such a level of intimacy.*

Harlow sat straight up. The shade was back.

"Stella," Harlow called, keeping her voice low. "Who is in my room?"

The AI responded quickly. "Yourself only, Harlow."

The shade stared out the windows, apparently watching the snow. *I am here, but not here. It is an odd existence.*

One thing they'd been able to uncover in ORAIS's general archives was lore about the Ravagers, which confirmed that a powerful elemental's presence on a planet would disturb the more paranormal elements, like spirits. The author's hypothesis was that on planets like Okairos, which derived much of their magical force from aethereal power, a Ravager would possibly change other spirits' essential nature. Finn guessed this might be why the ghosts, and this shade in particular, seemed so attracted to Harlow.

"Where did you live when you were alive?" Harlow asked. "Do you remember?"

The shade turned. *You are still trying to figure out who I am then.*

Harlow nodded. "Shades typically haunt people they have a personal connection with."

The creature smiled, which was a fearsome expression, given its otherworldly beauty and its sharp canines. *These are not the right questions, Harlow.*

The shade dissolved, to her frustration. What had it said to her in Lithraea's Way? *Seek the truth of this world, and your place in it.* Well, she was trying, but until they got into Connor's office and the command center, she doubted she'd have much more success.

Someone knocked at her door. "Come in. I'm up."

Larkin stuck her head inside. "Good. Thought you'd want to come see. I got Connor's office open—*and* Stella and I got the internet working."

"That is correct," the AI added. "I was integral in helping Larkin establish an internet connection, but we have not yet activated the link."

Harlow could swear the AI's flat voice sounded affectionate. If anyone could kindle feelings in a robot, it was Larkin. Harlow dressed quickly, which was easy because Finn had organized all the clothes she'd chosen from Aislin's closet by color.

Larkin shook her head when she emerged from the bathroom. "You look like one of those vintage fashion photos in that outfit. Like you belong in an apres-ski photoshoot."

Harlow glanced down at the monochromatic ensemble of champagne boots, combined with her beige sweater and leggings. She did look like she'd chosen clothes out of an *Ordinas* winter photo spread. She shrugged—it was fun to look put together and feel warm and comfortable at the same time.

"It wasn't a dig," Larkin said, her voice gentle as they made their way down the hall. "You look like yourself for the first time in a long, long time."

Harlow stopped in the lounge to make a quick latte. She'd become a bit addicted to them, here at ORAIS. "What does that mean?"

Larkin hoisted herself onto the counter while Harlow busied herself making them both a drink. "It's like you've come into your own or something. You seem more comfortable being yourself, ever since the bridge. Did the shade help you?"

Harlow made a noise she hoped would be interpreted as affirmative, concentrating on making a pretty design in Larkin's foam.

"Awww, a heart." Larkin grinned.

Harlow tweaked her nose. "Love you, sissy."

Larkin wrinkled her nose, rubbing it. "Don't call me that."

Harlow kissed her cheeks in apology. "I do love you though, Larkin." They set off for Connor's office once more, mugs in hand. Harlow bumped her sister's shoulder lightly. "I'm glad you're here."

Larkin just smiled. "Me too."

Outside, for the first time in days, the blizzard had slowed to flurries. The long hallway that connected the residential section of the facility with the research wing allowed a dazzling view of the surrounding peaks through its floor to ceiling windows.

Larkin slowed down, squinting at something off in the distance. "What is that?"

It was the first time since they'd arrived at ORAIS that there was a clear view of the landscape. Harlow stopped behind her sister, trying to find what she saw. There it was, just beyond the perimeter boundary, skirting it closely. Movement. Harlow's heart thumped with anxiety. Whatever was out there wasn't an animal. It was moving too quickly for that.

"Stella," she called. "Can you bring up the cameras on the north peaks on the main research terminal?"

"Of course, Harlow," the AI answered.

They rushed to the terminal, only to find Finn staring at the screen. "It's not the Vespae," he said as they approached.

Harlow and Larkin crowded next to him. The movement was gaining momentum, and the way it skirted the trigger for the perimeter alarms was reason for concern.

"Could be the Dominavus," Larkin reasoned.

"It's not," Ari said, entering the small foyer that led to the various offices and labs. He was damp, his cheeks flushed from the cold. "We wouldn't see the Dominavus coming until they hit a vulnerable point in the wards. I've studied their tactics. This isn't like them. Whoever that is wants us to know they're there —my sense is that they want us to be afraid."

"That's messed up," Larkin murmured.

Above her head, Harlow and Finn made eye contact. She knew instantly they thought the same name: Alain Easton. It was the only thing that made sense.

"Stella, bring up the wards' force," Finn commanded. "Full strength, please."

"It is done," Stella replied, after a long pause.

Ari watched Finn carefully. "I think it would be better if I ran patrol for a few days, since I can move unseen. The rest of you should stay in."

Harlow looked around for Larkin, who'd disappeared, while Finn thought Ari's proposal through. For a moment, he looked as though he might argue, but eventually he nodded. "We need to finish here and leave quickly. Tangling with whoever's out there isn't worth it."

Larkin emerged from the observatory. "In that case, what I just discovered might be of use." Everyone turned towards her. "I think I unlocked one of the terminals in the command center."

Ari grimaced. "Fill me in? I need a shower and a meal after my run. It's fucking cold out there."

Finn clapped a hand on his friend's shoulder. "Of course."

Harlow followed Larkin into the observatory, while Finn and Ari exchanged information. Harlow looked back over her shoulder. Though she couldn't make out Finn's words, she read "Alain Easton" on his lips. She kept walking, lest she be accused of eavesdropping. Finn would be desperate to keep everyone here safe, and Ari was his trusted second when Cian wasn't around. It was best to let them talk things out.

In the observatory, Larkin sat in a rolling chair, hunched toward a computer screen. "I wanted to see if I could get the command center online. Its sensors could tell us more about whoever is out there. But I couldn't access that part of the system, not yet anyway. The decryptions I was running last night gave me access to this..."

Harlow laughed when she got close enough to read the screen. It was a radar projection for the next two days. Larkin had managed to turn the weather on. Her sister gave her a withering look that shut her up immediately. Harlow pulled up another chair, while Larkin paused the radar progression that played on loop. "See those blue sections?"

Harlow nodded, grateful to have escaped a sisterly scolding for laughing at an inappropriate time.

"Watch them," Larkin ordered, playing the loop again, clearly still peeved that Harlow had laughed at her. On the screen, the blue splotches went from being tiny dots to covering the area surrounding ORAIS for a very brief amount of time, minutes probably.

Larkin paused the projection again, right when the blue dots covered ORAIS. "In two days, there will be a storm that should generate a rare kind of lightning—I don't really know how to explain it other than that it won't be a weather phenomenon, but a magical one. The lightning will be pure celestial energy, pulled through the limen. When it strikes, it will counter the effects of the iridium deposits for about two minutes."

Harlow nodded, touching the screen as the timelapse projection started over. "Here, right?"

Larkin nodded. "Yes, that's it. If we calibrate the computer, we should be able to track it more accurately. I think Ari will be able to do that. It's a little beyond me, but Nox taught him how."

"What is this phenomenon?" Harlow asked.

Larkin stared up at the ceiling, as though she could see the sky, or maybe the limen. "I don't really understand it, but there are times when the limen sort of aligns more closely to us than others, and it pulls celestial power into the world."

"So what does that mean?" Harlow asked, not understanding why this mattered.

Larkin shook her head. "Not much beyond the iridium

being temporarily neutralized. We should be able to teleport out, if we want to."

"That will make us vulnerable to Alain and whoever he has with him," Finn remarked, coming to stand behind Harlow. His arms wrapped around her shoulders as he watched the radar projection again.

Larkin sighed. "It's a risk. For sure." Her shoulders slumped a little as she bit her bottom lip, obviously racing to think through alternatives.

"We'll do it," Finn said. "But don't turn on the internet until shortly before we leave, okay? There's a real possibility my dad has that kind of thing tracked. I don't want him to know we've been here, if we can help it."

Larkin nodded. "Great. Let's go plunder his office for secret information." Harlow got up to go, but Larkin pulled her back into her chair. "Hold on, I just want to check if the rest of the terminal unlocked. There's some cool old planetary tracking systems in here that I want to check out."

Her fingers flew over the keyboard. The radar screen disappeared, and another appeared. Harlow didn't understand what she was looking at. The screen was split in two, showing what she assumed were tracking outputs. One showed deep space and a tiny pinprick of a planet; the other looked like some sort of terrain, though it was largely topographical lines and dots, changing features all the time.

"What is that?" Finn asked, pointing to the screen.

At the bottom of the page, in a pop-up window, was a message, dated several weeks prior to the current date. Larkin clicked the button labeled, "OPEN." Finn and Harlow both leaned closer to read. A chat window appeared. It started with a string of numbers and dots, followed by the words: *Population prepared for conquer.* Underneath it, in a message time-stamped only fifteen minutes ago, was a reply. *Received. Delegation assembling.*

Finn froze, his skin turning a deathly shade of gray. He staggered backwards, swallowing hard, his eyes glazing with panic. "The Ventyr are coming."

The room was silent, but Harlow's ears rang with the terror coursing through her. "Did Connor send this?"

Finn stumbled into a chair and slumped into it, covering his face with his hands. He didn't seem capable of answering her.

Larkin shrugged. "I don't know how to tell."

Finn shook his head. "He wouldn't. Believe me."

Larkin looked as though she wanted to argue, but Harlow raised a finger as an indignant expression darkened her sister's face. "Finn knows his dad, pal. He has no illusions about Connor's honor or goodness."

Again, Larkin looked like she might argue. Harlow sighed. "Connor doesn't like to share power."

Larkin's expression softened. "But with things the way they are, mightn't he think the others could help him get the Vespae under control?"

Finn's tone was gentle. "You really don't know my dad, and I'm so glad for that, but he'd let the whole world get eaten by those creatures before he let the Emperor have this world. He sees it, and everything in it, as *his*."

As that disturbing idea rocketed through them, Harlow watched the topographical map change abruptly. What looked like ancient ruins formed and disappeared in a mere moment. An idea occurred to her. "Is that the limen?"

Finn glanced at it, his eyes narrowing to a squint. He needed his glasses, badly. "It very well could be." He sat back, thoughtful, then asked, "Stella, who's logged into ORAIS for the past three months?"

"I'm sorry, Finn. That information is not available at your clearance level." The AI sounded apologetic. Whoever programmed her had taught her good inflection and emotional reaction—she was likable.

"Worth a try," he muttered, standing. "Our approach is two pronged, then. Someone needs to set up the algorithm to track the storm. Larkin, can you get started?"

Larkin pulled a hair tie off her wrist, yanking her hair into a ponytail as she turned back towards the computer. "Yep. You'll send Ari to help me?"

Finn nodded, motioning to Harlow. "We'd better get started on Connor's office."

# CHAPTER THIRTY

Connor's office was exactly how Harlow pictured it would be: decorated in heavy, dark woods, shelves lined with books, uncomfortable leather furniture. Apparently, Aislin's vision for a luxurious, comfortable research station had not extended to his space. A massive set of windows looked out on the mountain range below. Harlow tried not to stare outside, watching for Alain.

"This place has 'villain's lair' written all over it," Harlow said with a curl of her upper lip.

Finn's laugh was dry. He obviously agreed.

They got to work. Harlow took to the bookshelves, Finn took his father's desk. After only a few hours, the room was a mess, and they'd found nothing of interest.

"I'm going to check on Ari and Larkin," Finn said. "Want more coffee?"

Harlow flopped onto the stiff leather chesterfield, grimacing at the hard surface, and nodded. When Finn had gone, she laid back, staring at the ceiling. "There's got to be something here," she reasoned out loud. Sometimes talking to herself helped her visualize a problem better. "Otherwise, why would the door have been so difficult to unlock?"

They'd been through everything. Finn had even searched the desk for hidden compartments and found none. Harlow sat up to perch on the edge of the chesterfield, staring at the shelves. The place really did look like a villain's lair. Like something out of an Auvray Deville film. A spark of an idea lit in Harlow's mind. She dropped onto her hands and knees, crawling around the perimeter of the room, staring at the floor.

As she did so, Finn returned. "What are you doing?"

"Looking for the villain's lair. Like a Deville film."

Finn caught on. "Like the one on the mountain, with the lingerie models?"

"Not that one," Harlow murmured, concentrating. "That would be too obvious for Connor. The one with the casino and the evil professor. Did you see that one?"

She didn't hear Finn's answer over the thrill of discovery rushing through her. There it was: a deep scratch in the floor that arced out from the bookshelf.

"Aces," Harlow breathed, using the iconic spy's catchphrase. "Look what we have here."

"Seventeen hells," Finn murmured. "A fucking secret door. I don't know whether to be impressed or cringe."

Harlow snickered. "Right? It's so predictable."

They rushed to and fro, pulling every book from the shelf, trying to trigger the secret door. Nothing worked. Finn paused, assessing the scene again. His eyes drifted back to the scratch on the floor, then back to his father's desk several times, like he was trying to catch hold of a fleeting thought.

"Why didn't I think of that?" he murmured, searching through the debris he'd scattered on the desk. He pulled what looked like a library card out of a book, then began pulling books from the shelves opposite the door itself. He let out a pleased little grunt, which brought a smile to Harlow's lips.

She stepped back from the shelf, whispering, "It's going to open."

Finn slid the card into a nearly invisible sliver, right at the base of one of the shelves. The way the shadows hit the corner, she never would have seen it. But as the device that read the card made a soft clicking noise, the shelf she had searched first popped open, revealing concrete stairs that delved deep into the bowels of the observatory.

Sconces on the walls lit the way. Harlow started down, but Finn shook his head. "Wait a sec, okay?" He didn't wait for an answer, but jogged out of the room with the card. When he returned, he grinned and waved a walkie talkie. "Better not disappear into a secret passage without telling anyone where we're headed. Ari will keep an ear out for us."

"Where'd you find that?" Harlow asked, pointing to the walkie talkie as he led the way down the stairs.

"Under all the ORAIS sweaters. My mom and I used to use them to play hide and seek when I was really little." He sounded wistful. "Before my dad started training me, we'd come here as a family once a year. I didn't know what this place was—it just felt like an adventure. We took snowmobiles to get here, and it was just the three of us."

The stairs were steep, and Harlow had to watch every step carefully. The stairwell gave her the terrible feeling she was going to topple over. Before she gave it a second thought, she'd manifested her wings, just as she'd done on the bridge. Her shadows danced happily around her fingers, as though thrilled to see her wings. The fabric of the lovely sweater she'd chosen ripped, regrettably, but Harlow didn't feel as though she was going to fall, and she could concentrate on Finn's words.

"I don't know why Connor paired with Aislin. He's never had any interest in her as a person. When I was little, she was magical. Fun."

He paused for a moment. The stairs spiraled ever downward,

and now, the smooth wood-paneled walls gave way to rough stone. The sconces were fewer and farther between, with just enough light to keep them from plunging into pitch black darkness. "Careful here, the steps turn to stone as well. They're narrower."

As she followed Finn down, he spoke absently, as though he'd forgotten Harlow was there with him. "When Connor decided I was old enough to train, it was like she disappeared. I never saw the version of Aislin that told stories or played games again. It felt like she blamed me for choosing Connor's side."

Harlow wondered if it was all right to ask him anything, or if she should just let him speak. She decided it was better to interact, especially as he'd trailed off. "So, she didn't approve of Connor's methods?"

Ahead of her, Finn shrugged. "I don't know that she necessarily disapproved of his methods, but she acted as though I'd betrayed her." His head hung.

Surely he didn't feel shame for that? Harlow burned with anger. Of course Finn had taken that on. She caught his elbow, stopping him. "You were a child, and she was the adult. You did nothing wrong."

Finn didn't look back at her, but he nodded once before continuing on down the steps. He didn't say anything else. They walked for what felt like forever, until Finn paused, turning. His laugh was dry, as though he was frustrated with himself for just figuring something out. "We could make this faster, you know?"

Harlow shook her head. "Noooo, it makes me motion sick when you whoosh me around..."

"Come on," Finn cajoled. It was easy to see he was trying to banish the sad thoughts about his mother. He turned motioning to his backside. "Hop on my back."

Harlow couldn't deny him. She retracted her wings, letting them dissolve into nothing, then hopped on to Finn's back. With nothing more than a brief hiss of air, they arrived at the bottom of the staircase. Harlow gasped, feeling a little woozy as she caught her balance.

The staircase opened onto a wood deck that jutted out into a lake. Bioluminescent jellyfish undulated within it, casting a soft blue glow up from the water. Behind the deck, a glass enclosure held what they'd been looking for: shelves of books and maps, and rows of wood filing cabinets. This was Connor's cache of information.

In the distance, Harlow made out an outcropping of rocks, where water flowed slowly down into pools that rose with steam. "Hot springs?"

Finn grinned, leaning towards her to whisper in her ear. "Yes, and they're the perfect temperature for skinny dipping. We'll have to come back later." He raised his eyebrows, a wicked gleam in his eyes.

While Harlow deeply appreciated the warmth licking through her abdomen elicited by that gleam, in the back of her mind she worried. He was always rushing in to help someone, always setting aside his own pain to make things comfortable for someone else. She was concerned about how long he could reasonably keep putting his needs after others.

They still hadn't really talked about what had happened to him when he was with the Vespae. She knew the basics, of course, but he'd never opened up. Though she'd tried to make space for him to talk to her, especially since coming here, he was so deft at moving the conversation in other directions she often didn't notice that he'd evaded her until they were deep into another subject entirely.

The ease with which he put her off was troubling, but she didn't want to push him. After all, when he did talk to her, he told her things like the story about Aislin he'd remembered in the stairwell. His timeline for what to share was different than hers, and that wasn't always easy to respect.

Harlow took Finn's hands in hers. "Do you feel like you can talk to me?"

Confusion clouded his eyes. "Of course. Why would you ask that?"

"Because you don't always talk about the things that hurt very much. All that stuff about your mom? You've never told me any of that..."

One of Finn's hands flew to her face, his thumb grazing her jawline. "I love you so much, Harlow. You're so good to me."

He was doing it now, changing the subject. In moments, they'd decide it was time to go search through Connor's books and files, and he'd be forgotten again.

"You don't have to do that," she murmured. "We can talk about you."

His eyes slid to Connor's office. It was obvious he thought they needed to move on. "I know," he said before pressing his lips to hers. "Thank you."

"Okay." It wasn't what she wanted to say, but she understood. It was often confusing for her to understand how someone else processed their feelings, but she wanted to respect Finn's timelines, even if they weren't comprehensible to her. She changed the subject, gazing into the cavern pool. "Where do the jellyfish come from?"

Finn shook his head, moving towards the glass room. "I honestly don't know. I've never been down here before."

The large glass doors to the archive were unlocked, but sealed tightly enough that they took a big push from Finn to open. Soft reading lamps turned on as they entered. Inside, the warm humidity of the cave turned to simply warm air. The archive was obviously climate controlled and operated on its own sensors. Finn tried several times to access Stella, but she did not respond.

The archive was organized in a large "U" formation. The windows to the cave were empty, but the sides and back wall

were layered three stacks deep in shelves. The biggest old fashioned card catalogue Harlow had ever seen sat against the back
wall of the archive. Directly in front of it, in the center of the
room, sat a round, elegantly constructed counter height table,
with stools tucked under it. A huge, softly lit drum shade was
suspended on a gold wire from the ceiling. At the center of the
table was a small electronic device, accompanied by a tablet.

"What's that?" Harlow asked, pointing to the tablet and
device.

"A holographic projector," Finn answered.

"Okay," Harlow replied. "You should try it out, obviously.
What's our strategy here?"

Finn thought for a moment before answering. "Let's spend
an hour or so just getting the lay of things. Explore what's here,
then we can start honing in on what might be important. I can
start with the projector."

Harlow nodded. "That works perfectly. I'm probably better
off with the books."

Her first order of business was to search the card catalogue
to see what system had been used to organize the books and
various documents. It was none of the alpha-numeric systems
she recognized, but instead a simple chronological numbering.
Subjects could be cross-referenced, but obviously, whoever had
created the sections knew their significance by heart. Harlow
would have to struggle through the catalogue, or would have to
search the stacks manually. She fought the urge to grumble. This
was the kind of thing she'd been raised to understand.

After some close examination and a few basic cross-refer-
ences, she started to recognize a pattern. Searching for a broader
topic like "The Order of Mysteries" yielded several sections, and
in each, she found accounts of different Okarion cities. She
searched several more basic topics and found the same thing
each time. The numbered sections were based on location.

This made things tricky, as she wasn't even sure where to

start, or what they might be looking for. She sat down in the stacks to let her mind wander. It was a good feeling, one she was familiar with, and enjoyed. The smell of the books, the satisfying feeling of being surrounded by different colored spines. It was all very, very pleasing. But she did wish there were a better system of organization, and she couldn't resist a moment of self-indulgent grumpiness, missing the librarians at the Temple of Akatei library in Nea Sterlis. It would be so convenient if someone could just fetch her what they thought she might need.

She laughed at herself, but stopped short. *The Warden*. She had the copy Morgaine had given her upstairs. The human girl had suggested she look for the missing pages... She'd hoped they'd find them here, but what if she'd been too literal, looking for the actual pages? What if there was a copy of *The Warden* here?

Harlow rushed to the card catalogue, nearly tripping over her feet as she went. There was no luck, but she wasn't discouraged, because in looking, she discovered something else. The card catalogue did not reference *any* book titles, only topics. She started a manual search, scanning up and down each shelf. It was tedious work, and she missed having her headphones and phone to keep her company while she scanned the seemingly endless spines. But after a half-hour of searching, she found it, sitting as though it had been waiting for her.

Connor had a copy of *The Warden*. Though she was tempted to jump into the book, her first order of business had to be to determine where *The Warden* had been shelved—what was the location this section was based around? There were several journals here, many discussing similar topics to what she remembered from *The Warden*, a planet where the industry of war had reigned for centuries, so much so that the entire culture of the place had been based on it. She might not know the name for the place, but she was certain now that this was the section for the Ventyr's home planet. *Now* she felt comfortable satisfying her urge to examine *The Warden*.

She pulled it out carefully, holding it open just enough to examine the pages without endangering the spine, as she assessed the book's fragility. It was a good copy, with no apparent damage, or anything that might make the book susceptible to damage from normal use. In fact, it looked almost new, so she flipped straight to the page where Ashbourne and Lumina's story had left off. It continued here, but not at all how Harlow had expected.

She forced herself to read the story again, reminding herself of the war between the Ventyr houses, and the star-crossed lovers, Ashbourne—the Ash she knew—and his former lover, Lumina. The sadness of the story drew her in, tugging at her heart.

*It seemed, for a time, that the two Houses had come to a stalemate. Soon though, Notus devised a devious plan to end this diplomatic conflict so that the great Houses might return to the nobler enterprise of eternal war. As Lumina valued her freedom so highly, second only to her love for Ashbourne, Notus suggested she be exiled to the realm of Sirin—a dark world, populated by creatures so ingenious that the Ventyr could not conquer them. And so Lumina and Ashbourne were separated for all time.*

This was where the story had been redacted in the copy she'd received in Nea Sterlis, but here, it was whole. Eagerly, she read on.

*To ensure that their punishment continues for all eternity, if Fate allows them to find their way back to one another, House Anemoi's mages were forced to lay a most devious curse upon them. Should the star cross'd lovers ever meet again, they will not recognize one another. The curse was woven so skillfully, so cruelly, that even the desire—should they have it—to speak of their shared past to the other will be hidden from them. As such, the two do not even know they are cursed. They might search for one another still, in fact. But in this plot to separate Ashbourne and his Lumina, I have found one significant flaw.*

The thumping in Harlow's chest beat harder, especially now that she knew that Ashbourne was Connor's younger brother—Finn's uncle. He'd said the Ravager he was following was headed to Sirin—but she'd forgotten that's where Lumina would be. She had no way of warning him about what he faced now. What followed confirmed for Harlow that whoever had written *The Warden* must have been well-versed in spellwork:

*A curse cannot be crafted without a loophole, though I cannot determine what this one might be. It would be deeply personal to both parties, that much is certain. A bright spot, however, may lie in the fact that Lumina was sent to Sirin, specifically. There she may find help of a different kind, for Sirin is the home of the Vilhar, more specifically, the remnants of the spacecraft Avalonne. The line of House Feriant lives on—on Sirin, and those fey creatures may have the power to break this curse, once and for all.*

*If they cannot, the Oscarovi and their devices built to channel elemental power may be able to help her...*

Harlow skimmed through the rest of the pages that were missing from her copy of the book, but only found the author's brief history of how the people called the Oscarovi obtained the ability to channel aethereal power, after a prolonged adjustment period to living with the more advanced Vilhar. She could hardly focus on that information though, returning again and again to the sentence, *The line of House Feriant lives on—on Sirin.*

She clutched the book to her chest, rushing to the center of the archive. Finn had the holographic projector working and was examining a truly stunning model of a star system she didn't recognize. She set the book down, opening it to the page in question, tapping the relevant section.

"You found *The Warden.*" He began to read the new portion immediately, his eyes squinting at the tiny print.

When he looked up, she asked, "Have you ever heard anything like this before?"

He shook his head, but gestured towards the projector. "No, but this might be able to help."

He typed a few things into multiple search fields on the tablet's screen. They reminded Harlow of research databases, allowing you to search for multiple factors, rather than just one. Immediately, three results appeared as links on the screen.

Finn tapped the first, and the star system dissolved, replaced by several figures. All had different humanoid qualities, and were in various stages of turning into a very familiar looking giant bird, the Feriant. Their features were intensely familiar to Harlow now.

*They looked just like the shade.* Similar to the humanoids on Okairos, but sharper in their facial features, a bit taller, and a touch longer in limb.

Harlow let out a low whistle. "Who are they?"

Finn had been scanning through the text on the screen. As Harlow leaned towards him, she saw the pages he was reading weren't typed text, but images of handwritten notes. Now, he read aloud, "The Feriant are one House that comprises the Court of Winds. Though we do not know much about the fey courts, as they are a secretive and ancient society, we learned from Sirin to avoid any world they may have populated or are currently visiting. We made a mistake on Sirin, in thinking that they, like us, were interested in ventures of colonization.

"That mistake was our downfall. The Vilhar and the Oscarovi do not agree on much, but on one thing they adamantly held to: Sirin is theirs and theirs alone. We trapped them on Sirin as retribution, closing all portals to the limen. It is likely they will find ways to open them again, but it gave us time to retreat and recuperate."

Finn and Harlow were silent for a long moment, letting the information sink in. Finally, Harlow said what they must both be thinking. "So the Feriant aren't even a result of being part Ventyr."

Finn shook his head. "I don't know how it's possible. There's nothing else here about it, but my parents *knew*. They must have known." He stared at her, his eyes wide, almost awestruck. "You're part fey, and they wanted us," he gestured between them, "to *breed* the kind of warriors that could resist their own people." Finn's lip curled in disgust at the thought.

So many things made more sense now, they'd only had part of the puzzle before, with the Scroll of Akatei, and the revelations they'd found about the Heraldic and the Feriant. There were so many ancient layers to all this, it might take years to pull them apart and understand them completely. One thing was clear right now: the Illuminated had gone about things all wrong, but they'd done so thinking they were doing good—that they were protecting Okairos from their own kind. From a world of endless wars and conquering. She couldn't quite wrap her mind around the idea.

To help make sense of things, Harlow asked, "Who wrote that?"

Finn swallowed hard. "My mother. This is her handwriting." His grip on the tablet shook.

Harlow took it from him, setting it aside. They needed to talk about Aislin, that much was clear. "I don't mean to be rude, but your mother has always seemed very uninterested in things like politics. Why would she have been writing things like this?"

Finn's jaw twitched. "The woman you know—it's a shadow of the person she was when I was little, who I believe she was before I was born."

"I'm so sorry," Harlow replied, without missing a beat. She didn't need to know the particulars of this. It was obvious he mourned the loss of the mother Aislin had been, at least for a little while, when he was young.

"Thank you," Finn said, his shaking hands steadying. "I've always blamed myself."

"I don't think it was you, sweet boy," she replied, keeping her voice soft. Slowly, his eyes drifted to hers. "I think the more obvious answer here is that Connor is to blame."

He nodded. "I know. I just..." He paused, letting out a huff of air. "Before my parents came to Okairos, my mother was a diplomat. She was also one of the Emperor's mistresses. It wasn't uncommon for a woman of their culture to be both, and she was powerful in her own right. When the Emperor took a new territory, he sent her into smooth relations with the home governments, easing them into the Empire, so to speak."

Harlow grimaced; it sounded like uncomfortable work. Finn laughed at her reaction, seeming to know exactly what she thought. "Awful, isn't it? But she was a proud woman, and good at what she did. I believe she thought she could do the same here, but when the situation changed, when Pasiphae and my dad altered the trajectory of the envoy's plans, she lost her status, even though she and my father shared the Claim."

A hiss of air released from Harlow's lungs. "He Claimed her to control her. To cut her out."

Finn nodded. "That seems like my dad. He might have loved her, or at the very least admired her, but she was loyal to the Emperor. I doubt he trusted her."

Harlow realized why Finn had resisted Claiming her now. She deeply regretted how hard she'd pushed, but of course, she hadn't known any of this. The openness on Finn's face closed. Harlow was beginning to understand the push and pull of his disclosures; he needed breaks after sharing something so raw.

She looked back at the figures of the Feriant. "What else did you find?"

Finn clicked an arrow that functioned as a "back" button and the Feriant dissolved. Now schematics for something that looked like a spaceship appeared. The Illuminated forbade the construction of any such thing, but scientists believed they had the capability to build them, and they were an intense focus in literature and film. This was unlike anything Harlow had ever seen, however. It was like a train, a city, and a spacecraft, all at once. Beautiful in its gothic construction, elegant beyond belief, and enormous.

"This is an artist's rendering of what the Avalonne might have looked like before it was irreparably damaged on Sirin," Finn explained, after reading through what looked like some complicated schematics. "Nearly four thousand years ago, it crashed on Sirin. Or rather, it made an emergency landing, and never left. It carried with it a host of people, the Vilhar, space travelers..." he squinted, then pinched the screen to make the text larger.

Harlow didn't bother to hide her smile. Finn was adorable with his glasses, but he was even cuter without them.

"Stop laughing at my obvious farsightedness," he said with a cocky grin. His cheeks flushed, revealing that he was a little embarrassed by the attention. Harlow was glad to see him acting like himself.

"Okay, so the Vilhar were explorers, from far outside our solar system. The Ventyr really aren't sure where they're from, but they landed on Sirin a long-ass time ago and never left. The planet has been in a certain degree of turmoil ever since. Nothing else about how they might have gotten here, or the Feriant."

"What's the last link show?" Harlow asked.

Finn clicked it, the ship dissolving now, replaced with another star map, though this one showed several solar systems, with four planets highlighted in red. One was Okairos. Finn scrolled through them, a different highlighted planet showing with each swipe of his fingers. They were labeled: Okairos, Sirin, Interra and Earth.

"These are all the populated planets the Ventyr have occupied or interfered with, though not a record of everywhere they've visited. Interra is supposedly their home planet—where my parents came from. They never told me the name..."

Harlow now had a label for the section she'd found *The Warden* in. "Oh," she breathed, as her thoughts came together. "Oh."

Finn waited, knowing she was having an epiphany.

"This place. ORAIS. It's to monitor all the places the Ventyr have been. To keep the elder Illuminated informed about their potential whereabouts."

Finn's head slowly bobbed up and down. "Yes. *Yes.*"

Harlow's eyes drifted back to the planets in the projection. "Did the Ventyr conquer all these places?"

Finn shook his head. "No, these are the planets deemed close enough to Interra to investigate colonizing. Obviously, my parents were involved with the Okairos envoy. It says here that the Earth envoy was to leave shortly after they did, but nothing about how it went. I guess when they cut off contact with the Emperor, they never found out."

"So it's possible the Ventyr have Earth's citizens under their control—the way they wanted to do with us?" Harlow asked.

Finn nodded. "It's possible. Though, of course, they failed with Sirin, so maybe Earth wasn't a successful venture either. It's really hard to know."

"It doesn't matter," Harlow said. "I hate to agree with anything Connor has ever done, but he was right to stop them from coming here, and I agree with you that he's not the one who contacted them. Who else had access to these facilities besides your parents?"

Finn thought for a moment. "All four of the elder Velariuses, Alaric's parents and Petra's. Beyond that, I don't really know. Alaric and Petra never came here as kids, but I know their parents did."

Harlow groaned. "The Rogue Order was monitoring Leopold Velarius' movements. Did Alaric tell you?"

Finn shook his head. "No, we mostly spent time talking about how happy he was about being a father."

Harlow's chest ached at the thought of her sister's bondmate being excited for the baby. She squeezed Finn's hand. "I guess he's expressed a lot of dissatisfaction with both Pasiphae and Connor. The Rogues were always worried about your parents and Pasiphae, but they thought they were predictable. They think Leopold and Petra's parents might want more than what we've always assumed Connor and Pasiphae do."

"They want total domination—of humans, of the lower Orders." Finn sighed, his cheeks blowing out like a balloon. "That tracks with what the Knights have gathered, though I'll admit, I haven't taken the reports very seriously. The three of them have always been so... *uninvolved*."

Harlow shrugged; he would know better than she did. She was only reporting what Thea had told her. "The problem is, they have nearly unlimited resources..."

Finn covered his face with his hands. When he looked up, a muscle in his jaw twitched slightly. "We have to go to Nuva Troi and tell Connor. He's the only one who'd know where the Ventyr will come through—and how to stop it."

The room was quiet for a long moment, before Harlow nodded. "I really wish I didn't agree, but I do."

# CHAPTER THIRTY-ONE

L arkin and Ari made incredible progress, setting up an
algorithm that predicted when the celestial lightning
strikes in the incoming storm would be intense enough
to disrupt the magical dampening field caused by the iridium
deposits. Their estimation was that they'd have three to five
minutes notice before the conditions would be perfect, and that
they'd narrowed down their appearance to a two-hour window,
coming only a day from now.

After talking things over for nearly an hour with Larkin and
Ari, they'd ended up in the same place. They were headed to
Nuva Troi. Because of the intense wards on the city, they would
not be teleporting directly in, but would use the moments
before they jumped to connect to Nox, via the dark web. It
would be traceable back to ORAIS, but they'd be gone before
anyone could track them more closely. Nox should be able to tell
them exactly where to teleport in, how to get into the city safely,
and the rest wouldn't be *easy*, but it would hopefully be fairly
straightforward.

After the decision was made, everyone got to work on their
own tasks. Harlow returned to the archives to look for more

information about the origins of House Feriant and the Vilhar. After a long hour of searching, both the stacks and the card catalog, she gave up on finding more about those specific terms. Perhaps she needed to widen her search. Going back to *The Warden*, she hit again on the word "fey"—which she'd always understood to be associated with fictional heroes like Rhiannon, and her warrior companions, the Adar.

While the winged warriors had seemed fanciful to her as a child, after seeing the shade—and learning to manifest her Feriant form in various ways—she couldn't deny that this word had to be associated with her, and the Striders, and she wanted to know more. So she began again. The card catalogue yielded only one result, which was familiar to her: *The Violet Book of the Fey*. It was shelved in an anomalous section, tucked deep in a corner where she hadn't had the opportunity to spend much time. This bookcase was dedicated not to one location, but to various folklore.

As she ran her hand over the cover of *The Violet Book of Fey*, nostalgia hit her hard. The embossed gold illustrations of the faeries on the cover nearly had her in tears. They'd had this series of books as children—Selene had read to Thea and Harlow from it nearly every night when the twins were babies.

Harlow was transported back to her and Thea's attic bedroom in Nuva Troi, witchlights dimly lit, bobbing on the ceiling, as Selene's melodious voice carried stories of the many fey courts over their sleepy heads. Harlow missed Nuva Troi fiercely, and though she knew she'd find the city changed, she was ready to go home. She was ready to see her family again, and fight with them for the world that could be.

As she turned to walk back to the projector, something caught her eye—a volume stuck behind the various colors in the "Books of the Fey" series. Harlow pulled it out carefully; she only had to look at it to know it was very old, and not a facsimile or reproduction. A very careful look inside revealed Aislin's handwriting. This journal didn't find its way into what Connor likely considered the most useless part of the archive on accident —surely his wife had hidden it.

Harlow picked up *The Violet Book of Fey* and the journal, and brought them to the table at the center of the archive, powering up the holographic projector with the tablet. It took a few moments for everything to load, and Harlow looked carefully through the journal. The book was remarkably well preserved, and after a cursory glance Harlow strongly suspected Aislin had written much of it before coming to Okairos. It described the Ventyr's many missions into the limen once they had the means to travel there. There was only one reference to how they'd formed the first portal, and it was disturbing:

*Ouriel will never forgive Lucien for stealing the starfire from her. I fear this will come back to haunt us. I warned Boreas time and again about turning his children against one another, but he would not listen. My influence on him wanes, and I will be sent with the envoy to Okairos—away from him, and more importantly, away from Orynthia, who hates me. I cannot blame her, and if Boreas cannot see the cuckolding beneath his nose, her utter devotion to her people and the insufferable General Ithaina, then hells take him.*

Aislin had been a woman scorned before she met Connor. Against her own better judgment, she wondered what Finn's father had been like back then. She turned pages, looking for information.

*Conoch is a good leader, and his points about the tiresome nature of always being at war are well taken. I believe Pasiphae will align with him, as will Penemue and Leopold. As for myself, I find I do not care either way. Return or stay. Conquer for Boreas or ourselves. What does any of it matter? I will never have a child of my own. If I can bear a beast for my husband, the babe will be his from the moment it leaves my breast.*

That stung to read. Part of Harlow hated sympathizing with

Aislin. She'd done so many terrible things, and was the source of so much of Finn's pain, but here it was in clear letters: she'd known Connor would take Finn from her, turn him against her. There was something deeply sad about that. The whole situation was terrible.

The projector was ready to use now, but Harlow skimmed through more of the journal. At first, she didn't know what she was looking for, but quickly realized that she wanted to find something redeeming in Aislin. She wanted to find any point at which Aislin was someone Harlow could admire, or at least respect. But there was no evidence of any such thing in this journal: it was page after page of heartless commentary on conquering Okairos. The woman had thought little of the people who'd been here when she arrived. As Harlow read, she became certain Finn's mother hadn't seen them as people at all, but tools.

Her stomach turned at the thought. She'd thought she might show this to Finn, but now she was tempted to put it back where she found it and forget she'd ever seen it. Just as she resolved to do so, her eye caught the word "Vespae," and a chill ran through her as she read on.

*... and they call the creatures Vespae, believing them to be demons of a sort, sent to punish them for their wickedness. The humans on this planet are insufferably naive, but it serves a purpose. They are weakened, and will soon be vulnerable enough to accept our help.*

*I must admit, this was a bit of genius on Pasiphae's part. Conoch wanted to simply strongarm our way in, but she is a clever one. Letting the creatures into this world while we build strongholds in the remotest regions has proven to be wise. When the Heraldic dynasties fall, we will rule them easily. The trouble will be sending the Vespae back, as their world was destroyed, pulled into a dying star shortly after we let them into the limen. Pasiphae suggested finding them a new world, but we have only enough pure starfire to open one last portal, and we've agreed we'll only do so in the direst of circumstances, if our project here fails.*

*Pasiphae's cleverness shall likely save us again, as she and Penemue have devised an advanced Vascularity that shall act as a net, trapping the creatures in the limen...*

Everything past that discussed what Harlow already knew. What she'd already lived, watching Rakul Kimaris cut the love of his life down from the wretched Vascularity in Nea Sterlis. He'd had to do that because the Illuminated had let the Vespae into Okairos to begin with... *on purpose.*

Hot, furious tears slipped down her cheeks. They'd started all of this, created all of this death and destruction. And the Vespae? They were horrible, vicious creatures, but they too were victims of the Illuminated. Harlow grabbed the tablet, typing, "Vespae home world" into the search bar. The projector whirred to life, making a quiet little noise as it showed her a 3D model of something named "Planet 2361: DESTROYED." The caption said only, "Planet 2361, origin of Vespae, destroyed."

This had to be why the Vespae were searching for ORAIS: they wanted to know how to get home. They would not find the answers they sought here. And though she felt deep sympathy for their loss, and the cruelty the Ventyr had shown them, Harlow could not fathom what the creatures might do if they learned they could never return to their home.

She wondered if Alain Easton knew about this place, if with all his resources, he'd found out the same things they had in the past few months: that the Illuminated were not who, or what, they'd portrayed themselves to be. If, in his own way, Alain thought he was changing things for the better. A stab of guilt for killing Mark pierced her, like an arrow through the heart. Not because she was sorry she'd done it, she wasn't. It had been entirely necessary, but because it had only made things worse—if she'd just found another way—if Mark had... Maybe it would all be different now. Maybe they could have helped each other.

The idea broke something inside her, just a little. There had been a time she'd truly loved Mark, and she thought he'd probably loved her too, twisted as he'd been. If Alain had been on the same trail of information they were on for all this time, or longer, it would explain why Mark had tried so hard to get access to the Order of Mysteries' secrets. Her mind spun with the myriad possibilities, trying to weave them in everything else she'd just uncovered.

Harlow didn't know how long she sat staring at the projection of Planet 2361. Her mind couldn't make sense of the problems they faced, the enormity of what stood in front of them. After everything Connor, Aislin, and the elder Illuminated had done, she despised the thought of allying with them. But the Vespae weren't a foe the Fifth Order could fight.

And if the imperial Ventyr were also on their way here... There was no choice. There was nothing else they could do. They would have to ally with Connor and Pasiphae again to make the world safe. She hated to think of what they would ask for in return.

Someone touched her arm, their fingers feather light, but she startled anyway, shrieking. Finn grabbed her before she could tumble off her stool. "I'm so sorry. I called your name three times. You didn't hear me." He motioned to a plate of food. "I brought you lunch."

Hysterical laughter bubbled out of her. "Thank you."

He nodded. "You were thinking hard. What about?"

Now that he was here, and she had a plate of food in front of her, she realized she was starving. She motioned towards the journal, still open to the page she'd left it on, and the projection. As he read, she comforted herself with the sandwich in front of her. It was the only thing to do.

# CHAPTER THIRTY-TWO

F inn called Ari and Larkin down the moment he'd seen the depth of their problems. They went over everything Harlow had found, and when she'd spent her last word, showing them how deep their problems went, they too simply stared at the projection of Planet 2361.

Ari paced. "This doesn't even touch the issue of the Ravager. We still don't know where it is, or what it might do."

Larkin's eyes followed her friend. "And, we don't know the true extent of what an incubus can do. So we don't know what Alain is capable of. "

Harlow spent a few minutes trying to find information on both those subjects, both in the card catalogue and in the projector's database. Nothing came up, but that didn't surprise her. She had a growing theory that Connor had siloed various caches of information by topic in different locations, so that even if someone he hadn't authorized got into one cache, they would not have access to all his machinations or secrets.

She sat back down. "Nothing here. My guess is anything on the Ravagers or the incubi would be kept somewhere else. Locked down where Connor could keep an eye on it."

Finn didn't seem to hear her. "We are, I'm afraid, well and truly fucked." And then he laughed. "This is literally chaos. What are we going to do?"

She'd never seen him behave this way before. Finn always had an answer. He always had some way to take a step in the right direction to solving a problem. It was one of the things she found so comforting about him. But here he was admitting that this was all too much, that he didn't know what to do next. That he, Finn McKay, commander of the Knights of Serpens, was out of ideas.

Both Ari and Larkin stilled, each as perplexed by this reaction as Harlow. Someone needed to say something, think of something, because their little group was on the verge of spiraling into despair. Harlow took a few deep breaths, rewinding her thoughts some, going back to the moments before Finn had declared them well and truly fucked.

"We need access to another cache," she reasoned aloud. "If we're going to get the Fifth Order all the information they'll need to mount a defense of any kind, or at the very least some kind of bargaining chip, they'll need the full picture. We have to find out more about the Ravagers and the incubi."

Finn's eyes darted to her, the despair that clouded them clearing. "Yes," he murmured. "Yes, of course." He took her hand, squeezing it gratefully. "The Fifth Order can bargain with Connor and Pasiphae, their fighting force to align with the Illuminated's, in exchange for a more equal world."

"They'll agree to reform," Ari snapped, looking as resentful as Harlow felt. "They'll never agree to destroy what they've built for humans and the lower Orders."

"We'll end up right back where we are now," Larkin said, her eyes unfocused. "Right back in this terrible place, over and over."

Harlow didn't necessarily disagree with her sister, but her tone was so strange, so hopeless. So unlike *Larkin*. She worried that more had happened to her sister while they were separated than she was letting on. Harlow reassured herself with the fact that Enzo and Riley would be able to help with that soon. In fact, it could be even sooner.

"You're not coming with us to Nuva Troi," she said.

Larkin startled. "What?"

"You and Ari need to go to the Grove and tell the Council all of what we've found out here, *and* that we're going to find out the rest, everything Connor knows about the Ravagers and the incubi, in Nuva Troi."

Ari nodded. "His office. If you can get in—"

Finn interrupted. "Nox can get a message to the Fifth Order. They can come to the table with all the relevant information, and make a deal with the Illuminated on equal footing at least." He pulled Harlow into a giant hug. "Good job, babygirl. You figured it all out."

Harlow snorted. "It's just our next step."

He kissed her, his lips lingering over hers long past what was appropriate for the fact that they were still with Larkin and Ari. When he pulled away, he smiled, his eyes clear and confident once more. "We only ever need one more step. That's how you solve a problem this big, one bit at a time."

"Okay," Ari said. "I'm going to get back to my nap then. I have a feeling there won't be much sleep in my near future, and you all don't need me, do you?"

Finn shook his head. "I'm going to get us packed. We'll need to move fast, and travel light since we can't teleport into Nuva Troi."

When they'd gone upstairs, Harlow turned to Larkin. "Are you okay with this? With us separating?"

Her sister wore that same faraway look as before, as though she were lost in a world of her own. But she nodded. "Yeah, sure."

Harlow reached out, touching Larkin's cheek. "What's going on up there?"

Larkin smiled at her. "Nothing, sissy. I'm fine."

Harlow wanted to smile, but her lips wouldn't move. "Are you? You're acting strange."

Larkin shrugged, her mouth turning down in a frown. "It's an apocalypse, Harls, and I've been through it these past few months. What do you *want* me to act like?"

Harlow wasn't sure how to respond to that, but she felt instantly terrible about having pressured Larkin. "I'm sorry." Her words were so quiet she was certain Larkin hadn't heard them, because she was already walking away.

"I'm going to go make sure the tracker Ari and I set up is doing okay," Larkin called from the stairs. She didn't sound mad at all, in fact, she grinned at Harlow, blowing her a very Larkin-like kiss from the stairs.

Harlow got up, searching through the desk near the door for paper, pen, and envelopes. She sat down to write a letter to Enzo, letting him know that something seemed wrong with Larkin. He could help her figure things out. They were close, and Larkin might be able to hear him and Riley in a different way than she could her big sister. She tucked the letter into her back pocket to give to Ari later. The thought of going behind Larkin's back was unpleasant, but protecting her was what was most important.

# CHAPTER THIRTY-THREE

The next morning was hard. The closer their teleport window got, the more afraid Harlow became that splitting up was the wrong choice. Finn found her pacing in their bedroom.

"You know Ari won't let anything happen to her, right?" he said, gently trying to stop her from wearing a hole in the plush rug.

"I trust Ari," Harlow said. "Did you give him the letter for Enzo?"

He hugged her tightly. "Of course."

He hadn't quite understood why she felt so compelled to send it, but he hadn't questioned her either. Harlow got the sense that he was remaining as neutral as possible in all this, which made her feel a tiny bit patronized, even though she was certain that wasn't Finn's intent. The trouble was, Harlow wasn't sure she was being rational. She had no evidence that something was *wrong* with Larkin, just a feeling that something wasn't quite *right*.

Harlow buried her face in the sweater-clad muscles of Finn's chest. He smelled like comfort and strength. "Do you think I'm being overprotective?"

"Probably," he murmured into her hair. "But it's completely justified. I feel the same, and talking to Enzo could only do her good."

She raised her face to be kissed, and he happily obliged, his hands sliding up her back and into her hair. He deepened the kiss, and just as the tension that had knotted through her shoulders and spine began to loosen, Stella interrupted. "You have one hour until the way opens."

"Thanks, Stella," Finn replied. "I wish we had more time for this. It was nice to be here, wasn't it?"

Harlow nodded, pulling away from him to put her hiking boots on. They would not be able to teleport directly into the city, and there would be a walk through the suburbs to get to one of the locations where there were guarded openings in the wards for refugees. If they could get through to Nox, she would get them a more specific location. If they couldn't, Ari had given them the last coordinates he'd had, with the warning that Connor was rotating them at random intervals to keep the Vespae from predicting where the wards might open. It was a smart strategy, but it did make their journey difficult.

When she was laced up, Finn handed her a much lighter pack than the one she'd brought from Sanctum. In just a few hours, if all went the way it was supposed to, she'd be home. Or at the very least, back in Nuva Troi. As was becoming their family's parting custom, she and Larkin had spent time together last night, playing cards late into the evening, but today they were focused.

Ari and Larkin had spent the morning monitoring the incoming celestial storm. As Finn and Harlow made their way to the observatory, Harlow sensed something in the threads.

"I think I can feel the storm," she said softly, falling behind Finn to look at the sky. There was nothing there but a gloomy, gray day, and snow on the craggy peaks. Finn looked back at her, over his shoulder, waiting. "Feels like the aurorae."

He held a hand out for her, which she took. "The lightning that's coming is similar to what causes the aurorae, the clash of celestial power with our atmosphere. It's just a slightly different manifestation."

A bolt of lightning hit one of the peaks, illuminating the clouds across the narrow valley ORAIS was positioned in. It was followed by a roll of thunder unlike any she'd ever heard. Rather than a low, rolling vibration, this thunder was a high-pitched crack, and then a skittering hiss that hurt her ears.

On the peak the lightning-kissed snow began to crack and move. Finn's eyes followed it for half a second and then he yanked her arm as he started to run. "Move. Now. The storm is going to create a series of avalanches."

Harlow let herself be dragged, casting her gaze back over her shoulder to see the first rush of snow fall down the mountain. It was far enough away not to concern them, but she saw the problem. The storm would move right over them, meaning there was every chance that ORAIS would be hit, even though it sat lower than the nearest peak. There wasn't time to figure out if that would be safe, or if the building could withstand the pressure of falling snow, and possibly rock.

This might be their only chance out.

"It's starting," Ari shouted.

They rushed into the observatory, where Larkin typed furiously on a computer screen that hadn't been on the last time Harlow checked. She was getting in touch with Nox, or trying anyway.

Larkin shook her head. "She's not answering. I started early because of that." She flung her hand at several terrain maps.

"The storm's been causing avalanches, all across the range. They're more massive than anything I've ever seen," Ari explained. "We've gotta get out the minute we can."

"How long?" Finn asked, watching another avalanche in real time on the terrain map. Because it was little more than lines, it was hard for Harlow to envision how bad it actually was, but the tension in Finn's shoulders told her this wasn't a mere inconvenience.

Larkin's typing paused as she clicked into another screen. "Six minutes until it's directly overhead. From what I'm seeing, we'll have moments to get out before we're buried. Look, they're picking up in frequency." She pointed to something on the screen, a series of numbers that were rapidly increasing. Harlow had no clue what she was looking at, but she believed her sister.

"Okay," she replied. "Then let's get ready."

Stella's voice broke in as the lights in the observatory turned from their usual pleasant golden glow to flashing red. "Southwest perimeter ward, broken. Hostiles moving at speed toward the facility."

"Stella, lock all glass down," Finn ordered. "Clearance code 412-alpha-1018."

"Code accepted," Stella replied. "Hostiles still incoming. Count six."

"Can you determine their species?" Finn asked.

Stella didn't answer.

"Four minutes," Ari murmured, pulling Larkin up from her chair. "If you haven't got her yet, you're not getting her. Get to the center of the room."

Larkin nodded, distress clouding her features. She strapped her pack on, then hugged Harlow tight. "Ari will open the observatory top in a second, which will give us the clearance to teleport out. Love you. See you soon, okay?"

Harlow kissed her sister's face. "Love you," was all she could manage, she was shaking so hard.

"Hostiles on the roof," Stella said. "Five Vespae drones and an incubus. They are moving quickly toward your location, Finn."

"Shit," Ari swore, running his hands through his long hair. He stood next to the command center, ready to enter the code to open the roof. "If we open it, they'll get in."

Finn shook his head at his friend. "It's the only way, Ari. We'll be out before they can get in. When it's time, do it, and get your ass over here."

Ari nodded. Finn hugged Larkin. "Love you, kiddo. Keep the big guy safe, okay?"

Larkin nodded, grinning. "I can do that." She glanced down at her watch. "Thirty seconds." Ari made eye contact with Larkin and in unison they nodded.

At the same moment, heavy footsteps scrambled over the roof. Harlow's heart beat out of her chest. She hugged Finn tighter, tempted to close her eyes until it was all over, but something caught her eye by the door to the observatory.

The shade leaned against the doorway, smiling. *Have you figured it out yet? Do you know who you are? Do you know who I am?*

Finn couldn't hear it, but he saw the shade at the same moment she did. And then everything happened at once, in a muffled blur.

Ari yelled, "Time!" and ran for Larkin.

The roof opened, moving so slowly Harlow worried they wouldn't make it.

A message appeared on the screen Larkin had been typing on—Nox had responded, but it was too far away for Harlow to see, and there wasn't time to run to the terminal. Finn stared intently at the screen—perhaps he could see it. He only struggled to read things that were close without his glasses.

Six dark figures appeared, their faces obscured by the incredible show the celestial lighting put on in the sky above.

"Now!" Ari bellowed. "Go now."

The shade moved as the Wraith gave the signal. It smiled at Harlow, then disappeared inside her sister. Harlow lurched, not knowing if Finn saw what she had. But it was too late—his arms were wound tightly around her as she struggled—they were jumping.

*See you soon, little bird*, the shade murmured in her head as the world dissolved, and Harlow finally recognized its voice.

The Ravager had taken her sister. It had Larkin.

~

SHE HAD NO SENSE OF ANYTHING OTHER THAN HER rage. That *thing* had tricked her, made her think it was some sort of distant relation to her, made her trust it, and now it was inside her sister. Harlow didn't know how it was possible, but she'd seen it with her own eyes, heard it call her "little bird," just as the Ravager had. There was nothing but pain and fury, her shadows curling around her, concealing the world from her. And, she had the vague sense she was making noise, howling like an animal in pain.

Hands shot through the shadows, followed quickly by Finn's face. He took hold of her shoulders, shaking her hard. "Stop screaming," he hissed, rotating her body by force and clapping one hand over her mouth and the other around her abdomen. She was pinned to his chest, and he was murmuring something in her ear, something soft and comforting, but she could not hear it.

Harlow slumped against him, sobbing silently. Her shadows retreated, licking at her fingers, trying to soothe her pain. Finn took a few steps, though she couldn't see where they were through her tears. Vaguely, she heard a door opening and closing. Finn let her go, whispering for her to stay put.

There was nowhere to go. She was immobilized by the knowledge that she'd lost Larkin again. Already, the shock of what had happened receded in her mind. Harlow worried she was getting far too good at accepting the terrible things that happened to her. She forced air through her lungs, then scanned her body, bringing her attention to each muscle group. In the first days after losing Larkin and Finn, Sam and Tomyris had been the ones who'd coached her back into the present moment, not allowing her to spin out, or panic, promising her that she'd do her loved ones more good with her head on straight than she would by languishing in her despair.

They weren't here now, but they were just a short distance away, along with the rest of her family. The maters would know what to do. Nox would be able to contact the Grove. This wasn't as hopeless as it seemed, though it certainly wasn't good. It was like Finn said, they had to just keep chipping away at the behemoth pile of shit that kept piling up in front of them.

Something about that image made her laugh. Tears still slid down her cheeks, but the world crept back in. She stood in a desolate back hallway of a miserably sparse home. The furniture she could see from where she stood was sleek and modern, and everything was gray. Gray cushions on the couch, gray tile on the floor, gray baseboards, walls, and ceiling. The place was oppressive in its grayness.

Finn stood in front of her, keying in a code on a lock that led to the basement. The lock opened and he leaned down. A red laser scanned his eye, and the door popped softly open. When it did, Harlow was surprised to find that it was not the normal household door it had looked like from the outside; it was metal and nearly eight inches thick.

"Where are we?" she whispered, remembering that Finn had begged her to be quiet.

"Lemosyne Estates," Finn replied, naming a popular human enclave in the suburbs of Nuva Troi. That, at least, explained all the gray. Humans had gone through a period of loving the color in recent years, seemingly a reaction to the vivid color palettes immortals typically favored.

Finn took her hand, pulling her into the stairwell. He

pushed her forward, urging her down the stairs, before closing them in, the heavy door shutting with a soft click, followed by the sound of several bolts snicking into place.

When soft lights lit beneath their feet, Harlow replied. "The suburbs?"

Finn pushed gently past her, guiding her down the stairs. "Yes. This is a safe house. Nox directed us here..." He trailed off. The muscles in his shoulders contracted.

The staircase went down three flights, but Harlow could see another door at the bottom. "Did you see it?" she asked as Finn moved a bit quicker.

When they stood in front of the next door, he finally looked back. "Yes. What did it say to you?"

"See you soon, little bird."

This door took another code, and this time, a tiny bit of blood from his thumb. When the door opened, he said, "The Ravager."

Harlow only nodded. There was nothing to say. She needed to keep working on getting herself under control, so she focused on her breath, as sconces, low to the ground, lit the shining wood floors beneath their feet. These, at least, were not gray, but pale bleached wood.

"Petra got to decorate this place about five years ago," he murmured. "She was into a 'beachy' look at the time."

Beyond yet another door, and another coded lock, the hall finally gave way to a large room, with a window that looked out onto a view of Ambracia Bay. Harlow couldn't understand it. She was utterly turned around, trying to remember where Lemosyne Estates actually was. It *did* overlook the bay from some sections, the houses here small but costly.

The bay was blanketed in winter gloom, the sapphire water churning angrily far below. The windows were obscured by rock, set back far enough that it was doubtful anyone below could see them, but they let one of Nuva Troi's most impressive views into the little room.

When Harlow tore her eyes away from the sea, she found two white couches, covered in soft linen fabric, facing one another. An enormous driftwood coffee table with a glass top sat between them. Beyond them was a fireplace, a refrigerator, an open door that led to a small bathroom, and a bed covered in the same white linen as the couches.

Finn held the only thing of value: a phone. He already had it powered up and was sending text messages as he made himself comfortable on one of the couches. He glanced up. "This will take a while, with the wards up. I've gotta hack through a bunch of shit before I'll get to Nox. You should rest."

She stared at him. "Are we going to talk about it?"

He looked back down at the phone, his fingers flying across its touchscreen. "We shouldn't have taken her with us. You were right."

"Is that what you think I want? For you to tell me I was *right*?"

Finn didn't look back up. "Isn't it?"

He was shutting her out. "No," she replied, ice in her voice. "It actually isn't. I'm not your mother."

That got his attention. Anger flashed in his eyes as they glowed, and then immediately receded, softening as he saw her— really saw her. "I know." He set the phone down and got up, taking three long strides to get to her. "I just... fucking lost her again, Harlow. Why can't I keep any of you safe?"

The way his voice crackled over each subsequent word melted the icy anger she'd felt only moments before. As his arms went around her, and she hugged him in return, she sifted through the moments she'd shared with Larkin for the past few days, full of little inconsistencies. Her strange moods, the time she'd called her sissy when Larkin knew she hated it, and then further back to the shade, all it had said to her at ORAIS—one remembered phrase slamming into her.

*I am here but not here.* The shade had said it to her, and so had the Ravager. It had given her clues, and she missed them all. But why, why had it been kind? Why had it helped her on the bridge? Why did it want her to find the truth of who she was, the origins of the Feriant? And why in seventeen fucking hells had it taken her sister?

Finn kissed her forehead. "I need to get back to this. The sooner we get to Nox, the sooner she can get in touch with the Grove and we can find out where Larkin is." Harlow nodded. Her limbs felt heavy, weighed down by exhaustion. "Babygirl, you're crashing," Finn said as he guided her to the bed. "Lay down for a bit and I'll have news when you wake."

He bent down when she was seated, untying her boots like she was a small child. With every passing moment, she felt the shock of what had happened take over. She was not doing as well as she'd thought.

"Maybe I'm not cut out for this kind of thing," she mumbled, her words feeling thick in her mouth. "I'm not a hero."

Finn stood, then unzipped her jacket, gently peeling it from her shoulders. When he had her free of it, he steered her towards the pillows, lifting her feet to tuck her into the soft blankets.

"There are no heroes, Harlow," he murmured, climbing in next to her.

She cuddled in next to him, watching as he typed and typed on the phone, glad he'd gotten in bed with her, rather than going back to the couch.

"There's you," she breathed as sleep took her.

# CHAPTER THIRTY-FOUR

They didn't hear back from Nox for several hours. It was just after dawn when the phone buzzed, a sound that Harlow had forgotten existed. She was awake, watching the sea, but Finn slept. In fact, he was so asleep he didn't hear the phone. There was no identifying number on the screen, but Harlow assumed that only people who were trustworthy had the number.

"Hello," she said softly.

"Harlow?" It was Nox.

"Yes," she breathed. "Finn is sleeping. We made it to the safehouse in Lemosyne."

"Thank all gods," the shifter breathed. There was a small ruckus in the background as Nox whispered to whomever was with her, "They're safe."

"Are we good to talk?" Harlow asked, curling up on the couch.

"For a few minutes. I sent Finn the information he asked for."

"Okay," Harlow said, slowly, drawing the syllables out as she thought. Nox was usually so specific about things, precise to a fault, at times. The fact that she'd been vague meant she was worried the line could be compromised. Harlow proceeded with the caution, though she had to ask about Larkin. "Have you heard from Larkin and Ari? Did they make it to the Grove?"

Nox was so quiet Harlow worried she'd lost the connection. "Nox?"

"I'm still here." The shifter seemed to be thinking.

"We know, Nox," Harlow murmured. "What happened?"

The Wraith made a small humming noise, apparently relieved she didn't have to try to break the bad news to Harlow. "She completed the jump safely. Then said, *I'll keep her safe,* before disappearing."

Harlow let out a long breath. "Thank gods."

"You trust it?" Nox asked. Whispers in the background let Harlow know that at least some of her family was probably listening in.

"Hi everyone," she said before answering.

"Just me and Mother," Indi's voice chirped softly.

"No," Harlow said, relieved Selene wasn't there. "I don't, but if it wanted her dead, it could have killed her a thousand times."

There was a long pause, and again, Harlow worried they'd lost connection. "Ari said the same," Aurelia replied, sounding distant. "It's not much comfort, but it's some."

"We're going to lose you in a sec," Nox interjected. "We'll talk about this more tomorrow."

"Okay," Harlow replied. "Love you."

A chorus of "love yous" got cut off as the line really did go dead. She would see her family tomorrow and find a way to fix this.

Harlow resisted the urge to begin listing all the things that had gone wrong at this point. Instead, as Finn slept, she clicked into the folder icon on the screen of the phone. It was the only icon, besides the usual ones for settings, text, and compass.

There wasn't even music, news, or any of the gossips' apps on this thing, and those usually came standard with phones.

Inside the folder was a complete write-up of the Knights' progress in Nuva Troi, as well as a time and geolocation for the ward's opening. They had until this evening, which was awful, because the wards would open inside Nuva Troi's biggest nekropoleis. Ghasts, poltergeists, and shades would all be coming out, at exactly the same time. Harlow repressed the urge to protest; there was no other option. Instead, she shut the screen off.

She felt a little guilty for having pried into what she considered Finn's private business, but reasoned that it had been necessary to determine if it was all right for him to continue sleeping. She glanced briefly at Finn's slumbering form, wondering if she should wake him, then decided against it. They both needed as much rest as possible today. While she loved their family, being surrounded by them again would take precious energy reserves to navigate, and they both were running low.

Harlow fetched a bottled iced latte from the fridge, checking its expiration date. It was still good. As she walked back towards the couch, Finn stirred—sometime in the night, he'd let his glamour go and he rested in his true form, his wings spread out behind him, spilling over the side of the bed at awkward angles. Much like the many ways Axel slept that looked impossibly uncomfortable, Harlow couldn't imagine how he slept that way, but his face was the picture of peace.

His eyes fluttered open, dark in his true form. "Did Nox call yet?"

Harlow leaned on the bed, laying her head on the pillow close to his. "Yes. Larkin jumped Ari to the Grove, and then disappeared. The Ravager promised to keep her safe—whatever that means."

Finn nodded, his eyelids heavy. He yawned. "What about us?"

He was obviously exhausted, fighting his urge to be Knights' commander. "We don't go 'til tonight," she explained, stroking his brow, which was more prominent in this form. The opalescent, almost blue skin that covered his body glowed softly with her comforting touch. "Nox sent over the coordinates and her report."

Finn nodded sleepily, snuggling deeper into the covers. The room was pleasantly dim, cozy and soft. "You read it, okay? Get caught up on what's going on."

Harlow's eyes widened, just a little. "Really?"

"Yeah, could you?" He buried his face in the pillow, but his arm snaked out to pull her into a hug. "Love you," he mumbled before falling back into what Harlow hoped was a deeply restorative sleep.

She watched him sleep with fascination—he'd never slept so deeply in the entire time they'd been back in each other's lives. As she extricated herself from his heavy embrace, she thought of the thick doors and many locks that separated them from the outside world. It took all that to make him feel safe. That wasn't just the stark fact that the world had gone to shit, it was how Finn lived.

And now he was trusting her to read Nox's report for him. Harlow flexed her hands as she stood, staring at the engagement ring that she never, ever removed. Spending her life with Finn had always been something of a blurry, happy thought, until now. Now, it felt real. The shift between them since she'd gotten him back was nearly imperceptible, but it had made their relationship real in a way it had never been before. Raw, messy, even ugly sometimes. But they just kept trying.

They'd *keep* trying. They'd keep having each other's backs, and fighting when they didn't agree. It wouldn't be a perfect picture; they weren't some ideal. They were a perfect mess—and they were going to make it through this. She knew enough about stories to know this was meant to be her darkest hour—the point when she should feel unable to go on. The odds were certainly stacked against them, in nearly every way possible. There were no clean solutions left to any of their problems, and worse, disaster lurked around every corner.

But for the first time in months, that didn't make her feel unbearably heavy. She was terrified about what might happen to Larkin, but even the tiniest grain of hope was enough. Harlow didn't know what the Ravager wanted, but if she was right that it had been with them, watching them, since its release from Nihil, she wondered—really wondered—if what it wanted was utter destruction.

Harlow pulled a throw blanket from the arm of the couch and tucked herself into a corner where she could see the ocean, sipping her iced coffee, opening the file Nox had sent Finn to update him on what they'd learned so far in Nuva Troi. She assumed the most important information wouldn't be here: Nox might be confident in her ability to hide digital trails, but she'd never risk their operation when she and Finn would be in the same place in a few hours.

As expected, not much in the report was shocking or a secret. The first item was a long list of important places that had been destroyed in the fighting when the first wave of Vespae had come through the city, before the Order of Mysteries had gotten the wards to hold. She was sad to see that the streets surrounding the Monas had taken so much damage. It had been mostly residential, and longtime family friends had lost their homes.

There were also lists of places Nox had tracked the five rings symbol they'd seen marking certain windows last summer. They were cropping up more now, as a beacon of hope, but also an indicator that help for humans could be found within. That was, perhaps, the most depressing news. Humans had a curfew, and had been strictly forbidden from trying to use any aethereal power. They were expelled from the protective wards that surrounded Nuva Troi if they refused to comply.

Hives of Vespae had been tracked carefully. They were surrounding the city, gathering in the suburbs. In fact, there was one not far from Lemosyne Estates. They would have to pass near it, and through the city's outer ring nekropoleis to get to the ward opening later. Harlow shuddered thinking of it. She'd been blessedly free of ghasts for nearly two weeks and had no desire to have them chase her down again.

But by far, the worst news was that all of the gossips were back up and running, and they were calling the gathering of refugees in Nuva Troi, "the winter season." Harlow glanced through a few of the low points Nox had pulled out, shaking her head. The fact that there were members of the lower Orders socializing right now showed just how far removed they were from the realities of the world.

A sorcière Harlow had known since childhood had been quoted as saying, "As long as the wards hold, we're gonna party like the world is ending." At that, Harlow groaned aloud. A year ago she might have rolled her eyes, but she'd have moved on quickly, distracting herself with other pursuits and the idea that there was nothing she could do. Everything was different now.

Finn sat up, his head tilting. She'd woken him reacting to the foolish witch's words. "What time is it?"

Harlow looked at the clock on the end table. "A little past noon. Are you hungry?"

He leaned forward, his wings tensing behind him. "I might be."

Heat flushed through Harlow. His skin glowed softly as he looked her over. "Don't you want me to tell you what Nox sent over?"

"Not particularly," he said, swinging his legs over the side of the bed.

When he stood, the sheets fell away to reveal his naked body. In his true form, he was taller, broader, even more muscular than his humanoid alternae, and he was clearly not interested in hearing about anything other than her from the looks of things.

He strode into the bathroom, giving her a show of his sculpted behind. "Why don't we see about a bath for you?"

Harlow rose without another word, compelled by the rippling movement in his wings, the clenched muscles of his ass, and the sound of water running. They had time—for a little while longer, they had time.

# CHAPTER THIRTY-FIVE

A ri had described the devastation in Nuva Troi, but there weren't words to prepare Harlow for *this*. The damage in the suburbs had been light; the horror here was the profound emptiness. There were no children playing on the streets, no sledders in the parks, and no one was out shoveling snow. Typically, Harlow loved the city best, with its crowded, glittering glory. But in deep winter, the suburbs were always her favorite because of the sheer amount of people making the best of the cold.

Now, as she and Finn quietly made their way through the empty streets, the devastation of Okairos seeped into Harlow. Where were all the people who lived here? Her heart knew the answer, and it shuddered erratically as she followed Finn through back alleys. Traveling inconspicuously here was difficult, as even back alleys were wider than in the city, leaving room for trash trucks and Harlow's ultimate favorite: weekend garage sales. Harlow had never felt so exposed in Lemosyne Estates, which had been one of her favorite places to search for treasures on hot summer weekends.

The journey was quiet at first, and then the buzzing noise of thousands of Vespae seeped in. They were everywhere, essentially unavoidable the closer they got to the nekropoleis. But the day had been bright, sunny, and cold, and it seemed to have lent them a bit of luck so far. As the Vespae did not enjoy sunlight, most they encountered were in a dull stasis, huddled in groups, facing one another.

A mere hint of movement caught Harlow's attention in a deserted playground. She and Finn both froze. It was only a suggestion of pursuit, no footsteps, no brush of fabric, nothing more than a ghost of a sound. But it stopped when they stopped, and moved when they moved. A harsh wind kicked up, sending fresh snow flying in the air, the metal swings creaking back and forth.

*Can you tell where they're coming from?* Harlow asked, hoping that Finn's hyper-sensitive hearing might be able to discern more than she could.

*We've got two tails,* he replied. *Both moving alone.*

As he communicated this to her, a single drone crashed through the doors of the little visitors' center next to the playground. Its movements were erratic, as though it weren't moving on its own will. It made straight for Finn, who shouted, "Run! I'll meet you at the nekropoleis."

Harlow hesitated. They'd talked about what to do if something like this happened, but she didn't want to leave him. The logic of letting him fight the drone alone was solid. It was just one. He could use his speed if he had to, though they'd avoided both that and teleporting to keep a lower profile, not wanting to be tracked if the Illuminated were using CCTV or other monitoring devices to locate refugees—or seditionists.

"Harlow," he growled between punches. The drone wasn't fighting particularly well, but it was slippery, seeming to evade and pester, more than attack. He was distracted by her presence, unable to fight well if he knew she was standing there just watching.

*Better to be a moving target*, she remembered. She forced herself into a jog, out of the park, glancing back only once as she exited the park, but Finn had disappeared from sight, though she could still hear him fighting in the distance. Harlow got the strong sense they were being purposely separated, and she didn't like it. She decided to make one lap through the block she was on and go back for Finn.

Halfway around a block of nearly identical homes, movement in her peripheral vision caught her attention. She turned slowly, hoping to find Finn, but instead came face to face with a Vespae queen. Her wings were beautiful, whole rather than ragged, though her clothes fared no better than any of her counterparts. They were in tatters, looking like they'd been spun from spider-silk. Her face was freshly scarred, as though someone had dragged talons across it recently. It was the queen who'd tried to communicate with Harlow at the attack on Sanctum.

The queen's head tilted, and Harlow braced for the clicking noise that would call her swarm, but there was nothing. The queen moved slowly, carefully, as though she didn't want to startle Harlow. Her rigid brow tightened a little, as though she might be frowning.

Harlow couldn't make sense of what was happening, and her instinct was to run. But the queen's eyes searched hers, bright and intelligent. There wasn't a hint of the Vespae's usual menace in her demeanor. She'd tried to communicate before— might she try again? Harlow kept her voice low and even, putting effort into trying to replicate the buzzing noise the Vespae made when they were resting. "What do you want?"

The queen's head tilted further, her eyes widening some as she looked closely at Harlow's mouth. Despite her disheveled state, Harlow was surprised to find that the creature smelled like spring—like a field of wildflowers and sweet grass. She made a few soft noises, ones utterly different from the calls Harlow had heard in the past. They didn't sound like words, but there was no denying they were language. The Vespae queen *was* trying to communicate with her.

Harlow nodded, hoping to indicate that she was trying to understand. The queen nodded back, her eyes lighting. But then she shook her head no, repeating the same phrase again and again, pausing to nod then shake her head after each time. She was asking if Harlow understood her.

Harlow shook her head no, finally. The queen's shoulders slumped in obvious frustration. Harlow remembered that Alain Easton had somehow been communicating with the Vespae, and wondered how. "Do you understand me?"

The queen's eyes lit up again. She nodded vigorously.

Harlow looked around, thinking quickly. Did she have a pen in her pack? She wasn't sure, but she also didn't want to startle the queen with movement she might mistake as hostile. "Can you read our words? Write?"

This time the queen thought for a moment. She held up a finger as she spoke, which Harlow took to mean "I'm answering your first question." The queen nodded.

Harlow smiled. "You can read our words."

The queen looked horrified by the smile, staring at Harlow's teeth. Harlow stopped. "My apologies. I am happy you understand me."

When the queen looked confused, Harlow tried again. "It brings me joy that you understand my words." Still confusion. Maybe happiness and joy weren't clear concepts for the Vespae. She tried another approach, on a hunch. "It brings me peace that you understand me."

The queen nodded, pressing her hands to her chest, a low comforting buzz emitting from her mouth. Her eyes glazed over with bliss. Peace was a concept the queen understood, and obviously she found it as positive as Harlow did. Harlow kept her mouth closed this time, but nodded as she smiled, pointing to her mouth, then said, "Peace."

The queen nodded again, then held up two fingers. She was answering Harlow's second question about writing. Now she moved her head in an odd fashion, it wasn't a nod, or a shake, but somewhere in between. Then she pointed to her long fingers and curved talons.

"Oh!" Harlow exclaimed. "It's hard for you to write."

The queen nodded. She said several things, her buzzes and clicks repeating softly, as though she were talking to herself. A muscle in her face twitched.

"There's something you want to tell me," Harlow intuited aloud. "But it's complicated."

The queen nodded.

Harlow didn't know what they were going to do. A crash nearby startled them both. She heard Finn cry out, followed by the sounds of fighting. The queen let out a shrill noise, then a series of clicks. The queen looked at the sky in a way that obviously expressed frustration with her swarm but there were sounds of retreat. Finn called her name now, though Harlow didn't want to answer. It wouldn't matter if she said she was all right, he would come, and he would scare the queen off, or try to fight her.

Harlow took a risk and touched the queen's arm. "They'll be here soon, but I want to talk to you. What do your people want? Can you try to tell me?"

The queen nodded, crouching down. Her forehead moved again, this time expressing intense concentration. The snow was dirty, but the queen made big letters in it. The one word she wrote was not a surprise, it confirmed what Harlow had supposed at ORAIS.

"You want to go home."

The queen nodded, making several noises of distress, and movements with her body that indicated pain, then a motion with her hands that looked like a fish swimming along a straight path, followed by the noises that meant peace.

"It's painful to be here," Harlow translated. "You want to go home."

The queen made her "sort of" head motion again, then repeated the fish hand motions and the peace noise. Harlow tried again. "It's painful to be here, and you're looking for a way home."

Now the queen nodded, waiting expectantly. Harlow did what she knew no one else probably would, she took the queen's hands in her own. This did startle the creature, but she did not react violently; she made a lower noise than the peace noise, but similar. Harlow decided this meant it was all right.

She couldn't tell the queen that her world had been destroyed. Not when she was asking for help and Harlow had none. It felt like a betrayal, but their communication was so tenuous that she couldn't tell the whole truth, not until she had a solution that wouldn't devastate them both.

Harlow looked up into the queen's eyes, and told the best truth she could. "I will find the way. It's what I'm here to do." The queen nodded, then slid one of her hands out of Harlow's to write in the snow again. Her letters were messy, but they spelled out ORAIS. The queen pointed to Harlow, then herself several times.

"You were with Alain at ORAIS."

The queen nodded, she made a noise that was unmistakably angry, hitting her chest, but pointing away from Harlow. Then she pointed to Harlow, making the low noise that didn't quite mean peace again.

"Alain?" Harlow breathed, wondering if she was catching on.

The angry noise.

"Harlow," she said, pointed to herself.

The queen made a slightly less pleasant noise now, but it still resembled the positive noises the Vespae made. Harlow took it to mean, "You're not my favorite, but you're fine enough."

"Did you see what I found out about your planet?"

The queen nodded, squeezing her hand. There was no mistaking the sorrow on her face. She needn't have worried about lying. The queen already knew. She spoke quickly, moving her hands in ways Harlow couldn't make out. Then, she drug her talons across her face. Harlow remembered the way the first queen at Sanctum had hurt her.

"The others don't want to work with us?"

The queen shook her head. Finn and the queen's drone were getting closer. Harlow had to think fast. The queen had been to ORAIS, seen what Harlow had and she was reminding Harlow of the discord between herself and the other queen.

"They don't believe you. The others don't believe you that your planet was destroyed."

The queen nodded, making the noise Harlow now associated with Alain.

"Because Alain told them something else."

The queen nodded, dragging a finger across her throat. It was just a guess, but Harlow thought the queen meant that Alain had killed her people, the ones that had been with her. Likely, he'd done so to keep them from telling. Harlow wondered how the queen had escaped. There wasn't time to discuss that now. Footsteps approached from all directions: Finn's and the queen's drones, or perhaps her guard. They'd been found.

Harlow tightened her grip on the queen's hand. "We don't have to fight. Let me try to help."

The queen nodded, pointing to the word "HOME" in the snow. Finn was close now, and so were the queen's people. They were out of time. There would be a fight if they stayed.

"Go," Harlow said, releasing the queen. "I'll do everything I can to help."

The queen pressed a hand to her chest again, and made the full peace noise, as she looked up, into an upstairs window of the house. A figure stood watching—one Harlow would know anywhere.

"Larkin," she shouted.

Her sister stepped away from the window, and the queen shot into the air, calling to her approaching guards. Harlow rushed through the shattered glass of the kitchen door, racing towards the stairs at the center of the house. Larkin stood on the landing, but from the unnatural set of her shoulders, Harlow knew the Ravager had her.

"Please let my sister go," Harlow begged. "I'll do anything you want."

"You're already doing what I want," the Ravager said, with Larkin's voice. "And besides, I'm not hurting her."

Harlow knew better than to rush the stairs. The Ravager would just use Larkin's ability to teleport away. "Why did you help me? Why did you help Ari?"

Larkin's head shook. "The time for questions is over, little bird. We will see each other again when there are answers."

"Wait," Harlow cried out, desperate. "Are you going to kill her? Please. Just tell me the truth. Are you going to kill my sister?"

The Ravager inside her sister sighed deeply. "I am so very tired. Aren't you?" Larkin disappeared.

Harlow was still staring at the spot she'd stood when Finn crashed through the front door. Her entire body felt as though it might go limp. "Larkin was here."

Finn's head swiveled wildly, searching for Larkin. Noise from outside suggested another swarm had found them. The keening cry that threatened to build in Harlow's throat died as Finn grabbed her hand. "We have to go."

# CHAPTER THIRTY-SIX

Outside, the air vibrated with the noise of approaching Vespae. Finn glanced down at Harlow, whose hand shook in his. "We have to take a risk now, okay?"

She nodded, too upset to think. He took hold of her and they blinked out, reappearing inside a gas station. The electricity was off and across the street, Harlow spotted the entrance to Nuva Troi's largest nekropoleis.

"Are you all right?" he asked as he searched the empty gas station. The shelves had been ransacked.

Harlow shook off the moment with Larkin as best she could. "Yes. But before you found me, the Vespae queen that tried to talk to me at Sanctum, before I found you..."

Finn glanced up from a few aisles away. In a flash, he was next to her, hugging her. "Hey," he murmured into her hair. "Keep talking to me while I see if I can find some salt. We have to keep moving."

Outside, the sun was going down. They didn't have long until the ward opening. "The queen. She was at ORAIS with Alain. They found the information we did. She knows their planet was destroyed, but the other queens don't believe her. I think Alain is lying to them, manipulating them into helping him cause chaos."

Finn nodded. He held a bag of rock salt aloft, smiling. "In case the shades or poltergeists get too frisky." His cheer was fake, but she smiled back in kind. It was all they could do. "He's not causing chaos, Harls. He's making a power play. I have a feeling he wants the Illuminated's reign of power ended as much as we do—he just wants to be on top when it ends."

A sharp pain shot through Harlow's chest. She'd been holding her breath while Finn spoke, and her heart was beating in an uneven rhythm, her lungs pulling sharp gasps of air in. The ceiling felt as though it was lowering for a moment. Harlow closed her eyes, crouching down and unzipping her jacket so her neck and chest could get some air.

Finn crouched next to her, breathing slowly. "We're going to get through this, babygirl. One step at a time, okay?"

Harlow let her eyes drag up from the dirty tile floor to his. "Do you actually think we can do this? Can we win against all these odds?"

"The truth?" he asked.

She nodded, even though she wasn't sure she wanted it. Finn's analytical take on things was most likely grim right now.

"When I look at it objectively, no. We don't stand a fucking chance." Tears sprung in Harlow's eyes. Deep down, she knew this. "I don't know though, Harls…" he trailed off, his stormy eyes sparkling. Here in this dark, abandoned gas station, outside the city they both loved, at what felt like the end of everything, Finn's eyes were sparkling. "I know we can do this. It's not even a question for me. We're going to win—*because we have to.*"

Outside the gas station, ghasts appeared, and at least one poltergeist, attracted to Harlow's grief. Expensive sigils on the door kept them out, but as soon as they went out there, the ghasts would be all over them. Finn stood, pulling Harlow to her feet. He didn't pick the bag of salt back up as he stared at the growing crowd of unquiet spirits.

"If they're using the tracking equipment I'd use, they may already know we're here," he said softly. He wasn't talking to her, but to himself. He glanced down at his watch. "The wards are opening soon. We're blinking in."

Harlow's head tilted as her mouth opened, though to say what, she didn't know. Before she could think of anything to say, he covered her mouth with his, and they disappeared between.

They reappeared in the nekropoleis, along a row of impressive crypts, but Harlow didn't have time to admire the scenery. Ghosts streamed out of every crypt, attracted not only to Harlow, but apparently to the wards themselves. There was nothing to see, but Harlow felt the massive amount of magic being used to keep the wards up, a dome of power over Nuva Troi. She'd never seen anything like it before. The biggest spell she'd ever witnessed was the Vascularity in Nea Sterlis, and though the wards were less complex, the sheer area they covered was impressive.

Finn held her to his chest, his arm tight around her waist. The ghasts solidified as they neared Harlow, her fear growing by the moment. At Sanctum, one had been able to touch her, and now there were hundreds of them, filling the narrow lane between crypts. They were no longer silent, noise accompanying the hideous feats they performed with their rotting bodies.

Across the lane, the wards opened, a sliver of light that shimmered in the threads. "Fuck," Finn swore. "I miscalculated."

Finn grabbed her hand, pulling her towards the sliver of opening in the wards. They had less than a minute to get through. Several vampire ghasts, who'd likely died a hundred years ago from the vintage of their clothing, hissed at them. Their rotting flesh was livid with dark, oozing liquid. The pack of vampire ghasts were closing in on them, though the others materializing mostly milled about, terrifying, but not necessarily violent.

The vampires, however, obviously intended to inflict harm. Their ravenous howls attracted shades, who crept out from several crypts, their hollow eyes roving over the living flesh in their midst. Harlow had no idea how she'd mistaken the Ravager for a shade. Her fear of the dead had kept her from observing them too closely, but she saw the difference easily now.

Finn pushed her behind him. "Get on my back," he growled as he shifted into his true form.

He was going to barrel through them. Every second that passed, the ward-opening grew smaller. She did as he asked, holding tight as he sped through the creatures surrounding them, using his head as a battering ram and his wings as a barrier between her and the spirits they plough through. He shifted back as they crossed through the opening, just as it closed.

It was a bit like teleporting. There was a moment of blank contraction and then they were inside a crypt, gasping for air, both of them sweating from the side effects of having passed through the opening just a tiny bit too late. Inside the crypt, there were four huge Illuminated guards, armed to the teeth with human-made weaponry. It was the kind of tech Alaric called "terrifying in its genius," and was beyond illegal to even speak about, though of course the dark web was full of schematics. Apparently, Connor had found a way to actually produce them.

One of the guards, a redhead, sneered as she stepped forward. "Look what we have here. Finn Fucking McKay."

Harlow glanced from guard to guard. None wore even a shred of empathy on their faces. Which was supposed to help them? They all wore vicious expressions, and she found it hard to believe that even one of them might get them out of this. Finn stepped in front of Harlow.

The redhead took out a pair of zip ties and waved them in

Finn's face. "Put these on her, and then on yourself. Kimaris is gonna promote me to the Dominavus for this."

Harlow's heart sung at the mention of Rakul's name. Maybe they'd take them to him, and this nightmare would end. Vivia had to have made it back by now, and the two of them could help Finn and Harlow escape.

The tallest of the guards shook his head. "Fuck that, Marshall. You're not even close to a promotion. I've been short-listed for the Dominavus twice."

Marshall rolled her eyes. "All the more reason to let me take them in."

Harlow suspected Marshall was the one who was meant to help them, but she worried about Nox's choice in guards. The Illuminated woman was rude, and not particularly convincing. Even Harlow thought it was a stretch that the other guards would just let her take them in. She held out her hands for the zip ties though, the faster they got this over with, the better.

Finn held eye contact with her for a moment longer than necessary, flicking his eyes to Marshall as she and the tall guard argued. He pulled the zip tie closed, but not too tight. Harlow lowered her head in a slow nod. They agreed, Marshall was their best bet, whether she was the person who was supposed to help them or not. At the very least, they could overpower her easily when they were alone.

Marshall was a distracted mess, arguing with the tall guard, rather than watching them tie one another up. "C'mon Penemue, you're a nepo-baby and you'll get any position you want, eventually. Don't be an asshole. Let me take them in."

Finn's eyes widened at the use of the tall guard's name. This was Alix Penemue, the only son of Rosamund Penemue, the former governor of Falcyra. After spending months in Falcyra, Harlow had heard her fair share of rumors about his cruelty. They couldn't go with him. He was too well matched with Finn as a fighter, for one thing.

The other two guards appeared to have lost interest. They'd taken their places on watch. One by the door, one watching a dimly lit computer screen, which appeared to show a heat map of the nekropoleis. There were several Vespae moving through the graves, hot on Finn and Harlow's trail, but the ghasts and shades had disappeared. Harlow wondered about the Vespae. If the queen had called them off, why were they still following? But, of course, there was more than one swarm in the area.

Alix Penemue shook his head. "I'm not arguing about this with you, Marshall. I outrank you. Get back to work."

Harlow held her breath, waiting for Marshall to form another, more clever argument, but nothing came. The redhead grumbled a bit, then went back to a post by the window. Harlow's heart sank. She made eye contact with Finn just as Alix Penemue drew the butt of his gun back, then slammed it into the back of Finn's head so hard, he crumpled to the ground.

Harlow screamed and Penemue grabbed her roughly, tearing the zip ties off her, replacing them with metal cuffs. The second they were on, Harlow knew they were in trouble. The cuffs were made of iridium. She wouldn't be able to shift.

A long whimper escaped her lips as he clamped another set onto Finn. The other guards laughed, even Marshall.

"Gets 'em every time, doesn't it?" the redhead said. "We give shits like you a minute to think of all the ways you're gonna escape, and then you feel the death metal and..." she drew her finger across her throat, making a choking noise. "Makes doing this drudgery bearable, honestly."

The other two laughed again, obviously agreeing. Alix Penemue didn't laugh. His face didn't move one stony muscle as he dragged Finn towards a door at the back of the crypt. He opened it, revealing a dark staircase that only had one possible outcome: the catacombs under Nuva Troi.

"Follow," he commanded.

Harlow did as she was told, though everything in her

screamed that if she went down those stairs, she wouldn't surface again. She wasn't sure she had another choice.

Marshall stepped forward as she went, gripping Harlow's arm hard. "I hear it goes better if you don't fight him too hard." She waggled her eyebrows at Harlow suggestively.

Harlow spit in her face. The redhead punched her. Pain bloomed across the bridge of Harlow's nose, sending her to her knees. Ahead of her, Penemue pushed Finn down the stairs, his body thumping the entire way down. He turned, pushing Marshall back, who was spooling up for another punch.

"Don't spoil her face," Penemue said with a smirk.

Marshall laughed harder now, and Harlow knew that laugh. It was one she'd used, the one that held no humor, but relief. Relief it wasn't going to be her that got hurt. She'd used that laugh when Mark got mean with other people in front of her. It was something she'd regret her entire life, laughing when someone else was about to be hurt, rather than herself. But at least she understood.

As Alix Penemue pulled Harlow off the floor she looked Marshall directly in the eyes. "I'm glad it's me this time, instead of you," she whispered. "Maybe someday you'll forgive yourself for this."

The anger fell off the woman's face like a mask. Only shock remained. Behind her, Penemue laughed into her ear, low and cold. "There'll be plenty left for Marshall, don't you worry."

Harlow stared into the redhead's eyes as Penemue dragged her away. It was the only thing that gave her strength, knowing that even for a few moments, she was giving *that* woman relief, even if she hated her. The other two guards kept their eyes carefully ahead, as they had for the entire interaction, pretending not to see. As the darkness of the staircase closed around her, she shut her eyes.

When she opened them again, they were standing by a golf cart, deep in the catacombs. It was an odd sight, so out of place for the surroundings, but it did make sense, she supposed. Penemue was loading Finn into the back, and then shoved Harlow forward. "Get in."

There was a bit less cruelty in his voice now, but Harlow wasn't lulled into complacency. She'd fight every single second of this. She didn't move.

"I'd rather you not be passed out for this," Penemue growled. "Get in the cart."

He glanced back up the stairs, as though watching for the other guards. Was he hoping they'd peek in and see his cruelty? Or was he just satisfied that they'd hear him, whatever he was about to do, with their preternatural hearing. Her stomach turned, and every step was painful, but once she was seated in the cart, Penemue didn't lay a finger on her. So it was worse then; he had some secret lair down here, likely where no one would hear her scream.

She considered trying it anyway, just to stall for more time, but the cart lurched forward and she had to spend all her energy staying upright. There were no lights down here, and the golf cart's headlights were weak, so Harlow could see very little as they sped along. There were forks in the maze of tunnels every twenty to thirty feet, and Harlow didn't know how Penemue knew where to go until she noticed the red lines painted on the path.

Unconsciously, she began watching the lines, focusing all her attention on them. When they took an unmarked turn, her stomach dropped. She'd started to convince herself that Penemue was probably all talk, and that Connor would want them brought back in good condition. Who would risk making him mad? Not even Rosamund Penemue's heir.

But then, Finn was only knocked out. He was probably already healing. And he was who Connor would care about, not her. Her suspicion that Alix had a lair of his own down here seemed more likely to be true with every passing moment.

They'd picked up speed, so when the cart slammed to a halt, Harlow lurched forward.

Penemue kept her from flying out of the cart, his arm slamming into her chest. "Get out," he ordered, his voice a murmur.

Harlow didn't move. She was frozen by her own fear. Penemue shook his head, then began unlocking the heavy wooden door in front of them with several combination locks. Harlow struggled against the iridium manacles around her wrists, to no avail, then tried her best to summon her shadows. Nothing worked. The iridium muffled her access to the aether, and Finn was still out cold.

She was a little surprised that when Penemue had the door open, he dragged Finn in first. Harlow jumped out of the cart, rushing to follow Finn, to try to stop whatever Penemue would do next. Finn lay in a heap in front of her, but Penemue was nowhere to be seen. The door slammed shut, the sound of whirling locks sinking her spirits even further. Harlow spun to face Penemue, determined to be brave.

The Illuminated grinned at her, opening his arms. "I'm so fucking glad to see you."

Harlow took several steps backward, in horror, nearly tripping over Finn's body. A ward went up around the door, a strong, sorcière-made ward. And then Penemue's face began to melt. Harlow's vision blurred. She blinked several times and when her sight cleared, Meline stood in front of her.

"Sorry!" her sister cried. Meline grabbed her, hugging her hard, kissing her cheeks. "That was *so* messed up. I'm sorry."

Harlow stood stock-still, completely stunned. The illusion had been *perfect*. Her mouth fell open as Meline pulled away from her. She didn't know whether to laugh or sob.

Meline ran to a spiral staircase that grew out of one corner of the room. The floral carving on the alabaster stone reminded her of something, some*where* familiar. "Are we under the Order of Mysteries?" Harlow breathed.

"Yes," Meline said, before calling up the stairs. "I have them, come quick."

Sam and Tomyris rushed down, and Harlow thought she would lose her mind with relief. Tears fell on her cheeks as her breath shuddered through her. Tomyris gave her a quick, fierce hug, before beginning work on Finn, celestial power flowing through her hands. It took Harlow a moment to register that Tomyris was using her alternae. Instead of the curvaceous, muscular Ventyr woman Harlow was used to seeing, she watched as a woman with all of Tomyris' sharp, angular features, with umber skin and long, ebony hair tied back in a bouncy ponytail, worked to revive Finn.

"Who did her ponytail?" Harlow asked as Sam hugged her tightly.

Her friend's grin was wide. "She did it herself. Your sisters have been giving her tutorials. All her idea—when she found out they used to be influencers."

"Used to be?" Harlow murmured.

Sam nodded, watching as Meline handed things to Tomyris from a duffel bag that served as her medical kit. "Those two are great friends... But yeah, your sisters refused to get back on socials. They've quit."

It wasn't so surprising, she guessed, given all they'd been through, but it was a little odd. The twins had been public figures since they were in their teens. The second the maters let them have social media, they'd already had brand identities planned. An era had ended in Nuva Troi society if they weren't going to be the perpetual "it" girls that everyone looked to for fashion and beauty advice.

But Meline was wearing completely practical clothes even now: a black, funnel neck winter coat, sensible thick leggings, and tall, compact snow boots. She looked stunning, as always, but there wasn't an accessory on her. Her sister had changed. Harlow didn't know if it was for the better, but she looked well.

Happy, even. Some of the shock of the past hour wore off and Harlow was able to give Sam a rundown of what the last few days had been like and what they'd found at ORAIS.

When her story wound down, Finn was awake. He sat up, rubbing the back of his head. He looked at Meline, narrowed his eyes and then shook his head. "You hit me, huh?"

She grimaced. "I had to make it look real!"

He shook his head, but started to laugh, pulling Meline into a hug. "You had me fooled. That was great work."

Meline hugged back, and Harlow thought her heart might burst. When she replied with, "Love you, big brother," Harlow burst into tears.

"Aww, Harls," Tomyris bellowed. "Don't start on the waterworks." Tears pricked her big brown eyes though, and she stood, wrapping Harlow and Sam both into a giant hug.

"I missed the two of you so much," Harlow blubbered as Finn and Meline both wedged their way into the group hug.

They didn't stand that way for long. Meline hurried them upstairs. "Go on, I have to go handle Alix's demise. I have a trick up my sleeve to make Connor believe you've escaped back to the suburbs."

Finn, who was halfway into the first spiral, turned. "Is Alix Penemue still alive?"

Meline rolled her eyes. "I didn't become an assassin while you were gone. He's knocked out in a broom closet in their headquarters under the Temple of Raia offices. He won't wake up for another four hours, and I'll be three hours gone by then."

Finn nodded. "You have it all figured out then."

Tomyris clapped a hand on his shoulder. "She's good at this. Really good."

Harlow hugged Meline. "Love you to the moons," she whispered in her sister's ear. "See you wherever home is later?"

Meline cupped Harlow's face in her hands. "You sure will, pal."

Then her sister shifted back into the enormous Illuminated asshole, Alix Penemue, who shook his rump like an agitated chicken and clucked a few times. Meline laughed in Alix's voice. "I just love making dudes like this look like incompetent fucks."

Meline-as-Alix disappeared back through the door, and Harlow stood watching, speechless at the effortlessness of it all. Sam smiled at her. "She can expand her illusion now to others. Up to about a half hour, which is all she should need."

Finn looked down the stairs at Sam. "What do you mean?"

Tomyris grinned, her white teeth shining in that feral way that reminded Harlow that she was an expert fighter. "She's got two of the sorcière we're sending into the 'burbs on recon gussied up as the two of *you*. They're about to go put on a little show for the cameras. 'Harlow and Finn' are about to escape the great Alix Penemue and stuff him in a closet."

Harlow was impressed; she caught Finn's eye and his head shook in amazement. "Why'd we even come back?" he said with a wry smile. "You all have everything handled."

Sam took Harlow's hand. "Come on, your moms are waiting upstairs. They've been staying here for the past few weeks, instead of Alaric's."

Harlow followed Sam upstairs, bringing up the rear, while Tomyris explained, "Aurelia and Selene have been looking for everything we can find on the Ravagers. As soon as we found out how Larkin was taken, we came here."

"And have the maters found anything?" Finn asked.

"A bit," Sam answered, turning to wink at Harlow.

Harlow shook her head. If anyone could work this out, it was Selene and Aurelia. It felt like it took forever, and about twenty spirals, but Finn opened a door into a back hallway so familiar it brought back Harlow's childhood.

The Order of Mysteries smelled of cedarwood, wax, paper, and the merest hint of vanilla absolut, which was an odd change, but pleasant. It was less odd when Selene wrapped her arms around Harlow, surrounding her with her own sultry scent. Vanilla absolut was one of Selene's favorite perfumes, and she smelled of it now.

"Darling," Mama whispered in her ear.

"Let me hug our girl," Aurelia interrupted.

Sam and Tomyris backed away, smiling at the happy reunion. "See you tomorrow," Sam mouthed. "Morning run?"

Harlow shook her head, shooting Sam a mock-glare, mouthing back, "Not a chance."

Tomyris blew her a kiss as they walked off. Selene threw herself at Finn, who'd apparently just been hugged by Aurelia, as he still looked slightly bewildered by the parental attention. Bewildered, but pleased. Harlow was pleased as well. Seeing her entire family just as excited to see him as they were to see her was just the balm she needed after the day she'd had.

# CHAPTER THIRTY-SEVEN

Walking down the halls of the Order of Mysteries brought back all kinds of memories, and not just because she'd spent so much time here as a kid, but because nearly everyone her parents trusted most was *here*. Their friends, and their friends' children, and sometimes their children as well.

"What are they all doing here?" Harlow asked as the maters led her and Finn to Aurelia's apartments.

All of the Order of Mysteries' representatives and their staff had quarters in the Order itself for times when there were multi-day rituals, or events. As the Order operated as much as an academic unit and artists' atelier as anything else, their compound in Nuva Troi was nearly the size of the Alcaia liberal arts college next door.

"We're safer together," Aurelia answered. "As well, we decided to come back here to help the administration at Alcaia."

The Order and the university had a close relationship, so that didn't surprise Harlow. "Are things all right there?"

Selene smiled. "The students protested a lot at the beginning. They argued for letting more refugees in..." Mama's eyes got misty.

Aurelia finished. "There was a massacre."

Finn stopped cold. "The Vespae?"

Aurelia placed her hand on Finn's arm, deep empathy in her eyes. "No, darling."

His jaw clenched as his eyes fell to his feet, his cheeks flushing red as people passed.

Aurelia took his hand in both of hers. "No one here blames you, Finn."

Selene added her hand to her wife's. They were making a scene in the hallway, and from the performance Selene was putting on, this was utterly strategic. They were quite a picture, the penitent Knight and the wise sorcière matriarchs. It was working; people looked on them with sympathy as they passed. A few spared a glance for Harlow, but not one person said hello.

Their eyes slid past her as they had for the past two years. Harlow shook her head. She knew the way to her family's rooms here, and she wasn't going to ruin what Selene and Aurelia were trying to do. She waited until a few people came to speak to Finn and the maters before slipping away. She looked back over her shoulder to find Selene's eyes following her.

Selene's smile spoke of understanding. She knew how unfair it was that they could accept Finn, but were still holding a grudge against Harlow for dating Mark. Selene had been the subject of similar treatment when she was young, and apparently a bit of a rake. As family lore went, Mama had broken the wrong heart right before she met Aurelia, and it took several decades to build their reputation with the Order of Mysteries again.

Harlow's people were wonderful, but sorcière were slow to forgive. As she made her way through the arched limestone hallways, she ignored every curious look, and the accompanying freeze out. Just as she pressed her palm to the electronic lock at the Krane's quarters, a voice called out her name.

She turned to find Avery Hargrove jogging after her. The curvaceous, beautiful witch was another of Mark Easton's exes, and a close friend of Larkin's. Avery, who was usually elegant and reserved, threw her arms around Harlow.

"I heard about Larkin," she murmured, before pulling away. "Not many people know, don't worry. But your moms asked me to help look through the archives for information on the Ravagers."

So they were jumping right in. Still, Harlow was glad for the hug, and glad for Avery's hand slipping into hers. "I'm so glad you're okay, Harlow."

"You are?" The words slipped out before Harlow could think better of them.

But it was clear Avery understood. "I know everyone's still deep in the habit of freezing you out. It took three years for me. Given everything you've done for them, I'd say you have a few more days, tops." Avery's round cheeks lifted towards her sparkling brown eyes in a smile. "And if I'm wrong, fuck 'em. You have Finn and your family, the Knights, the Feriant Legion... and me."

Harlow hugged Avery again. They'd never been friends, never even tried, but she was grateful for this moment. It felt like coming full circle.

Avery made it a few steps before turning back. "He deserved to die, Harlow. Thank you for what you did."

Harlow's heart stopped. She had no idea Avery knew what she'd done last spring. The other woman pressed her hand to her heart. "There are others of us—women he hurt before he found you. Every one of us is grateful to you, Harlow. You are our hero."

Harlow stood there for a long time after Avery disappeared around a corner, stunned by what Avery had said. She stood there so long, in fact, that Selene and Finn rounded the corner. They'd lost Aurelia, apparently. As arch-chancellor, she was likely needed for some Order business.

"What are you doing out here still?" Selene asked, pushing through the door. "Mommy and I have a dinner we're committed to this evening, and Nox and Indi are on patrol 'til ten, so the two of you are on your own."

Harlow laughed. "We literally came through a wasp's nest of danger to get here, and you all have *plans*?"

Selene let out a frustrated little breath. "Scoff all you want, but it's taken a lot for Lili and me to pull the Order together."

Harlow softened her expression. She hadn't meant to sound so harsh. "I know. I was being silly—or trying anyway."

Selene's brows furrowed slightly. "I didn't catch that." Selene really was just like her sometimes. Harlow had the same trouble catching humor, occasionally. Selene's brow smoothed and she hugged Harlow. "I'm just so glad you're here. There's food in the fridge, and we'll talk about what we've learned tomorrow over breakfast. You two get some rest." And then she was gone.

"In and out like a whirlwind," Harlow remarked.

Finn was staring at the living room, just beyond the foyer, surrounded on three sides by books and arched stone windows that looked out on a courtyard. A giant overstuffed sofa in the living room was covered in a dark tapestry fabric depicting unicorns frolicking in a forest. The wood floors were covered in plush patterned rugs in cool jewel tones, and the chairs that flanked the couch were all a lush eggplant velvet. Several oil portraits of animals dressed in historical dress graced the wall opposite them and Finn seemed perplexed by the whimsy of it all.

It was nothing like the retro-minimalism of ORAIS, or the opulent, serious furniture his parents had in their estate. This was Selene at her weirdest. At home, above the Monas, things were colorful, but understated in comparison to this. Lush wallpaper covered the hallway walls, depicting mythical creatures, lurking amongst the flowers in an ancient garden.

"This is something," Finn said, clearly at a loss for words.

Harlow nodded. "See why I wanted to decorate in all neutrals?"

He laughed. "I like this, but yes."

She took him down the hall to the kitchen, where the cabinets were painted a high gloss emerald green with gold hardware. The tile was shaped like dragon scales or arches, depending on how you looked at it.

"Really?" she asked. "You like this?"

Finn smiled, picking up a framed photo of Harlow and Thea when they were five and seven, respectively. They were dressed in little pallyras, for a Solstice ritual. "I *love* this. It feels like home."

She nodded. "This has always been our second home. I just haven't been here much since Mark. Come on, I'll show you to my room."

"You have your own room here?" Finn seemed astonished. He solved his own disbelief moments later. "Because Aurelia is arch-chancellor?"

Harlow shook her head. "No, everyone has room for their whole family."

Finn frowned, his analytical mind working overtime. "But... the building isn't big enough for that."

Harlow raised her eyebrows. "This is the Order of *Mysteries*, Finbar." She began walking down the hall, towards her bedroom. "The building has had a life of its own since its inception. So much magic, all in one place, it defies logic a lot of the time."

"That's not possible," Finn said, following close behind. "That's not how magic works. There's a science to it."

Harlow stopped in front of the door to her room, smirking. "That's what the *Illuminated* believe. Again, we are the Order of Mysteries. Where did you think the name came from?"

He shrugged, frowning so deeply she worried he might crack his forehead. "It's just that..."

The door to her room opened. Her hand wasn't on the doorknob. In fact, both of her hands were clasped firmly in front of her body. Finn's eyes widened as he entered the room. "What is this? I had no idea you had the talent for illusion."

"I don't." There was nothing in her bedroom but a giant bed, a crystal chandelier, and clouds that were slowly changing colors from a deep sapphire to an even deeper emerald green, giving the fantasy of a dark, duotone daydream. They hung from the ceiling, and puffed up from the floors.

"First, it's not an illusion." Harlow sat down on the bed, looking around, pleased to be back after so long. She hadn't known what she'd find when she opened the door. The sorcière had rejected her thoroughly for the past two years, but apparently the Order of Mysteries *itself* had not. "And second, this is a little different from what it was like when I was younger. Back then, the colors were lighter, and there were some posters on the wall."

Finn sat next to her, staring at the clouds as they shifted in slow motion. The chandelier dimmed to a low glow. He laughed, a deep belly laugh that rumbled through her. "Is it... reacting to us?"

Harlow raised her eyebrows and lowered her voice, as she climbed onto his lap. His arms went around her, his hands gripping her hips, drawing her closer to him. "What would it be reacting to?"

His answer was a kiss, his lips pressing to hers, gently at first, then harder as the chandelier lowered the lights further.

Finn wrapped one arm around her, his fingers splaying out across her back as his tongue slid against hers. His other hand dug into her hair, pulling hard at the nape of her neck, eliciting a whimper of pure bliss.

She broke their kiss, tracing the lines of his face with her fingers. "Today was pretty messed up." Finn's smile was sad. He nodded once. Harlow brushed kisses on his brow and his lips. "Will you help me forget it?"

Now his smile reached his eyes, his arms tightening around her as he scooted back on the bed. Soon, he was resting against the upholstered headboard, his knees cradling her smaller body against his. Nestled between her legs, his desire for her grew, but Harlow was in no rush.

She kissed him again, tasting lust on his lips as her hips moved slowly, tantalizingly. She pulled her sweater off, then unclasped her bra. He moaned at the sight of her nipples stiffening in the cool air of the room. Her hips ground against his harder now as she leaned back against his knees, guiding his hands to her breasts.

"You are so beautiful," he murmured, his words sweet as he pinched her nipples, sending a delicious bite of pain through her.

"I need to remember what we're fighting for," Harlow insisted, punctuating her words with another roll of her hips. He stared at her for a moment, wonder in his eyes. Her arms twined around his neck, and she whispered in his ear, "Show me. Fill me with it."

When she pulled back, his eyes glowed faintly, and his fangs emerged. The Claim was brutal in some ways, but it was also pure energy, the combination of both aethereal and celestial force. *Life*.

Finn maneuvered her quickly, lowering her back to the bed as he pulled her leggings smoothly off her, and then the rest of his clothes in quick succession. He kissed his way down her abdomen, slowly, his tongue making a languorous journey towards the pulsing core of her. There was nothing in the world she wanted so much as his mouth on her, now, but he teased her, skipping to her thighs, which he showered with attention. His mouth, his fingers, his face, all caressing her skin in a fever of missing the spot she wanted him most.

Beneath his ministrations, she writhed, attempting to guide him to her preferred location for his efforts. Still, he teased her, his fingers sliding into the legs of her panties, pulling them away from her body enough that air hit her sensitive flesh. Air, but not his touch.

His mouth fell over the fabric covering the slick heat gathering at the apex of her thighs, his tongue sucking and caressing her through the fabric of her panties, stoking both her pleasure and frustration to an inferno.

And then he stopped, yanking the fabric from her as he slid up her body to kiss her mouth. He sank into her, the head of his cock spreading her wide.

"I love you," he murmured as he moved slowly inside her, sliding inch by tantalizing inch. "And if you and I are all that's left at the end of this, I will have everything I need."

She pulled him deeper inside her as her mouth crashed into his, their movements frantic and desperate. Venom filled her mouth as her fangs protracted, and when her mouth fitted against his neck, he mirrored the motion, piercing her skin at the same moment she sank into him.

Finn roared against her neck, his cry muffled as his venom flowed into her. Euphoria lit her from within, and her entire body burst into dark, inky flames. Wings sprung out from her back as her fangs released from Finn's neck. They were levitating several inches above the bed, and she felt the difference in her body, the strength of her Feriant form flowing through her as her pleasure crested.

As the moment passed, they fell back to the bed, crashing awkwardly into one another, laughing. Finn pushed her hair back as he adjusted slightly to lay beside her, rather than atop her. "Your ears..."

She felt them, and though they were fading back to their

usual rounded tips, she felt the arch that had been there. "Did I shift completely?" she asked.

He shook his head. "No, not into whatever the shade was, but a little bit like it."

"Weird," she breathed, smiling. "Bath or food next?"

He scooped her into his arms. "Bath."

# CHAPTER THIRTY-EIGHT

B reakfast was a whirlwind of catching up amongst piles of food, all of Harlow's Nuva Troi favorites, in fact. Chocolate croissants from Lupin, coffee from Cerberus, and all the family chatter she could wish for. As she watched her sisters and the maters orbit around one another in the kitchen, grazing on the spread of fruit, cheeses, and pastries, her heart ached for Thea and Larkin.

Harlow tried to apologize for what had happened to Larkin, but no one would hear it. In fact, the maters thought the whole thing might be good, rather than an utter failure on her part. Finn squeezed her hand to reassure her, seeing that the explanation hadn't helped with the guilt she felt. Instead, they urged she and Finn to catch them up on all that happened since they separated.

The maters were most interested in hearing about the Vespae queen, and Harlow wished she could tell them more. Selene pulled her blonde hair into a tight bun, and Harlow knew instantly that her mind was already spun out in a million different directions, cataloging search terms for later. Nox, who had buzzed off all her ebony hair, jotted several things down in her phone as she listened to Harlow. The quiet shifter fit into their family life seamlessly.

Harlow watched as she and Indigo interacted, so deeply in love they were like extensions of one another. It was a different kind of love than the one she and Finn shared. They were so similar, dressing in the same edgy, stylish clothes that were as utilitarian as they were fashionable, and even speaking in a similar cadence that had Harlow wondering how Meline felt about things. She and Indigo had always been so close.

The longer she watched them, the less she worried. It was obvious the three of them were the best of friends. Harlow noticed that Meline's face went carefully blank every time Ari's name was mentioned. He was settling in all right, from the little they'd heard from the Grove. Nox and Meline loaded the dishwasher as Nox reported out to Finn. It was a little like being in a cross between a family meeting and confabulation of all the organizations they were affiliated with.

Harlow stopped listening to it all, happy to be sitting on a countertop, safe in a kitchen she'd been in thousands of times over her life. She pulled Indigo into her arms, wrapping her legs around her sister's slender body and kissing her short, dark hair. "I missed you," she murmured in her sister's ear. Nox and Meli were talking so animatedly to Finn she risked a question. "What's going on with Meli and Ari?"

Indi glanced over her shoulder, her eyes rolling. "All drama, all the time."

Harlow suppressed a smile, at the same time her heart ached. "They're a couple of big personalities."

Indi nodded. "I'm glad I get to *stop* being a big personality now."

"I heard you retired from the it-girl life."

Indi leaned back, her head falling on Harlow's shoulder. "It was always more Meli's thing than mine, but it just got to be too much. Neither of us meant for it to take over our lives. It was better to delete and move on."

"You deleted your accounts?" Harlow asked, incredulous.

Indi broke free of her embrace, grabbing her twin's hand. Even with their different styling now, they were so alike. "We deleted everything. It's just the Monas' socials for us now. We're going to use our savvy to make it better than ever when all this over."

Meline nodded. "We are. It's gonna be epic."

"I wish we didn't have to go," Indigo said. "But we all have shifts to get to, and the maters need to get you up to date on the Chandelnuit plan."

Harlow was thoroughly confused. Chandelnuit was a ritual to celebrate the return of the light, not a party, at least for the sorcière.

Finn looked as though he might have an idea of what was going on. "They're not actually having their annual party, are they?"

Selene nodded, kissing Meline goodbye as she slung a messenger bag over her shoulders. "See you after I'm done with the kiddos," Meline said.

She was off to teach the sorcière children how to teach their human friends magic. It was a strangely brilliant plan: because the Illuminated valued children so much, they weren't monitoring them in the slightest compared to the adults. So the sorcière taught their own children how to help their human friends learn to use aethereal power, and the human children taught their parents.

Nox and Indigo had a lab, where they monitored the gossips, socials, and the dark web for useful information. They weren't coming up with much more than they'd already reported to Finn, but they were in the middle of decrypting a video missive from the Fifth Order, and they were eager to get back to it.

When the others were gone, Finn and Harlow followed the

maters to Aurelia and Selene's office. Outside the glass doors that led to the courtyard, a flock of dark-eyed juncos fought for spots at the feeder. This had long been Harlow's favorite room in the Order of Mysteries' residence. It felt like the Monas, with the same white bookshelves, a similar celestial fresco painted on the ceiling, and a chandelier fashioned to look like a golden orrery that depicted their solar system.

Harlow stared at the chandelier as Selene brought up a folder labeled "Ravagers" on the digital whiteboard. It was hard to imagine just how far away planets like Interra, Sirin, and Earth must be, when they weren't even in their solar system. There weren't any comfortable chairs here, only Selene and Aurelia's desks and room for pacing, so the four of them stood in front of the whiteboard.

The old-fashioned telephone on Aurelia's desk rang, nearly scaring Harlow out of her skin. Aurelia answered, said "mmhmm" a few times, then "I'll be right down." She hung up, and turned back to the group. "Nox forgot to tell you that she has phones ready for the two of you. You'll need them, so I'm going to pick them up."

"What else are you up to?" Selene asked with a wicked smile.

"You can explain things to the children, darling. Apparently, Merhart Locklear is on his way over as well. The Order of Masks may finally have agreed to join us."

Harlow was relieved to hear that. "What about the Order of Night?"

Selene shook her head as Aurelia kissed her goodbye and disappeared. "Most of them are with the Illuminated. Athan is leading the charge now that Berith is gone. Kate and the others had luck though—if the Illuminated don't agree to our terms, the Avignonne vampires will join us, as will Castel des Rêves."

Finn's face opened up into the happiest smile Harlow had seen since he'd returned. "Really? That's wonderful."

Selene smiled. "It seems we have a chance. Our alliances are stronger than they were in the Great War. We won't fail this time."

"Show us what you found," Finn said, stepping closer to Selene.

Harlow tracked the files as Selene scanned through them, noting citations from dozens of books about the origins of aethereal power and theorems regarding elemental beings. She stopped on a scan of an ancient book with an unusual foldout that expanded the page to three times its usual size. The drawings on the foldout were precise, nearly architectural in nature, though the written language was not one Harlow recognized.

"What is this?" Harlow breathed, stepping closer to the screen as Selene enlarged the image.

"The Santvara Manuscript," Selene said, as though that explained everything.

Finn looked to Harlow for a clue, as wonder caused her mouth to gape open. "This is it? You found it? Where?"

Selene looked like a cat who'd swallowed a bird whole. "Some of the children found it tucked in with a skeleton."

Harlow snorted. "In the crypt?"

"Yes," Selene laughed. "They were playing—"

"Hide and Freak," Harlow finished. The lost look on Finn's face deepened. "It's like 'hide and seek' but in the crypt—and the Santvara Manuscript is practically a legend, said to show the origins of the aether."

She stepped forward examining the image, then pointed to a section that clearly depicted symbols for limenal space. "See here, these symbols are kind of universal to indicate something about the limen, the aether in particular."

Finn tilted his head slightly, then pointed to some of the smaller depictions of cities. "Is this meant to represent the way the limen sometimes replicates real places?"

"Yes!" Selene nodded. "And these symbols are common alchemical markings that show how aether gives way to life, and those who use magic give back to the aether." She pointed to each of the symbols as she described them. "It's like a formula."

Finn glanced at Harlow. "This is stuff you already knew about?"

Harlow smiled. "Identifying this kind of 'stuff' used to be part of my *job*, Finn."

It was ages since she'd thought about her work at what had felt like a completely mundane job, identifying occult texts and archiving them for both the Monas and the Order of Mysteries. She and Thea both. Harlow bit her bottom lip to keep from tearing up. That all seemed so unreal now. Like it was lifetimes ago.

Finn didn't say anything, just took her hand and squeezed. Selene watched, a look of satisfaction passing over her face. Finn had passed a test with her, one neither of them had expected he'd take today, but from the look on Selene's face, it had been an important one.

"So," Selene continued. "This is the part we're interested in, though really, the entire book is fascinating—this is what's relevant."

She enlarged part of the image to show intricately detailed clouds of aether moving into screaming faces, much like the ones Harlow had seen in Nihil when the Ravagers escaped. She didn't recognize the symbols the author had used now, except for the ones that referred to "limen" and "aether."

"What is this?" she asked Selene.

Selene's face was drawn and serious now. "A disturbance— the aether is sentient, as you know. It operates as a whole, a collective of ideas connected to all worlds. It is meant to be infinite and regenerative. But if it's disturbed, the author theorizes here that sometimes it individuates."

Selene zoomed in on another part of the image that depicted an angry, monstrous creature stepping out of the cloud of faces.

Above its head was a luridly drawn alchemical symbol Harlow knew all too well.

"That represents the isolation of an element," Harlow explained. "Though I don't think I've ever seen it look so—"

"Angry," Finn finished, squeezing her hand.

Selene took a deep breath. "It's not a particularly positive depiction, but we believe this is meant to represent the way a Ravager is created. It would appear that when first isolated, the aethereal energy is often quite distressed."

"And powerful," Finn mused.

Selene nodded. "You can see how it might be mistaken for an Elemental."

"Technically it is," Harlow said. "Aether is the primary element in all things."

Selene reached towards her face, stroking Harlow's cheek with her knuckle. "My smart girl."

Finn let go of Harlow's hand. "So what about this makes you optimistic about Larkin?"

Selene still stared at Harlow as she answered. "The Elementals your father's people imprisoned are not young. The rest of the images here indicate that the first period of isolation is the worst for the creatures; after that, they develop as people would, as individuals."

"And what would make you think this one isn't angry with us? Why wouldn't it be after what Connor's family did?"

Selene raised her eyebrows at Harlow. "You know the answer, don't you, darling?"

"Judge people by what they've done," Harlow said, tilting her head at her mother. "Not by what you think they might do."

Finn watched them carefully. Harlow hugged Selene with one arm. "It's one of Mama's big life lessons."

"One I learned the hard way as a young woman," Selene explained. "Several times, in fact. I used to jump to many conclusions—and it never failed to get me into trouble."

"It took Larkin without her permission, without telling us why," Finn said, looking at the two of them as though they were taking a bizarre leap of logic.

"I didn't say it made perfect choices, Finbar," Selene said. "But it's reassured us twice now that it will not hurt her and that she's safe. You said she looked well when you encountered her yesterday."

Harlow nodded. "That's true. And it helped me, on the bridge, and with figuring things out about the Vilhar—and the House of Feriant. It's actually given us quite a bit to use against your parents—not to mention the incident with the queen yesterday."

For a brief moment Finn looked as though he wanted to return to the point that the Ravager had stolen Larkin. Eventually, he shook his head. "You're right. We don't even know that it completely understands why just taking her might be a problem for us."

Harlow had another idea. "Or it does understand, but it needs *her*, specifically her. She's a dream walker, Finn, and if the information we have about it is right, it may not have much time before its presence here starts changing Okairos."

Selene clapped a hand over her mouth. "And it knows her, Harlow. How many times has she been to the limen over the years, visiting Ash? We have no idea how its senses work. It could know her."

It all made sense now. The Elemental's immediate recognition of who and what she was, its selection of Larkin as its host. "But what is it here to do?" Harlow asked.

Finn grimaced. "I can't believe I'm about to say this after everything we've been through—but do you think it's trying to *help* us?"

"Help us do what?" Harlow mused.

Finn shook his head. "I don't know—but I have a feeling Larkin might."

Harlow stared at the whiteboard screen as Selene closed the file, and opened another. "I really wish we could ask her."

"At least there's reason to hope," Selene said. "Now, let's talk about the plan for the Chandelnuit party. We're going to need to be precise—and the two of you are going to have to play your parts perfectly, or this won't work."

# CHAPTER THIRTY-NINE

After lunch from Gastro Lupo, Harlow looked through her new phone. Nox had set everything up so that Harlow's socials were all ready to go. Finn sat with her on the couch in the Order of Mysteries apartment, her feet on his lap. On the surface it looked like he was catching up on Nuva Troi news channels, but Harlow knew better. He was going over every facet of the maters' plan, trying to figure out if it was a good one.

"I know you don't like it," she said, after watching him pretend to scroll for a half hour.

His jaw did that little twitchy thing. "It's *not* the same as before."

"No," she said, poking him in the belly with her toe. "It's safer."

He sighed. That much was true. "You don't need my permission—"

"I don't," she interrupted. "But I'd like to know if you think it's a solid plan."

He dragged her onto his lap, in one fell swoop. "It's a solid plan. Much as I hate the gossips, they're our best tool right now. Go forth and be photographed."

Harlow popped the last of her parm fries in her mouth and grinned. "This is going to be *really* weird."

"It is," he agreed. "Call if you need anything."

～

HARLOW'S TASK FOR THE DAY WAS TO RETRIEVE WHAT they'd need to crash an Illuminated party, from home and Enzo's atelier. Nox had it on good authority that Connor believed Harlow and Finn had escaped Penemue, back into the suburbs. He'd sent troops into the wasted neighborhoods, searching for them, and the real Alix was enduring hours of "questioning" with a Dominavus intelligence officer. Harlow was to get into the atelier, and then the Monas, bringing all the jewels and dresses they'd need home with her.

Rakul had been in touch, and he would keep the Dominavus off her trail for the day, leaving Harlow to be caught sneaking around Nuva Troi by the gossips. As they had no idea when the Imperial Ventyr might arrive, they didn't have time to have quiet, never ending talks with Connor about the logic of banding together with the Fifth Order. The Illuminated needed to *see* the tides had turned against them before they presented their plan, and the information about the incoming threat.

The maters had come up with an ingenious plan with the twins, who might have retired from living their lives in public, but who definitely knew how to work the gossips to their own advantage. Harlow's trip out was practical, but it was also an opportunity. Sam was coming with her, to help transport the items back, and Harlow was glad for the company as they stepped past the light wards on the Order of Mysteries.

It felt a little like stepping onto a battlefield, except now the battle would be fought in ways that had typically been used against Harlow. She and Finn had manipulated the gossips a few times over the summer, but nothing quite as calculated as this. All Harlow could do was be grateful that while Nuva Troi winters were cold, they were marginally better than Falcyra.

Winter in Nuva Troi was one of Harlow's least favorite times of year. The sky was a heavy, dreary gray, and the plows had piled snow over and over all winter, making it gray as well. But today, big fluffy flakes had been falling all morning and her walk with Sam felt magical. An added bonus was that Harlow's toes were warm, something that was literally impossible to achieve in Falcyra. Both her and Samira's moods were lifted by the warmer temperatures alone.

The other Strider hadn't spent much time in Nuva Troi, so Harlow pointed out her favorite shops and cafes as they walked. The streets weren't as busy as they usually were this time of day, and the amount of buildings that had been destroyed in the fighting before the wards went up was distressing. Harlow tried hard not to stare, as it would mark her as having just arrived, and there were soldiers patrolling in pairs on every street.

With everyone bundled up against the cold, Harlow and Sam were just another couple of girls in ball caps, sunnies, furry boots, and puffy jackets. The soldiers weren't looking for them —that was the Dominavus' purview. Still, Harlow did have to at least try to look like she was attempting to sneak around. To help this pantomime, Meline had dressed the two of them in what she called "dime a dozen" gear for the winter season, and no one had spared them a second look.

They stopped for coffee at Cerberus, and while Harlow kept her sunnies on in the coffee shop, she caught a few people looking at her longer than was polite. The coffee shop was busy, and for all intents and purposes, life was going on like it always had. After months without reliable power, it was bizarre to be standing in the white-tiled, posh coffee shop, listening to jazz.

She started to sweat a little and unzipped her jacket a little, taking off her gloves and shoving them in her pocket. Her sapphire engagement ring caught the light. A blonde swan shifter at a nearby table stared at the ring, before getting out their phone. Harlow kept her sigh quiet. This was all part of the plan. The ring had been photographed dozens of times over the summer, and it was just one of a few opportunities the twins had suggested for her to be caught—and turned in to Section Seven. When both she and Sam had lattes in their trendy insulated mugs, she slipped her gloves back on.

Outside Cerberus, Sam took a long drink of her latte. "I am never going back to Falcyra. Did you ever notice how awful Audata's coffee is?"

Harlow snickered as they walked towards the atelier. "Yeah."

When they were a few blocks away, their boots crunching on the snowy paths of Riverside Park, Sam asked, "Did it work?"

Harlow shrugged. "Hard to know. The blonde shifter definitely clocked my ring."

Sam nodded. "And did you see the redheaded vampire?"

"No," Harlow replied, feeling almost like they were gossiping, having a totally normal girls day out.

"He was filming you under the table," Samira said. "Is this what your life is always like?"

Harlow thought about how normalized it had been to simply be *watched*. Everywhere she went, someone took photos or videos. "Yes."

Sam's eyebrows raised. "When did it start?"

Harlow shrugged. "Always. Since I was a kid. Even before Aurelia's position with the Order, the maters were always a big deal in the lower Orders."

"Wow, that must have been really hard."

Harlow paused, watching the river for a moment, trying to figure out if Sam was being sarcastic. The fresh snow, combined with the river, the familiar wrought iron light posts, and the cobbled paths made the afternoon seem like something out of an old movie. "Do you mean that?"

Sam laughed, stopping next to Harlow to watch the river. "Yeah. What a fucking trip to have someone watching you all the time. Most kids don't grow up like that."

"No," Harlow mused as they kept walking. "I guess they don't."

They crossed through the park and made it to Enzo's without any more attention. Stopping at Cerberus had been a wise idea.

"How close is the Monas?" Sam asked as they entered the atelier.

"Just a couple blocks away," Harlow murmured absently.

The sight of the atelier's blue walls and plush patterned rugs elicited an ache in Harlow's chest for Enzo. Sam's mouth fell open as she wandered between the rich handcrafted wooden racks, staring at the clothes. "This is all so beautiful. I mean, I've seen his work in magazines, of course, but in person..."

"You didn't go to social stuff much growing up?" Harlow asked.

The Strider laughed. "No, my mother was an Ultima, and her mother before her, and so on. Social events are rarely a thing for us. Don't get me wrong, I've never minded it. I love my lineage, but I think we should party more, if it means wearing stuff like this!"

Harlow laughed. "Then change it. When everything else changes, tell them you want to go to more parties—*have* more parties."

"Oh, we have parties," Sam said, waggling her eyebrows at Harlow. "Just not fancy-dress."

Harlow watched as her friend tried on several dresses, all of which looked beautiful on her. But she settled on a tuxedo for herself in a neon pink velvet that would contrast beautifully with her dark skin, and another in a sleek black satin for Tomyris.

"What are you going to wear?" Sam asked as Harlow bagged her clothes and what she'd gathered for the maters, Finn, her sisters, and Nox.

Harlow looked around. "I honestly don't know. Nothing feels right. Enzo always helps me."

Sam grimaced. "I'm not much help, am I?"

"It's not that," Harlow said, sinking into a chair by Enzo's collection of fashion books, the ones Thea had helped him put together before his grand opening, the ones that had put his business on the map. "I just miss them all so much. I miss our lives before all of this happened, even though I wouldn't go back, even if I could."

Sam wandered between the racks again, admiring the clothes. "I know just how you feel. I don't want to go back either, but the last few months have been a lot."

Harlow stood, remembering that there was one more room. "Come see Enzo's vintage reserve," she called.

Sam followed her into Enzo's office, which was painted the same blue as the main showroom. Back here, he kept some of his most special items—ones his mother had worn to events— preserved behind huge glass frames, like a giant catalogue of her life.

"He must really miss her," Sam said, looking at the clothes.

Harlow fought back tears, thinking of Clarissa Weraka. "She was amazing. The most talented witch I've ever known, and one of the kindest people in the world. She'd be so proud of him—of us. And she'd *love* you and Tomy. She was Selene's best friend growing up."

Sam had paused behind her, staring at something. Harlow stepped closer to her as her friend turned. She wheeled out a covered garment rack, grinning at Harlow. "This has your name on it."

Harlow looked at the tag, and indeed, it did. She turned the tag over and her breath caught. "It's my wedding clothes."

Sam looked over her shoulder. "Oh my gods. Are you sure you want to look?"

Harlow's chin trembled. She didn't really want to, not without Enzo. But she'd wanted his help, his advice about what to wear to a big fancy event, and here was her answer. She unzipped the cloth that covered the rack. Inside were several hanging bags, each carefully labeled in Enzo's precise handwriting. *Engagement party, options one and two. Bridal shower, options one through three. Bachelorette party, only one option. Wedding day casual, one and two. Wedding day robe, antique.* Harlow stopped at her wedding gown. She wouldn't look at it. Not without her best friend.

There were two more bags after that, one was her "Going away suit" and the other read, "reception, one and two." She pulled those out, zipping the rack back up.

Sam nodded, seeming to understand. "You'll do the rest when he gets back."

Harlow tried to agree. She'd felt so hopeful for the past few days, despite everything, but all of a sudden the danger of the situation they were in crashed into her. *What if it all went wrong?*

Sam hugged her. "Hey, it'll be okay. I'm going to take this stuff back to the Order okay? I'll meet you at the Monas?"

"Okay," Harlow said as Sam teleported out.

They'd agreed to walk here, and teleport back for convenience. Harlow opened the first reception option and sighed. She and Enzo fundamentally disagreed on whether blush was a beautiful nude for her, his very wrong opinion, or ugly, her correct assertion. She set the floor length sheath dress aside, which was unfortunate, as the cut was gorgeous, but likely hard to walk in without alterations.

She took a deep breath and stared at the ceiling as she unzipped the second option. "Enzo, please know exactly what I would have said yes to."

When she looked down, she gasped. It was nothing short of phenomenal—and perfect for the occasion. She drew the jump-suit out first. It was a beautiful shade of midnight blue, cut simply in a halter style with a plunging neckline and a high waist, with wide legs that would allow for freedom of movement. The jacket was the stunner of the ensemble though: a floor length cape with sparkling raptors embroidered into it.

She looked closer at them, realizing Enzo had done the work himself. They were a perfect representation of her Feriant form. She zipped the suit back up and put her jacket back on. There wasn't time to try the suit on, but knowing Enzo, it would fit perfectly.

Harlow took the back alleyways to the Monas, carrying the suit carefully so as to keep it out of the mud. Every step closer to their back courtyard set her heart racing faster. The street behind theirs was sad, the house directly behind the Monas especially, as it had been a part of the courtyard's landscape, and now the gorgeous old townhome was crumbling. It had been a rental for many years, so they hadn't known any of the tenants well, but the building itself had been so familiar to Harlow that seeing it in this state broke her heart.

When the back door unlocked, she stood in the threshold of the doorway for a long moment. Going inside was sure to feel strange. She moved slowly, hanging her coat and the suit in the mud room. As tempting as it was to linger, she forced herself to run upstairs, moving through the apartment quickly, not stop-ping to look at the photos in the living room, or go upstairs to her and Thea's bedroom.

If she started down memory lane, she was likely to get lost, so she went directly to the giant safe in the maters' vibrant peach bedroom. When she'd gathered all the requested jewels and handbags, she began the work of carrying them downstairs in Aurelia's gigantic canvas shopping bags. It took far too much effort to get them all ready to go somewhere, she decided on her last trip upstairs.

Somewhere in the back of the apartment, something stirred. "Sam?" Harlow called out. Maybe the Strider had misjudged her jump back. The noise stopped abruptly, but no one answered.

Harlow felt for her connection to Sam in the threads, but it led across the city. She was still at the Order, not here. Harlow found another connection instead. Larkin.

"Larkin?" she whispered, then out loud. "Pal, are you here?"

Larkin stepped out of her bedroom. She'd changed clothes, and there was a long scratch on her cheek.

"Gods," Harlow cried out, shooting forward. "Are you okay?"

Larkin stepped back, her eyes wide and glassy. "Don't," she whispered. "It will come back."

"Are you okay?" Harlow whispered.

Larkin didn't make eye contact with her, it was as though she were purposely trying to avoid looking her way. "I am." She touched her cheek. "I ran into a branch. No fighting."

Her little sister didn't sound like herself. Her voice was flat, but not tired.

"Trying not to catch its attention," Larkin said. "It's nearby —reading."

Harlow thought fast. "Downstairs."

Larkin didn't answer, so she took it as a no. There were plenty of other book stores on the Row though, so it could be anywhere.

"Staying here, so it can read, and I can be somewhere familiar," Larkin's voice was so quiet Harlow could hardly hear her. "Thought you were at the Order with the others."

If the Ravager was coming back anyway, they didn't have time for this. She took the risk and teleported the short distance down the hall, and grabbed Larkin. She was prepping for a second jump when Larkin shook her.

"You can't," she hissed. "I have to stay. I have to help."

"You *want* to help it?" Harlow asked.

Larkin smiled, and though she looked tired, the expression was genuine. "Yes..." She stared at something behind Harlow now. "Couldn't we just tell her?"

Harlow spun. The shade stood behind her now, shaking its head. And then it disappeared. When Harlow turned back to her sister, she knew the Ravager had taken her again.

"Why can't you tell me what you're up to?" Harlow demanded.

"It's not all worked out," the Ravager answered, shaking her hands off her sister's shoulders. "You'll have to trust that Larkin trusts me."

Harlow stepped back, trying to at least give the illusion that she was respecting the creature's space. "That's difficult to do. She doesn't seem much like herself."

The creature said nothing for a moment and then Larkin's eyes cleared. "I can't tell you what's happening. I promised."

"But why?" Harlow pleaded.

Larkin threw her hands up helplessly. It wasn't a "typical" Larkin move, but it was recognizable and natural. The creature wasn't puppeteering her. "To be honest, I don't completely understand its logic, but I do understand what it *wants*."

"What?" Harlow shrieked, infuriated.

Larkin shook her head. "I *promised* I wouldn't say... But it isn't bad, okay? Don't you trust that I know the difference between right and wrong?"

Harlow gritted her teeth. "Yes, but I'm worried it's influencing you. That it's been watching you your whole life, visiting Ash in Nihil, and it knows how to manipulate you."

Larkin smiled sweetly, a sad look in her eyes. "I know why you'd think that—and I get it. But that's not what's happening." She took Harlow's hands in her own. "Can you understand why it wouldn't trust Mother, or any of the Illuminated?"

Harlow nodded, unable to speak without screaming. When she got a hold of herself she asked. "So what do you want me to do?"

"Whatever you're planning for Chandelnuit. Just go with the plan."

"You know what the plan is?" Harlow asked, incredulous. Larkin shrugged in response. More secrets then. "And when this is over, I get you back?"

Her sister smiled. "Of course."

"No," Harlow replied. "I want to hear it say it. I want its word."

Harlow wasn't sure why she insisted, but Larkin had emphasized that she *promised* the Ravager so many times now, it stood to reason that promises meant something to the thing.

Larkin's eyes changed again. "You want my word?"

Harlow thought carefully. The amount of times Larkin had said the word promise was odd. Her sister was like a walking thesaurus. "No, I want your promise."

The Ravager inside Larkin smiled. "You are learning, aren't you, little bird? The importance of nuance, the dance of words. Your ancestors knew the power of semantics. Of promises." It gazed beyond Harlow now, to some faraway place. "So many of your kind have wound words like weapons, twisting the bonds between us the wrong way."

Harlow wasn't sure what it spoke of now, but she wondered. "Did the Vilhar create you? Were they responsible for your individuation?"

The Ravager smiled at her again, speaking in unfamiliar terms and circles. "You are right to wonder, but no. Not me, but another, younger part of me. Even now, it calls to us." It took Harlow's hand in Larkin's. "I told you the truth before, little bird. I don't remember who I am any longer. Now, you must go."

Harlow started to walk away. It would probably be better to

meet Sam downstairs. She spun on her heel. "You didn't promise that you'd return Larkin to me safe."

"As I said, clever. I promise you, Harlow Krane. I will not harm Larkin, and she will be returned to you." It paused, as though thinking. "She is my friend. Perhaps my only one, unless you are as well?"

Harlow raised her eyebrows. "I suppose all that depends on how things turn out."

"An exchange then," the Ravager said, clapping Larkin's hands together in apparent delight.

Harlow thought of the stories in *The Violet Book of the Fey*. If the Ravager was anything like the foes Rhiannon often encountered, making bargains was a bad idea. "Let's just stick to your promise about my sister, and we'll see where we end up."

"Clever and wise," the Ravager said, obviously pleased. "Your friend has arrived." And then it disappeared, taking all traces of her little sister along with it. Harlow's eyes fell closed, her heart thumping hard. She hadn't even realized she was sweating, or how hard her heart had been beating, she was so focused on the Ravager.

Harlow had no idea if what she'd learned was good or bad news. She was as confused as she'd been before, but it was a small comfort that it promised not to hurt Larkin. She hoped she'd read her sister's signals correctly, and that assurance was binding.

"Harls?" Sam called from the mud room. "Need help up there?"

"No," Harlow yelled back. "I'm ready to go."

# CHAPTER FORTY

arlow had never been to an event at the Illuminated Order, the main headquarters, offices, and archives for Connor, Pasiphae and the other ruling Illuminated, and their staff. She hadn't known there even was a place for events in the building. She sat in Aurelia's office, after reporting her encounter with the Ravager, examining schematics for the Illuminated Order building.

Merhart Locklear had brought them the day before, as an act of good faith and commitment to the Fifth Order's cause. One of Nuva Troi's rare dolphin shifters, who also happened to be an architect, had made the drawing for them, after using their echolocation to map the building, down to its sub-basement levels. Harlow was nearly startled into dropping her cup of Duke and Duchess tea when Indigo rushed into the room.

"Have you seen it?" Indigo looked and sounded so much like Thea in that moment that Harlow had to blink a few times to clear the image from her head.

"What are you talking about?"

Indigo picked up Harlow's new phone, unlocked it, and

brought up the Section Seven app. Harlow rolled her eyes. "Are you serious?"

"It seems strange to me that you *wouldn't* be monitoring it," Indigo chided.

"Really?" Harlow laughed. She was a little annoyed by how fast her sister had forgotten the way the gossips had bullied her. "I'm not actually looking forward to this part."

Indigo sighed. "I know they're cruel to you—and I am sorry to tell you that hasn't changed—but... just look."

Harlow did as her sister asked, and there it was: the pinned story was about her, with a photo taken from outside the front window of Enzo's atelier yesterday. The caption read, *Harlow Krane returns to the city, looking like a drowned kitten, as she ransacks Enzo Weraka's gorgeous atelier.*

She braced herself for the sinking feeling of dread that came with a Section Seven encounter. It didn't come. In fact, she felt nothing at all. Worried she might be dissociating, she moved through her body awareness exercises—she didn't need a meltdown of any kind today. Chandelnuit was tomorrow, and she needed the rest of the day to be calm and quiet so she could optimize her focus and her reserves of power.

She found it wasn't exactly true that she felt nothing; she felt slightly annoyed about being called a "drowned kitten." She looked objectively adorable in the photos. But there was no real sting to it. Section Seven was doing what they'd expected them to. Harlow read the story. It was as they'd planned—they'd been spotted at Cerberus, and Section Seven tracked them to the atelier.

Finn rushed in, his cheeks flushed. He'd been sparring with a few of the sorcière when she returned from her trip out, and she hadn't wanted to bother him. "Are you okay?"

She looked up from her phone, nodding. "I'm fine. It's just Section Seven being Section Seven. It worked just how we planned, so that's good."

Finn shook his head. "Not that—though that's good—the Ravager. Selene just told me."

Harlow nodded. "Yes, I'm fine."

Finn sat in Aurelia's desk chair, rolling it over to where Harlow sat at Selene's desk. "Why didn't you come tell me?"

"I'll let you two talk," Indigo said. "But Harlow, we need to talk next-steps." Harlow and Finn both nodded as Indigo left.

"You were having a nice time," she said slowly, wondering if she'd hurt his feelings. "I wasn't hiding it from you, I just— things have been hard lately."

He took her hands, kissing them. "Thank you for thinking of me that way. You can tell me anything though, okay?"

The last thing she wanted to do was make him feel bad. "I know I can. But I really was okay."

He paused, his eyes searching hers. "You changed while I was gone." Seeing that she was about to explain herself, he shook his head. "It's not a bad thing, I just didn't understand 'til now. You don't need me to guide you through all this rebellious intrigue stuff anymore."

Harlow let a deep breath cleanse any remaining tension from her abdomen. "It's not that I don't need you. I just know more than I used to. I'm intermediate now. You're still the expert..." She nudged his knee with hers. "But I'm catching up fast."

He smiled as he cupped her face in his hands. "You never cease to amaze me, you know that? The way you learn things and adapt so fast. You're incredible."

"Thank you," she replied. "Do you want to look over these schematics Locklear brought over and tell me if you feel like they're accurate?"

He nodded, moving straight into examining the building. As he peered at the pages of the rolled out paper on Selene's desk, Harlow let the compliment he'd given her sink in. She'd never been with anyone else who saw her quite how Finn did—who saw how smart she was and liked it as much as anything else about her. She didn't think Kate had minded that part of her, but she'd never said so. Mark had hated it, and tried to squash it every chance he'd gotten. It's why she hadn't applied to grad school after graduation.

Her eyes rested on the Alcaia brochures Aurelia had brought her, after her return from Enzo's. Finn looked up from the schematics. "These look very accurate to me, I don't see any potential mistakes."

His eye followed her gaze, landing on the brochures. "Are you thinking of applying?"

Harlow shrugged.

He scooted his chair closer to her again. "I think you should —if you want to, that is."

"We have to get through all of this," she waved her hand at the schematics, "before I can even think about that."

"You want to though," he urged.

"Maybe," she replied.

She was spared from having to discuss it further. Selene and Aurelia entered, followed by Nox, Indigo and Meline. Selene pulled up the internet on the whiteboard, swiftly opening window after window of sites that had picked up the Section Seven story about Harlow.

"So what's next?" Selene asked the twins.

They looked at one another, both of them grinning the same wide, dimpled grin. "Now we craft the narrative," Indigo said.

Meline added, "We tell everyone you're back, and why."

"How?" Harlow asked.

Indigo moved to the whiteboard, her hands flying over the screen, bringing up all of Harlow's social accounts. She had nearly a million more followers than she'd had before.

Harlow's mouth gaped. She hadn't had the courage to open her social apps, even though she'd known they'd use them at some point in all this. "What is this?"

Meline held out her hand to Indigo. "You owe me. I told you she didn't know."

Indigo reached into her pocket and handed her sister a flat, shiny rock that the two of them had been passing back and forth since they were children—whoever had it had some kind of privileges between them, one of their mysterious twin rituals.

When that was taken care of, Indigo explained, pushing her glasses back up her nose. "It started around Yule. People wondered what had happened to you, and when we left socials, a lot of our followers followed you instead."

Meline nodded. "It's been a big topic on message boards. A lot of people are just waiting to find out where you are and what you're up to."

Harlow glanced at Finn. "You're sure this is going to work? Don't you think they'd rather hear all this from him?" Finn had always been the popular one between the two of them, and she didn't resent it.

Indigo picked up Harlow's phone and handed it to Meline, who started scanning through various windows. "*You* were romantically involved with a human, *you* have been targeted unfairly over and over by the immortal-idolizing gossips. Believe it or not, they want to hear from you—not us, or Finn, or anyone else. They'll believe what you say, because you never try to spin shit."

It made sense, but it was still a little hard to believe.

Meline shook her head. "If you don't believe her, you should read the comments on this Section Seven story. People are defending you, saying that you and Finn are the "couple of the century" and Section Seven should stop bullying you."

Harlow could hardly believe that. Making fun of her had been something of a pastime. Meline handed her phone to her, pointing at the story. Harlow braced herself, but her sister was right. There were seven hundred comments already, and the vast majority of them defended her.

"This is super weird," she said after a few minutes of reading. She locked her phone. "What changed their minds? People used to love to rag on me."

Indigo sighed. "That was before the Illuminated showed their asses, Harlow. I'm not defending how people acted before, but the context has changed. After all this is over, it will change again."

"You don't have to do this forever," Meline added, seeing that Indigo's tirade had made Harlow more worried, not less. "People are looking for someone to trust in all this. I know it looks like people are just going about their normal lives, but they're messed up inside."

Nox smiled in her quiet way, pushing the sleeves of her hoodie up. "They're looking for a way to help. You can give that to them."

Finn smiled at her, nodding. The maters both looked anxious, but nodded as well. They were all on the same page then. Harlow took a deep breath. "Okay. What should I say? Or post?" They hadn't planned this part. The twins said it was better to wait and see what the gossips posted, and what the response was. Now they had it.

Indi grinned. "I have the best idea, do you trust me?"

Harlow mirrored her sister's grin. "Always."

～

THEY ENDED UP IN THE CRUMBLING RUIN OF THE townhouse behind the Monas, with a pizza and a half-burned dining room chair. Snow drifted on the floor of the burned out dining room. Indigo dressed Harlow in a vintage Gastro Lupo t-shirt, and nothing else.

The chain had been hit hard before the wards went up, and the Illuminated had refused to help rebuild, even though it was hands down everyone's favorite pizza, immortals and humans alike. An odd coalition had sprung up around the restaurant, a mix of Okairons from all walks of life who just wanted their parm fries and MeatLovers Classic.

They'd started reproducing the vintage style of the Gastro Lupo tshirt to make money, and had been able to open two of the restaurants back up, both of which had the five link chain that had come to represent the five groups of people who lived on Okairos—and equality—on their doors. Gastro Lupo had become the unofficial restaurant of a growing movement in Nuva Troi calling for change. Not necessarily the kind of change the Fifth Order sought, but their supporters at least believed that the ways they'd been doing things weren't working, and they were quite outspoken about it.

It was mostly very, very powerful people, who were in no danger from the Illuminated, but plenty of average folks, immortal and human alike, were picking up their Friday night pie from Gastro Lupo, and their social media accounts had *millions* of followers. Of course, Indigo knew their social media manager, and she'd let the shifter know that Harlow was about to tag them.

The photo was eerie: Harlow sitting cross-legged in the destroyed dining room, untouched snow drifted around her, in just her Gastro Lupo t-shirt, taking a big bite of the pie. The caption read, "I'm back. If you believe, like I do, that we can't go on like this, meet me outside the Illuminated Order tomorrow night at dusk for Chandelnuit. Let's show the Illuminated what a unified Okairos could look like."

She posted it when they got back to the Order of Mysteries, worried they hadn't given people enough time as she set her phone down. Effective protests took time to organize, she knew from listening to the Rogue Council, but time wasn't a luxury they had. They could only hope this would be enough. That having eyes on them would remind the Illuminated that the rest of the people on Okairos far outnumbered them, even with the vampires on their side.

~

HARLOW DRESSED QUICKLY IN THE CLOTHES MELINE had left out for her, a lavender cropped wrap sweater and a pair of gray joggers with the puffy boots she'd worn home from ORAIS, and ran downstairs to meet Finn in the lobby of the Order. They were headed to the Three Besoms for what would look like a date, but was actually an opportunity for the world to see them.

He was leaned up against a huge marble statue of Akatei. Like her, he was wearing gray joggers, a hoodie, and a puffer jacket. He was looking at his phone when she walked up holding her jacket. When he caught wind of her, he looked up, his eyes taking in the outfit.

"Holy shit," he breathed, as she walked up.

"It's just sweats," she murmured as he took her hand, twirling her around.

His laugh was sultry. "It's not. Gods, you are so fucking hot."

Her heart fluttered as her cheeks warmed.

He helped her into her coat, brushing kisses over her face as he zipped her up. "Can we please go back upstairs?" He took her hand. They had to do this, and it was possible it would be fun, but it wasn't a real date, and they both knew it.

The evening air was cold, snow falling harder than it had earlier in the day. All over the city, lights came on in the dark, setting the snow aglow as they walked towards the bar, hand in hand. Snow caught on Harlow's eyelashes. Meline had done her face, so there was no danger of her makeup smudging.

Something called "fresh face makeup" was apparently all the rage right now, along with the casual dancer-off-duty style she wore. The usual tendency to dress up to go out had gone out of style over the winter, as people saw dressing to the nines as a bit gauche, considering all they'd lost. It looked too much like a celebration, apparently.

Someone had hung strings of faery lights across the street the Three Besoms was on, and it was so simple and beautiful, Harlow's breath caught. Finn stopped, looking down at her. A little laugh fell out of her, as tears sprang to her eyes. The Three Besoms' building was half destroyed. Tonight was a fundraiser for the bar, and the street was crowded with shifters playing music with humans. Vampires danced with humans.

Harlow turned, holding her phone up as she clicked into her stories, raising her phone to show both her and Finn's faces. "Hey, Nuva Troi," Harlow said. "Wanna meet me and Finn at the Three Besoms for a drink?"

Harlow locked her phone, not bothering to look at the post from earlier. She needed to concentrate on what came next. She searched the crowd for Sam and Tomy. Eyes that strayed to her and Finn were wary at first, then friendly when Finn started saying hi to everyone and shaking hands.

"I'll get us some drinks," he said. "There's Sam. Go do your thing."

Sam waved at her. She was standing near two elderly sorcière, with graying hair: Holly and Tori Suvari, the sisters who owned the bar. Harlow hugged them both. They'd been friends of her parents forever.

"What happened?" Harlow asked.

Holly shrugged. "Same thing that happened everywhere. The bombs hit the bar, instead of the bugs."

Tori added bitterly, "No one's allowed to use weapons for years, and then the Illuminated try to train humans in a couple of days. Things went like shit."

Harlow nodded slowly. "Would it be okay if me and Sam helped with the bar?"

Tori threw her hands in the air playfully, obviously trying to have a sense of humor about the situation. "I don't know what you can do, unless Finn's going to pay for a new bar."

Sam winked at her, as Harlow laughed. "We have something a little different in mind, but it'll probably be a bit of a spectacle."

The sisters shrugged. Sam and Harlow took their jackets off, handing them to Holly, who looked like she wanted to tell them they were going to catch cold.

Sam stepped forward with Harlow, towards the building. "This is a little bigger than the tomb in Austvanger."

Harlow raised her eyebrows at her friend. "Think you can handle it?"

Sam grabbed her hand. "I know *we* can."

They pressed their free hands to the building. Behind them, a slow hush came over the crowd in the street. The music stopped playing, all eyes on them. Sam whispered a countdown. "Three, two... one."

Harlow put everything she had into this. Later, Finn would help her regain her energy, but this was an important step in their plan. People had to see a taste of what the Striders could do. Indigo had leaked rumors about the mysterious Striders and their talents, leaving out the fact that they turned into giant birds that could kill the Illuminated. Just a bit of mystery to get people interested, and the hint that Harlow and the friend she'd been spotted out with were both Striders.

The building had collapsed inward onto itself, which meant most of its parts were still there. Harlow and Sam had spent the afternoon examining the original plans for the building's construction, as well as all the improvements the sisters had filed with the Building Commission over the years. They'd come up with a version they thought they could bring the Three Besoms back to without exhausting themselves completely.

Now, Harlow's shadows mingled with Sam's. It was nothing

like when she and Finn made love. This was platonic love, strong and steady, fueled by all the things that made Harlow and Sam's friendship great. Slowly, as sweat beaded on each of their foreheads, the building went back up, its bricks rearranging above their heads.

Perspiration beaded on Harlow's chest and lower back. Sam hummed one low note, which helped her concentrate. She was sensing the inside of the building, watching it go back up from the inside out in her second sight.

"It's done," she breathed, pulling Harlow into a hug.

When they turned to look at their work, the Three Besoms looked as it had a hundred years ago. It was missing the rooftop conservatory Holly and Tori had added fifty years ago, but otherwise, it looked much the same as it always had. A cheer went up behind them, the roar startling Harlow.

She'd completely forgotten they had an audience. They turned to find Holly and Tori rushing for them. And then there was a crowd, hugging them, thanking them. The music started back up, and Harlow spotted Finn by the bar. His eyes shone with pride, but he waited to hug her until people had the chance to say thank you, that they would come to the Chandelnuit event tomorrow.

A big bear shifter Finn had invited approached the sisters. "I'm Max Persad," he said. "Finn said you might need a building inspector tonight." He pulled some hard hats out of a bag he carried. "Shall we go check things out?"

The sisters nodded. Tori shouted, "Drinks are on the house. We'll donate the money to someone else!"

Holly hugged Harlow. "Thank you for this. I know people have been hard on you since your fling with that human boy. No one who drinks here will keep on with that."

Harlow was speechless. The Three Besoms was an Order of Mysteries institution, as were the sisters who owned it; what they said went. While Harlow hadn't expected this reaction, she appreciated it. This action had been calculated to get people to come to Chandelnuit, not for Harlow's benefit—but as she made her way through the crowd, it sounded like it had worked on both fronts.

Sam and Tomy had moved nearer to the musicians and started dancing. When Finn found her in the crowd, he took her hand. "Hey, Krane. Do you wanna dance?"

It was the exact way he'd asked her to dance at their primary school graduation. There was only one thing to do: answer in kind. She punched his shoulder and nodded. "Sure, McKay. Nobody else is asking."

As he twirled her around in the snowy night air, he grinned. "You're the girl of my dreams, Harls. Always have been." He pulled her close. "Always will be."

# CHAPTER FORTY-ONE

F inn and Harlow stayed up until the wee hours, recouping Harlow's powers in multiple ways. Afterwards, Harlow slept for most of the day. Finn was off making sure that all their plans were on the right track, and she was starting to get ready. Just as she was about to dress, Meline burst into Harlow's bedroom. "Have you seen your post from yesterday?"

Harlow picked up her phone. There were over five hundred thousand likes, and the comments continued to roll in by the thousands. Most said versions of "see you there." Many told the story about what she'd done at the Three Besoms, though Harlow noted a fair amount of the people telling the story hadn't even been there.

Harlow could hardly believe it. She'd been avoiding her socials because she didn't want to face potential failure. But she hadn't failed. It had all worked.

Finn returned, as Meline was choosing comments for Harlow to respond to.

Meline's phone rang. She held up a finger and answered,

murmuring "mhmm" a few times before hanging up. "They're coming, on foot, with candles. A *lot* of them."

Finn grabbed the jacket for his tux. "Is everything else in place?"

Meline nodded, glancing back at her phone, which buzzed wildly in her hand. "The others are here too. Sam's bringing them up."

Harlow fought back tears. She hadn't known if this part would happen, it was such a risk—but they were going all in, all cards on the table. Their people on the ground were ready, and now, so were they. Everyone had arrived from the Grove. In minutes, all of Harlow's family and friends would be reunited for the first time in months.

Finn slipped his jacket on and stared at her. "You look amazing. You *are* amazing. No matter what happens tonight, I am so proud of us."

Harlow took Finn's hand and kissed his palm. "Let's go greet our guests. We have a party to get to."

The Order of Mysteries was nearly empty but for the group standing in the ballroom. Aside from the children, who were all in protective care, everyone else was already headed to the Illuminated Order. From Nox's reports, the streets were full.

Harlow watched with mixed feelings as Meline hugged Ari, then Cian. Everywhere Harlow looked, there were faces of people she loved. Petra had already taken Axel down to where the children were, and he was happily playing with his new entourage of fans. She hugged Kate and Audata, and the rest of the Striders. Riley kissed her cheek, before heading for Finn.

"You found it," Enzo said, pushing through the crowd. His hug was so tight and warm, she nearly forgot to be scared. "You didn't look at the rest did you?"

Harlow shook her head. "Just this and the blush dress."

He laughed, then seeing something behind her, kissed her cheeks. "Look who it is."

Harlow turned, hoping, and then burst into tears at the sight of her pregnant sister. "You are perfect," she sobbed as Thea moved towards her, looking every bit the picture of Aphora in her "Mother" aspect. "You shouldn't be here though."

Thea pulled her into a hug, her pregnant belly between them. "I am *exactly* where I need to be."

Alaric materialized behind them, making eye contact with Harlow. "The slightest hint of danger—"

"And you get her out," Harlow agreed. "I don't want you two going in." She shook Thea's shoulders gently. "Do you understand? They'll have wards up to keep people from teleporting."

Thea nodded, exasperated with both Harlow and Alaric. "But when Pasiphae sees me..." she patted her stomach, which was a sizable bump now.

"She's gonna flip," Harlow said. "So you know the plan then?"

Thea nodded. "Yep. I can't believe I'm going to speak for us all."

"You're the swan of the season," Harlow said.

"*You're* the one they're coming for," Thea replied as she took Harlow's hand.

Everyone had gathered around them and they moved into the agreed upon formation, Harlow and Thea behind Finn and Alaric, their friends and family surrounding them.

Harlow made eye contact with Cian, who looked at their phone and then nodded. Then Aurelia, who also nodded.

"Let's go," she said.

The entire group teleported at once. There was a brief moment of darkness, and they appeared in a clear spot in a huge crowd of people. They were standing in front of the Illuminated Order's enormous building, with its harsh curving lines, imposing and forceful as the Illuminated themselves.

Inside the building, in the elegant lobby, the Chandelnuit

party was already going strong, despite the crowds gathered out front. Sequins and satin glittered in light from the hundreds of tapers that lit the room. From the street, Harlow could see piles of food on the buffet tables, amongst ice sculptures and fountains of sparkling wine.

People outside the wards were starving, and not one person stood near the buffet table. Harlow glanced at Finn, whose face was so drawn with anger, she thought he might burst into flames. His eyes glowed with cold fury as he stared at the Dominavus, who stood guard out front. She knew he was wondering what she was: had Rakul managed to turn any of them to their cause? They hadn't had much communication with Rakul and Vivia, as their involvement was part of their element of surprise.

They'd let so much be open, let so much be known, so that the world would see the Illuminated for what they were. If not the world, at least all of Nuva Troi. For twelve blocks the city streets were full of people, all carrying candles or flashlights, ready to be lit. Harlow nodded to Alaric and Ari, who gave the signal to light their candles. As the dark streets filled with pinpricks of light, a hush came over the crowd. No one spoke for long minutes, letting their silent vigil speak for them. Harlow watched as the shifters who played music in the corner of the lobby turned. Each of them stopped playing, staring outside at the people gathered.

The noise from the party died, meeting the silence that waited for them in the street. Vampires and Illuminated alike stopped to stare, first at the musicians, and then at the crowd. Harlow spotted Connor, who grabbed hold of Rakul Kimaris' arm. Behind them, Vivia was dressed in an elegant silver velvet gown. Her eyes met Cian's and she nodded once. They were ready.

Connor pointed to the crowd, still speaking angrily to Rakul, who stayed very calm. The Ventyr took his Argent wife's hand, and together they left the party, walking through the lobby as the crowd inside parted for them.

When they came outside, Rakul spoke in a booming voice that carried over the crowd. "Go home. It's cold, and you should all be inside."

Finn stepped forward. "Tell my father to come out. I'd like a word with him."

Inside the building, the crowd of Illuminated and vampire party-goers shifted. Connor McKay emerged on one end, and Pasiphae the other. Both stared out the windows at their sons. Connor was obviously furious, but Pasiphae merely looked concerned.

"No," Rakul said, staying preternaturally calm. "You may come in, but no one is coming out."

Finn looked back at Harlow. Thea squeezed her hand. She was ready. Alaric and Ari parted to let the two of them through. Inside, Pasiphae clapped her hands over her mouth at the sight of Thea's round belly. In the candlelight, Harlow's eldest sister, dressed in a flowing white gown, looked like Raia the Mother incarnate.

A cry went up over the crowd as Thea and Harlow walked up exactly three steps, just enough so the entire crowd could see her. She held up her hands and they fell silent. "Thank you for coming tonight, all of you. My sister's call was quite compelling, wasn't it?"

There was laughter in the crowd. They liked Thea.

"Like Harlow, I've spent the last few months with the Fifth Order. And while you don't know them now, you will soon. We are here tonight to demand the Illuminated give over their stranglehold on power, and help us usher in a new age of democracy."

Thea touched her belly. "I want my twins born in a world where they're safe. A world where the Illuminated don't decide what they deserve."

Someone in the crowd called out, "And what does Alaric want?"

Thea smiled. "Alaric and I, along with Finn McKay and Petra Velarius, signed over our personal fortunes to the Fifth Order this evening, just before we got here. We want to live in a new world together, as equals—a world where humans have an equal voice to immortals. Where we decide things together, from here on out."

The crowd whispered to one another. This wasn't what they'd expected. Thea turned towards Pasiphae, who stood with one hand pressed to the window. "Will you come and talk with me about this future?"

Connor rushed towards Pasiphae, shouting something at her, but the crowd inside was too thick and she had been moving towards the door the entire time Thea was speaking, her eyes on her daughter-in-law's pregnant belly.

Pasiphae stepped outside, pushing past Rakul to meet Thea on the steps. "Yes, I'll come hear you out."

The crowd sent up a cheer, and Thea guided her towards Alaric, and the three of them teleported out. Harlow rejoined Finn, who stood on the bottom step. "One down," he murmured as she took her hand.

Connor finally made it out onto the steps and the rest of the party streamed out behind him. "Pasiphae doesn't speak for all of us," he shouted.

The crowd behind Harlow was displeased by this proclamation, but the Illuminated and vampires on the steps looked smug.

Connor spoke again. "Go home, all of you, before this turns ugly."

Finn shook his head. "Perhaps you should take your own advice, dad."

Connor stared at his son, aghast that he would speak out against him so directly, in front of so many people. Harlow looked down at Meline, who had her phone out and nodded up at her. This was streaming on all the gossips, *and* on Harlow's livestream. Millions of people were watching.

Finn spoke again. "Happy Chandelnuit, dad."

It was the signal. Lights shone on the rooftops of the buildings surrounding the Illuminated Order, and then came the sound of glass shattering—hundreds of windows breaking as sorcière in the audience broke every window in the square, directing the shards into the empty fountain behind them. It was a spectacular sight on its own, but what happened next sent chills down Harlow's spine, despite the fact that she'd known it would happen.

In each broken window appeared Fifth Order snipers, and a rush of air from above caused everyone to look up. The Feriant legion came first, sweeping low over the crowd. Then came the griffins and alicorns, the flying chimera, and the cockatrice. Last were the wyverns and the firedrakes, all of whom landed on the rooftops, staring down at the crowd below like gargoyles.

These were what the Humanists had brought them, the reason why the Rogue Council had so readily agreed to align with them: the Humanists had been manufacturing weapons that rivaled those of the Illuminated, and they had a full force of trained Heraldic adults among them.

The aerial units and snipers were not all the Fifth Order had to reveal. At the front of the crowd, the lyons, tygres, stags, and pantheroi shifted, their Heraldic forms much larger than their mundane animal counterparts. Civilians in the crowd surrounding the immediate vicinity of the Illuminated Order building shed their coats, revealing more weapons and fully armored soldiers. While the Rogue Order had been a sanctuary for refugees, the Humanists had built a small army, and joined with the fighters the Rogues had gathered, they were an impressive show of force.

They stood silently in the dark. Further off, Fifth Order

volunteers helped the true civilians to get off the street. If fighting was to follow, they wouldn't risk children and the elderly. Many adults stayed though, standing at the back of the trained forces of the Fifth Order, obviously willing to fight for the new world Thea had spoken about.

Connor had the good sense to be stunned into silence, as did the rest of the Illuminated. The maters had planned this with the Order of Mysteries and the Fifth Order down to the second, and so far it had gone off without a hitch. Every piece had fallen into place, and now all they could do was wait. If Connor would agree to talk, they could move forward in relative peace. If not, the war would begin here—tonight. Someone showed Connor their phone, likely telling him that they were still broadcasting, despite the fact that the crowd was thinning.

He stepped forward, coming down several steps, glaring at Finn. "You've made a good show, boy. Now come inside, and let's talk reasonably about this."

Finn lowered his voice. "Send the rest of them home, dad, and I will. You don't want anyone else to hear what I have to say. And you won't be talking to me about what happens next, you'll be talking to *them*."

The First Council of the Fifth Order stepped forward, with representatives from each immortal Order, as well as several humans, including Piper Winslow, who looked very, very satisfied right now. They were flanked by the Feriant Legion, their official guard.

Connor looked back at Rakul. "Arrest them all."

An expression of extreme satisfaction crept over Rakul's face as the Dominavus shifted positions to reveal Petra Velarius at their head, geared up and armed just as they were. She grinned wickedly at Connor as she directed the Dominavus to stand in front of the Council, which was now surrounded by the world's most elite soldiers. Petra stepped forward to stand next to Finn as the realization of what had happened dawned on Connor.

Rakul had turned his most elite fighting force against the Illuminated, and what was more, he'd turned over their leadership to Petra Velarius, whose estrangement from her powerful parents was well known. Harlow tamped down the urge to feel smug. They hadn't won yet.

Connor looked back, his face a mask of horror as Vivia Woolf transformed before his eyes. She was the oldest, and therefore the strongest of the Argent, longer than a city bus, and nearly three stories tall. "Know when you are beaten, McKay," she said as her alternae solidified.

She lowered her head, turning it slowly towards Rakul, which gave Connor an up close look at the inside of her mouth, which she opened slightly now, showing her rows of razor sharp teeth. A tiny wisp of smoke curled from her nostrils before a dart of flame shot through her teeth, singeing Connor's shoes.

He leapt back from the flame, stifling a yelp, his eyes wide. It was as though he'd just remembered that he'd killed her children and grandchildren, not to mention her mother. The arrogant prick had really believed that she'd forgiven him until this very moment. Harlow looked forward to hearing how Vivia had managed to convince him of that, but having seen her way with people at Sanctum, she'd fully believed in her ability to do it.

Rakul hopped onto his wife's lowered neck. He was still spellbound, unable to shift into anything other than his canine form, which wouldn't help him now. "You really shouldn't have fucked with my marriage, Connor. Or given me my own elite crew of soldiers to make unfailingly loyal to me, and me alone... I have a feeling your son is about to enlighten you regarding several other mistakes you've made. We have bigger problems to deal with than your pride."

Connor fumed, clearly not knowing what to say as Vivia lifted her husband away from him. She growled once for emphasis, and Harlow was pleased to see Connor shove his hands in his jacket pockets to hide their shaking from the crowd. The Argent leapt into the air to join the rest of the Heraldic, who peered down at the Illuminated and vampires.

Harlow had been watching the interaction between Vivia, Rakul, and Connor so closely that she'd stopped paying attention to the rest of Connor's people. Some backed away, likely planning to disappear into the building, and out the back; many had already gone. Those who were left were spun up with fury. The vampires hissed and growled, their fangs bared.

"Don't let them do this, Dad," Finn warned. "So few of you can't stand against us."

Athan Sanvier stepped out from behind his people, snarling, "We'll kill you all."

The House of Remiel streamed into the crowd, screaming. Finn shook his head, as several of the younger Illuminated shifted into their true forms, following their vampire friends. The Council was teleported out immediately, as this had been something they'd planned for.

The ground force surged forward to meet the Illuminated and the House of Remiel, meeting in a clash of fangs and claws. Harlow shed her cape, her shadows surrounding her, her wings spread out behind her in a dark blaze of glory. A vampire lunged for her, and she met him, two shadow blades springing from her hands, crossing in front of her as she sliced his head from his shoulders in one clean, quick motion.

Connor stared at her like he'd never seen her before. Harlow grinned at him as she stepped forward to fight another vampire, shoving one of her blades into her chest. Another she decapitated as it screamed, launching itself at her in an erratic fashion that revealed its lack of training. She remembered a time when vampires like this had terrified her, when Athan Sanvier had kidnapped her and menaced her with people just like this, from the House of Remiel.

Now, it was almost comical how amateur they seemed. She had learned to fight truly dangerous creatures, and while she might not be an expert at it, these city vampires were no longer something she had to fear. Her wings beat with the pleasure of this realization as she rose a few feet above the steps. The others coming toward her turned and fled. It had all happened in a matter of moments, she realized, as she caught sight of Connor's shock, alongside Finn's pride.

"They're easier to fight than the Vespae," she remarked as Connor stumbled away from her.

"You are so hot," Finn growled, before grabbing his father's arm. Connor had been trying to get away. He dragged him up the steps, Harlow following close behind. While the others fought, their next task was figuring out how the Imperial Ventyr might enter, and *when*. Finding out who had called them was another problem, but not high on their list of things to take care of immediately.

"Forget about them," Finn hissed as Connor looked toward the crowd. "The Fifth Order will slaughter your people in minutes."

Even now, the Heraldic were holding their own and gaining ground on the Illuminated. The vampires were easier to kill, and there were hardly any left as it was. They'd either fled or had been turned to dust.

Connor laughed. "So you have the Dominavus. I have troops everywhere, being called into duty at this very moment. This fight is far from over."

Finn drew his father close. "You won't want to waste them on us, Dad. Boreas is coming, with an envoy. Where will they enter?"

Connor went deathly pale. "What did you say?"

Harlow stepped closer to Finn's father. "You heard him. Where will they come through? They're coming—we don't know when, but someone sent them a message from ORAIS. We need to do whatever it takes to make sure they can't get in."

Connor shook his head. "They can't get in—the portal is—"

His eyes went wide, as though he'd realized something horrible. His eyes met Finn's, wild and furious. "Where the fuck is your mother?"

He swung around, rushing into the building. Finn ran after him, Harlow close behind. Connor stood next to the elevator, pushing the button repeatedly.

"Dad," Finn said, touching his father's shoulder. "Dad, that won't make it come faster."

Connor's breath heaved through him in panicked shudders. "She's going to let them in, boy."

# CHAPTER FORTY-TWO

islin had signaled the Ventyr. Of course she had. It all made sense. Harlow nearly groaned. "Can we teleport down there?" The portal had to be in the basement archives.

"No," Connor snapped. "Of course not."

All the ground they'd gained, the way everything had come together, began to slip apart in Harlow's mind. They hadn't known exactly when the Imperial Ventyr would arrive. They'd assumed it would be soon, but neither of them had assumed it would be *tonight*. Harlow glanced at Finn, who took her hand. His brow furrowed, and his jaw clenched. He felt it too, the unraveling of their progress, the way the plan was unspooling away from them, the threads pulled in directions they hadn't predicted.

The elevator opened and the three of them rushed in. Connor opened a panel next to the usual buttons and pressed his left thumb to it, swearing. "I never should have trusted her. Two thousand years together and she's still a fucking snake."

"Or unhappy," Harlow murmured.

Connor glared at her, his chest puffing up. Finn stepped

between them. "She's right. Maybe if you'd tried a little harder with her she wouldn't have betrayed you."

Connor shook his head. "Us. She betrayed *us*. Hate me all you want, call for reform or my head with your Fifth Order, but do you know what the first thing Boreas' people will do when they get here?"

Harlow and Finn were silent. Smooth jazz played in the background as the elevator slowly descended into the bowels of the building.

"They'll string me, you, *her*," Connor pointed at Harlow, "and every single one of the people you love up first. If you think I fucked this all up, you may well be right, but what happens next—I promise you, Finbar, you can't even *imagine* what the Ventyr are capable of."

Harlow wondered when Connor McKay had shrunk. He'd always seemed taller than her, but for the first time ever, she realized that wasn't true. They had only moments to pull their shit together and he was focusing on the wrong things. "How do we stop them from getting in?"

Connor's head swiveled, as though he were shocked she was speaking to him directly. "What?"

"You said Aislin is going to let them in. How do we *stop it*? What's the mechanism to close the portal—I assume she has a way of opening a portal down here—right?"

Connor sighed, pinching the bridge of his nose. "Once she opens it, it can't be closed without a weapon capable of wielding pure starfire. That's why we didn't open it. It was meant for us to use when we had the population subdued."

"There's no way to close the portal once she opens it?" Finn asked.

"Right," Connor said.

Words Connor didn't need to say hung in the air: this was their only chance. They had moments to change everything, to get the world set right again, or at least get it back on track.

426

They'd all come this far, with vastly different motives, only to have underestimated the foe that could actually beat them. They'd all ignored Aislin for years, assuming she was vapid and uninterested, and it had come back to bite them all.

The elevator dinged, and the doors opened into an enormous room, filled with archways of heavy wooden shelves filled with books and scrolls. Each arch was a long hallway. Connor marched down the center, Finn and Harlow at his heels. Behind them, the elevator door closed, called back up. Harlow couldn't help but wonder where it was going, and who might be headed their way next.

The room opened up to reveal freestanding metal safes, with more shelving along the walls containing glass boxes, full of curious items. Beyond the metal safes, a single desk stood in front of a primordial stone arch. Inside the arch, a silver liquid swirled. There was something menacing about it that turned Harlow's stomach. Something was *wrong* about the magic of the liquid. She felt into the threads and found no connection to aethereal power, nor any celestial power either. The liquid was something else, something awful.

Finn stared at it. "The blood of the universe."

"What?" Harlow didn't know what that was.

"It's what's left when you rip a hole in reality the wrong way," Connor growled, stalking forward. "Sometimes they're like a howling storm. We got the quiet kind. Don't worry, she hasn't got it open yet."

Aislin sat at the desk, swearing at the computer in front of her. She'd managed to get the screen unlocked, but was apparently having trouble with some aspect of whatever came next. She spun in Connor's chair, saw them, and continued typing.

Connor reached her in a burst of speed, dragging her from the computer by her hair. He slammed her against the eldritch archway. "You couldn't even open the portal right, could you?"

Blood oozed out of her mouth, and as angry as Harlow was

with Finn's mother, this was abhorrent. She stepped forward, meaning to stop him, but Finn pulled her back, shaking his head. "Don't go near it. It's worse than the barrier in Nea Sterlis. You won't just end up in the limen, it will destroy you."

"Why the fuck would you do this, Aislin?" Connor screamed at his wife.

She laughed, spitting blood in his face. "Why the fuck wouldn't I?"

Next to her, Finn's chin jutted out. Harlow grabbed his hand, her stomach roiling.

"I should kill you," Connor screamed in her face, holding her inches from the terrifying liquid.

"Go ahead," she said, her eyes dead. "It won't stop them from coming."

"We've already stopped you, Mother," Finn said, stepping forward. He held out his hand, towards his father. "We stopped her, Dad. You don't have to kill her."

Connor moved backwards a hair, taking them both to slightly safer ground. He pushed Aislin to the floor, where she collapsed. Harlow thought at first she was crying, but she wasn't. She was laughing.

"You haven't stopped anything, you fools. I took the wards down while you were in the elevator. This city will be cleansed by the five swarms that I called here a week ago." She turned to Harlow. "Your people are already dying."

Before Harlow could do anything, Aislin moved, using her own burst of speed. She pressed three buttons on the computer, and the silver liquid cleared. The way was open, directly into the limen, a swirling maw of dark clouds. Somewhere in the distance, deep within them, the sound of a force marching in lockstep echoed through the archives.

The portal was open, and there was no way to close it. Harlow's face threatened to crumple. They'd come so close, but they'd lost. There was no escaping the fact that the Imperial

Ventyr would stream into this world, a plague worse than the Vespae had ever been. But they could run. Retreat now, and live to fight another day. They could regroup, find a way to fight them. They could, couldn't they?

She turned to Finn, her eyes pleading. "We can fight them," Harlow said, her chin trembling. "Let's go get our people and start clearing the city."

Finn nodded, taking her hand. He turned to his father. "What do you say, dad? Can we work together?"

Connor's face changed then, and Harlow saw the father Finn might have had. The one he'd needed all these years. He clapped his hands on each of their shoulders. "Yes." He moved to the computer. "You won't be surprised to know that I have a missile aimed at the building. It's on a satellite."

He was wrong—that *did* surprise Harlow—but apparently not Finn, who nodded.

"It won't close the portal, but it will slow them down a bit. We're going to need to evacuate the city quickly."

Finn started to argue, which they didn't have time for. Still, Harlow whipped out her phone, frustrated to find she had no service.

On the floor, Aislin laughed. "The three of you, against the Empire. You're fools."

Finn glared at her. "And you are my *mother*. You should be ashamed of yourself."

Aislin stood, smiling. "I am not ashamed of anything but you." She stepped over to the computer, placing her hand on Connor's arm. "I disabled your satellite missile days ago. Stop this now and meet your fate with honor."

Connor McKay looked as though he might cry. It was the first time Harlow had ever seen him look sad. "I loved you once," he said, his voice low, as though he meant his words for only her.

"Don't spend your last breath on lies," Aislin spat.

The elevator rang in the distance, curtailing Aislin's words.

Footsteps rushed towards them from two directions. Harlow just stared at Finn. They'd been grasping at straws for the last few minutes, but there was no way forward.

She took Finn's hand. "Remember the bridge?"

He nodded once to her—he understood. The day on the bridge, just outside Lithraea's Way, he'd taken her power, channeling it through the Claim. They'd whispered about it in the dark in the days after, wondering what would happen if they tried it again. It had all been theories, playing with ideas in the dark of night.

Tonight, they would do the same, only she would channel *his* power, all of it. It would destroy them both, but also this room, this building. It wouldn't close the portal—she didn't think she and Finn could conjure pure starfire—but they might get close enough to damage it and slow the Imperial Ventyr down enough to give the Fifth Order time to regroup.

Harlow's heart ached to think of all they'd miss. Seeing Alaric and Thea's children. Watching Enzo and Riley grow old together and Petra and Kate defy all odds, and change the world. Seeing what Cian would do next, with their precious, beautiful life. Tears slipped down Harlow's face, as she thought of never seeing Axel again. She hated that the maters wouldn't know what happened, that she wouldn't get to see the twins become the women they were meant to grow into, but most of all, she was sorry she didn't get to tell Larkin any of the thousands of things she needed her to know.

In Finn's eyes, she saw all her hopes and dreams begin and end. They would die together, and for all she'd wanted more, this was a good way to go. Harlow never feared death the way others did. She'd always walked a little too close to it. For years, she'd thought that was a flaw in her construction, something she needed to fix. But now she was at peace.

They would die, but they would not go easily, and they

would go together. Whatever was beyond this life, they would meet it as one.

And then Alain Easton emerged from the stacks, followed by five Vespae queens. "The portal is open," he said, with a satisfied smile. "And you've brought me your son, and Harlow Krane. Very good, Aislin. Very good indeed." He turned to the queens. "Take them."

Two of them broke off, tearing Finn from her grip, while just one caught Harlow in her grip. The other two took Connor. Harlow didn't even have time to cry out. She glanced towards the portal. The aether was parting, and in the distance she saw the enormity of what Aislin had done. What looked like an entire army of Ventyr marched towards them. They were still so far off, and something about the perspective within the limen was distorting.

"What are you doing, Alain?" Finn asked, struggling against the queens who held him.

"Winning," Alain Easton said with a grin. "Humans will be treated differently when the Empire arrives, and I'll be given the resources to create more children. More incubi."

Connor rolled his eyes. Unlike Finn, he didn't struggle. "You're a fool to believe that," his eyes fell to the floor. Almost to himself, he muttered, "We're all such fools."

Harlow didn't think she'd live to see the day she completely agreed with Connor McKay, but she did now. Behind her, the queen that held her made a soft noise that sounded like a purr. Harlow twisted in her grip, tearing her eyes from Finn and Connor. It was her queen, the one she'd made friends with. "Did you tell them?"

She shook her head, but spoke to the others. The other queens made noises, and the one that held her responded. Harlow couldn't be sure, but she thought they might be arguing.

Aislin, who now stood next to Alain Easton, cringed. "What are they saying?"

Alain shrugged. "I can hardly understand them. They're brutes, really."

Harlow struggled. "They're not. Tell them the truth, Alain."

The queens quieted, staring first at her, then at Alain.

He scoffed. "What truth?"

Behind Harlow, her queen made a version of the low purring noise, shaking Harlow slightly. Harlow glanced back at her. She nodded—Harlow was being allowed to speak.

"That their world is gone. Destroyed." The queen let go of her. Harlow pointed to Alain. "You told them they could go home if they helped you, didn't you? Tell them the truth, Connor."

He nodded. "It's true. Your world was destroyed shortly after we let you into this one." He had the decency not to apologize, or explain further.

She turned. "I am so sorry. You've been used, horribly. You can never go home."

Harlow wasn't sure how much of the nuance the queens understood. The one who held her, the one Harlow had started to think of as *hers*, placed a hand on her shoulder, her talons sharp, but gentle on Harlow's bare skin. She spoke to her sistren, quickly. They released Finn and Connor immediately, each going into a momentary silence.

Alain and Aislin both had the sense to look nervous. "What's going on?" Alain asked.

The queen that had held Harlow pressed a hand to her chest and buzzed the word that meant "peace." Harlow smiled at her friend. "Get out of here. Get your people out." She lowered her voice. "Finn and I are going to destroy the building, and hopefully the portal. I won't see you again. Please, look for a way to find peace here, with our people."

The queen nodded, and then hugged Harlow tightly,

smelling like the freshest spring day, and then they were gone, running for the elevator. Finn and Harlow rushed toward one another. Alain shifted, his incubus form monstrous as he sprang for Finn, and Aislin for Harlow. Connor dove for his wife, but missed as she ducked him, shoving his head hard against the corner of the desk.

Aislin lunged for Harlow, grappling with her. She was much stronger than she looked, and within moments she had Harlow's arms pinned to her side. Harlow wasn't sure why she didn't just shift into her true form. Connor did, and he was on his wife in moments, but he couldn't seem to pry her off Harlow.

"Help Finn!" Harlow screamed.

Connor looked as though he would argue, but he did as he was asked.

Aislin laughed. "The Emperor is going to love breaking you."

Harlow stopped fighting, letting Aislin's grip tighten around her. "Does that scare you, little girl?" Aislin murmured in her ear. "I hope it does. You took my son from me when he was a child. You replaced me as his confidant. I *never* would have let you live, and now I will get the pleasure of watching you die slowly, in glorious pain."

Harlow sighed. "Why do people like you always need to make some big, awful speech?"

Aislin sputtered, her grip on Harlow loosening slightly.

"Seriously, do you ever think it just gives people like me the time to kick your ass?" Harlow didn't wait for an answer; she just shifted, using her beak to toss Aislin against the wall hard enough to kill a human, but only hard enough to send the Illuminated woman into unconsciousness. Harlow was somewhat relieved. She would die in moments with the rest of them, but Harlow preferred not to have killed Finn's mother.

She turned to join Finn's fight, trying to find the place to insert herself where she wouldn't accidentally hurt him. He and

Connor were losing to Alain, and quickly. She had to figure something out. Alain punched into Connor's chest. He crumpled to the ground, his heart in Alain's hand. A hole gaped in Connor McKay's chest, but somehow he still gasped for air.

"Dad!" Finn screamed.

Now was her moment. Alain and Finn were separated. She dove forward, taking Finn gently in her beak and tossed him away from the incubus. He slid across the room, towards his mother, but was already running back. She had moments, and Alain was already reaching for her, wrapping his horrible arms around her neck. It worked—her airways were beginning to constrict, despite her strength as the Feriant.

She shifted back into her humanoid form, slipping out of Alain's grip and behind him in a quick and surprising movement, a shadow sword in her hand. She shoved it through his rib cage, willing it to lengthen until it was a longsword growing out of his brain. She yanked it out, swiftly. He was still conscious, but unlike Mark, or Aislin, Harlow didn't take any time to spout off arrogant words. She just shifted back into her full Feriant form and ripped the head from Alain Easton's miserable body, tossing it into the breach between worlds. It rolled towards the Ventyr and she let out a fierce cry, hissing into the aether.

They were still so far away, but they stopped as the head rolled towards them. Harlow shifted back. She would end this in her humanoid form, though she kept her wings. Finn crouched near his father, who was still breathing, but barely, and who whispered something she couldn't hear before he shuddered and stilled completely.

"I'm sorry," she said softly. "We have to do this now, or we won't be able to do it at all."

Finn kissed his father's forehead and stood, coming to stand with her. "He's gone."

They didn't need words. They'd said them all. She took the power he offered her, her shadows multiplying around her in dark, inky flames, the feathers of her wings shining with dark light that amplified into something bigger, brighter, the more it grew inside her.

"My goddess," Finn said as he fell to his knees before her, wrapping his arms around her waist. "May we meet again in the next world."

The power in her grew, like a dark star imploding. She wondered if that was how this would work. If the portal would survive, but when she was at full capacity she'd draw everything, including the approaching Ventyr, into whatever void she and Finn were headed for. She closed her eyes and held Finn tight, focusing on the pinprick within her heart, the one that would suck them all into oblivion.

"Not so fast," said a familiar voice.

Harlow nearly jumped out of her skin, she was so startled. It was a dangerous time to be distracted. Finn pulled back a little from her, lessening the sense that they were about to hurtle the world into a hungry, cosmic maw. She and Finn turned to find Larkin, standing next to the shade—or rather, the Ravager.

"I told you they'd be willing to sacrifice everything for their people. Is that enough for you? Do they pass your stupid test?" Larkin crossed her arms, looking supremely annoyed.

"They did well," the shade said aloud. It took the form of the Feriant again. "I am sorry we didn't get here sooner. The wards blocking this place were more serious than I anticipated."

"We could have just taken the elevator," Larkin sniped. "But no, you wanted to make an entrance."

Harlow still burned with the combination of celestial and aethereal power. "We don't have time for this. Get my sister out of here. Now."

"I can close the portal for you," the Ravager said. "And take the Vespae with me. I know a place where they will be happy."

Finn stood. "We truly do not have time for this bullshit. The Ventyr are coming, or don't you see them?"

The shade shrugged. "We have time."

"You *know* a place?" Harlow sputtered, still stuck on that turn of phrase. What in seventeen hells was going on?

"Yes," the shade insisted. "A world full of plants to eat and some nasty incorporeal creatures that they can fight if they want to. They can have the whole world to themselves. Here—let's ask them if they want to go."

The shade reached out and pulled Harlow's favorite queen out of thin air. It was one of the most disturbing displays of magic she'd ever seen. The shade spoke in the Vespae's language. The queen nodded vigorously, turning to Harlow with what Harlow thought was her try at a smile.

"See," the shade said. "They want to go."

"You told her about the nasty incorporeal creatures?" Harlow asked, hardly believing they were discussing this. Finn watched, stunned speechless.

"Of course," the shade replied. "She says they need something to make life interesting, or someone to murder—something along those lines. I admit, I don't really understand some of the nuances of their language."

This was, without a doubt, the strangest thing that had ever happened to Harlow, but she wasn't about to let a good turn of events go to waste. "You can actually do this?" she asked. "And you'll just help us? Why?"

The Ravager took Larkin's hand, their eyes softening to a glow as they looked at her. "Because I want to go home. I have not enjoyed being an individual. Your sister helped me to find a way to rejoin the aether. I will deliver the Vespae to their new planet, and then cease to be... this."

The Ravager looked at Larkin as though she were the only person who'd ever understood them. Harlow got it. Larkin made a lot of people feel that way. It didn't make it any less incredible.

"You don't want to destroy everything?" Finn asked, somewhat incredulous.

The Ravager reached out, putting a hand to Finn's cheek. "As Larkin's television shows have taught me to say, 'take the win,' McKay."

Larkin snickered and the Ravager turned to her. "Was that the right way to use that phrase?"

She nodded. "Yes, you finally got an idiomatic phrase right!"

"Just in time." The shade wrapped its arms around Larkin, pressing its forehead to hers as it spoke. "Thank you for everything, little Walker. Visit us soon. You know the place."

Again, Larkin nodded. For reasons Harlow could not comprehend, she was overtaken by emotion. The Ravager *had* called Larkin its friend; perhaps it was hers as well. Inside the aether, the Ventyr were moving again, gaining ground. They were close enough now that they would breach the portal shortly.

"Perhaps you should release some of that power into there," the Ravager suggested, waving a long arm at the shadow flames licking at her fingers. "I don't think it will make you feel very good to keep it inside. Give me a moment to fetch our friends."

Harlow stepped towards the portal, careful to stay away from the transparent barrier. Though the "blood of the universe" or whatever that had been was gone, she'd learned a valuable lesson in Nea Sterlis about the way such breaches could suck a person in, and she'd had quite enough of being separated from Finn. She glanced back at him. "Hold onto me?"

He nodded, steadying himself as he wrapped his arms around her waist, whispering in her ear, "I can't believe this is happening."

"Right?" she breathed. She was grateful, but she felt as though someone had spun her in circles for hours and then sat her down and told her not to puke. Finn's arms tightened around her as she leaned forward, feeling the pull of the barrier.

Harlow's arms shot through the barrier. The first of the Ventyr were close enough now that she could make out their features. They looked like people she knew and loved, but they were not here to help—they were here to conquer.

Still, they looked like Finn, Petra, and Tomyris—and the rest of her Ventyr friends, so much that she knew they were likely related, even if distantly. So Harlow shouted, "Run," into the breach, before letting her power go.

To the warriors' credit, they did, scattering as her dark flames licked at their feet. When she and Finn turned back, the shade had returned and there was a slit in the fabric of reality, different from the portal; more like a window to another part of the world. Again, Harlow was stunned by the magnitude of power the Ravager wielded.

"It will heal," the shade said, as though that explained everything. "This will hurt a little," it added, before time itself twisted.

It did not hurt a little. It was excruciating. Harlow's ears and eyes both began to bleed, as did Larkin and Finn's, all three of them sent to their knees as the Vespae streamed out of the hole in reality into the breach in a painful fast-forward. There was no other way for Harlow to describe it.

If humans had thought the Illuminated were gods when they arrived on Okairos, Harlow now understood the feeling completely. They'd never stood a chance against this being. They were only lucky it hadn't wanted to stay on this planet. The amount of magic it used to manipulate time was horrifying. Harlow felt the aether being sucked directly from the breach to power this feat.

The hole in reality shut as the last of the Vespae stepped through. It was Harlow's queen and as time slowed to a normal pace, she gave Harlow one last farewell, her dark eyes glowing with the joy of going someplace where her people would thrive.

"Goodbye, Larkin Krane," the shade said as it stepped through the breach, following the queen.

"See you later," Larkin said, wiping her face.

The portal closed, as though it had never existed at all. Finn took her hand, then Larkin's. "Are all our problems—solved?"

Larkin shrugged. "Seems like we saved the world."

Harlow rolled her eyes, wiping blood from her cheeks. She probably looked horrific right now. "I can't believe the two of you are *joking* right now."

That was a lie. She could believe it quite easily. They walked towards the elevator, arm in arm. "Wait," Finn said. "Where's Aislin?"

Harlow looked around. She was gone, but she'd been injured in her fight with Harlow, and there were bloody smudges leading to the elevator.

"Guess we have one more thing to do before we throw a pizza party," Larkin said as they stepped onto the elevator.

# CHAPTER FORTY-THREE

They found Aislin at the top of the building, in Pasiphae's office. She stood near the blown out windows, looking out on Nuva Troi. Plumes of smoke rose everywhere, and the sound of fighting still rose from the streets. Harlow briefly thought that they needed to get downstairs and fight, before she stumbled. Finn caught her, his hands trembling, just as hers had done.

They'd almost burned themselves out in the basement. Neither of them were going anywhere to fight. This was their last stop for the day.

Larkin squeezed Harlow's hand, her eyes full of concern. "I think I'd better go find someone to tell about all this."

Harlow nodded, staying back while Finn moved slowly towards his mother. She opened her phone and dialed Nox's secure comm line. "Go tell them it's over, pal. You can wait in the assistant's office if you want."

Larkin hugged her. "See you in a few."

Harlow waited until her sister was closed into the inner office on the floor, never so glad to see her sister shut into a room with no windows. Cold winter winds whipped through the building. Falcyrans called this last bit of winter, "the brutal season." Harlow thought it was the perfect name for it.

"So, you ruined everything," Aislin said. She stood too close to the edge of the broken windows, but Harlow wasn't worried. She was one of the Ventyr, after all.

Finn moved slowly towards her, as though he worried she might fall. "Step back from there, please."

"Why?" Aislin shrieked. "So you can punish me? Send me to some prison for the rest of my life? I've spent my entire life in prison. This is the end."

Harlow didn't understand. Being married to Connor couldn't have been easy, but it wasn't a *prison*. Was Aislin really this delusional?

Finn's mother laughed. "Oh, she doesn't know. You didn't tell her."

"No," Finn said. "I made a promise to you, didn't I? I didn't break *my* promises."

Aislin took another step towards the open air. "I release you from secrecy. Tell that girl what kind of family she's marrying into—what your legacy is, Finbar. Tell your precious Harlow who you're destined to become."

Finn turned to Harlow. "Connor spellbound my mother when I was a child. She tried to leave with me, tried to open the portal and take me back to Interra, so he kept her from ever using magic again."

Harlow's mouth fell open in horror. Spellbinding was terrible magic. She held a hand out to Aislin. "Come with us. My mother can help you."

"No," Aislin said.

She stepped into thin air. Harlow screamed. Finn stood still, frozen in fear. It took a moment, but Harlow crept to the edge to look over. Finn couldn't move, but she had to look, she had to be able to tell him his mother was gone.

And she was. Gone, but not dead. There was no trace of a

body below. It was dark, but there was still enough light to see that much. Harlow frowned, and then remembered: the horrible thing about spellbinding was that in order to curse someone else so deeply, you bound your life force to the spell. Which meant if you died, the spellbinding wouldn't survive either. Which meant that somewhere, Rakul Kimaris was also free.

Had Aislin known when she jumped? If so, it was a cruel thing to do to Finn. *Finn.*

Harlow scrambled back from the edge. "She isn't dead. Connor's death broke the binding. I don't know if she teleported, or flew aw—"

He grabbed her and hugged her so tightly she couldn't breathe. They clung to one another, alive. Alive and whole. Battered, blood all over their beautiful clothes, but *alive.* Larkin was right, after months of trying to figure out how to overcome what had seemed insurmountable odds, everything had worked out.

Finn's grip on her loosened. "We made it."

"Yeah," she said, a laugh bubbling out of her.

He looked out over the city they loved. "It's a mess out there."

Larkin poked her head through Pasiphae's office door. "The word is out. Indigo says you should post on your story to tell people."

Harlow grimaced, but she sat down on the floor, pulling Larkin and Finn next to her. "If I have to go live to be an apocalyptic influencer, so do the two of you."

"Maybe you should clean your face up?" Finn suggested as he reached up to turn a lamp on. He brought it down to sit in front of them. "It's not the best lighting, but..."

Larkin shook her head. "No, the twins said you should look awful."

"Well?" Harlow asked. "Do I look awful?"

"Yes," Finn and Larkin answered in unison.

The two of them were never going to let her live this down. She hit the "go live" button in revenge. "Hi, Nuva Troi," she waved at the screen. People were popping on by the dozens. "It's me, Harlow."

# CHAPTER FORTY-FOUR

In the days that followed the Battle for Nuva Troi, there were massive losses to contend with. Hundreds of people had lost their lives. Again, Harlow was shocked by how lucky she'd been. Her entire family was safe, though some were having a harder time adjusting than others.

The Illuminated had scattered, leaving the world to pick up the pieces, though for the time being, they were mostly picking up the mess the Vespae had left. It wasn't perfect, but the Fifth Order took over, as a provisional government in Okairos and Falcyra, allowing Avignonne and Castel des Reves time to discuss how they wanted to proceed in international cooperation. It was a complex set of politics, and Harlow was happy she didn't have any part of it.

Pasiphae would go to trial, but she had already entered a guilty plea, and had turned over her own fortune, in exchange for leaving a little to Alaric, "for the babies." He didn't take it, and the Fifth Order held it in trust for him, starting a generous scholarship fund for students who wanted to learn music, the way he'd wanted to when he was a young man. Now, he took up the guitar, and played every day for Thea and the twins that grew inside her. They were blissfully happy.

For about a month after the Battle for Nuva Troi, the Kranes, the Knights, and most of their friends stayed at the Order of Mysteries together. It was as though they needed the comfort of seeing one another every day. Soon though, people drifted slowly back into their old lives. Enzo and Riley to the apartment above the atelier. The maters and Meline went back to the Monas, which had opened back up. Nox and Indi moved into Harlow's penthouse until they found a place of their own. Kate and Petra moved in together, and Audata was moving to Nuva Troi for good.

Cian left for Avignonne with Vivia and Rakul, on an extended trip to their homeland. They sent postcards frequently, and Harlow enjoyed hearing about their travels. Only Harlow and Finn stayed at the Order of Mysteries with Alaric and Thea.

One morning, just as spring took hold of Nuva Troi for good, Harlow stopped into Selene and Aurelia's office in their quarters at the Order of Mysteries. Finn was in there with Axel asleep on his lap, typing away at a spreadsheet. He was dressed casually, in slouchy gray sweatpants and his My Girlfriend is a Witch t-shirt. His hair had gotten long again, and it was falling in his eyes as he tapped away at the keys of his laptop.

Finn pushed his glasses back up his nose as he looked up. He was so beautiful it hurt to look at him sometimes. "Have time for a walk?" she asked.

"Sure," he replied with a smile. "You break the news to buddy though."

Harlow kissed Axel as she pulled him off Finn, setting him down in a patch of sunshine. He barely even woke, letting out a small mew in protest.

Out in the sunshine, Finn smiled down at her. "You look beautiful today."

Harlow blushed a little.

"The ballet-core look you've pioneered is really catching on," he said, bumping his hip to hers.

It was true, she'd sort of re-popularized athleisure. Section Seven loved it, for now anyway. Harlow kept hoping she'd get to stop with the influencer life soon, but so many people reached out to her in legitimate need, and she'd been able to coordinate help for them. She saw now why the twins had a hard time giving it up. It was hard to believe that had all been just a year ago. That the season had just been a year ago. There would be no official season this year, or ever again. No one needed it anymore.

She and Finn walked in quiet peace for a while, her feet moving without thinking. The path they walked was a familiar one for her. The cherry blossoms were just blooming, and the air was hazy and sweet with spring. While the Fifth Order worked to figure out how the world would be governed, everyone was just muddling through the frequent changes in rules and regulations. Still, in many ways, life had gone back to something similar to what it had been before.

Except now their planet was lonelier. They'd lost so many people. Cities sat half empty, and people were finding their footing with one another. When Harlow had spoken to Piper Winslow, a few days prior, at their now-weekly coffee date, the human told her she thought it would be years before Okairos recovered from this one year. It had been strange the first time Piper asked her to meet, and they spent most of their time arguing, but she thought someday they might actually be friends.

"Where's my girl?" Finn asked, pulling her back to reality. She hadn't realized she'd stopped—but they'd reached their destination, so it was okay.

"Right here," she said, pointing to the house. "This is where I wanted you to come with me."

Finn stared at the house they'd taken her first "influencer" photo in. It was just behind the Monas. "I'm confused."

"Welcome home!" Harlow said, grinning.

Finn was perplexed. "What?"

"I sold the penthouse to Nox and bought this," Harlow explained.

Finn grimaced. "Why? We could have lived in the penthouse. I don't think anyone can live here—ever."

Harlow pushed through the garden gate. "Well... not now, but with some work..."

He smiled at her, looking like he was going to call her his sweet summer child. "We have no money, babygirl."

Harlow tapped his nose. "We actually do. As a part of the home-grant program Piper's heading up with Cian, destroyed homes in residential areas are very cheap. You know they want people to move back to the cities, to help improve infrastructure and efficiency."

"Yes," Finn said. "But even if it were dirt cheap—"

"Which it was!" Harlow interjected.

"Even so, it wouldn't be enough to do the renovations needed to make this place safe," he explained. It was clear he was trying to be gentle with her.

"Finn," she insisted, using his name as a plea for him to just shut up and listen. He stopped staring at the crumbling building in front of them to look at her. She pulled out the blueprints in her bag and spread them out on the stone front porch.

"These are a set of architectural directions, okay? When I applied for the grant, I talked with the architect Cian hired to guide people like us."

"People like us?" Finn asked.

Harlow grinned. "People who are going to renovate."

Finn sighed again. "I—"

"Finn!" Harlow yelled. He shut his mouth as she dragged him up the steps, and into the front hallway. "Did you forget I could do this?"

Her shadows flowed out of her, winding around the broken staircase, mending and weaving the wood back together. In a few moments, Harlow had broken out in a mild sweat, but the stairs were whole and gleaming again.

He broke out into a laugh. "I—yeah. I did sort of forget that. Gods, you are brilliant, and I'm a bit distracted..." He nuzzled her neck, murmuring all the apology she needed.

She grabbed his hand, dragging him away from her neck. "With our powers combined, I think we can get a roof on this place in no time, Mr. McKay."

He laughed. "Okay, babygirl. Let's do it, but what are we gonna do with all this space? There's five floors. This place is a literal mansion."

Harlow's eyes sparkled as she told him her plans for a family home: Alaric and Thea on the top floors, Haven's offices in the middle, and them on the ground floor walkout. She used her shadows to build a little model out of the wood splinters and dust on the floor.

"Do you love it?" she asked when she was done painting her picture.

"I do," he said, wrapping his arms around her, as the model fell back to dust. "And I love you, Harlow Krane. Let's get married."

"We are getting married," she said with a smile.

Finn shook his head. "No, I mean today. Let's get married today. Tonight. I don't want to wait for a better time. There is no better time than right now."

Harlow pulled out her phone and began typing.

"What are you doing?" Finn asked. "I just asked you to marry me now."

Harlow smiled up at him. "I know. I just told the group text. Should be set up in an hour. What do you want to do 'til the wedding?"

Finn shrugged. "Maybe get a roof on this place."

Harlow grinned. "You'd better kiss me first."

And he did.

# Epilogue
## Four years later.

Harlow's sneakers crunched on the dried leaves that covered the cobblestone walkway on Antiquity Row. Summer's heat had finally drained away, and the crisp breeze that ruffled her hair smelled faintly of roasted chestnuts and caramel apples. Fall blew into Nuva Troi with cold nights, softening light, and an air of possibility. It was the start of a new cycle, and in Harlow's opinion, the most magical time of the year.

The golden afternoon sun cast a glow on the shiny "I Voted" button pinned to her sweatshirt. She'd squeezed her vote in right after her final for HIST 4423: The Rectification of Historic Inequality in Nytra. It had been the most brutal of her exams, but she was grateful not to have another paper to write. Dissertation topics beat a slow drumbeat in her mind, thrumming for attention. She'd have to narrow things down soon, and the thought of choosing drove her to distraction.

It wouldn't hurt to check the election results one more time. At the very least it was a good way to turn her busy mind away from her dissertation. There were at least four hours until the polls closed, but she was desperate to know who'd win Nytra's election for representatives to the planetary parliament. She let her feet carry her towards the Monas as she refreshed commentary on the results so far, her phone's notifications going wild as she took it off "do not disturb."

A wall of muscle sprang up before her, taking her by surprise. Strong hands caught both her arms and her phone as it went flying.

"Watch where you're going, Krane," a deep voice rumbled.

Harlow mock-glared into stormy, slate blue eyes, before snatching her phone back. "Don't act like you didn't run into me on purpose."

Finn grinned, brushing a kiss to her temple, his dark hair falling into his eyes. "Damn right I did." He inhaled as he bent to brush another kiss to her ear. "Why do you smell so good?" One hand, free now that she'd recovered her phone, slipped under her sweatshirt, as he pulled her into a hug.

Canvas grocery bags hit her in the leg as Finn nipped at her ear. Harlow glanced down. "Did you go shopping *again*?"

He sighed, a little growl vibrating through him. "No one is following my spreadsheet."

Harlow suppressed a laugh. Finn had added a spreadsheet to their friends and family sharedrive that was *supposed* to govern what everyone brought to their Election Day celebration party. Apparently, he'd caught wind that everyone was going rogue, bringing dips when they signed up for hot appetizers, and generally mocking his attempt at organization.

She raised up on her tiptoes to kiss his cheek. "Sorry, sweet boy."

A chill breeze ruffled some papers sticking out of Finn's grocery bags. Harlow snatched them out, as they walked arm in arm towards the Monas. The pile of papers were get-out-the-vote flyers, stuck to a clipboard attachment on Finn's tablet. She peeked at the tshirt he was wearing under his leather jacket, which read "ASK ME HOW TO REGISTER TO VOTE."

"Any luck getting Nuva Troi's youth to register?" she asked with a sly grin. He was the Election Office's top registry volunteer, exponentially blowing his quotas every week by simply getting out and about with his flyers, tablet, and a wide variety of novelty t-shirts.

He nodded, checking his watch. "There's still a few more hours..."

Harlow sighed as they pushed the doors to the Monas open. The smell of books and Selene's signature perfume hit her nose all at once. The store was uncharacteristically empty for this time of day.

"Hello, darlings!" Selene called from atop one of the brass ladders that ran the gamut of white painted shelves on this level. "Could you flip the 'open' sign over and lock the door?"

Finn reached back and did as Selene asked immediately—he was always eager to please her, a fact that brought a bittersweet ache to Harlow's chest. They still hadn't heard a peep from Aislin, though there were rumors everywhere that she and Petra's parents were mounting a secret campaign against democracy. The world was changing rapidly, but some of the Illuminated were still holding onto the past with an iron grip. Aislin obviously hadn't come to Connor's funeral four years ago. Not many had, other than their friends and family.

Aurelia poked her head out from the back. "Finn! Could you share your spreadsheet with me again? I can't remember what we signed up for..."

"We're the chips and dips, darling," Selene interjected as she glided down the ladder.

Finn sighed. "Actually..."

Selene raised an eyebrow and Finn's mouth shut. He took his tablet from Harlow, handing her the grocery bags. "Could you take these home for me? I'm going to go see if I can get a few more registrations."

Harlow smiled. "Of course." As he leaned in for a kiss, she added, "And you're going to the store again, aren't you?"

His face was a mask of innocence as he unlocked the door to the Monas and disappeared down the street in a flash of speed. Harlow locked the door, shaking her head at the maters. They'd signed up to bring dessert and Harlow knew neither of them had forgotten. "Did you *have* to mess with him that way?"

Selene snorted. "Yes, bun. We absolutely did."

Aurelia leaned against the doorframe to the back office, shrugging. "It is a rite of passage."

Harlow sighed. "It has been *four years*."

Aurelia pushed off the doorframe and crossed the store in a few long strides, snaking her long arms around Selene's waist. "The blink of an eye."

Selene nodded, tears pricking at the corner of her eyes. "A happy blink, though, and we love that boy."

Harlow walked towards her parents, pausing to be squeezed and kissed as she made her way towards the back of the store. Her parents absolutely did love Finn, and despite her chiding, it thrilled her that they teased him the same as they did their daughters. He, Alaric, and Nox were treated just exactly as the girls had always been: endless cups of tea and an ear to listen when they needed something—coupled with the gentle ribbing and pranks that the maters had been notorious for, before what most people now referred to as the Conflict.

Four years later, and the Kranes, along with the rest of the world, were still recovering. So many people were lost, so many lives shattered in ways that simply rebuilding didn't make up for. But most people made the effort anyway, even when no one seemed to agree about how to solve their problems. Piper Winslow, at once of their recent coffee dates, had opined that it would likely be decades before any real recovery was possible.

It had surprised Harlow when the former Education Councillor, who now headed up a task force in Nytran Intelligence, asked her to coffee three years ago. After the Conflict ended, she assumed she'd never hear from the woman again. But Piper had called when they had Haven up and running again, wanting to form a better relationship—and strange as it was to think about, they had. The human's insight was invaluable to Haven's progress, and she'd introduced Finn and Harlow to several of their board members.

Thinking of Piper, Harlow spotted the new Wesley Arden book. She chuckled, thinking of the way that Piper had messed with her by pretending she'd never heard of the last bestselling series from the author. Those days seemed like a dream now. She took the book and rang it up at the register, filling out the form that would have it sent to Piper's uptown flat.

While she finished scrawling a wry note to the human, the maters finished their end-of-day routine. Meline and Indigo emerged from their upstairs offices to help close down the shop for the day. They were running the shop with the maters full time now, and the four of them made a splendid team.

"How'd the midterms go?" Meli asked as she trudged down the stairs. Her eyes were rimmed red and puffy. She and Ari had broken up a month ago, and she was still in the crying-and-ice-cream phase.

"Good," Harlow replied. She had the feeling her sister wanted to ask something else, but was hesitating.

Indi squeezed her twin's hand. "She wants to know if Ari's coming tonight."

Harlow glanced between the two of them and then the maters, who were pretending not to listen. "No. He and Larkin took the Woody on a road trip up to the lake for the long weekend."

Meli nodded, tears welling in her eyes. "That's good. I'm glad he has his best friend."

Indi hugged Meline, their fair and dark hair mingling as Meli's shoulders shook. It was hard to watch. Meline and Ari were both too good natured to have had a dramatic breakup. They'd fallen out of love, and held on for too long, not knowing how to be apart after everything they'd been through together. Larkin had texted before the dreaded HIST 4423 final, letting Harlow know the Woody was fine, and that Ari was as much of a mess as Meline.

Finn thought they'd be friends again in a few months, but Harlow hesitated to make that prediction. They'd always be family to each other—but *friends* might take a while longer than that. It was good, in her opinion, that they were taking a little time to process. And no one would be a better balm for Ari's heart than Larkin, who had become his best friend.

Harlow gave her sisters a long hug, kissing both their foreheads in turn. Their arms went around her and she felt the maters' eyes on them, the heavy feeling of savoring even the sad moments with one another filling her heart with the bittersweet pulse of living, rather than only surviving.

In her pocket, her phone buzzed. She stepped away from her sisters to check it. It was Enzo, sending a photo to both her and Finn in their group message of the baby, who had Riley's luminous eyes and Enzo's wicked smile. Her nose crinkled as she smiled, sending a barrage of hearts with the message that said, *Kiss Sarai a million times for me!* She clicked out of the group message and opened a new one between only her and Enzo: *Please check Finn's spreadsheet before you come. He's freaking out.*

A photo of several bags of cupcakes came through almost immediately. *Riley would never pull the shenanigans Lili and Selene have been.*

*Thank you,* she responded, after sending another barrage of 3D hearts.

Of course Riley would never. They were too considerate for that. She glanced up. Meli was wiping her eyes, smiling a watery smile. "I won't cry through Election Night. Promise."

Harlow reached out and tugged Meli's long blonde braid. "It's okay if you do. Everyone understands."

Meline took a deep breath, then nodded. "I actually think I'm going to give Ari a quick call."

Selene looked as though she wanted to argue, but Aurelia shook her head slightly and her mouth shut. After Meline disappeared upstairs Indi squeezed Selene's arm. "Believe it or not, they're actually helping each other with this. They know they're not getting back together—they just have to find a way to move forward—and it's hard."

Selene nodded, kissing Indi's forehead. "Okay, bun-bun. You know best."

Indi shook her head. "I don't believe that for a second, Mama. I've gotta run home before the party. See you all in a bit."

Aurelia smiled, placid as a bovine on a cool spring day as Indigo rushed out the back door. The three of them went to watch her, as Nox zoomed up on her motorcycle.

"They're going to be late," Selene said with a pleased smile. She loved the fact that three of her children were so happily paired. "Do you know she told me Nox wants to have children when they're forty or fifty? Won't that be lovely?"

Harlow nodded, grinning at Selene. "Just a steady stream of babies for you to love."

Selene cupped Harlow's face in one hand. "I don't mind about you and Finn, darling."

"I know," Harlow replied, making brief eye contact with Aurelia. Selene did mind a little, but she tried hard to hide it. Still, she had the twins, Sarai, and another baby on the way right now, and Harlow knew it would be enough. "I've gotta run. See you soon?"

The maters both nodded and Harlow made her way out the back door and across the courtyard to the garden gate that connected their backyards. When she passed through the arched gate, a little body rushed towards her, attaching themselves to her legs.

*River.* "Auntie!"

Harlow crouched down. "Hey, pal."

"Phaedra's in the treehouse and said I can't come up," the littling said, voice muffled, as their face was buried in the stretchy fabric of her leggings.

"Oh no," Harlow said softly, glancing up at Thea, who reclined across the yard in a hammock under the big oak tree that spread over the entire yard. She pulled the blanket River had clearly cast off when Harlow had arrived over her swelling belly. She shrugged, shaking her head, but she didn't get up—she was on bed rest for the last month of her pregnancy. Besides, whenever the twins fought there wasn't much anyone could do—they just had to work things out on their own.

Harlow abandoned the grocery bags and picked the four year old up. They were getting a little too big to be carried around, but it made them feel better to be held. She walked under the tree to stand under the treehouse she and Phaedra had built together. "Hey, chicken," she called up. "Why isn't Riv allowed up with you?"

Phaedra's dark head popped out, her great brown eyes the same as her twin's and Alaric's. "They do not have wings," she explained. "It isn't safe."

"I would be careful," River replied with a pout. "Don't boss me so much."

Phaedra's Strider abilities had manifested when she was two, and River's had not. It had been something of a struggle between them. Thea watched, a faint smile on her lips. She was so beautiful when she was pregnant, and *happy*. Harlow was excited for another baby, despite the resurgence of Selene's reassurances that it was all right for her and Finn not to procreate.

"If you can't share the treehouse, Phae, then you'll need to come down," Thea called from the hammock.

The little girl stepped onto the front porch of the treehouse, spread dark wings behind her, and glided down to the ground, holding her hand out to her twin. "Want me to take you up?"

River nodded vigorously, scrambling out of Harlow's arms and into their sister's, who teleported them both into the treehouse the second Riv's hands met hers. Phaedra was generous with her magic, and soon the sound of laughter suffused the yard. Thea's phone dinged and Harlow looked over as she read a text message.

"Cian's staying in Avignonne with Rakul and the others for another week," she murmured.

The firedrake had been training young Heraldic shifters with the Dominavus all over the world for the past few months, and it was long past time for them all to come home, in Harlow's opinion. She missed them. Thea turned her phone around to show Harlow a photo of Cian with Kate, Petra, and a very pregnant Audata—the firedrake had their arms around Audata's cousin Fernando. Everyone was grinning like wild, laughing their asses off about something.

"Oh," she said softly, handing the phone back to her sister.

"They'll be home soon enough," Thea said with a smile, then slapped her leg playfully. "You're something of a mother hen, you know that?"

Harlow slid into the hammock next to her sister, laying her head on Thea's shoulder as they swung in the warm afternoon sunlight. "I've been feeling a little wistful lately."

"Mmmmm," Thea responded. "You get that way in autumn. Always have."

Axel jumped onto the hammock, mewing loudly at the two of them before settling in between them for belly rubs. Thea adjusted her blanket over her big belly and then proceeded to scratch the cat's chin with her long nails, while Harlow gave the required belly rubs. In moments, the cat was asleep.

"Do you think it'll show this year?" Harlow murmured, not

wanting the twins to hear her. The moons were waxing, and the veil between Okairos and the limen was at its thinnest.

"The shade?" Thea whispered back. "It hasn't for two years. Maybe it's gone. Larkin can't find it when she walks."

Harlow glanced up at Thea, who had half her mind in the treehouse, monitoring what the twins were up to. "I think that's on purpose, don't you?"

Thea's smile was wan. "You think she visited too much after things ended and wore out her welcome?"

Harlow shrugged. "I think maybe it sensed she wasn't moving on." The shade visited Harlow for the first two autumns after the Conflict, checking in to find out how Larkin was doing, but avoiding her. It had never stayed long enough for Harlow to find out why it was avoiding her sister, but maybe this year she would.

Thea pointed to a stain on her sweatshirt. "Is that coffee?"

Harlow laughed. She'd spilled on herself during her final. "Yeah, I should go change."

Alaric came down the back steps from the Haven office, located on the first floor of the townhouse they shared, carrying two huge folding tables across his broad shoulders. "When's Finn coming home?"

"When he's bought the grocery store out, I assume," Harlow called back.

Alaric set up the tables, then came to give his wife a kiss. When he was finished with that, he pointed to the stain on Harlow's sweatshirt. "After you change out of that, could you take a quick look at the Lilac House plans?"

Harlow got up, letting Alaric replace her in the hammock. Axel woke with a grumpy chirp and jumped down, obviously prepared to follow Harlow into the house. "Sure, did you email them?"

Alaric shook his head, pulling his wife into his arms. "No, they haven't been scanned yet. The architect's office dropped them off earlier. They're in the office on the conference table."

Harlow nodded. "Okay." She walked across the yard, gathering up the grocery bags and appreciating the bright autumnal foliage. The leaves had finally all turned—the year was going dormant in a blaze of glorious color that warmed her to her toes. Everything about fall was magic.

Axel purred loudly, rubbing his face against her legs as she walked into the ground-level apartment she and Finn shared. Harlow deposited the groceries on the giant antique island, salvaged from one his parents' country homes that had been half burned to the ground in the Conflict. The kitchen, as it turned out, had been one of the only rooms to survive, this island his only keepsake from any of his parents' homes. Everything else had been turned over to the Fifth Order, and soon would be property of the planetary parliament.

When she'd asked why he wanted this, he'd told her the story of his first memory of Cian, bandaging a skinned knee on this very island, and many memories after that of talks with the firedrake in the country cottage. His parents had rarely gone there, but sent him there often with Cian. Four years into their marriage, and Harlow still didn't know all of Finn's stories. She mused over the thought as Axel hopped up to the island and rolled onto his back on the rustic hunk of wood.

The house was quiet, everyone either outside or getting ready for the party. She watched Thea and Alaric in the hammock, keeping an eye on the twins as they played. Her own twin sisters were coming through the garden gate, laughing, though Meline's eyes were red. Nox trailed behind Indi, eyes glued to her phone, but laughing at whatever the twins were. Behind them, the maters seemed to have forgotten something and were bickering over who'd go back to get it. From her kitchen window, Harlow snapped a photo and sent it to Larkin.

*Miss you. Love you. Hug Ari for me.*

The response was nearly instantaneous. *Happy Election Day. Love you.* Then, a selfie of Larkin and Ari at the lake. They were in a canoe, with a cheeseboard between them. They were fine. Everyone was okay.

*Then why was her heart beating so irregularly? Why did she feel like at any moment, the peace she felt might simply dissipate?* Axel rubbed his head against her arm on his way to the little bay in the kitchen window, behind the sink. It was one of his favorite afternoon spots, as the sun would shine through soon.

Tears filled her eyes as she watched him flop over. She bit her lip, trying hard not to cry. Today was a happy day, not a sad one.

*You have been through much. I am told that it takes humans a long time to process grief and sadness as great as yours.*

Harlow spun. Behind her stood the shade, though its form was barely corporeal. "You're here."

*Yes*, the shade responded, coming to stand next to her. *How long has it been since we last saw one another?*

"Two years."

*That long?* The shade's eyebrows raised. It still took the form of the fey woman, the Feriant, with elegant, dark-feathered wings wrapped around its shoulders like a cape.

"Why do you appear like that?" Harlow asked. She'd never gotten the chance to ask before.

The shade's incorporeal body rested impossibly against the quartz of the kitchen counter, its wings parting a little to reveal a beautiful gown, cut low between its breasts and flowing to the floor. It wore a pendant with a complex pattern that Harlow couldn't quite make out. *To remind you that the universe is wide. That this world is not alone. That there were beginnings and endings before, and that there will be many more before the end.*

"Going with cryptic, then?" Harlow said with a wry laugh.

*I suppose you would think so*, the shade said with a sly smile. *But I didn't come to talk of the war. Your part in that is done. I came to see how you fare.*

Harlow didn't miss the implication that a greater war still raged, outside of Okairos' bounds. She was glad to hear her part was done, but wondered if she asked... would it tell her? She'd long puzzled over the piece of the prophecy that Morgaine Yarlo had given her in Nea Sterlis: *Awaken the Fifth Order and the seventh ward shall break, and in so doing balance returns. The terror of the Ravagers ends when gods walk the earth as mere denizens.*

The Fifth Order had awoken, but what about the "seventh ward" and gods walking the earth? She'd searched all the archives she could for two years after the Conflict, needing to make sure nothing else was coming for them. But she'd never come up with an answer. This might be her only chance to find out. "What happened to Ashbourne? And the imperial Ventyr? And what about all that stuff about 'gods walking the earth' and wards breaking?"

The shade stared out at the yard for such a long time that Harlow thought it might not answer. *I told you Harlow, you've played your part. You will not see them again. This world is safe, and I, its guardian.*

The shade's words held a note of finality to them, and she knew by instinct that it would say no more on the matter of the prophecy. But it did explain the terror of the Ravagers ending, she supposed. It had been a while since things felt this big—she'd grown used to her mundane life. It struck her that she was glad of it. Glad to be done, and even glad to be protected by the shade, the Ravager—whatever it was now.

"Why?" Harlow breathed. "Why would you do that?"

*Because the people here still try. They still strive for better. They have not given up.* It paused. *Because Larkin still lives. Because you do.*

"And do your brethren feel the same?" Harlow asked, a sheen of sweat breaking out on her back at the thought of the other Ravagers.

*Their focus is elsewhere.* The shade touched her arm, nothing more than a memory of touch, rather than actual pressure. *You have not answered me. How do you fare?*

Harlow sighed, understanding the shade wasn't going to tell her more. "Some days are better than others, though objectively the world is moving on."

The shade nodded, a sage look in its dark eyes. *You cannot forget all you had to do to get here.*

Harlow nodded. She'd thought she'd handled things so well, from killing Mark to everything that had happened after. But when regular life started up again, the dreams started. The nightmares she woke from screaming. The hollow look that haunted Finn, and the eyes of everyone she loved from time to time. The days got easier, and the dreams were less frequent. But even now, there was still the pervasive feeling that it might all disappear.

"Will it ever stop?" she asked. "The remembering?"

The shade's sharp features narrowed. *No. But your life shall be long, and it will become easier to bear.*

"Thank you," she whispered. The shade's form was loosening.

*You will recover, Harlow Krane. And you will thrive.*

The shade's words held the weight of a portent, and once more, she was grateful. "Will I ever see you again?"

*No,* the shade said. *Tell Larkin that I said goodbye.* It took one of her hands, its touch like a whisper.

"I will," Harlow promised.

*I wish you well,* it said as it disappeared, a smile on its incorporeal lips. This time it did not fade into limenal space, as it had done in the past. It broke apart, as though dissolving into tiny pieces. Harlow used her second sight to watch it go. On the other side of the veil, in the limen, pieces of the creature that had once been an Elemental force so terrifying it had to be locked up for centuries floated into clouds of aether.

*We will not meet again,* voices said, a chorus in her head.

Harlow's spirit body rose above the maze at the center of the limen. All that was Nihil was gone now, but the labyrinth remained. Harlow returned to her side of the veil. When every trace of the shade was gone, Harlow turned to look at Axel, who was snoring in the window. He had fallen asleep during the shade's visit. She bent over the kitchen sink and sobbed, not really knowing why, just that it felt better to let the excess emotion out than force it to stay inside. When her chest stopped shuddering, a slow calm came over her.

She splashed cold water onto her face, movement in the yard catching her eye. Enzo and Riley had arrived and Riley was passing the baby to Selene. Enzo was headed her way. He poked his head in the kitchen door. "Hey—" he took a long look at her face. "Were you crying?"

Harlow didn't want to explain about the shade. "Today just felt like a lot."

He took two long strides across the slate floor and hugged her tight. "I did the same earlier. Cried over my kitchen sink, I mean. Just to get all my big feelings out."

She pulled her face away from the cashmere of his ochre sweater. "I'll get snot on you."

He smiled, his brown eyes sparkling. "Can't have that. Want help picking something out?"

She nodded and he followed her through the large room that made up their dining and living room space, decorated in her favorite cream and beige textures. The space was a combination of rustic and elegant, with art covering the walls, all Finn's selections, and some of the paintings he'd been making in the studio.

Enzo selected a sweater dress in the same cozy cashmere as what he wore, though in a dark gray, rather than ochre. Both sweaters were from a collaboration between himself and a Falcyran sheep farm. Then tall boots and thick socks. She changed quickly, while listening to gossip he'd picked up in the atelier, laughing softly at the mundanity of it all, at the pleasure of telling tales about their friends—Jareth Sanvier was dating one of Riley's exes and there was some salacious rumors about the lyon shifter and one of the press secretaries for Nuva Troi's gubernatorial candidates.

When she was dressed, they walked arm in arm out to the kitchen. Finn had just returned and was organizing massive amounts of food on the tables in the yard, with both sets of twins' help. Alaric was setting up the holo-projector and election counts flickered as he got the settings just right for an outdoor evening.

Harlow leaned her head on Enzo's shoulder. "Are you sad about giving up the arch-chancellor position?"

Enzo shook his head. "No, Aurelia was right. The Orders should have elections as well, and I didn't want it. My mom would be proud, don't you think?"

Harlow nodded, thinking of the Werakas. "Both your parents would be. They always talked about the idea of elections when we were kids, don't you remember?"

Enzo's smile betrayed the ache he must be feeling as well. "I do." He hugged her hard. "I'm glad you do too."

They clasped hands, walking out into the chill air of the early evening, Axel weaving between their feet. It was already getting dark, and friends trickled into the yard. Sam and Tomy waved as they dragged in their portable stove for a bonfire. Finn turned away from his mountain of food. Harlow had to admit, she was impressed with his vision.

He grinned when he saw her, hugging Enzo for a brief moment before Phaedra and River dragged him away. "Well, what do you think?" He asked, turning her towards the party. He'd strung lights across the yard and Sam had just gotten the bonfire crackling merrily. A group of shifters who worked with Haven's building group played folk music on string instruments.

"It looks great... Oh, I forgot to look at the plans the architect brought over for Lilac House."

Finn kissed the top of her head. "I reviewed them. You're going to love them—it's everything we talked about."

Lilac House was the biggest of five multi-generational, secure housing complexes that Haven was building for people who were still displaced from the Conflict, or who were experiencing hardship due to immortal retaliation. It was an unfortunate reality, but not everyone was excited about democracy, and some vampires and Illuminated were not reacting well to its implementation. Haven was Finn, Cian, and Alaric's full-time business now. It would be the real legacy of the Knights of Serpens. When Harlow was done with school, she planned to split her time between The Monas and Haven, like Thea did.

"A life of service and books," Finn had called it when she applied for Alcaia the year after Larkin's conservatory acceptance. It was an accurate description, and she didn't intend to waver from it. She had long years ahead of her, and she couldn't think of a better way to spend them than helping those that would shape the world into a better place for everyone.

Finn's arms tightened around her waist as they watched Axel play with River and Phaedra, who had conjured silvery moths for him to chase around the yard. The sounds of their friends and family chatting as election results rolled in were comforting. Twilight descended and Finn pulled Harlow into a chaise with him to watch the moons rise. She rested her back against his chest as he cradled her in his arms.

People clapped as Nytra's candidate was announced, but to Harlow's surprise she hardly noticed, she was so entranced by the moons. She glanced back at Finn to find him staring at the sky as well.

When he caught her eye, he smiled, one finger twitching to point at the waxing crescents above. "A new beginning," he murmured.

A smile spread slowly over her face as Axel hopped into her lap. "It's perfect."

A chill wind cooled her face, as Axel settled in for a nap and Finn relaxed behind her. Harlow's second sight showed the connections between every person at the party, strong and glowing with love. The smell of leaves and magic floated on the breeze. Just above the Monas, the moons rose in the sky. It was going to be a beautiful night.

THANK YOU SO MUCH FOR READING THE IMMORTAL Orders. If you are interested in reading more books in the The Tapestry (the metaverse that Okairos exists in) then I suggest reading *The Hollow Plane* next... *Especially*, if you were intrigued by Ashbourne the Warden and his lost love, Lumina.

# Extra Content

*Get your all access pass now*

My newsletter squad gets access to a library all of the maps, character art and bonus content that I share over the years, in addition to seeing covers and character art early, in-progress sketches of art and covers and exclusive sneak peeks of my books.

## JOIN HERE

https://allisoncarrwaechter.myflodesk.com/jointhesquad

# Author's Note

It's really hard to know where to start to say thank you. I typically save the best for last, but I think in this case, we should start with you, the reader. This series changed my life. You changed my life. Thank you for reading, reviewing, telling your friends, your moms, taking photos, making videos, and all the millions of things you've done to tell the world you loved this series. It's made all the difference in the world. I hope you'll love the new worlds we visit as much as this one, but if you don't, thank you **endlessly** for loving this one.

Thank you next to Doug. For the room to take this big next step. For all the support and love, and your expert knowledge with both the espresso machine and the air fryer.

To Sooz, who better not be reading this, thanks for letting me watch soaps as a kid and believing in me even when you're not sure about my next wild scheme.

Holly, Victoria, Nicola and Chels: You saved this one, babes. You save them all, but this one needed saving. Thank you for all you've done for me.

Kenna, thanks for cleaning up after me and my commas, and for all the encouraging notes along the way.

To The Coven for always being there, whether it's laughing over penis popsicles or telling me how to author, I appreciate you all so much.

Charlie, I might have made it this far without you, but I doubt it would have been so fast. Thank you for your friendship and your support for both myself and indie authors.

He Who Did the Least But Claims the Most goes last: Nev, thanks for sharing your desk with me. You're generous to let me have so much of it for my tippy-tapping. Sorry the noise disturbs your nap time.

Printed in Great Britain
by Amazon

40172727R00270